PC41: CASCADE EFFECT

BY

J.D. BELL

Copyright © 2020 J.D. Bell
ISBN: 978-1-936507-88-7
An ACOA Publication
www.aconspiracyofauthors.com

PC41: Cascade Effect
A Conspiracy of Authors Publication
www.aconspiracyofauthors.com
Copyright © 2020, J.D. Bell
ISBN: 978-1-936507-88-7
Cover Art: Copyright © 2020, Lazette Gifford

First Print Edition, January 2020

TABLE OF CONTENTS

CHAPTER 1

"Good evening," he said over the gun barrel.

I knew him, the man sitting in my big rattan rocker. He ran a bookstore over on 13th street, north of the university. He was a big man, once. You could see his barrel chest and his long waist under the sweater and the tweed jacket he was wearing.

I'd been to his bookstore. His place was a fixture among the college kids and the semi-pro academicians — the eternal postgraduates. He had a back room with a dead espresso machine, three Mr. Coffee brewers, and the proper sort of dilapidated couches and decayed club chairs arrayed for intense conversations. He opened promptly at nine every morning and threw everyone out at eleven in the evening.

He'd taught philosophy back when WSU was Wichita Municipal University, in the late 1950s. But he'd done more than teach. There was a 'love me' collection of black and white photos all over the backroom walls. In one cluster Wolff was fishing with Hemingway in Cuba; sitting with Hemingway again, in Paris. Both were dressed in the dapper suits of the 1930s, and then again, wearing the ragged olive drab of the Liberation.

In the next cluster of photos, he was drinking with Dashiell Hammett in a night club. Lingering over coffee and a cigarette with Jack Kerouac. A single uncredited photo of a very young Sinatra at a table in a night club.

Some of the pictures were of actors that had lit up marquees, some were of statesmen taking the air. You could watch him age in the photos, his hairline receding and his hands getting liver spots in the silver halides. The photos stopped at around 1964-that was the last date I saw. Bobby Kennedy giving a speech, without Wolff in the picture. Not quite 20 years ago, now.

I had taken it all in. The low-key, typewritten, labels identifying each of the cultural lights in the black and white photos. There were posters from plays in New York or London, one-sheets of French films, an Opera one sheet. It was a trophy room. I had glanced around again, finished my so-so cup of coffee and left.

He hadn't struck me as needing that sort of status by proxy. Like water-boys who rub shoulders with the championship football team in the photos in the display cases in the student union. But a lot of glossy pictures with typewritten labels had said otherwise.

My brief was to 'watch.' Never mind the why. I swung by the store about every fortnight, bought a couple of books, did not drink the coffee, and then went home to my furnished apartment. Three months of this and nothing to report.

Now Benjamin Wolff was gaunt, with sparse white hair and dark bags under his deep-set eyes. The jacket hanging off his shoulders, the cravat trying to hide his thin neck. Not matching any of the photos in my thin dossier, not at all.

He was also sitting in my rocking chair, in my front room, with my cat in his lap, and steadily holding his gun pointed at my face.

I had an armful of groceries and two Sunday newspapers. I had a Swiss Army knife and a handful of change in my trousers, having left both guns I was issued locked in the pantry. I thought about throwing the groceries at him and taking my chances. Then I heard a safety snap, off to my left.

He smiled at how still I'd suddenly become. "An associate."

"I see." I leaned over and slowly set the bag on the floor. Then I stepped back. I could feel the other gun change position when I stepped to my right. I had the gunman clocked, but he was just outside my reach.

"Please don't." Wolff said, gently shaking his gun at me. "I might miss, but Lyn won't. And I think you should hear me out."

"Yes," I said. "Anything for guests." I walked slowly away from the bag and sat down on the lumpy couch, laying the newspapers carefully on the cushions. My attention was focused on Wolff to my front.

"Who feeds you?"

I sat back into the couch, crossed my leg, and kept my hands carefully on top of my knee. I took my time answering. "A House, on the Hudson."

I was startled at the question direct, but not quite surprised. I knew there was a reason they had sent me here on a 'watching brief.' Besides the fact that I had terribly screwed up in my last posting. Director Vittorio was notorious for not telling his people everything they needed to know. He had a theory that the best way to keep people 'keen' was to keep them slightly in the dark.

"The Registry?"

I shrugged, nodded to one side. I didn't admit anything, nor did I mislead. He was close, but, not close enough; in more than one sense of the word. The Registry was familiar to me, but to use his archaic formulation, they didn't feed me. Sometimes we fed at the same table, elbow to elbow as it were, but they didn't feed me.

I felt his gunman inch closer when Wolff proposed me as a representative of the Registry. Eager?

"You are, of interest, to them?" My tone was dismissive; after all, we were someplace out in the great fly over. 'Civilization dribbles out west of the Kaatterskills.' I'd heard one of the Registry's drones make that observation once when we were at table. Motive enough to stay in my quarters at the House and eat takeout and avoid what passed for conversation among my peers.

The indifferent insult brought Wolff forward slightly in the rocker and 'Lyn' was well within the length of my lance now. Enough.

>Now< I pushed, and a migraine sparked, becoming a carbon arc at the base of my brain. The cat took flight, clawing his way up the front of Wolff's chest and raking his face as he went up and over the back of the rocker. I reached out and squeezed Lyn's Sahasra node, she blacked out, instantly. Lyn was female, I noted absently. I took Wolff out in the next breath, again pressure upon the Sahasra.

Lyn's automatic didn't go off, which was a most excellent thing, the landlord having firm notions on damage deposits, renter's hygiene and noise. But Wolff's did. His was a large bore, spring needle gun, two millimeters; it made about the noise a hardback book makes when you drop it three feet on to the kitchen tiles. The needle went into the ceiling, knocked a divot about the size of a pencil eraser out of the plaster. I doubted that the landlord would notice it in all the other stains and spots. How someone could stain a ceiling with what looked like cheese sauce was beyond me.

That was another of Vittorio aphorisms, that an impoverished agent was again, 'keen'. Every disapproved expense came out of the agent's compensation, and most expenses not budgeted beforehand were not approved. Like damage deposits. Or rent.

I took a length of leather shoelace from my pocket and hogtied Lyn, carefully depriving her of her hoard of weapons, tools and – snacks? Then I turned her head to the side; if she came to, unattended, she had less chance of aspirating vomit.

PC41, my cat, stalked over to Wolff and sat on his chest.

>regret< came through the fading migraine.

I walked over and retrieved the antique spring gun Wolff had leveled at me. Took the pulse at his throat, his left wrist, and his right temple. Then I stripped the kidskin gloves from his hands and manipulated the knobby, swollen, joints. His knuckles were half again bigger than they should have been, with a limited range of motion, and his hands were chilled. Swollen joints, compromised circulation. A quick pat down showed a block of needles for the gun, a stockman's pocketknife, some pills in a pill case and a worn, calf's leather wallet. No snacks. I placed my collection on the couch.

I felt him climbing up from the stun. First, he became aware of ego, then his body, and finally he opened his eyes to the world. PC41 patted his face gently in apology, claws carefully withheld.

"So, perhaps, not of the Registry; after all," he said, his voice rough. "A Sangsue, in any event."

I winced, not a friendly term at all.

"I rather prefer the term D'draig-llai, or even Selai, if we are exchanging epithets." I reached out and stroked PC's back. "And you are of the Longue vie."

"Not much longer now, eh?" He looked over to where Lyn lay on her side, her face turned away. He sighed.

I didn't look away from him, I would have known if Lyn was stirring herself or if there were others about. I should have known they were here in the first place. Too complacent by half, I suppose. Focused on the promise of the crosswords in the Sunday papers, not on the now. Away from the House, you can get careless. It is never safe in a House where Registry Marshals and the thrice-damned Eisenring sit at Table, not by any means. But the dangers there are...different. People vanish, disappear without a splash or a flurry. When you are out on assignment, among the clueless secular population, you relax your guard.

"She should be alright," I said, backing away, his own antique covering him. "A bit muddled and hungover, very much like a cognac drunk, but alright."

"I should be honored, that they sent a," he paused, his eyes twinkling through the pain and his confusion. I began to understand why he might be a figure to reckon with in the middle of the pageantry of the century. "Sangsue, to put this old man down."

"How long have you been ill?" I sat at the end of the couch again, slowly stowing the items I had gathered from Lyn and Wolff on the Sunday papers. I intended to remove them to a kitchen counter and the folded paper would do. Lyn's pistol was in my pocket.

He blinked, his eyes fluttering as he reconsidered. "Not quite the year," he said slowly. "although the symptoms had not come fully on until late this last semester."

"Two-fold attack, I should say. Metal contamination, light metals? Then a biological agent that established itself, a cold or a mild flu. Your immune system was compromised. Mimicking Lupus. Any facial rash?"

"No, joint pain and irritable bowel. I have lost a lot of weight over this last summer. Are you physician as well as executioner?" He was irritated. Like a lot of the people I rub up against, when you counter their expectations, it puts them off-balance.

Lyn was stirring, testing her rawhide hobbles.

"It varies, day to day," I said. PC41 turned his head, to look at me. I nodded, slightly. "I have your parole?"

"Scholar and a gentleman as well?" He closed his eyes and searched for his gloves with his knobbed hands. "My parole."

I got up. I walked over to my groceries and produced a can of tuna.

>satisfaction< push-purred through the fading veil of the migraine. First things first, as always.

I am an operative of that thrice-damned Eisenring. The Unity Eisenring. The 'old firm' as it was and not the Feckless Provos. Was an operative, may still be an operative, certainly I am still owned by the Unity 'Ring. Despite what you hear, neither the Unity 'Ring nor the Feckless Provo Eisenring are a pack of knuckle dragging Luddite inquisitors. At our best we are a last defense against cross-contamination of the world-lines. At our very worst we manipulate the amount of information, trade and hardware flow in such a way as to benefit us and friendly Houses. We are corrupt, self-serving, bureaucratic, humorless and often clueless. But we serve a function. It's a function people sometimes forget or bristle at; and then comes the White Death or the English Measles and everyone wants to close the gates forever.

Which the Dai will not do.

I went into the kitchen and placed the items I took off of Lyn and Wolff on the counter. I picked up my abandoned bag and put the rest of the groceries away. Then I started a pot of coffee. I hadn't known that Wolff was of the hidden world when they gave me the brief. Hadn't considered it. It was just a make-work assignment to keep me away from Croton house.

I should have realized. I should have gathered from the pictures of him that he had been aging particularly well. The oldest picture that I could date offhand was likely taken, in Paris, just before the stock market crash of 1929. The women's hats gave it away. And he didn't look to be a teenager in that picture. In fact, he looked to be slightly older than Ernest. I placed his Borchardt needler on the counter alongside of Lyn's 9mm.

I took a magnet that was holding a note on the fridge in the kitchen, placed it on a flyspeck upon the side of the freestanding cabinet. There was a click and the cabinet opened slightly. I pulled it all the way open and took a carefully unlabeled, tightly sealed tin off the top shelf along with my modern needle gun – half the size of Wolff's Borchardt. I took my needle gun and slipped it into my right trouser pocket. I was going to start wearing a holster again.

Then I used the tin's attached turn-key to pop the vacuum and peel the vacuum strip off. I slipped a canned tea cake from the tin out onto a cutting board. It was from the Smoke, the Estuary in Little England, not the London of AngTerra. I got a packet of patent headache powders down from the pantry as well. Then I closed the closet and put the magnet back on the fridge.

I'd installed the lock when I took the place. The lock retracted a spring-loaded pin when I placed a strong magnet against a particular point on the cabinet. Removing the magnet allowed the pin to engage a plate in the door of the cabinet. To a snoopy landlord it would just be a jammed closet door. No visible locks and it acted like it was swollen shut. It was not truly secure – but I had mistakenly thought this assignment was a waste of time and not an operation.

I don't like to share my sundries.

Except with enemies I should like to be friends with. I have no shame and less scruples.

"Lyn, do you prefer tea or coffee?" I said, with my back to her. The soft stirring behind my back as she tried to slip her bonds stopped. "I have loose tea, Gunpowder, I believe. I have a tea cake with raisins and a packet of headache powder."

I turned and looked directly at Wolf. "Coffee?"

"Yes, please. Black. You have tea cake?"

"Well, I have a tea cake, sealed in a tin from Fortnum and Lewis, that seal is reputed to last 10 years. Not as good as fresh, but it will do."

"Excellent manners, Anglo tucker, and if the smell is correct, good coffee." Wolff turned his head to look at Lyn laying on the floor to my side. "Lyn will have a cuppa coffee, a slice of cake, and that packet. And she will give you her parole, won't you Lyn?"

"Yes." Her flat grey eyes promised mayhem; a slightly crooked nose underscored the promise. "You have my...parole." She was not happy. PC41 sat down to give himself a thorough cleaning and watched her all the while. She was a mouse that merited his attention.

CHAPTER 2

It was not a particularly happy kaffeeklatsch. Lyn was uneasy about the headache powders, but she was green around the gills and under orders knocked back a cold glass of water with the powders mixed in after I cut her bonds. PC41 settled his feet under him, making the classic observing cat pose, and kept a very close eye on her. Which also made her uneasy. So uneasy she forgot that she was going to be suspicious of my coffee and my tea cake. Wolff wanted to know more. And I settled in after serving him and taking care of myself, I was wanting to know more myself.

I ate my scrap of tea cake and sipped some more of the coffee. I leaned back in the ratty sofa and rested my cup on my left knee. Unremarked, by my right hand, I had my gun, I'd left all of their weapons on the counter of the kitchen. "I suppose I should properly introduce myself. I am Braxton, Josiah Braxton. Although I will answer to Joe or simply Braxton quite cheerfully. I am a middling strong, churched, D'draig-llai. I sometimes rub elbows with the Registry, but I answer to a far different wing of the Hudson." If you can call the Joint Eisenring a 'wing' of Croton on the Hudson.

I regarded PC41. Today he was a slightly orange tiger, later tonight he might be smoke grey. It varied, day to day.

"My operational handler gave me a suitcase with dubious identification, insufficient funds, vague but contradictory instructions. The usual. I was to establish myself locally, observe and then report back on you and your bookstore. I don't know why. Questions were discouraged."

Much of that was true. The very best lies are half-truths.

"You," Wolff said, "were remarked upon the very day you came into my bookstore. And every sortie since that day. Not quite a student, not quite the lost civilian looking for a proper chain bookstore, not quite anything. But quite suspicious," he said, as he set his cup down upon the floor and then leaned back in my rocking chair. Well, the Landlord's rocking chair. When I left this place, I would leave it behind me; along with the lumpy couch.

Wolff continued, "from our brief conversation I have realized that you are churched and from my somewhat unhappy recent experience, a more than middling Sangsue. Much more than middling, Mister Braxton."

"So why should I be tasked with surveilling you?" I glanced at Lyn out of the corner of my eye. I had not remarked on her when I scouted the bookstore on that first day, a mistake.

"I do not have a ready answer." Wolff replied. "I have been many things to many Tables. Some enterprises have prospered under my hand, some have not." He clasped his hands about a knee. "I was dying before I was poisoned, as old men sometimes do. I had nothing in train; I had not made the egotistical gesture of writing a memoir. What secrets I know I planned to take to my pyre. Or they were not my confidences anymore."

"What Tables? What House did you stand in?" This was important, to me. It might give me a reason for my watching brief.

He grimaced, shook his head. "It truly does not matter. A White Plague; then the fires that came after burned away what stubble that was left from that Plague." His face stilled. "I hunted many monsters, Talented and Gifted, churched and un-churched. The Sangsue were a particular project of mine." He smiled at me, the way you smile to underline a threat.

"I see." I got up and pocketed my pistol. I looked to Lyn. Her cup and saucer were in her lap, handy to fling them at me upon need. Her parole was given, but she was a Medji. The Medji are very flexible in their concept of parole. "I have not been tasked with more than an observational brief. But I will advise my controller that things have changed."

I backed away from them, retrieved their weapons and kit from the counter, and placed them on a rather rickety occasional table by the door. Then I slightly opened the door with my left hand without taking my eyes off them, my right hand was in my pocket with the pistol. PC41 did not move from his place on the rug, but his purr grew louder. "I should bid you goodnight and I will see you tomorrow, after I consult with Control." I nodded at them, gestured to the table and retreated into the kitchenette.

Wolff nodded. He made a small motion with one hand and Lyn stood smoothly, leaving her dishes on the arm of the ratty chair. She walked stiffly to the door, took up her side arm, checked, cleared, and holstered it. With the same smooth motion, she tucked away her knife, then collected Wolff's wallet, pill case, needle block, stockman's knife and the Borchardt. She stepped into the doorway and then waited for Wolff to follow, her eyes fixed on me and her back to the opened door.

Wolff stood stiffly, awkwardly. He nodded to me and walked carefully to the door and took his antique weapon from Lyn. They left my apartment, closing the door softly behind them. Her snacks were left on the table.

I leaned against the refrigerator, out of the line of sight of the half-windows in the living room and listened to faint steps in the hallway outside my door.

Ten minutes passed and then twenty. PC41 got up, stretched and walked deliberately to the bathroom. I shot the deadbolt on the door, gathered up the dishes and placed them in the sink. I took the groceries from the sack, put them away in the open pantry, while I assessed what I knew, and what I had learned.

It was Monday. I had stopped by Rector's News downtown. I'd passed a pleasant ten minutes with the clerk, who sported a black flat-topped cowboy hat this day to my delight and picked up the newspapers he'd held for me. I'd made his acquaintance the week I arrived, browsing for reading materials, entertainments and places to dine that avoided Golden Arches or the like.

The Kansas City Star from yesterday and the London Sunday Times from last week were still on my kitchen counter. I stripped out the crossword puzzles, then threw the rest in the bin. I looked at the puzzles, then I carefully folded them away. Likely not tonight.

I opened the locked cabinet again and took a Weitbrecht coupler out. I sat down at the desk to share the wealth of my uneasiness. I placed the handset of the telephone upon the audio coupler and dialed a local number that would connect to a House on the Hudson. Encrypting the call with the coupler.

It was late on that Monday night, the 16th of August 1982. I took pleasure in dumping this development into Vittorio's lap.

The date was important, though I didn't know that then.

CHAPTER 3

They picked up at the second ring. "Braxton for Vittorio," was all I said. The silence was complete. I sat down and composed my thoughts.

"Vittorio." How one can be briskly slimy over an encrypted phone is quite beyond me.

"Wolff was in my apartment this evening."

"You made contact. Your brief was – "

"He made contact with me. I had minimal exposure to him, but he knew I was churched."

"Poor tradecraft on your part." I rolled my eyes.

"No. He had been tipped off, thought I was of the Registry and not your... establishment." Vittorio was Unity 'Ring, on loan to a Joint Eisenring section operating in North America. Like I was. Director Vittorio was notorious among the Old Firm for being a cheap bugger; having sticky fingers, a roving eye and being not quite as bright as a box of hammers. Which is why he was the Director of a moth-eaten desk of Eisenring culls west of the Kaatterskills, and not at Croton House. "Entered my hide and had me under a pair of guns, his and a Medji he called Lyn. They were not aware of my...nature."

"Termination?"

"No need, as of now. He is dying. I think he was poisoned. Appears to be a binary agent, a tailored biological with a toxic accelerant. I would estimate it was administered within the last year, certainly in the last eighteen months."

"You are certain?"

"As well as I can be, absent a workup for biologicals, neurotoxins and heavy metal contamination. I would hazard an opinion of the origin of the attack: Hanse, specifically *Xternen de AngelegenheitenBüro.*" I gave him the full title, which should have taken him between wind and water. It did.

He stopped breathing. I waited. He coughed. "This is not the first death we have encountered."

I smiled to myself. Keeping me in the dark, keeping me 'keen'. Ha! Bites you in the arse every time, Vittorio.

He sighed, fumbled the handset, and continued. "There is a dossier in a bank safety deposit box. You have the necessary documentation and keys in a packet that your contact gave you. It will read you into the current operation. I needn't remind you of the necessity to restrict any access to this file."

"No, Director Vittorio," I said, knowing that I was going to read Wolff in as soon as I got my hands on the dossier. I hung up on him and went to bed, with the Times crossword. I had a premonition that this might be the last time I'd have the chance to indulge myself. Sufficient unto the day and so forth.

After an early and scant breakfast, I let PC41 loose upon the unsuspecting neighborhood. I took a taxi downtown to a middling bank. I had a car, you cannot operate out west of the Kaatterskills without one, but I thought I might avoid observation using a taxi. In the packet the contact gave me there was a ring of keys and a set of identification that would give me access to three largish safe deposit boxes. I was supposed to be only accessing box number one, but bugger that for a lark. I emptied all three into a stack of folded banker's boxes I'd brought with me. The bank was quite happy to help me with removing them from the deposit room.

I went home, by taxi again. In one of the safe deposit boxes there had been a locked, leather Gladstone bag. In the bag were twenty-five thousand in American dollars and twenty thousand in English pounds; a Little Englander 9mm with no proof marks or serial numbers and a fifty-round box of 9mm cartridges. There was also a 'zeme 1.1mm needler and an extra century block of needles for when the one in the needle gun was exhausted.

There was a very large stack of expanding file folders, secured with cloth ties and wax seals. They filled the other banker's boxes.

Wax seals. I was thankful that I was not handling vellum and straining my eyes with copperplate script. Bureaucracy, the curse of the Eisenring, be it Unity or the Feckless Provos.

The typed onion skin reports behind the seals covered a great deal of Wolff's life and his career from 1902 until 1952. That was when his last 'legend', Major Carleton-Wolff of the Territorial Army's London Division, retired and emigrated to Canada with a medical discharge.

The Major shortly then came south to the United States and 'died' of natural causes in 1953. Benjamin Wolff had surfaced about six months before his cousin's tragic demise, establishing himself as a PhD Candidate in the University. He took his doctorate and quickly became a tenure track instructor, then bought into the bookstore. The story had been that he, Benjamin, had rattled about Europe in the prewar period dropping out and back into one of the English universities. University of Durham. After some lackluster middling wartime service with the Royal Canadian Ordnance Corps in the ETO--under another legend as phony as Major Carleton-Wolff--Benjamin completed a Baccalaureate degree at Durham and emigrated from England to the States, getting his Graduate Degree in philosophy from Duke University in the late 40's.

Benjamin had used the photos I had seen to give him a smooth back story. They were true as far as they went, he had been there as Benjamin and not Major Carlton-Wolff and I would lay odds that there were very few official photos of the Major in existence.

The popular lights in the photos might remember Wolff's face, but many of them were dead or scattered to the winds when 'Benjamin' surfaced well after the war. Their memories of times in a world gone by would be suspect. He was as well established in his cover as you could be with as much exposure as he had before the war. I wondered if anyone ever questioned his collection of photos and his apparent age.

PC batted at the window of my garden apartment. I got up from the desk and let the gourmand in. I pushed at him, ignoring the instant migraine, >anything<. He stalked over to the favored corner of the couch; PC was a 'he' this afternoon. Also, a Persian, today.

>kippers< He proceeded to clean his whiskers. >satisfaction<. His purr rumbled through the apartment. >sleep<.

CHAPTER 4

That early afternoon I drove to the small storefront strip where Wolff's bookstore was. It had a coin laundry, a liquor store, a dry cleaner, and a Chinese restaurant. Wolff's store had thrice the space and about four times the traffic of the rest of the establishments on the strip. I parked my car and strolled in with my document laden dispatch bag. It was a quarter after ten and there were three people nosing through the shelves, a dogsbody making coffee in the back and Lyn at the cash register.

"You." Her eyes still promised mayhem. I let it pass.

"Is Mr. Wolff about?" I asked, placing my hand upon the counter.

She looked at the clock. Slumped. "He has an apartment above the store." She glared at me again. "He had a bad night after- "

"I am sorry for that. But I had a longish call to that house after you left. I will need to see him as soon as convenient."

Lyn tapped her short fingernails on the antique register. "There is no help for it, is there?" She stepped out from behind the counter. "Eric, come cover the register." The accident in the back stopped fussing with the coffee makers and came through the bead curtain. He gave me what he thought was a 'hard' look. I had my mid-level bureaucratic face on; I was perhaps a zoning official or a revenue agent. Nothing and nobody to remember.

"Is there a problem, Lyn?"

She rolled her eyes at him. "Just paperwork and such. Do not let Mister Raymond put any of the issues on reserve, he has not paid us for last month's comics."

We walked through the store, to the back and she unlocked a sturdy door, behind the door there was a small hallway with a table along the wall, then at the end of the hall was a door to the alley outside and a flight of stairs going up. She motioned me ahead, up the stairs. I smiled and nodded. She was at my back, but well within my hand, even without PC41 extending me.

There was landing at the top of the stairs, another sturdy door behind which was a cozy apartment that seemed to run the depth of the mall and twice the width of the bookstore. Wolff was sitting in a robe, in a well-worn club chair and paging through a thick album of photos.

"Good morning Mister Braxton," he said, not looking up from the album. "I have a pot of tea, fresh, if you would like."

It was afternoon, but I didn't quibble. "Not this morning. I spoke to the House last night. I was instructed to read you in." I lied.

His hand stilled. "Really." I think he knew I was completely exceeding my brief.

I sat in a chair, the twin of the one he was sitting in. Lyn hovered for a moment, Wolff looked at her over the top of his reading glasses and flicked a hand at her. She started to speak, checked herself and quietly left. He took off his reading glasses, folded them, then rested his hands upon the open album in his lap.

"I told the Directorate that you were being poisoned, slowly. After a lot of useless and unimportant palaver, they decided that it was necessary to know who was doing this and put a stop to it."

He leaned back in his chair and slightly smiled. "I'm

gratified that they are taking such an interest in me. I am also curious as to why I am important enough to warrant wasting your valuable time?"

"According to my sources, you were an officer in the British SIS. In particular in the British Commanders'-in-Chief Mission to the Soviets, BRIXMIS, in the occupied zone."

This startled him. His eyes locked on mine for the longest second, and then shifted to see something far away over my left shoulder. We sat in silence for what seemed like a very long time, then he spoke. "My memory is not what it used to be, so I have been going through my photo albums trying to understand the predicament I'm in. In my lifetime there's been no coincidences, every action has a beginning point and an end point. I thought that the source of my trouble was a faction well within the hidden world. Now, I wonder."

"In the last 18 months, Sir," I had without thinking about it, dropped into my 'after action' report tone, "21 members or former members of BRIXMIS have died or unaccountably disappeared." I held out a file folder to him. "The details are in here, but they were all assigned to the British Military Liaison Mission in Germany at one time or another." He took the folder from me. The first page and a half of the folder was the usual Bum Fodder of the Official Secrets Act, Unity BUMF Rendition. It boiled down to, 'If you talk about this, we will kill you'. He skimmed the threats and cautions and then went to the next page. It was a list of names, dates of service, branch of service and date of deaths.

"The operatives' service dates range from 1945 to 1980," I said. "Saving two, they have all died since January 1981."

He put his glasses back on and began to run a gnarled finger down the lists. "I know some of these names; some I served with, three were transiting to that assignment as I was being sent to SIS on permanent TDY. The rest of these, I have no idea. Is the only linkage that we all were in BRIXMIS?"

"Deeper in the dossier, there is another linkage. You all were in the north of the GDR at one time or another, in Bezirk Rostock."

"Rostock." He glanced at me over his reading glasses. "You think this is a KGB operation? Or a German Democratic Republic-HVA one?"

"I might think so, except for the fact there are reports concerning similar deaths and disappearances among the French MMFL, the USMLM of the Americans and, surprisingly, the Soviet SOSMIX. All of these quasi-diplomatic Missions have been suffering a greater than statistically normal rate of 'retired', reassigned and active members dying or going absent in recent months." I leaned back in the chair. "Very few of the missing or dead of the other occupying powers seem to have a direct connection to the Rostock District, but there are some commonalities."

Wolff flicked through the dossier and quickly read the summary for BRIXMIS. "Braxton, there is a large horsefly in the ointment. This Major Carleton-Wolff, who was a sol-distant cousin on my mother's side, did come to visit me in 1956. Lamentably, he died from a heart attack that fall." He looked up from the dossier. "That was my BRIXMIS legend, the trail should have gone cold there."

"But now you are dying, again."

"I cannot imagine why. Anything I knew, anyone I knew of, anything I have done is thirty-six and more years in the past."

"Perhaps not." I crossed my legs and struggled to keep from dozing off. Solving the puzzle and disconcerting Vittorio had cut into my sleep; mucking about with banks and long-winded dossier summaries had made my scant breakfast a distant, miserable, memory. "A short time before the deaths started, there was an incident at a gate in Rostock Gamby on the *Hanzevijver*."

"Well, now." He sat quietly. "That puts a different piece on the board. The Hanse and the Common Lands."

CHAPTER 5

We spent much of the afternoon, going through the BRIXMIS dossier page by page. Several of the deaths were suspicious only because they came in close proximity to the others. Others were mundane.

"McMurry here, I think we can disregard him." Wolff tapped a name midway through the list. "I knew him slightly when he was a Captain, very fond of his whisky and no soda. It says here that he retired as a Major in '68, passed over twice for promotion. Died of cirrhosis of the liver."

"And Leighton?"

Wolff shook his head. "That one is dodgy as all hell. He locked his house, leaving his passport and his dog behind, drove up into the highlands of Scotland very close to the Bridge of Orchy, parked his Land Rover in an isolated spot and promptly expired. Massive un-specified heart failure they opined. They did not find him for three -bloody-weeks in high summer! A scant hundred feet from a foot path, and no one noticed him, the reek, or his Land Rover? This beggars my imagination. How could they have any idea what did for him after three weeks in a sealed car, in the summer? It could have been 'elf-shot', for all they knew." He was indignant at the terrible tradecraft, not only a lie but an incompetent, undeniable lie; an insult direct.

"That was the last one on the list. Twenty-one men, five missing and eleven deaths that were either completely natural or 'not proven'. Four deaths that lay well within the possibility of enemy action." I scratched out the last name and put my pencil down. "Down from twenty-one endings to just four."

"Five." Said Lyn. Pecking away at her Sweet and Sour pork, using chopsticks. She looked at Wolfe, gave me a flat glare and went back to her takeaway.

Wolff grunted, shuffling his papers like a dealer squaring the deck. "Yes. Five. And I have no idea still what linked us all together." Wolff had dressed for lunch-a very late lunch, or an early dinner. He had sent Lyn out for Chinese and produced a large bottle of chilled home brew. Commenting that the sediment was conducive to keeping one 'regular in your habits' and to be avoided if at all possible, he carefully decanted the amber liquid into the pitcher and left a quarter inch of sediment and beer in the bottom of the bottle. We each had a schooner of the brew; it tasted more like a heavy cider with a touch of carbonation than a pilsner. Different but good. Lyn was still measuring me for a shallow grave somewhere in the countryside, but the beer seemed to mellow her somewhat. Or maybe it was that PC41 was not present.

"Start again." Wolff said. "The incident at the gate."

I flicked to the opening narration of the 'Incident'. As provided by the Eisenring.

"Three people entered the gate on the 'zeme end. The wicket was a single gallery; the Walker of the three had to be very chummy with the transporters or one of the couriers had to be a Walker as well as a transporter. It was one of the oldest kinds of wicket, slightly adapted for use by either an independent Walker or by someone using a limited *Fähremeister* docent provided by the Gate Base Operator. No mechanical trolleys, nothing out of the ordinary."

He nodded.

"Midway in the path, something happened. Reportedly

one of the transporters opened fire on one of the others with a heavy spring needler. He tried to seize the packet of his victim and escape. This was observed by one of the surviving personnel, identity redacted. This was at the gate at Rostock Gamby, in the Hanse Confederation homelands, coming from the 'zeme Commonality lands. It was a commonly used, though minor, gate. Its primary utility was that it had a 'book' for the Hanse, 'zeme and Terra. Limited capacity but a quick turnaround if you wanted to, say, gate from 'zeme to Terra through the Hanse. You would idle at the Hanse terminal, waiting for the gate energies to 'still', then go through the wicket again to arrive at Terra.

At the same time, someone tried to breach the *gatehus adit* chamber lock at Rostock Gamby in the Hanse with a small demolition charge. The gate subsequently ruptured and none of the transporters or the 'Ring close overwatch at either end of the Gallery survived. No bodies were recovered." I turned over the page and continued. "Two of the four gate Systems Operators at the Hanse terminal and one of the stand-by docents at the 'zeme Commonality end survived the collateral damage and were able, eventually, to provide us with this bare bone description." I leaned back and dropped my pencil on the tabletop. "That someone used a demolition charge close to the *adit* terminal, indicates either a callous disregard for the possible side effects or an abysmal ignorance of same."

"And how long was the Veil disrupted?" Wolff asked.

"A month on 'zeme, sixteen weeks apparent on Hanse. That particular gate is inoperable even now: its paths to Terra, 'zeme and Hanse are closed. Forty gates across the northern hemisphere on 'zeme and the Hanse were damaged or disrupted to a greater or lesser degree. Terra is much the same. The Hanse were very irate, to say the least. The Commonality was apoplectic. And the Calendar has not achieved a consistently successful hand-shake synchronization across all the gates. AngTerra, 'zeme, Hanse, Little England, Sindu, the lot."

That was another thing both Eisenrings were supposed to guard against, use of firearms.

Modern weapons within a Gallery had wildly unpredictable effects. Time flowed oddly enough within a Gallery in the best practice; add even primitive gunpowder-matchlocks or anything else-and strange things happened. Which is why the two Eisenrings still trained at bronze age martial arts and the guards within the Galleries carried edged weapons, crossbows or pneumatic pellet guns and spring guns with heavy needles. Like the Borchardt. Local conditions often made the accuracy of light needles or pellets chancy. Much like shooting through water. A short sword was certain.

Lyn spoke up. "And the sapper?"

"He-."

My pager chose that time to go off. It gave me a number: Croton on the Hudson, here in AngTerra. Vittorio. I looked up at them. "Do you have a pay phone near here, I'd rather not use your phones."

Lyn spoke, looking up from her congealing plate. "The laundromat is your best choice. Red Wall's payphone is perpetually out of order." I nodded my thanks, struggled out of the antique but surprisingly comfortable chair, and left the apartment.

I walked down the stairs and went through the bookstore, composing my coming interview with Vittorio or one of his minders. The pager was in my weak hand.

At the cash register there was a strikingly tall woman. Her dark hair was cut close about her head, in not quite a military crop. She wore a blazer that was not readily available here and now, some non-descript but business-appropriate slacks, a large purse slung across her body, from her left shoulder to her right hip. No earrings. Her hands were splayed out on the glass top, ringless, her fingers white from the restrained anger I heard in her voice. English was a third choice for her, you could almost follow the translation tree in her pauses. As I passed behind her, she flicked an eye to check me, dismissed me, then went back to butting heads with the marginally competent Eric.

"I will see Wolff this day, this very day, this very instant. I do insist." The forcefulness of her words was belied by a squeak in her voice. She leaned forward to poke Eric's chest with her left index finger. He batted it away, leaned in his turn to try and intimidate her, which was laughable; he was a head shorter. She then grabbed his t-shirt collar with her right hand and twisted it, not tight enough to make a difference-or even much of an impression. He grabbed her wrist and found he could not quite break her hold. They rattled the cash register, the counter and the display case as they seesawed back and forth. I had thought her older, from her clothing mostly. The business casual wear gave the impression that she was some years older than Eric, but I could tell now that they were of an age. He was wearing a worn-thin Dr. Who t-shirt and jeans out at the knees; while she had the Burberry wool blazer. They scrabbled for dominance like primary schoolchildren.

Then she made a left-handed grab for the pistol tucked away under the back of her blazer.

This had been entertaining. Amusing enough that I had slowed to watch what was happening. Much like watching a very public breakup or someone being 'had' for public intoxication. Harmless. But I drew the line at 'weapons drawn', particularly as inept as her draw with her weak hand was proving to be. Just as likely to shoot herself as him-or worse yet me.

Eric was frightened and angry and worst of all embarrassed; he was winding up to punch a woman taller and stronger than he was with his weak hand. I caught his eye as I stepped in close behind her, looking past her shoulder. His red face paled in an instant and he stopped.

She froze. My weak hand had the pager cupped in it pressed to the back of her neck and a very obvious gun barrel was in the small of her back right above her holstered pistol. She eased her left hand away from the pistol in the holster, almost as slowly as a Kata performance. I approved of her caution. When she felt the slight snap my pistol's safety made, she rattled off several choice words in a language I happily understood.

I raked her charkas with my auric tools, giving her a light jab with the pager and letting it buzz for good measure. Misdirection. Convincing her that I had a stun gun at the nape of her neck charging up for a solid shot and not something more. I raked her again, pinching a charka and making her lightheaded. Then I dropped my pager to the floor and stripped her gun from her holster, slid the pistol into my left trouser pocket.

Eric saw my gun then and made a slow grab for the phone at the side of the register, his hand missing the phone entirely.

I shook my head. He stopped. "Eric," I said, "do be a good lad and lock up the drawer. Then precede us up the stairs to Mister Wolff's apartment."

"I am not supposed to leave the-."

She tensed to make a move on me. I 'leaned' on her chakras, while my free hand was pressed against the back of her neck. The pager vibrated angrily on the floor at the side of the counter, much like a rattlesnake. Vittorio was getting anxious. She started to slide down the front of the counter, her hands grabbing it as her legs gave way.

I smiled into Eric's face, nodded my head towards the back hall and the stairway.

"Yes…Sir." He gulped. He didn't lock the drawer, but I decided to overlook that lapse in the coming report. He edged from behind the counter, his eyes fixed on us. Then he turned and scampered to the door that secured the hallway leading to Wolff's apartments.

A quick glance about the shop, no one had any interest in us; I pushed her to follow Eric. "Now after him, if you please. Dama. No theater," I said, in Low Hanse.

She stumbled a bit; from the physical push I gave her and the 'push' I gave her charkas. She was also shocked to be addressed in the prevailing dialect of the Hansatic Commons. I faded back from her, far enough that she would be uncertain of connecting if she ventured an attack.

Lyn met us at the base of the stairs leading up to the apartment; with a shaken Eric huddling behind her, two steps up. She had a small needler in her right hand down by her leg.

"She needs to see Wolff," I said, "if she knows where he is…" Lyn nodded and motioned Eric around us with her free hand while her eyes remained focused on the woman in front of me. Eric did not yet present a problem, which was fortunate for him and convenient for us. He slowly stepped around the Hansatic woman, dashed past me and disappeared back into the shop. "Is he-" I nodded at the fleeing Eric. "going to be a problem?"

Lyn shook her head. "I have strongly discouraged him from involving anyone else. I think he took it to heart."

Right. Eric being instructed by the focus of his midnight crush, 'taking it to heart'. Well, I will reinforce that. "Very good, lead the way." And Lyn backed up the stairs.

CHAPTER 6

Wolff was standing in his parlor. He was behind the chair in which I had found him with the album and our briefing papers put safely away. Lyn backed through the opened door and took a position off to the right of the door, her eyes still on the intruder. I nudged the Hansatic woman into the apartment. Then I tugged gently at the back of her jacket to stop her. Then I put my weapon away. "You will pardon the familiarity, Dama," I said in her Low Hanse and began to frisk her from behind. This was not particularly effective or safe, but Lyn had her under one gun and I knew that Wolff had a gun ready behind the chair. I also knew that Lyn would not hesitate to shoot through me if necessary, or even if it wasn't necessary.

I had her pistol already. I took the purse off her shoulder and over her head, dropped it on the floor. I ran my hands over her body, gently pushed her arms into the air. There was a wallet in an interior pocket of the blazer and nothing else on her. I stepped back, flipped open the wallet. There was no passport; just a cheaply laminated photo ID, in German. It legended her as Inspector Johanna Marie Ledhrad. "West German Border Guard." I translated out loud.

"The *Bundesgrenzschutz*." Wolff said, he had a Prussian accent when he spoke German. Then he greeted her in Low Hanse and not the German of this milieu. "Welcome to my threshold, Dama Ledhrad. But of course, you sit at the table with *XternBuro* and not our West Germany." He had no accent in the 'Common Tongue', which did not surprise me.

She nodded her head. "I will not contest that fact." She replied also in Low Hanse. "And you are Dom Wolff, an agent in place for the Dai Commonality, the Unity."

"I was once engaged with that constellation, but quite some time ago. Do come in." He motioned to the chair I had so recently warmed. "Sit and let us visit a while." She walked slowly over to the chair without taking her eyes off Wolff and sat down. "Tea, perhaps, or I could brew some coffee?" She exhaled, nodded slightly. An offer of hospitality.

"I would treasure a cup of coffee," she said in stilted English.

Lyn coughed, stifling a laugh or a curse. "I'll start a fresh pot, we still have some crullers, you want me to lay them out as well?" She was not a happy Medji. Medji in a proper placement do not serve tea or coffee.

"If you please. And you Mister Braxton?"

I placed Dama Ledhard's weapon and her ID folder on a table by the door. "I must decline, I need to speak with some people." I nodded to Lyn and to Wolff and left.

I cornered Eric by a rotating comic book rack. "Lyn had words with you?"

"She did." He was trying to work up to being assertive. Assertive enough to call the police.

"Mr. Wolff was in the war, in Intelligence. Then after the war he had a role to play in protecting the West. Now he is semi-retired, and Lyn has been assigned to him." I let that dollop of lies percolate through his mind. "There is more happening here than I, or Lyn, may reveal to you. Do you understand?"

Appeal to his inner secret agent. I have no shame.

His eyes lit up. "Yes. Yes, I understand." He was eager to enlist. To impress.

"Excellent. All will be well, if we but keep our heads. I will return, shortly." I shook his slightly damp and sticky hand as if he was off on a SOE mission over Occupied Europe. I reiterate, I have no shame. As I left the store, I wiped my hand with a cheap handkerchief, discarding it in a trash can as I walked down the sidewalk to the laundromat.

The phone set at the laundromat was filthy, I wiped it clean with another handkerchief that I also promptly discarded and then I put some Weitbrecht couplers over the speaker and microphone of the handset.

"Braxton for Vittorio…"

Of course, the urgent message was that a Hanse operative had been observed at Wichita's airport. I informed Vittorio's aide that his news was a day late and a half-penny short. That a representative of the *XternBuro* was even now sitting and comparing notes with Mr. Wolff. This caused a great deal of agitation on their end and no end of satisfaction on my end. Keeping me 'keen' indeed.

"It would appear that information is leaking from your table, like thin broth from a colander. In any event I need to go back to Wolff's apartment before the *XternBuro* brings him over into their service." I hung up on the aide, uncoupled the encoders and nodded politely at the attendant.

I swung through the liquor store and picked up a six pack of IPA and a pair of the large Stella Artois bottles. I knew from Wolff's appreciation of my hoarded tea cake that a gift of a Pale Ale might not go amiss, while Stella Artois was about the closest available to a Hanse Brewmeister's pilsner I once encountered. Both were cold, which might have been a misstep, but they were only available cold. As was the Guinness Stout on offer by the shop, but cold Guinness is a mortal insult.

I breezed into the bookstore and up the stairs like I had free reign over the store. Eric only gave me a solemn nod as I went past with my large brown paper bag. He did push a button under the cash register, and I was quickly met by Lyn at the top of the stairs.

"And which of the secret services are we today?" She asked me, with one eye on the empty stairs behind me. "Uncle or Control?"

I gave her a very well-rehearsed poker face. "What are you going on about?"

"Mnph. He needs to rest an-."

"And how are they getting on?"

"He has pulled out the pre-war albums and is bringing her up to speed on Café Society in Paris-prewar of course. That man never meets a stranger."

I nodded. "My people are properly horrified. Do you have any back up?"

"No. We have not had backup for quite a while." She nodded at the bag, it clinked. "You intend to drink him under the table?"

"Hospitality. I am uncomfortable with all of us dining out and take-out Chinese again is..." I made the bag clink once again. "But a glass or three and then I can take Dama Ledhrad off to a quiet dinner and leave you to your devices."

"Too smooth, by half. Napoleon Solo, today." And she followed me into the apartment.

CHAPTER 7

Wolff surprised me by preferring the Stella, while Dama Ledhrad was delighted with the IPA. That was neither here nor there.

"Dama, how did you come across?" I asked Ledhrad, in English.

She turned from Wolff and regarded me with that level gaze the Hanse have prepared their children with since they were in pre-school. "I 'came across' at the Island," She replied in kind. "to receive my preliminary orientation to this milieu. It was, interesting." She was poised, sitting in his club chair and without a wrinkle in her blazer from wrestling with Eric.

I nodded. "How, if I may ask, did you come to have such a complete briefing on Mr. Wolff."

"He was the first one on my manifest. The living roster that is."

"And your list stems from-?"

"And you are?"

"Josiah Braxton." I was not forthcoming.

"You were not in my brief."

I smiled and nodded agreement. "I should hope not."

She tapped a fingernail against her beer glass. Looked to her right where Lyn sat, nursing a glass of water and with her pistol in hand, then looked to Wolff. "Dom Wolff, your protectors are-." She addressed him in Low Hanse.

"He is not, strictly speaking, my protector." Wolff replied in English. He was putting her off balance for a reason. He looked up from his photo album and smiled at Lyn. "So, you must take him as you find him. Mr. Braxton and my interests seem to run in the same direction, but I am not his principal."

She blinked at that.

"Why have you come calling upon Mr. Wolff," I said. "Or, rather, why do you have a list with his name on it?"

Her account of the 'incident' was much the same as ours, with some differences. The gate was a sanctioned entry point from the Commonality of the 'Zeme to the Hanse and from the Hanse to AngTerra. It had a properly licensed and bonded staff consisting of a *Fähremeister*, with the required fifteen-man security and customs detail comprising of an Eisenring detachment and an *XternBuro* office. These details were not included in our briefing papers. For a single Gallery wicket, it was rather over staffed. Suspiciously so, but the Hanse was a society that believed in full employment. Idle hands were frowned upon.

What happened in the confines of the gate was unclear to the Hanse, but two tried to exit where three were expected. They were being detained at the threshold proper, when there was an external attack upon the customs and security station. The gate 'scrammed', in her words, and the two who were detained at the gate disappeared into the energies, as did fully half of the attending Eisenring and *XternBuro* details. The external attack was repelled with significant casualties on both sides, but two of the attackers were arrested.

"To our shame, the surviving attackers were former *XternBuro* employees. Sojourners to be sure and not of the Common Folk, but once employed by *XternBuro* as facilitators among the *Gaiten*. We quickly came to the root of our concern, after debriefing them extensively."

"Hmm. I see," Wolff said. "And their goal in the attack?"

"They were to recover a particular *Auslander* who was being regularly employed as a *Gaiten* controller." She produced a crisply folded sheet of paper from another wallet in her purse. "He was one of fifteen identities that we became concerned about-there are seven names that are thought to be resident here." And she handed the list to Wolff.

"Unfortunately, Karsten Tauber was among the dead at the scene."

Wolff had taken a set of reading glasses from their case on the end table at his left hand. He stopped, the list in his hand. "And the others?" He put his reading glasses on and begun to work his way down the almost Gothic typescript. I could tell that particular name meant something to him.

"It took time to convince the survivors that it was in their best interest to cooperate fully." She shrugged in a practiced way. "Some upon the list of sojourners were dead. Regrettably, some had fled successfully. To Little England-the Isle of Alba to be precise-and points beyond, so I have been instructed."

Wolff sighed, cracked his neck. Then took off his glasses and folded the paper, carefully putting it away. "I find that I am very weary, Dama Ledhrad. Let me peruse this list and compare it to the information our resources have provided us." He waved at me. "Josiah will see to your accommodations and we will resume this discussion tomorrow."

And Lyn ushered us out smoothly. She would have made a grand chucker-out in the old neighborhood in the Estuary. I passed Eric, who was at his post. He handed me the roll-on suitcase that I had missed when I frog-marched Dama Ledhard up to see Wolff. He also handed me my pager. I nodded, thanking him for his service and shook his hand again, making a mental note to buy more cheap cotton handkerchiefs. Lyn made sure we were clear of the door and well on our way to my car before she went to lock up early. I could feel my ears burning as the door locked behind us.

We had watchers. I was relieved to some extent to see, in the parking lot and across the street, watchers. I had made it clear to Vittorio's aide that keeping Wolff healthy was in everyone's present interest. One of the watchers was deliberately displayed, for my benefit. He was the local stringer that had given me my keys and meager funds at the start of this soiree. It made it very likely that the rest of the observers were Vittorio's.

I took her to Portobello's, a Steak House of excellent local reputation. She was resolutely mute all the way there, one hand clenching the seatbelt and the other braced against the A-pillar. I parked the car and walked around to open her door. Her eyes were still closed.

"Dama Ledhard?"

"We are there?"

"Yes."

She swallowed. "I must apologize, but I am unfamiliar with-." She released her grip on the seatbelt. "It was not quite this exciting on the way to Dom Wolff's from the *Gaiten*."

So, she gated directly here from the Island-which I assumed was within Little England's mandate, Alba. From Hanse to 'zeme to Alba and then to AngTerra. Someone was being artistic in their traffic protocols.

I knew of six gates, covert but sanctioned and controlled, that were direct to AngTerra from the Hanse. I did not know of a gate to anywhere within the perimeter of Midcontinent Airport. I wondered if Vittorio knew.

"I am sorry for your distress." I held my hand out. She took it in her weak hand and slid out of the car more gracefully than she had stepped into it.

I had made a reservation from the phone in the apartment, as she was making her excuses to Wolff. It was mid-week, and they were not busy, and it was not very late in the evening: they would be delighted to save us a table.

Dama Ledhrad had been well trained, at least by someone with a clipboard and a check list. The ride in the extremely unfamiliar car, unsafe as well as unfamiliar by her lights, had disconcerted her. But by the time we entered the restaurant, she had regained her balance. She took in the greeter, the bar and bartender close by the door, the cluster of tables near but not too near the entrance, the kitchen swing doors and the fire exits. All in one casual sweep. It was a sweep that was from a three-ring binder: titled 'How to scan an unfamiliar room and note all threats and escape routes-There will be a test.' She was not as well seasoned as she tried to present herself.

We were seated and I asked for a cup of coffee while we read the menus. Dama Ledhrad seconded my request for coffee and opened her menu, right side up. She could read, English at least.

"Have you any questions?" I asked her, in English.

"Many, but my questions are not about the offerings in this." She tapped the menu.

"Order what you like, if you are uncertain..." The waitress brought two sets of coffee service and a carafe. She poured us both a cup and then left us to the menus.

Ledhrad closed her menu and laid it face down on the table. Picked up her coffee, cup and saucer as well, and sipped at it. "I am not terribly fond of seafood and I am somewhat unsettled from the journey."

"Should I order?"

"Yes. Please."

I got us a salad each with vinegar and oil. Then rare prime rib, a baked potato and steamed broccoli for me. I ordered her a small filet, medium well, roasted new red potatoes and glazed carrots. We both had ice water and coffee with the meal. The meal occupied us long enough to make us comfortable with silence between us. I ordered more coffee and addressed her in Low Hanse.

"I am of the Eisenring." She tilted her head at my declaration, inviting more. "I was given a watching brief over Dom Wolff, but events have overtaken that tasking. Have you noted the changes in his appearance?"

She considered for a long time. "No. His appearance closely matches the photos in our dossier on him."

That meant that someone had recently had eyes on him, and that it was someone from the Tables of the Dai that was feeding information to the Hanse. Or it was Hanse agents operating here in AngTerra, which was an even larger kettle of fish. "He is gravely ill. Perhaps a tailored infection and a toxin to impair the immune system's response to the infection. Our consensus is: that the attack is technically beyond either the Confederated Houses or the Unity. We thought it likely came from a Steelyard laboratory in the Hanse."

She did not like that. Not at all.

"And Nihon?"

Points to her, they were noted for offside attacks. Poison and the like. "We considered that possibility. But the other attacks-"

"Other attacks?"

We gazed at each other over the coffee cups. I had not seen the list she brought over. And she had not seen our list.

It took me less than fifteen minutes to read her in. From memory, I am proud to say. She was stunned. She had also memorized her list and recited it to me.

Of the remaining names, beside our Benjamin Wolff, on

both lists was Hugh Snow.

On my list he was a Captain in the British 5th Infantry Division, handling operational logistics for BRIXMIS. Transport, lodging, food and other supplies. And so, when the time came for him to cycle out of BRIXMIS his orders never came. He was 'lost' to his original unit; too good at the job with BRIXMIS. He stayed with the British Military Liaison Mission until 1951, providing logistical support and being privy to all of the operations in the GDR and much of Europe. Then he went home, mustered out, and became a minor businessman in a minor business in London. He faded away from the records, no family, no promotions, or fawning articles about his role in the minor business in the local Business paper. Then the minor business closed, and he found another job in an office park outside of Birmingham doing much the minor same thing. The last time he had an address and a tax return with the Inland Revenue was in the late 60's. He wasn't listed on my tally as dead, just 'not found'; 'gone to Australia', 'gone for a Burton'. But he was in BRIXMIS throughout much of the early postwar days and he was included as a footnote to the other list of 'missing'; it was well-nigh impossible to drop out of the sight of Inland Revenue, even in the swinging 60s, and that made him a person of interest.

On her list he was a duly chartered, registered, and bonded *Auslander* merchant; known for dealing in rare liquors, exotic foods and spices. And he was still paying his taxes and guild fees up to the last quarter before the incident. Then he vanished from the aegis of the Concierge, the surveillance program that kept the Hanse well ordered. That made him more interesting to the *XternBuro* than if they had found him dead in the street.

Other than Hugh Snow and Wolff, there was no other obvious cross-matches. She had five confirmed deaths, all unattended, and all either *Auslanders* or closely associated with an *Auslander*. We had our five suspicious deaths, including the declining Wolff. All had a link with Bostock and the British mission in the GDR.

I left a substantial tip on the card slip, thinking cheerfully about Vittorio and his quarterly budget, and escorted her to the car.

"Have you a hotel room?" I asked her in English.

She sighed. "No." She clutched her purse, which had her pistol in it; sans the magazine, which I had in my jacket.

"I have an apartment, with two bedrooms, close at hand. You are welcome to stay with me if you wish."

I could feel her eyes on me. "Why would I think this is a good thing?"

"You have made an impression on someone. I received a panicky message that an *XternBuro* agent had appeared at the airport, unescorted and wholly unexpected." I looked at her. "Someone slipped you around the normal routes and past the usual receptions and deposited you on the front stoop of perhaps the last living name on both our mutual lists."

She nodded slowly. "I would not be hard to replace, but it would be a nuisance." For both of us.

"And if Wolff was to die, tonight, you would be a person of interest."

"As would you."

"Um-hum." I nodded. "However, I have been well vetted and arrived here in the usual way." Of a sort.

"I agree." The undertone in her voice made it clear just what she was agreeing to, and what she was not.

I nodded again, wondering what PC41 was going to make of her-and what she was going to make of Him. Or Her, as it might be.

CHAPTER 8

P C41 was sitting regally in the middle of the living room of the apartment when we arrived. This evening he was a very large, short-hair, tuxedo with white markings on his chest and muzzle.

"There is a cat." In Low Hanse. She had taken three steps into the room, just clearing the doorway and allowing me to maneuver her single piece of luggage through it.

"He came with the apartment." I lied. In Low Hanse, flat lies can be quite believable. It is one reason they particularly abhor liars. "He is respectable, more so I fear than I am, at times."

She crouched on one knee and cautiously extended her hand to PC41. He took a step forward, sniffed politely and brushed his whiskers against the knuckles of the offered hand. Then he stood up, gave me an offended look, and stalked into the kitchenette.

"I am afraid that his dinner is quite late."

"I understand full well, He knows his priorities. And where is the necessity?" She smiled at me for the first time since I frog-marched her up the stairs to Wolff.

I let Dama Ledhrad find her own way to the 'necessity' and I procured a can of salmon for my other charge. The migraine sparked at the base of my skull. >different<.

I knelt and scooped his dinner out upon a small plate,

made sure he had water-he was a 'he' this evening-and carefully put the empty can away from temptation. His batting the empty can through the hallway at four in the morning was not something I wished to repeat.

>very< I thought. >very<

I was sitting in the rocker when she came back into the living room. "I have made my place-" She said in careful English. "in the unused room. You are to be commended, the necessity was sparkling, and your lumber room was well kept as well."

PC41 was on my lap, making what passed for a purr from a two and a-half stone cat. "You would prefer to use English?"

"I do not know how long I will be here, or who I will be dealing with."

"Using the local dominant language is a wise choice."

"You have a multiplicity of languages to deal with. Do you not?"

"On this leaf of the Veil, certainly. And on the rest of the worlds that the Dai can walk to, there perhaps are even more. Many are cognate to each other, a few are almost exactly the same. And there are languages that are quite unique."

She smiled at PC41. "I hear a strain of enthusiasm in your voice, you were once a student of languages?"

"I have a faculty with learning new tongues. But," I scratched at PC41's neck at the base of his large skull. His 'purr' increased, sounding much like the rumble of a Prestwich Motorcycle. "there was less of a need for a specialist in linguistics than for a general dogs-body."

"Dog's body?"

"A person who is at the bottom of the office list, who was assigned the routine and boring tasks."

"I understand." She looked me directly in the face for the first time since she had come into the room. "But you are not a routine functionary, now?"

"No, if I take your meaning correctly." I nudged PC41 off my lap and stood. "I had the bed simply made up, sheets and a bedspread, before I knew I might be accommodating guests. I have an extra set of pillows and a comforter in the closet in the hall by the 'necessary's' door."

"What is our plan for tomorrow?"

"We should breakfast, early, and present ourselves at Wolff's door. Hopefully he will have spent a quiet night and we may be able to develop a better idea of what is going on." I took her pistol's magazine from my jacket, handed it to her.

In the middle of the night, PC41 landed on my chest. >wake<.

I had my weak hand under the pillow as I laid on my back, lightly holding my needle gun.

>wake< And my head rang with his push.

I rolled off the bed and taking PC41 with me landed on the carpet. The house was quiet. I opened the five thresholds and 'listened', which made the migraine come on even faster.

"Where away." I whispered. PC41 was completely black now, sleek and half the size he-now she-had been when I went to bed and she had slipped out the screen window for her nightly rounds.

>door<. >DOOR<.

And I knew she meant the apartment door. I slipped out of my room and edged down the hall, my needle gun in my strong hand now and the migraine curling at the base of my brain.

As I got to the rather lumpy couch, I heard the lock snap open. It pushed against the security chain and in the dim light from the hall I could see a thin pair of metal cutters snip the chain.

>now<. I pushed.

And my awareness bloomed about me, washed past PC41 and the pair in the doorway. My awareness knew Ledhrad was at my back. Just as a hand fumbled the light on, just as I heard Ledhrad take the safety of her gun off, I knew what was in the doorway.

"Check fire, check fire," I said in a conversational tone, in Hanse, not whispering but not shouting either.

Lyn was frozen in the doorway, half concealing Wolff from us. He had a brown leather briefcase, almost twice as large as a messenger bag, under one arm. He was wearing a cracked leather jacket with a ripped shoulder seam. She carefully dropped her snips from her left hand and motioned at Wolff with her head. She was leaning against him, her right arm hanging loosely.

"I have come calling, Mr. Braxton." Said Wolff. "With an explanation, I should think, for part of what is troubling you and Dama Ledhrad."

CHAPTER 9

I enthroned Wolff in the rattan rocker again, released Ledhrad with a wave of my hand and gently closed the door behind PC41's dark grey back as he slipped through it. The hallway was carpeted with a particularly faded institutional grey, the light was dim, and she had a way of drifting like smoke.

I had, wisely as it turned out, slept in a set of trainers. I had not paid attention to what Ledhrad had worn to bed. I still have no idea of what she had appeared in when Wolff came knocking on my door.

Lyn was in much worse shape than Wolff. Someone or something had hit her a solid blow to the cheekbone. Her eye was nearly swollen shut and I think she had gotten another punch in the ribs. She wasn't breathing well.

I got a plastic bag and a handful of ice from the freezer and had her sit on the couch while I pressed the bag against her face. When I did that, I could tell what shape her chakras were in. She had a spray of needles in her right arm, cheap loads. Common neurotoxins, the most of them had not penetrated her jacket. The few that did were playing merry hell with her breathing.

"We need to get that jacket off; you got a spray."

"Fu'kin ay I did." She laid her head back on the couch and closed both eyes, allowing me to hold the ice bag against her cheek. I had enough energy to touch up her charkas. Once I did, she could manage to hold the ice bag against her face with her left hand. I unbuttoned the sleeve of the jacket. I then gently pulled the sleeve down and away from her right arm. I could see, even in the meager light of the living room, a spray of silver dots embedded in the denim.

I should have cut it away, but with the amount of detailed embroidery and patches on the jacket, I was afraid she'd fight me. I heard a thump in my bedroom and knew that PC41 had reentered my garden apartment by the open window in the bedroom. She came stalking out of my room, tiger striped in grey and light grey. Wolff did not notice, but Ledhrad did.

Dama Ledhrad had her gun in her hand and she was dressed for any eventuality, her bag over her shoulder.

I had her sit on the couch close to Lyn. PC41 did her sphinx imitation on the table where she could watch over all of us. I nodded to Ledhrad and went to dress.

Twenty minutes and a pot of tea with honey later, we were all much calmer. Lyn was so much calmer she was snoring, faintly. It was four in the morning, local time.

"What happened?" I finally asked Wolff.

"I keep some things off the premises, always have. It is a fair neighborhood, but someone occasionally tries to burgle my place when I am down in the store." He smiled slightly at Lyn, who was still snoring softly on the couch. "It never ends well for the sneak thief. But, at most, a salutary beating; nothing serious. And never repeated."

"I had Lyn slip me out and away from your 'mousers' and we went to one of my caches. On the way back-someone attacked us."

"Needles only?"

"They wanted to take me alive and concentrated on Lyn. I got two with my Borchardt." The antique needler.

"Will I need to call a clean-up crew?"

He nodded. "There were four, one driving a van and three to make the grab. The van and one of the three snatch men escaped. The other two I put down…"

I nodded. I got up and walked over to the pantry, got the coupler out and went to make someone's morning even brighter.

After waking Vittorio from a sound sleep to tell him that Wichita had gone active and we needed a sanitation crew. I went back to sitting in an uncomfortable kitchen chair from the 1950s, next to Wolff.

"What is in that dossier that makes this all worthwhile?"

"Karsten Tauber."

"The Gate operator," Ledhrad spoke for the first time in an hour. "The supposed target of the group that attacked the *gatehus*." She shifted uncomfortably in her chair. "We knew someone wanted him, for unknown reasons, but how would you know of him?"

"Oh, I know Karsten Tauber quite well," Wolff said. "I spent most of a fruitless year trying to run him down." He opened the brief and took out a large fistful of dossiers. On the front of one of the manila file-folders there was a faded black wreath enclosing a stylized eagle with a swastika in his claws. "His rank was *Standartenführer*, his organization the *Orpo*- the *Ordnungspolizei*- and he was a very, very wanted man. And from your account, Dama, he had been living a blameless, productive, life, in the Hanse. Since the year 1945, in our common era."

My mouth went dry. I knew precisely who Wolff was now, '*der Jager*'.

Wolff had made a career out of eliminating the Unchurched Talented; at first in the runup to the war, then during the war, and finally in the grey crumbling aftermath of the Thousand Year Reich. I was not a contemporary, but I had heard about *'der Jager'* from his peers. At 'table' as it was, they had swapped accounts of him taking down some of the best and the darkest of the *Allemagne Noir*. He was supposed to be immune or resistant to all the binding pedigrees. Resistant as well to the auric weapons of the Sangsue, although I was living proof that account was not reliable.

He noted that I'd had a moment of chilling clarity. He smiled at me, tilted his head sideways in acknowledgment. "Tauber was a churched *Allemagne Noir*. Not quite a Sangsue, but an educated connoisseur of the methods and side effects of Gestapo interrogations. And he was also well known to the secular intelligence agencies, for his activities in the *Orpo*." He handed me a large black and white. glossy, identification photo. A man in a light grey uniform with an Iron Cross on his left pocket, an Eagle in a light metal wreath on his left sleeve. Short dark hair, neither thin nor fat; satisfied with his place in the Reich. "The uniform was actually a field green; his hair was brown, slicked down with a pomade. No known distinguishing marks, we were not even certain he had had the blood group tattoo. *Orpo* was not SS, at least not completely. By the end of the war there was not a playing card's thickness between them." He took the glossy photo back from me. "We, the Occupying powers, turned an official blind eye to the *Orpo's*, the uniformed police, existence. The Four Powers needed an organization to manage the Occupation, you see." He smiled again and there was no humor in it. "But we made examples of the higher officers. And carefully purged all the specialized agencies in the police, 'to encourage the others'."

"Churched?" Ledhrad asked.

We had forgotten Ledhrad. A mistake.

I turned and looked at her. Her face was white and pinched, as if she had tasted something incredibly foul. She had her hand in the bag, presumably the hand with the gun. She looked at Lyn, then at Wolff and me.

"How much did your department brief you?" I asked her.

"Not enough, entirely not enough. It is against the banns to allow a Sojourner's petty conflicts to break the Peace of the Common Land, but to bring blood and red mayhem to the Land! To Spill The Blood Of The People! Yet you maintain that this is exactly what has transpired this last long generation?" Her voice broke, squeaked.

Long generation. I blinked. By our calendars the war was not quite forty years in our past. In the Hanse, a 'Long Generation' was something well over seventy years. It was much the same in the 'zeme, maybe sixty years for a long generation. Crossing the veil and time could and would slip. Under the Elf hill, again.

Wolff answered for us both. "Yes. The last great war on this Line has spilled its fragments into many of the Notes, into the Sheaf's of this Chord. Including the Hanse." He placed his hand on the dossiers. "We thought that the procedures in place for controlling the passage between our Notes, our worlds, stopped any contamination of the Common Land."

"No." She lapsed into a dialect of Hanse that I had no knowledge of. Her auras bloomed in the darkened room: horrified, disgusted, enraged, repulsed, frightened. I could see and thread my auric tendrils through her rising fields. I saw PC41 rise slowly to her feet, his fur bottling out and changing to slate grey. A black mist began to coalesce around Ledhrad in my eyes, shot through with boiling swirls of light. She shrank away from Lyn and tried to draw her gun from the bag, fumbling in her distress. PC41 slowly faded into the shadows of the room, each step he took brought him closer to the quivering woman. At each step we pushed. At each push she panted more, at each push she lost coordination, lost focus. At each push her auras rolled like silt in disturbed water.

"And how are you to report this, Dama Ledhrad? If you succeed?" Wolff was watching all this, speaking calmly. His hands firmly on the packet in his lap. "You will be forsaken, adrift, discarded, on this side of the Veil. Vanished beyond a succession of posterns and narrow passages, stranded among strangers. Lost to the Common Land and the Common People."

She cursed and flung her bag at me, tried to stand, and stumbled over PC to land flat on her back. Lyn woke up, scrambled for her own weapon-which I had carefully placed out of reach-and goggled at Ledhrad batting away at PC41. He was nuzzling her face with his claws firmly embedded in her blouse but not her skin, purring loudly; as loud as a two-stroke engine. Lyn tried to stand and then fell heavily back into the couch.

Ledhrad's accent in Hanse was cultivated, over educated even. Until she was pushed into a corner and then it slipped. Like a Sloan Ranger of the AngTerra milieu suddenly breaking into gutter cockney.

Wolff looked at me from the corner of his eye. I was ignoring PC41 nuzzling Ledhrad, watching Wolff instead. He was within my range, along with Lyn on the couch and Johanna Marie on the floor. "That, is a bloody peculiar cat."

I nodded. "Isn't it though." I picked up Ledhrad's bag and stuffed the few items that had fallen out back into it. Her wallet, lip gloss, packet of sweets, a packet of tissues.

That brand of gloss and the Burberry blazer she wore were from Little England; and any proper ops runner would have embargoed that. I checked and the Franco-German PPK was still in the purse. I watched PC41 crouching over her a moment longer, then turned to Wolff. "This is going to cause the Provos, the 'Unity and Croton-upon-Hudson mass apoplexy. Letting the Hanse in on the game."

When he heard, Vittorio might just take to his bed, turn his face to the wall, and die. A cheery thought. I stood and went to adjust Lyn on the couch, threading my web through her auras as I stuffed a pillow behind her. She smiled at me, murmured something, then her eyes closed, and she began to snore again.

I smiled down at Lyn; when she wasn't contemplating mayhem, she was pleasant in a tomboy way. I kept half an ear on Ledhrad, sobbing fitfully on the floor.

She was convinced, from what I could glean from her babbling through the sobs, that she was polluted beyond redemption. Forever unfit to rejoin the Commons. It was a possibility.

Between learning more than she ever wanted to know about the Dai and Sojourners; having to deal with obviously socially maladjusted and ill-bred strangers, riding in outrageously unsafe vehicles, having an otherworldly cat licking away her shameful tears, she'd had more than enough. One deeper sob and perhaps a prayer and she burbled into sleep.

>alright< I pushed. >enough< PC41 settled on her chest and began to purr, lightly kneading.

The migraine was much fainter each time. Which concerned me. >watch< And I felt a satisfaction. She liked Johanna Marie.

"Do you think-" I asked Wolff. "the people who ambushed you will show up on my doorstep?"

"I don't have an opinion either way. I suppose they might. They should have been here by now, if they had any proper tradecraft to their quivers. If it was not for the needle-gun, I would have ascribed it to simple coincidence. They were so poorly trained. It was an inept attempt in any event, two dead to an old man with an old gun. You know they had a van, but the driver in his desire to get clean away impaled it on a fire hydrant three blocks on. The driver fled on foot along with the other fool."

I winced. I hadn't known that. A dead body or two is one thing, a broken hydrant is something quite another. Television stations, for some reason, are just enthralled by the geysers of broken hydrants. "I suspect this location is rumbled, if not now then shortly. Do you have any suggestions?"

"Perhaps." He thought for a bit, nodded. "I know of a small horse farm, some miles north of here. A tenured professor's farm. They are, I believe, out of town competing in dressage and I know where they hide their door keys."

CHAPTER 10

It was a bit of an undertaking; stuffing the ladies, Wolff, PC41 and myself into my rental car. I recovered the roller suitcase which she had not unpacked, brought her blazer on a hanger and a comforter into the living room. Then I carefully enfolded Lyn's jacket in the comforter so we would not be contaminated by the spray and then put them in the boot of my car.

I half-carried Lyn and then Ledhrad out to the car, escorted each time by PC41 who a shadow among shadows was. I put them in the back seat with pillows and more blankets keeping them upright and warm. Both were shocky and even in the August night were chilled, Lyn from the neurotoxins and Johanna Marie from getting her world so thoroughly rocked. Wolff walked carefully to the car, by himself, with his dispatch bag in one hand and the antique pistol in the other. I had packed all my necessities in the messenger bag with a blood-red broad arrow and Longspee's Six Gold lions embossed on it. Money, several spurious IDs and matching credit cards, ammunition, two pairs each of socks, shirts, and underwear; the acoustic coupler and twelve cans of cat food-survival rations for herself, filled it. Regretfully I abandoned the 'sterile' canned rations I had in the cabinet, with the labels peeled away and the canner impressions inked over. I had procured them when I left Croton house for Wichita.

We were abandoning the car Lyn and Wolff had arrived in, I parked it down the block and made sure that it had nothing in it.

I noticed that Wolff was walking better than he had two days gone by. I wondered if the drastic 'push' I had hit him with on our original meeting had a beneficial side effect, or perhaps it was just the thought that it was 'someone' trying to kill him and not a natural decline that improved his step.

I hoped that my neighbors were still asleep and not paying attention to the peculiar goings on in my apartment. They would miss PC41; he had developed a successful trapline of scraps, bowls of cream and the occasional dish of gourmet cat food among the apartments.

When I made my report, it seemed Vittorio had been replaced. Replaced by someone who perhaps sat higher at a Table and who was not as prone to sputtering attacks of anxiety. I reported that we were shifting location, that there had been an attempt on Subject A, that I would make a more detailed report later this day. "Understood." And he hung up on me.

PC41, an orange tom in the early morning light, nestled in between the ladies and kept up a steady, rumbling purr. Wolff had his bag in the footwell, and his gun concealed under his folded coat, on his lap. Both of mine were concealed, but I had easy access to them.

I started the car. "Where are we going?"

"East." He settled himself into the front seat, buckled his seatbelt. "I'll give you your turns."

It took less than a half-hour to leave the city behind, cutting north and east from Central avenue after it left Wichita onto county roads, and then taking a graveled overpass over the turnpike to the east of the city. You could still see civilization on the horizon, gas flares from a refinery and the taller building's aircraft warning lights at this time of the morning, but it was distant. There were yard lights at most of the farms we passed, sold as security necessities by the power companies; some of the houses and outbuildings were brightly lit as the farmers began their day.

Wolff indicated a turn off. About half a mile of a graded dirt driveway deposited us at a small cluster of buildings. All were dark, a security light over the door of the barn was the only bright spot. It switched off as we drove up, the sun was about to rise, and the dawn trigged the photocell.

Wolff got out, left his bag in the car and walked up to the side door of the large attached garage. He unlocked the door and went in. He'd told me to wait for him to open the front door of the house. We would put the women in the house, deposit our baggage and then I'd put the car away in the garage.

"Will there be room?" I asked as we pulled up.

"They took both their van and their pickup," he said. "It is a large pickup, well capable of pulling a horse trailer."

He was just a minute or two in the garage and then the door to the house opened and he stepped out on the porch. I got out, opened the passenger door behind me and unbundled Lyn first. PC41 slid past her and trotted off into the pre-dawn light her tail straight up like a guerdon.

The house had a L-shaped couch, big enough to allow both women to comfortably sleep off the last hour they had gone through. I laid Lyn at the long leg of the couch and then went back and picked up Johanna Marie. PC41 strolled through the house like he owned it, he was male this morning, marking the corners with his chin.

Lyn, I knew, was knackered from the spray of needles and

the intervention to stabilize her. Ledhrad was just knackered. I wondered just why, aside from mine and PC41's 'push', she had dropped the plot and ravaged the scenery. She had not struck me as someone with that tenuous a grip on reality. I have never known a Hanse with anything but a Bulldog grip on reality. But as it turns out I have never known a Hanse like her.

PC41 finished clearing the house, slipped into the garage when Wolff and I went to put the rental away and disappeared into the dawn. I hoped he'd stay away from the livestock.

We got the rental and the garage secured and went back in the house. Wolff got a glass of ice water and sat at the kitchen table, with his brief before him. "I would like to know what sort of-"

I waved him off. "The shortest explanation is that I was seconded to a multi-agency operation against a cross-world contraband ring. Hudson House Registry, Unity 'Ring, Provo Eisenring and a few token Secular agents. We had expected to gather exotic weapons, electronics, recreational and medicinal drugs, dark information and perhaps poor honest slavers. What we found was proscribed biologicals." I sat at the table as well, where I could keep my eye and ear on the women. "And what I got was PC41."

"The cat."

"The smugglers had five smallish shipping containers concealed in a storage site within a warehouse complex. The containers were a meter tall by a meter deep by two meters long. Locked and sealed with varied counterfeit customs seals. Each one was marked; PC41 through '46. Marked with bogus shipping labels and equally bogus origination, transits and arrivals. We opened all of them; quite carefully. In four of the containers we found aerogel cubes, eight-by-eight-by-eight centimeters in dimensions. Thirty-nine hundred in total were estimated to be in the shipping containers we opened. The containers were refrigerated by a LP-gas powered cooler, ambient temperature was not quite freezing. The cubes were marked with barbed trefoils-biological hazard warnings. Also, fire, acid and poison pictograms. None of them had printed labels, just pictograms. We sealed each of those shipping containers back up, right smartly, after we saw the first layer of aerogels in the containers.

The fifth and last container was labeled PC41. Our breeching techs carefully cut the locks away and unlatched the door to see nothing. A light fog at the open door. And then the cat hit us like a bowling ball in a game of nine-pins. After all was said and done, he was sitting on my chest and I was mad as the Hatter."

"I am surprised they did not simply dispose of the beast?" The subtext was 'And you'.

I nodded. "That notion did occur to the onsite commanders, but it did not last more than the half an hour it took Ops-Command to get their thumb out, notify Overwatch that they had a biological container breach and make the request for a burning. Joint Eisenring AngTerra Overwatch denied the disposal request and ordered PC41 and I to be 'secured'. Bureaucracy can be a blessing sometimes." I turned my back on him, but I knew he was within my reach; Lyn was beginning to stir. "And, fortunately, none of the other operators were killed in that particular event-or they might have sent for you anyway." Or someone very much like you.

"Full manifestation?"

"Full manifestation of my gift ensued and then some. While I was sobering up, after the bureaucracy had made its temporary disposition, while I was still under the guns of my teammates, with PC41 nestled in my lap, the doors to the warehouse blew in. Detcord at the hinges, suppressive fire and all that. They were careful to keep their aim high, away from the containers. The customers had arrived and wanted their consignments." I shrugged. "Between one thing and another, the customers did not survive to be interrogated and the smugglers had been quite dead before we had opened the containers."

I'd never killed before, as a D'draig. It was not pleasant. It was draining.

"A story for another time," Wolff said.

"I take it," I asked him. "that you have a theory on why the sudden flurry of activity concerning the Military Liaison Missions?"

"Tauber was only one member of a large bag of un-hung villains that we were scraping up out of the rump and the rubble of the Third Reich. And he was one of many that just never turned up. We thought that he lay anonymously dead beneath a drift of bricks. Now-"

"Why try for him now? And who wanted him back?" I asked.

"Or who wanted him to remain there."

CHAPTER 11

Going through the gob of paper Wolff had brought with him did not provide us with much of any substance. We did find that several of the *Orpo* regional offices had noticed Tauber went missing in late December 1944. They made desultory inquiries and found that his office had evidently been eradicated by a single blockbuster bomb. This was unusual in that Bad Doberan, a former resort city near the Baltic coast and the site of his office, was not a priority target. What was left at that point of AMT-V assumed it, the bomb, was jettisoned from a British Mosquito raid on one of the ports in the Rostock region.

Terrible bad luck for Tauber and the city block his office had been in, they closed the file and stamped it finished. The casualties had been limited only by the time of the attack. One AM, local time.

"More likely Tauber had a demolition charge prepared, called a secret meeting of the local *Kirpos* and informants he had responsibility for and blew them to hell." Wolff carefully put the fragile onionskin documents back in a dispatch envelope.

"Hm. What gates do we know exist or existed in that section of Germany?"

"Officially; three crossing points to 'zeme, one to Little Englander-or to use the correct political terminology Greater France. Four in total. All within a ten-mile radius of Rostock.

They were not much used then, before or since; only one person could safely walk the critical path and carry maybe a rucksack. All were 'soft', or unimproved. Two-" He produced a very old notebook from a pocket in his brief. "two had been interdicted by Joint Eisenring operational groups in the 'zeme, two were in Rostock proper and had bombing debris covering their reported sites by May 1945."

"Any reports of gate effects from the ones buried in the bomb sites?"

"Not that I was ever made aware of."

I pushed away from the table. PC41 had batted at the kitchen window earlier and I'd let him in. Wolff had become hyper-vigilant when the 'cat' had stalked by him. PC had ignored Wolff, settled into the middle of the living room floor and proceeded to have a good wash. She was slightly speckled with hay.

I started a kettle of water on the stove, foraged through the cabinets until I found a box of tea bags. Lipton. Ah well. What sacrifices we make for the Unity. All the while I was trying to suss out my, our, next move. "I think," I said to the stove as I tended the burner under the kettle. "I think we should give up on Tauber as a blind alley. If he had been recovered alive, then we could have put screws to him, but as it is…"

"Something has changed, so many deaths, so many abscondments. Perhaps the starting point was not the fiasco at the gate, but before it." Said Wolff.

"Hugh Snow." Ledhrad suggested from the couch. I manifested and turned, very surprised to see her sitting upright and looking responsive. Lyn was still bleary; her auras muddy even in the half-light of the house. Ledhrad's auras, on the other hand were crisp. Crisper than I recalled them being. Her voice was cultivated, without the hint of the low accent that I had heard when she had the come apart. I closed my eyes and pushed at PC41 >what<.

If a feline could shrug; she flicked a set of whiskers at me.

"I think he has a significant role in this intrigue." She continued. "He is the only active token on the board that we are clueless about." She nodded at Wolff. "You, Dom Wolff, are of interest but you were not active until your door was rattled."

"So," I said. "We need to look closely at Hugh Snow."

She nodded, solemnly. "And I feel the need to apologize for my outburst." Wolff, PC41 and I waited. "I-" She swallowed. "I am in my first fifth of my first year as a probationary agent-employee of the *XternBuro*." She looked to her left, to Lyn, and then at the cat shaped lump on the carpet. Licked her lips. "I am a foundling, my parents dead and without extended family, a child of the whole. I was advanced for my age in my creche and selected early for the honor of service to the Common Land. When I completed my primary tutorials, I joined the *Xternen de AngelegenheitenBüro*." She gave the *Buro* its full jaw breaking title, in Hanse. "In addition to the Seven Principles of the Commons, I have completed an intensive programme in the four provincial dialects of English and a brush-out in 'zeme Creole-"

"Brush-up, Dama, is the phrase you are reaching for." Said Wolff.

"Thank you. Brush-up. I had not finished the *XternBuro* Station Qualifying programme or any of the follow-on training regimens, when I was tasked to cross the threshold, identify and then to secure Dom Wolff. A more experienced *XternBuro* team was to follow…"

The penny dropped for Wolff, and for me.

"How many gates did you pass through to arrive here?" He asked her.

"Six." Her eyes got that thousand-yard stare of the frequently sold. "I spent three nights at a location within ear shot of the ocean; qualifying with a decidedly obsolete sidearm, memorizing my identity papers and getting what they called an 'over-lay' in the patois that matched my papers."

Wolff gave me another sidelong look. "An over-lay?" he said. And essayed a rapid, short, spiel of German.

Ledhrad blinked, squinted, and replied haltingly in the same tongue. Grammatically correct but definitely not how a native speaker of German would have phrased it.

"Admirable," he said. "I think you have an idea on what was intended for you?"

"I was to inspire you to break cover. A lure." She paused. "I think I should like to have some tea, now."

I got up and procured her a cup and saucer and a teabag. She huddled in her blanket and regarded the steam rising from her cup.

"What were the instructions, should Mr. Wolff be deceased or missing?" I asked.

"I was to remain in the area," She said to the cup. "to not make contact with anyone except Dom Wolff or my intended principal, to closely observe the shop and the residence."

"You expect your principal and his team when?"

"What is today-the day after my arrival? Today."

We all sat in silence for a while. The day brightened outside the windows, but the light did not make much inroads through the curtains. I thought about using the phone and the coupler, but I also considered that our local establishment was a flaming colander and decided not to. Wolff's friends did not deserve to have their house firebombed. Lyn woke up, massaged and stretched her right arm where the needles had sprayed, then asked politely for a cup of tea and her side arm. I brought them to her. Wolff thought and sucked at his teeth in place of a pipe stem, staring holes through the tabletop.

"There is no help for it," I said. "There is at least one, perhaps three active players on the pitch. Someone tried to 'quietly' dispose of Mr. Wolff," I held up one finger. "someone then tried to blatantly dispose of Mr. Wolff and Miss Lyn-and how did you get to my house again?"

"He drove. On the left-hand side of the street." Lyn, sighed. "I was already having problems with the spray and-"

"Yes." I shuddered to think about that trip. "And I think Dama Ledhrad was a redundant attempt to flush out Mr. Wolff-or perhaps even if he has retreated here, Captain Snow. And in any event…"

"They were going to dispose of me, Dom Wolff and anyone who was associated with him." Ledhrad blew gently across the cup.

"Quite so, I am afraid." Said Wolff. "Quite so."

CHAPTER 12

We made free with the limited provisions in the kitchen. I fixed scrambled eggs, bacon rashers, toast, and coffee once we found the canister. Lyn picked at her food, and then cleaned her plate. She then pillaged half of mine and went on to make a bowl of instant oatmeal with a tablespoon of honey. Wolff had coffee and toast and regarded Lyn with astonishment marbled with affection.

Ledhrad had a scrambled egg lightly peppered and a further cup of tea.

PC41 was not hungry this morning and I had fears of an early morning raid on a chicken coop or a piglet or two. >not so< Came down the push to me. The migraine was faint. >large flightless pigeon<

>turkey< I offered the word.

>turkey< And smug was the emotion. I hoped they were not domesticated, but blame could always be shifted to foxes.

I canvassed the kitchen, the living room and the bathroom for clutter and traces of visiting elves. I had Lyn wash the dishes and I bagged trash while Wolff and Ledhrad tried to brainstorm where and what Captain Snow was about.

We left the place marginally tidier and cleaner than we

found it and our trash at a Quick Trip just off the interstate.

We were on the road back into Wichita when I remembered to turn on my pager. It rattled with about three urgent coded texts, I pulled over at a freestanding pay phone and used the coupler. "Braxton."

"You've been off the porch."

I didn't know his name, Vittorio's replacement, but I knew his voice. "Seemed a prudent idea. The Hanse operative came in through questionably dark channels, was given a criminally minimal preparation and afforded no introduction to our apparat. She was placed on us to pin, in the open, Wolff and anyone around him. She has told us that she was sent ahead of a more experienced *XternBuro* team."

Vittorio's replacement had some vulgar comments about this turn of events. "When were the Crows expected?"

"Today, sometime. She came from Wichita's MidContinent airport, but I am certain that she did not fly in. Is there a known gate there?"

He grunted, as if someone had punched him. "Not that I know of." And I felt sorry for anyone downstream of him in the local apparat, from the Dowsers to the useful watchers, for not knowing of the gate. Or knowing and not passing that knowledge up stream. "And the watchers we had covering the old man?"

"Unknown. He bypassed them and then came under attack by needle-boys. Possibly they were neutralized or just flaming incompetent." I didn't mention why he evaded the watchers.

"Old fool." I smiled at that. The replacement had, I thought, no idea who Wolff was or what place he held in the hidden world. That ignorance was a good thing. For me.

CHAPTER 13

The bookstore had two cranky customers in the doorway when we showed up. Civilians by the look of them. Wolff apologized, mentioned that he had been called briefly out of town, let them in. Lyn and I opened the shop.

There was some sign of strangers in the store, a haphazard search and the back door had been gently forced. Alarms were foxed, wires cut at the base of the stairs. There was not a sign of any watchers outside, which did not surprise me. Lyn led the way up the stairs to the apartment after we had cleared the shop and the coffee area.

The apartment was clear, but it had been expertly tossed. Wolff had several strong boxes where you would expect someone to 'hide' them. They had been found and expertly opened, then neatly locked again, contents untouched. He also had a small gun-safe at the back of a pantry in the kitchen. It had evidently been missed. The searchers found what they expected to find and didn't look deeper.

PC41 made an appearance and the two of us did a very thorough once-over of the apartment. Together we found a set of listening devices. They looked to be from across the veil, not obviously from the Hanse or any 'zeme tradecraft I knew, but certainly not local. I thought they were likely *XternBuro* and I left them alone. I'd go and alert Vittorio's successors when we were more settled and have them deal with the devices, meanwhile we would have our skull sessions elsewhere.

After we let Wolff and Ledhrad upstairs I sat her at the table and pointed out one of the more obvious mikes. She grimaced and muttered under her breath, confirming my opinions about the sources of the bugs.

I called the House from the apartment, through the audio coupler, since anything I said to the House went from my lips to the opposition's ears anyway. "Braxton."

"Wait one."

I took a notebook out of my jump-bag and wrote a note in Hanse. Showed it to Ledhrad. I was proposing a hotel suite with a conference room for the afternoon and then shuffling off into another hide for the evening. She nodded agreement and then carefully translated it into stilted printed English for Lyn and Wolff to read.

"Caerton here." Good to put a name to the voice.

"We are back in town. The location has been compromised and you will need to send a technical team to recover items of interest."

He grunted acknowledgement. "Our people?"

"Not a hair to be seen. I intend to displace immediately, hunker down for the night" I lied. "and contact you tomorrow once you have more people online."

"No help for it. We know of the wicket now. It is on the groundside of the aerodrome at Wichita."

"Oh." Aerodrome? Caerton was not of the Western Hemisphere Dai by his choice of words. Unity Cadre then, not Unity 'Ring at a guess. Not a 'Resource' either, but a Political officer, much like the Commissars in the Red Army. 'Groundside' meant the parts of an airport not close by the landing field and the hangars for the airplanes. So somewhere in the terminal or by the office park. "Have our visitors come through?"

"Not through that wicket. We think they might have

arrived via a flight from Atlanta."

"How very ordinary."

"You will inform us of your location."

"Mhn." And I disconnected the line. Not likely, chum. The only thugs I thought less of than the Eisenring was Unity Cadre and their political officers.

Wolff had made himself useful packing an overnight bag and looking to see if anything had gone missing from his apartments. Lyn had packed a medicine bag for him, retrieved a jump bag from the gun safe with clothing, weapons and money. And snacks.

We were in and out in twenty minutes and I put us all into the new rental. Still no watchers and I was a bit concerned about any staff for the bookstore. Wolff threw everybody out, one browser, one clerk and the two eternal philosophers camped in the back room. He had told them to spread the word that Wolff and Lyn were going to be out of town, that the store was closed for the time being. Family business, he explained.

He had a pair of bags, his niece 'Lyn' had a bag and we-Ledhrad and I-were friends giving his niece and him a lift to the airport. So it seemed. We did not have any obvious watchers on us at the moment. We went to a local rental place, not connected to the airport, and I used a set of ID and credit cards that neither the House on the Hudson nor either of the Eisenrings knew anything about and acquired a new sedan. We drove the sedan to a new hotel, with Lyn following in my old rental. Then I installed Lyn and company in a business suite. I dropped my old and likely compromised rental off at the airport. Took a shuttle bus downtown to a different hotel and then walked four blocks to the hotel that Wolff was staying in.

Paranoid, yes, but there were opposing forces in play that

were unknown. And the players on our side were none too trustworthy.

CHAPTER 14

"They were very interested in my scrapbooks." Wolff said after a light brunch from room service. I was paying for the room with a different set of cards then what I had rented the sedan with. Even if the various Eisenrings, Croton-on-Hudson heavy moggies or 'Enemies Unknown' were competent, it was not likely they would find us before we displaced to another site. "Several pages-" He continued. "had been razored out of them, pages from before the war."

"Can you tell who they were looking for?"

"I have the page numbers that they removed, and we can retrieve a microfiche sheet from one of my storage units to be certain, but I would say it was from late Weimar period Germany."

Um. That was very long ago indeed. "Where could we have access to a microfiche reader?"

"The library has several readers available in the basement," Wolff said.

"They have a genealogy department down there that gets a lot of usage." Lyn said from the other end of the conference table. She was paging through the drifts of paper Wolff had brought with him and hoovering up all the leftovers from brunch. Ledhrad and PC41 were sitting comfortably on a divan and watching the street six stories below. She was watching the street, PC41 was closely eyeing the pigeons on the window ledges. The pigeons were uneasy.

"You walk in," Lyn said. "Check out a census sheet with your library card and then you would view the sheet you brought in."

Wolff sucked at his teeth, in lieu of a pipe. "A bit complicated, and they might wonder if you were making off with the microfiche you checked out and cause a fuss. But it would still work, I would just tell them that I needed to check my own copies against theirs." Wolff nodded. "But to retrieve the microfiche we would have to go back to one of the storage lockers, and that one is the very locker we were ambushed at."

I looked to where PC 41 was sitting, she turned her head and gazed back at me. I shrugged. "They might not expect a return visit. At dusk, then."

"Why not later, after full dark?"

"Puts them on the back foot, we drive up bold as brass and rifle around in the storeroom, well out of view but very active, popping in and out with boxes and the like. Take three times what we truly want; then drop off a shrink-wrapped bundle of newspapers and a banker's box of junk from a pawn shop and drive off. It will give them pause, imply that we are well escorted, send them to scrabbling to recover the trash we dropped off. Exposing them to any of our watchers still operational. If they should try for a second round of grab and snatch, I and Dama Ledhrad will be there." I looked to PC41 again. "We might even net a Confidential Informant."

"As opposed to a Continental Op?" Lyn spread the last of the ersatz marmalade on a piece of toast. She was not going to let that joke die a natural death.

"Are all the Eisenring like you?" Wolff asked.

"It varies-."

"Day to day." Snickered Lyn. "Day to day."

CHAPTER 15

It took a bit to sort out what we wanted to present as bait for interested parties. The hotel had a bundle of Wall Street Journal's ready to go back to the news agent's, I paid for them. Then wrapped the bundle up, stuffed it in a pillowcase we filched from the hotel, leaving a pair of twenties on the bed for a tip, and put it into the boot of the rental. I sent Lyn out with sixty dollars and told her to purchase anything that caught her fancy from a local pawn shop and get a banker's box to put it in. Wolff was uneasy about letting her out on her own. He had more than a casual interest in her welfare. He gave me a dead level gaze when she went off on her errand. His promise of mayhem if she was at all endangered was coldly convincing.

I poked at the bear, gently. "More than a Medji."

He nodded, his eyes not leaving mine. "Much more. I'll thank you to remember and thank you to be discreet about that."

"I have a great deal of latitude these days about what I see and what I notice."

We left it at that.

Lyn came back in a timely fashion, empty handed having left the bait in the rental. We pressed a soda on her and then left the hotel.

No one followed us from that hotel, I was certain of that. An advantage of my peculiar condition is that I could, with exertion, perceive the intent of people close to me. The same auras that allow me to put a target to rest, or kill, also allow me to 'sense' if someone is untowardly interested in me. Before PC41, this 'sense' was haphazard and badly focused. And it was quite costly in the sense of shagging me out. Now it was like watching contestants flying banners in a floor dance exercise.

It wasn't infallible, it wasn't without a cost to me. I had to be within a certain distance to detect this 'interest', but between ordinary tradecraft, PC41 and I, we were as safe as we could be. And I just was mildly fagged from sweeping our back trail.

And there was a pair of watchers at the storage unit. A half block away, in an old stepside van, from the rolling gates to the storage compound.

The unit was self-service, basically a maze of small four-plex and eight-plex units with a rolling overhead door and a set of keyed padlocks at each door. It covered maybe half a city block at the outskirts of town, well-lit with but one way in and out through that keypad protected gate.

Our opponents had put two obvious watchers on the gate and called it proper. Wolff knew of another, wider gate at the back of the property, with a Chubb padlock securing the gate. This was for customers using the property to store trailers and boats.

To which Wolff had a key.

Of course.

His unit was, apparently, a ten-by-twenty storage space with a rollup door and a high-end Master's padlock. Behind the rollup door was another rollup door at right angles through a dou1ble-cored concrete wall affording entry into the ten by twenty storage space next door. Which had no apparent external doors. In that space, deeply set in concrete between steel I-beams, was a very large walk-in safe behind a Diebold combination lock and key.

"What are you storing here, Mr. Wolff?" It was not an old safe, not an antique and not something a rusticated agent would keep his memoirs in.

He smiled as he spun the combination wheel. "Things. A habit I cannot quite let go of."

We had noted pry marks at the hasp of the obvious rollup door on the first unit. They hadn't got anywhere with it since last night, but it was only a matter of time until someone procured the right tools.

He had several long guns on racks. British imperial issue I thought. Within the safe there were three battered filing cabinets; a shelf with nothing but banker's boxes of paper, heavy canvas mail bags with GR Mail locks and a triplet of footlockers at the back of the safe. The boxes were cryptically labeled with dates and operational names; *Spion Kop* 25/1/1900 caught my eye, but there were much more. From the later Victorian times to Elizabeth II. "It is no wonder that Croton and certain other Tables and Desks are nervous about you." I brushed at the dust layering the boxes. "I thought you said you had no secrets worth killing you over?"

"I fully planned to dispose of these, when the time was right. These are historical, mostly, and should not be a threat to the varied organizations. Perhaps an embarrassment, but not a threat." He unlocked a file cabinet and riffed through a set of manila folders. He chose one. "I have plans in place that discourage overt attacks on my person. Everyone within reach would be sadly discomforted if I were to step in front of a bus, but, simple old age would have vitiated those policies." Wolff was putting on the toff for some reason. Must have been the dust off of the files.

"The nesting pair of watchers have company." Lyn was at the false front of the rental unit, standing on a footstool at a judas port, observing through a birding scope. "They are agitated, looks like they may have figured out that we passed them by."

"How many?"

"Three, no four. A new sedan, now six little Indians. Six in total that I see."

I looked at Wolff. "You have what you want?"

"Yes."

I handed him a bundle of money, an address and the number of my pager. "We'll see if the back door is still open, if so, go to earth at that address, it is adequate but nothing special. Call my pager if you don't hear from me by midnight."

"And what will you be doing?" Lyn spoke without taking her eye from the scope.

"Don't ask." Wolff said to her.

PC41 had already faded into the dusk.

CHAPTER 16

They had not found the backway in or they did not know that Wolff had a key to the rear gate. He left; with Lyn driving, Wolff in the passenger seat and Dama Ledhrad ensconced in the back seat, with Wolff's collection of microfiches in a leather brief at her feet.

I faded into the maze of the storage park. It once had an onsite keeper, someone who lived in a small apartment and signed you in and out of the park. Now the apartment was locked and shuttered. I needed to draw the opposing force into the maze. I entered the unused apartment, used a torch and moved about the darkened rooms and then left from a side door with the torch held low.

They hesitated, arguing command and control I would guess, and then they threw a blanket on the barbed wire and three came over the rolling gate and into the park.

I'd noted the electrical mains for the park at the rear gate. When Wolff and company exited the park, I settled into an overwatch and waited. When our watchers were well into the maze and closing on Wolff's storage unit, I tripped the breaker with a hammer I had found in Wolff's unit. Most of the lights in the park flickered and died, there some light from outside but not enough.

I took them one at a time. Without a fuss.

The ones waiting outside the Storage park knew things

had gone seriously pear-shaped, their people had walkie-talkies that were going unanswered. They did the obviously stupid thing; they jumped in the van and crashed through the front gate, leaving some of the watchers behind in the second vehicle to cover their backs.

They knew that they had to 'rescue' their friends. The cops would be coming when the park's power went down and sent an alarm out, they also knew that someone might be holding or hunting their friends. As they came around the back corner of the first section of the storage park, in their badly damaged vehicle, one of their friends 'stepped' in front of the van.

Or, he appeared in front of the van, in the light of the one remaining head light. And they ran him over with a sodden crunch.

I will give them full marks for bravery, they stopped the van and jumped from its one working door on the passenger side. One ran to aid the downed man pinned in the undercarriage and one stood to cover them with a pump shotgun while the last of the three kept the motor running.

When the cops arrived, fifteen minutes later, the van's engine was still running. One man was pinned under that van, quite dead; two were sprawled in the corner nearest the van with their necks broken and the shotgun broken as well.

Two more were found in a more distant corner, dead from blunt force trauma. But unknown to the police, three were missing. As was the car the watchers had nested in. Missing, but known to be missing only to the Allemagne Noir.

And me.

An hour before midnight I got a pager call. It was not

Wolff. I wiped off my hands with a wad of cotton waste and walked over to the phone that was mounted on the wall by the shop desk. I called the number, directly, not bothering to encrypt it.

"Yes," I said.

"Braxton, where in the hell are you?"

"Gone to earth until you get some control of your enterprise." I leaned up against the wall by the phone and looked out of the garage door windows. I popped my neck and then looked at the man sitting in the chair by the desk. His eyes were open and dull in the faint illumination that came through the dirty windows from the streetlights, his mouth sagged open, his tongue lolling out.

Caerton was shouting over the phone and I heard it as a faint buzz in my ear. "Ass," I hissed into the handset. "your bondsmen have turned their coats. If you weren't dirty to begin with. You will be dead when They" I snarled that word at him. "sort themselves out. The Crows of the *XternBuro* are already stalking your household; then the 'Ring will sweep through like a grassfire through dry stubble."

He grew very quiet on the other end of the line. "Eisenring?" The one thing the Unity Cadre feared in this world or the next was the Eisenring. Particularly the Old Firm. Brushing up against the Old Firm didn't make old bones.

I laughed, slightly. "You didn't know? You didn't know whose Table I have my knees under? What Wolff was, and is; for all that he was sitting in the middle of your back garden? Caerton, take advice from someone who only has your best interest at heart. Cut your throat with a straight razor. It will be less painful than the 'Ring skinning you inside out." And I pushed down on the handset button.

PC41 drifted out of a shadow to sit at my feet. >sorry<

"I know. But I am a more than middling Sangsue. Time to leave."

CHAPTER 17

Where I had sent Wolff and company was an adequate but cheap motel at the far west edge of Wichita. Lyn knew exactly where it was, which was interesting in a 'I do not want to know more about how she knew'-way. Some questions are dangerous to even consider.

They had a weekly rack rate; tiny kitchenettes with a toaster-oven, a hotplate and a sink. A shower/tub with a window you could shove a small dog through. A local-calls only princess dial phone that went out through an automatic switchboard in the office and a TV with an indoor antenna. Double beds with paper thin sheets and flat pillows completed the setup.

I drove sedately out US-54 to the motel, circled the parking lot twice looking for all the wrong persons, then backed in next to our rental. It was well after midnight, local time. I sent PC41 out and about while I tapped on the obvious door, someone having dropped a torn sheet of typing paper on the sidewalk in front of their room.

Wolff answered the door with his gun discreetly by his leg and Lyn casually at his back.

"Well met," he said.

"Not by moonlight." I jingled a set of keys in my left hand. "I have news and an exhibit."

Wolff was not happy at that; he knew full well what I was,

and he had strong views on that subject. "I'll send the Hanse to the other room."

"It might be advisable. Let us not tarry, PC is vetting the neighborhood, but I want to secure the exhibit and then put the car around back."

"We noticed you cruising through the parking lot."

I nodded and went to open the boot. I liked this sedan, it was a marque of a Henry Ford product that had a roomy back seat, a radio, a rack of shotguns on the back of the front bench seat and a handy spotlight that ran off the cigar lighter. It also came equipped with many useful tools and supplies in the boot. Drop cloths, burglar's instruments, eighteen by twenty-inch bags woven of water-resistant hessian and a two-foot-long, inch-and-a-quarter diameter, heavy rubber hose: nicely weighted with sand. Everything one could want for midnight inquiries.

I had a drop cloth wrapped tightly about a lump snuggled into the deep well by the spare tire. It had flinched when I opened the boot, so I knew it was still warm and receptive. I grabbed the drop cloth at the back of the lump, dead lifted it out of the boot and dropped it not so gently on the walk. Once I would have needed an extra pair of hands to horse that wright clear of the car. But now...

I shut the boot and PC appeared. >nothing<

I nodded and pushed back >overwatch<.

She drifted into the shadow of the cars. I dragged the wrapped package across the walk and over the threshold into the room. It bumped one end, hard, at the threshold and gave a muffled gasp. Wolff had sent the women into the other room and was giving me a very cold eye.

"Is this entirely necessary?"

I did not answer; I was not in a mood to explain or

consult. I pulled a multi tool out of my pocket, flicked the knife blade open and started carefully cutting away the drop cloth.

Wolff stepped away from me, to where he could keep a weapon on my prize and on me. I was not concerned. I got the drop cloth skinned back from the shrouded head, but still swaddling my prize's upper arms. The head was in a hessian bag, more durable than a burlap flour sack, with leather shoelaces securing it tightly. I carefully snipped the laces away with the scissor in my multi-tool and lifted the bag away from my prize's head.

"Dom Wolff," I said in Hanse. "I give you Captain Snow, late of the Fifth Infantry, British Occupation forces."

Wolff, it turned out, had a fine command of obscenity, modern, outdated and classical. He also had a steady hand with that antique spring pistol, he didn't shoot either of us.

Snow had a bloody sock stuffed into his mouth, but it wasn't his blood-or his sock. He was taking deep, desperate breaths through his nose and trying to work his mouth around to spitting out the sock.

I clouted Snow on the back of his head with the closed tool. "None of that," I said in English. "or I'll let the cat nuzzle you again."

He looked at Wolff for something like mercy and then I think he recognized him, from thirty years ago. Or from a dossier he'd seen this morning. Hugh Snow slumped in his wrappings and shivered into an exhausted doze, the way a captured animal gives up the struggle.

"What-the-bloody-hell is this?" Wolff said quietly.

I patted Snow. "This is a member of the sideshow we are currently starring in," I let my hand linger on the back of Snow's neck and ever so lightly picked at the charkas that ran through there. He shivered and twitched from the attention, not truly awake but in a stunned confusion that I had found helpful. "he is a singular rarity. The first one of his kind I have had the honor to encounter. A Skrenner. A Skrenner Adept." I looked away from him and smiled at Wolff. "And he is in the Blinders. He has been looking for the way out of the Blind Spot since before Karsten Tauber was killed."

I took Snow by his slimy chin and forced him to open his eyes, with my auras curling about his face and neck. Forced him to look at me. "And he has found it. The Inflection Point."

"He seems saner than most." Wolff said, sitting on the bed as far away from Snow as possible.

I was only slightly surprised. "You've dealt with them?"

"Yes. Less than a half-dozen times a Skrenner, or someone who fed him, has been at the bottom of a problem I was tasked with solving." He de-cocked his pistol. "A Skrenner can read the patterns, suss out the possibilities, follow all the decision paths you might want to explore. It's helpful to have a hint of how things might be shaping up, to take an advantage if events break a certain way-or if they remain the same. You can even set things up that precede certain events, precursors like nailing a door shut or getting a transport pilot drunk, inducing outcomes that your pet Skrenner had seen as possibilities, if slightly remote. If that is as far as you take your 'gift' it can be an asset to your operations." He nestled his antique in his lap. "On the other hand, if you try to nudge an extremely exotic probability into existence-" Wolff shook his head. "bad things will happen. Bad, bad things. To you, to your principals and to people around the operation."

We put Snow in the bathtub and set Lyn to watching him.

I had driven the Crown Vic around to the back of the property, took off the plate with my handy little tool and flung it over the fence into the adjacent cemetery. I then collected PC41, who was not happy with either the local hunting or foraging, and we had a council of war. Wolff, Lyn, Ledhrad and I sitting at the battered kitchen table; PC41 sitting on the back of the stool in the bathroom watching Hugh Snow closely, his tail flicking like a metronome.

"A short time ago," I began. "after the actor got elected to the American Presidency, several pods of Skrenners here and elsewhere began to encounter dropouts or blanks in their matrixes. It is not unusual, I have since been told, to have one Clade or Aelde of Skrenners draw a blank in a short term or mid-term possibility skein. That is why if you are going to run Skrenners, you have several Pods and keep them isolated from each other. One pod might draw a blank but another under your hand might cover the blank skein quite nicely."

Wolff nodded; his eyes hooded.

"There were five-" I continued. "totally independent linages having difficulty in producing a lucid matrix. All the matrixes centered on AngTerra, including the one that was not in the Dai sphere of influence proper, a linage in the Hanse of all places."

Wolff leaned back against the rickety chair. "And you think that this has caused the spate of suspicious deaths?" Wolff asked.

"I don't have much of an opinion one way or another. The tea-leaf crowd was never a factor in my detachment's tasking. But I recovered one of the smash and grab boyos and the operational handler of that clusterfuck. And that merchant." I hooked a thumb at the bathroom. "Our Captain Snow was attached to the operation."

I leaned on the rickety kitchen table and pushed a grimy

packet of photos over to Wolff. "They had surveillance photos of you, Lyn, Eric-for some unknown reason-and several of your other regulars. Judging from the date stamp on the earliest prints they had been surveilling you shortly after you began to have health problems."

"You have people who can predict the future?" Dama Ledhrad spoke up.

"Not precisely. Or not with any reliability." Wolff thumbed through the glossy prints. "Your culture have card games, games of chance and skill. No?"

"We do, it is not forbidden but it is not encouraged."

"A Skrenner can see a pattern matrix or a decision skein that might lead to certain outcomes. Small changes in the pattern can make large changes much later in the matrix solutions."

She nodded. "Place a low card so it redoubles in value at the end of the trick."

"You have the gist of it," Wolff said. "Now attempt to play that hand with blind folds on the players and the dealer; and under rules that often change."

She scoffed. "It is not possible."

"Precisely. What is merely difficult and sometimes not quite useless becomes completely impossible and insanely dangerous when you are in a Blind Spot." Wolff turned the photos face down and placed them on a folder.

I was in a chair that had no comfortable place to rest my bones. "What they, and who they are is not at all clear to me, began to run into was Blind Spots in the Skein or Matrix for this leaf, for AngTerra in particular. In their forecasting, no matter if they used Divination cards, runes, hexagrams or vision drugs, there was a blank spot. A Blind Spot that lasts for about ten years."

"And you know this how?" Lyn asked me.

I looked at Lyn. I didn't reply to her question, I just looked at her. She understood and looked away. She had counted the opposing forces, and the solitary prize I brought home and drew the right conclusion.

"Ten years, more or less, from this last American presidential election there were six probable solutions emerging from the blinders. There were many paths, there always are, but six solutions had a broad consensus among the clades. One path had no appreciable change in the Leaf of AngTerra or it's close cognates. The other paths were not so sanguine."

Wolff tapped on the table. "Don't draw it out."

"The absolute worst: a full up thermonuclear exchange and nuclear winter, over all of the northern hemisphere on AngTerra. A resulting crash in the gates from the resonances of that exchange between five contiguous Leaves." I extended my first finger.

"Next: a massive 'conventional' war between the Warsaw Pact and the NATO alliance, destroying most of the Northern Hemisphere with the collateral damage to the infrastructure. Leaving a swath of rubble across Europe, the Americas and much of Asia north of the South China Sea." I extended my middle finger.

"An intense and high-tech irregular war. Striking with special forces at power, fuel and communication grids: destroying water supplies and sewage treatment facilities in the larger cities, wrecking most of the transportation rail grids and disrupting food production and distribution with terroristic attacks. The idea with this strategy is to not completely destroy the lands in order to take them, just wreck them."

I extended the rest of the fingers on that hand. "Nuclear, biological, or chemical weapons would be deployed to take down important political and economic centers. Snake heads;

cutting off the heads of the political entities. This path was a spur off of the irregular war possibility."

And I closed all the fingers of that hand into a fist. "Or just chaos."

"Just chaos?"

"The complete political, economic and social collapse of all the hegemonic states or multi-state establishments on AngTerra, 'Zeme, Little England, Imperial Sindu and, to a much lesser degree, the Hanse. Not necessarily linked to any sort of coordinated military action. Just random, spasmodic, destruction."

I looked at Dama Ledhrad, watching to see if she was going to melt down again at the threat to her homeland. "Widespread civil disturbances, producing a heavy military or paramilitary response by the relevant authorities. True civil wars, sporadic popular insurrections, secession movements and refugee surges because of disturbances; surges that will destabilize all the borders they come across." I looked to where PC41 was guarding Snow. "A war of all against all, with no goal and no end."

And in the silence, I nodded at Wolff. "And you were a prominent 'face' in the disjointed visualizations the Skrenner consensus had of the Blinders. As each one of the other 'faces' were removed, you became more prominent in the uncertain causal skeins and matrixes."

"That is…not reassuring." He pointed his hand at me, four fingers in a blade. The gesture of a cavalry officer. "And where do you appear in this drama?"

"Oddly enough, I do not appear. When I approached you, you dropped almost completely from the skeins, but the causal chains did not reflect your death or absence."

"You are a Blind Agent."

"An archaic term but yes, it would appear that I am. And

so is Dama Ledhrad."

"Me?"

"You appeared in several Hanse causal chains. Snow mentioned them, referring to you as a long-standing person of interest before you were out of school, which is why I suspect the Crows recruited you Johanna Marie. They wanted to keep anyone that-" I smiled grimly. "attracted the attention of the irrational but distressingly effective operatives of the Dai. Then after that November election, in our local calendar, you became in the eyes of their Dai contractors an Agent Unaware-again an archaic term-and disrupting the matrixes of probability for the Hanse. They still had you in their hands and I suspect there was a suggestion to quietly dispose of you." She inhaled sharply. Settled back into her chair with her eyes fixed on me. "I suspect that is why you were sent here, to die along with Wolff. A neat solution if not as certain."

"I would very much like to go lie down now." She rubbed her temples with her hands.

"There is more, although not as significant."

"Never the nonetheless," She said, standing slowly. "I shall lie down and try and find my center, to know my balance in the steelyard." That was an odd expression. She turned and walked away; her bag forgotten at the side of her chair.

Lyn got up and followed her through the connecting door to the next motel room, glaring at me over her shoulder as she went through the door.

"More?" Said Wolff.

"Snow is a Skrenner, an Adept, as I have said. A rare bird indeed. He was attempting to wrench the path into a new channel." I rubbed my thumbs along the edge of the tabletop, not looking towards where the Hanse and Lyn had retreated.

"He manifested long before the war. He is male and not female; reasonably sane, not certifiably crackers at any rate. And of an age that most adepts never want or hope to see. He is also of the Allemagne Noir."

Wolff face darkened even more. "Well." He exhaled. "I should like to interview Captain Snow." He stood up and cracked his knuckles. "Now."

CHAPTER 18

Snow was still alive. I had wondered if he would be, he had shown symptoms of acute stress, to the point I had adjusted his auric flow before I stuffed him in the boot of the Crown. I needed to eat soon, I was running low on energy and what I had was coming through PC41. I hauled Snow out of the shower tub and dropped him on the bathroom floor. He opened his eyes and dully watched me flick open my tool.

"Are you going to be a problem?" I asked him.

He shook his head no. I slit the drop cloth further away from his shoulders and cut the wires with the snips, I did not free his hands so much as peel his shroud away from his shoulders to ease his breathing. I sat him up and leaned him against the tub, plucking the bloody sock out of his mouth.

"Right. Now repeat what you gave up at the filling station to our mister Wolff here. Nice and straightforward. I'll know if you shade the truth. And. You. Won't. Like. That." I rapped his skull with my knuckle to underscore my last comment.

He nodded again.

Wolff squatted in the doorway with a thin knife held loosely in his left hand. I never saw him produce it. It was just suddenly there, the blade was worn away to a slightly crescent shape, it gleamed in the low light. The edge was razor sharp.

"Friend, Braxton tells me you claim to comb skeins with

your fingers. Is that true?" He was conversing with Snow, old acquaintances talking over drinks, his face wooden. Indifferent. That scared me more than if he had been ranting.

Snow nodded again. Wolff brushed Snow's face with the knife, lightly. A thin line of blood welled up, high on the cheekbone. He flinched away from the cut.

"Answer me directly when I ask a question, no dumb insolence." Wolff smiled. "You are a Skrenner, a Skrenner Adept no less?"

"Yes sir."

"I would find that hard to credit, but I have a great deal of confidence in Braxton. Let us explore your history before the end of the war."

"Sir."

"Illuminate me, how you came to be a tool for the Allemagne Noir."

Snow closed his eyes. "I was bred."

Wolff blinked, and his stance shifted a bit. The knife was still out, but the hunger had abated. "I see. What lineage?"

"Wettin."

"That is a broken staff."

"Not within The Gotha."

"So." This was news and Wolff did not like it. It was news to me as well. I did not have the slightest clue about Wettin. "And when the second war came you combed the skeins for them?"

"I was less then-" He shifted into High German to spin his tale.

"I have the gift," His voice was rough, screaming has that effect. "but it was for short horizons and narrow vistas. A day, a week, perhaps a fortnight, and then the sightlines blended into a haze of possibilities. There were better players, with longer horizons and wider stages. But that was not why they kept me at table." He looked at me and shivered slightly, the three of us knew what happened to those who were sent down from The Gotha tables.

"Go on." Wolff said, brushing the back of his hands with the knife.

"I could tell early, very early, when someone was…becoming less than reliable. When their skeins were tangled and sloppy, when they began to see paths and matrixes that never were. To know when they were attempting to urge actions on the tangled lines."

"That would be useful." Wolff approved.

"I did not essay longer horizons; I just watched the skeins flowing through our kennel. Then, one by one, all the Adepts that were kenneled with me fell into the blind spot."

"This was when?"

"Nineteen forty-three was when it started for our kennel. Luen Castle."

"And-"

"One by one their vision failed and so did they. Suicides, of one sort or another. The Gotha tasked me, only then, to look at the pathways. I had always averted my gaze from the longer horizons. I did not look for paths to victory, which may have been what kept me sane, but paths to escape."

"And the end came-"

"When The Gotha knew that there were no clear, sane, paths to victory, they set in motion escape and evasion protocols. They had previously suborned and incorporated much of the various branches of the Nazi regime: Military, RHSA and civilian political offices. Not at a high level, but high enough to be useful. Now they offered the ones they had suborned a way to elude the coming night, to coordinate escapes and to help fund them."

The Ratline. I cracked my knuckles, to hurry him along.

"And the regime, they leapt at the chance?"

"Assuredly. The Gotha carefully chose their clients. They preferred to approach the ones who were not owned heart and soul by the madness of the Reich, but who were focused only on the main chance and the profit to be had. Those clients also had resources to be exploited."

"You ended up in BRIXMIS?"

Snow nodded. "The Gotha had contacts with their counter parts among the Allies, they always did, blood trumps all. In the crumbling days after *Wacht am Rhein* failed, The Gotha quickly, silently, minimized their involvement with the higher ranks of the Reich." Which meant they killed those contacts that were not useful.

He paused, watching the knife Wolff held so lightly. "I was placed within the British army shortly before the end of that May, well after the surrender. I was fluent in English, sane, and I was notably discreet. What fates I had seen in the last days of my pod mates were quite enough to keep me focused on remaining in the background. I was tasked to pass 'clients' and The Gotha members through to a reception committee, to keep a watch out for Inquisitors-like you Herr Wolff-and discourage any refugees that did not have a provenience."

"And the traitor who snuggled you in your nest?" Wolff rumbled, leaning forward as if he longed to rip that information from Snow.

Snow shook his head frantically. "A ranking member of The Gotha procured me an English uniform, a dossier to study and a set of orders to establish me as a replacement. A Quartermaster. I never saw, that I know of, any of the Inquisitors who were cooperating with The Gotha."

Wolff was not happy that he did not have a name to put to the betrayal. Or a throat to put to his blade.

CHAPTER 19

"T his has all been very enlightening," I said, "but it does not advance the issue of the current Blinders."

"There have been problems-" Snow said, "with plaiting the skeins for some time. Slight problems. We have-or had-three to five pods functioning since the middle 1960's." He was more comfortable, now that he thought he was not likely to be killed out of hand. Wolff had backed off after he realized that Snow did not know who among the Inquisitors had betrayed their trust. "The pods were a check on each other, isolated from each other, blind reporting to a coordinating office." Nothing that I didn't know, he was stalling.

Wolff interrupted. "The Gotha?"

Snow was slow to answer, I pushed at him a bit. One hand on the back of his neck. "No. No, Herr Wolff. A joint commission; two Western Houses in Sable, an Eisenring independent action detachment and a section of the *XternBuro.*"

This I had not known, particularly the *XternBuro.* I thought to wring his neck, there and then. He had known I was Eisenring and assumed I had been 'read into' the operation. *XternBuro* and Eisenring in bed with the *Allemagne Noir.* It was distressing news to Wolff as well. I thought he had an idea of the who the Houses in Sable might be, one or both of them.

"After that American presidential election, on this sheaf, the small problems bloomed. All of the pods became liabilities. We then essayed a correction. The removal of Reagan."

"You tried to assassinate the president of the United States." Wolff was mildly incredulous.

"Yes. A covert direct-action correction of the cascading paths. The paths branching from that successful proposed correction were deemed stable for a thousand days and favored more subtle corrections thereafter. No one associated with his regime had been read into the necessity of the corrective action. It failed."

"Things became worse."

"Yes. Much worse." Snow licked his lips, the split from where I had gotten his attention earlier began to ooze blood again. "May I have some water?"

I glanced at Wolff, he had relaxed his stance and so I became the 'hard man' of the interrogation. "Be content," I said in my vulgar low German. "we are letting you breathe." And I pinched his neck, hard enough to leave bruises almost at once.

"Lyn." Wolff said offhandedly, almost under his breath. "Get him a glass of water."

Lyn had been close, closer than I realized, listening in. More than a simple Medji, of a certainty. "Mnh." She assented, stepped away from the doorway and went to the other motel room. Drew a glass of water from the basin there and brought it back. She handed it to Wolff and faded into the shabby wallpaper again. Medji and a ghost as well, suppressing her auras at need. Much more than a simple, sworn, retainer.

Snow drank from the glass, Wolff held it for him. I nodded slightly to Wolff and he winked ever so slightly to me.

"Wolff, we need to finish up this-debrief-and clear this location. Let me peel him and have done with it." I roughly grasped Snow by the collar.

Snow choked slightly on the water, his eyes rolling towards me. He had profited from observing a 'peel' at close hand and that observation had made him quickly, eagerly, forthcoming.

"We tried again," hissed Snow. "when he was in hospital. It failed, our operative suicided as he was taken by their security forces. But we left misleading tokens. The Ami's thought it was the Zenit Spetsnaz, the Reds thought it was a CIA coup attempt to install either Director Bush or General Haig as the President. I have no idea what they might think now."

"What next, Mr. Snow?"

"It was considered that lesser targets might be just as effective. Several persons of interest to the limited skeins we could evoke or discern were removed from the flow."

"You mean killed," I said in a very dry tone.

He rolled his eyes to me. "Yes. Killed. This cleared the flow for a…time and then it became rolled again. New persons of interest, new possibilities were identified and-"

"All were BRIXMIS?"

Snow turned his eyes to Wolff. "No, Herr Wolff. Not all were BRIXMIS. But the skeins where BRIXMIS actors came to the fore became more and more prominent."

"And has the 'flow' finally cleared?" I asked him.

"No. If anything, since Herr Wolff came to prominence, it has become even more rolled and murky. We are contemplating returning to more significant targets."

"This is why I detest dealing with Adepts," Wolff said. "They make small problems into insurmountable issues and then hand them off to-"

"Us." I trailed a thumb along a nerve from just before Snow's ear and down to the hollow of his neck. "He is delaying. Oh, my dear Captain Snow, what do you hope for? Rescue, a quick and easy end, a turning of the coat?"

"We wanted to clear the board of the lesser pieces and then move on," he said, ducking his head, hunching his shoulders against the blow.

I snorted. "The Amis would not easily let you close to their principal, again."

"The General Secretary of the Central Committee." Said Wolff, and Snow jumped even in his winding sheet. His pulse began to race under my thumb. "Who thought of this, The Gotha?" Asked Wolff.

"Not The Gotha. The Streltsy." Snow began to hyperventilate, and his eyes lost their focus, looking past us at the open door. "The Streltsy. The Streltsy and bent Inquisitors. The Gotha; Houses in Sable, Tables revealed, Cauldrons removed. Sable upon charcoal. Houses. Houses. Houses!" Snow's eyes were fully dilated, blood shot, then they rolled back into his head. He squealed and thrashed, thrashing his head back and forth. He tried to bite me, then bit his own lips until they bled, then blood ran from his nose and I could hear cracking noises from under the canvas drop cloth as bones broke. I grabbed his head, stopping him from cracking it open on the tub at the cost of skinning my knuckles. I compromised the neural pathways from his brain to a spinal node, the net sending fingers through the spinal column like long legged spiders; but still he thrashed.

"Throw it in the tub. Now." Wolff grabbed the kicking legs and I gripped him by the back of his neck and a handful of the canvas drop cloth, we wrestled him back into the tub. "Turn the shower on full and stand away." Wolff was not shouting, but he was firmly ordering, not wanting to attract any more attention than necessary.

I was surprised at the convulsions but not gob-smacked until smoke and steam began to spiral up from the writhing man in the filling tub. I took three steps back and began to fully manifest, spinning up my net around me and between

Wolff and the thing in the bathtub. PC41 had been watching the entire proceedings from the tank at the back of the stool. He blurred for the door, through Lyn's legs and under the bed.

"Back, the water may superheat and spray us." And Wolff dragged me back by the collar of my jacket and hip checked Lyn into the motel room. She turned and dashed into the adjoining room; I could hear her collecting Dama Ledhrad.

The body in the tub burned. Like metallic sodium in water, it burned; consumed, but with little heat or light. We stayed well outside the bathroom door. It took less than a minute and what was left in the tub was a soggy, scorched drop cloth mixed with blackened clothing and a few crumbling bones and a skullcap of hair. I looked up to the ceiling; there was a smoky grease stain on the acoustic tiles and yet the fire sprinklers had not drenched us. The shower was running full force.

"We should leave, and quickly," Wolff said.

I put away the gun I had drawn as a comfort. Nodded. "I think you have the right of it." I gestured to the tub with water still pouring in, steam eddying from it. "What-?"

He shrugged and hustled to the documents on the kitchen table, swept them into his dispatch case and then did a quick turn about the motel room, opening drawers and checking the waste basket. "Someone will come to clean the room, find the remains and someone else will come to deal with that-" He waved at the door to the bathroom, water was beginning to cover the remains in the bottom of the tub. "and the people who know what precisely happened will keep quiet and those who have not a glimmer will forget as quickly as they can."

"What happened?"

Wolff chuckled grimly under his breath. "Dickens and Krook, Mister Braxton. Dickens and Krook."

CHAPTER 20

I didn't ask what he was going on about. I patted my pockets to check that I hadn't lost anything in the tussle with the late Captain Snow and swept up everything in both rooms that might carry fingerprints-several glasses and a coffee cup-into a trash can and brought it with me. I reflected that I was spending an inordinate amount of time as a 'char' for the detachment in this affair.

Lyn was driving, PC41 was in the back seat next to Ledhrad and Wolff and I was in the front with the trash can between my legs. We pulled out of the parking slot in front of the rooms and quietly drove to the exit.

She glanced at me. "My driving is that bad?"

"No, just being tidy."

"Where to?" She asked the group at large.

"I am out of destinations and suggestions," I said.

"Let us leave Wichita altogether," Wolff said. "At the moment, I think, all of our opponents are at a loss for where we are. Let us keep it that way."

"Sounds good." Said Lyn and pulled out on to the highway. Turned right and headed west into the dark.

We rode in silence for a very long while; PC41 was purring and Lyn was humming softly under her breath, but the radio was off-a blessing-and I thought someone was snoring in the back seat. I looked over my shoulder and saw Wolff glancing through a microfiche with a magnifying loupe from his knife and a penlight. Dama Ledhrad was the obvious culprit for snoring.

"Wolff," I said when I saw a sign indicating that the highway was branching off. "you have any destinations in mind? The sign said that US 400 is going north to Dodge City."

"Might as well," Lyn said. "There will be motels and someplace to eat."

"Yes," Wolff said. "Take us to Dodge and we will hole up there. I have several credit cards with matching ID, what do you have Braxton?"

"I have a few sets; I also have cash. I did not know you had any."

"Again, a habit." He carefully stowed his makeshift micro-reader and the sheet of microfiche. He rubbed at his eyes. "Are you going to try and make contact with your control?"

I had not had the time to fill him in on Caerton's cluelessness and I didn't mention that Caerton was not precisely of the 'Ring. "I don't think it is advisable. The local detachment seems to be thoroughly compromised. Whether from the *Allemagne Noir* or one of the other factions I have not a clue." I rolled my stiff neck around, it crackled like dry twigs underfoot. "Absent any other goal, we hunker down and survive. I have a dead drop, a blind postal address, that I could use to pass on what Snow told us before his melodramatic end. But nothing else I would trust to use as a contact, and that drop is not secure."

"I thought as much." He sighed. "Dodge City is very near the very western rim of Cantry Ford in the 'zeme. There is a small postern there that would bring us to the Ford, where I have contacts still." He cracked his knuckles, shifted in his seat. "We should be at Dodge City in about forty minutes, I would think." He checked his watch. "I have just after three in the morning. Let us procure a box of alleged doughnuts and something hot to drink and then bed down for the day. Get up at sunset and go to the postern, transit, and then hunker down in the civilized outskirts of Cantry Ford, where you can get a proper cup of coffee and a pastry from a cadet branch of the *La Marquise patisserie*." He had a longing I had not heard in his voice before.

"*La Marquise patisserie*, a favorite of yours, in Paris?"

He chuckled. "Oh no, an establishment I actually have sometimes patronized in New Orleans. I first encountered them in the Cantry, but I did not know they had a foot across the veil. I was delighted when I visited New Orléans to find them there as well."

Ninety minutes later we had adjoining rooms in a chain motel with a connecting door; a dozen adequate doughnuts, two coffees, a tea and a hot chocolate. Lyn and Ledhrad ate a doughnut each, drank their tea and cocoa and went to bed. PC41 had a can of cat food in my bathroom and then drifted into the ladies' room.

"Wolff," I asked. "what the merry hell was that-the business with Snow?" I was on my second box of doughnuts.

"It happens, occasionally. With Skrenner Adepts." He was sitting in a chair with his head tilted back on a pillow, a leg resting on another chair. His eyes closed and his cup to hand. "You well know, better than most, that our bodies are an uneasy amalgam of energy and flesh. Many of the 'gifts' the Dai confront the worlds with are auric in one degree or another."

"That is a given fact."

"Skrenning is an internal manifestation, an internal process if you will, as opposed to an external expression of that gift. A practitioner can 'see' futures in patterns of the present and the past. Futures, plural. You may have a possible outcome, but there are many paths to that outcome; or you may have many outcomes from the path before you."

"Gambling, like you explained before."

"An offshoot, or perhaps a precursor to the gift. In any event they, Skrenners, are not well controlled and Skrenning is not well understood but common in its minor form. A fully manifested Skrenner Adept is rare and short lived, marginally sane and never stable-a condition which does not lend itself to any systematic study. Adepts do not reproduce at all, which is why I was surprised at Snow's contention that he was bred to it."

I had a dark thought. "Can it be forced? The gift?"

"No. That has been attempted, shown to be a fiasco of the first order, and its practitioners punished roundly by fate and the responsible local authorities for that attempt." He shifted in the chair and his free hand rubbed his upper thigh of the leg resting on the pillow, my net of auras saw an old knot in the flow. "It may have been particularly significant that our adept was male; most males of the Skrenner Adept clades who do manifest, do so as a result of a catastrophe in their lives-war in particular produces such. A female Skrenner of any sort, minor or Adept, will usually manifest upon menarche."

"Take enough candidates from known Skrenner lineages, force them through a lethal initiation of some sort, and collect the ones that survived," I said.

He opened one eye, focused on me. "Is that a speculation or an observation?"

"An observation of several different training regimes, for several different 'gifts. One I have endured and several I have observed."

He regarded me. "The Iron Ring I knew has changed, greatly."

I shrugged. "Snow and his end?"

"Any Skrenner begins with just seeing a possible path to a possible outcome. No more than that. For the Skrenner Adept it begins with seeing that path and often ends with trying to exist simultaneously across many possible endings. This co-location, being in one-two-three-many places at the same time demands energy from the Adepts. The energies involved can be and usually are lethal, though generally not as dramatic as Snow's end." He closed his eye. "We forced him, unintentionally, to inflate his visualization of the possible pathways, actors and events of the current crisis. He combusted, from the effort."

"You are having me on."

"Oh no. His auric body had converted enough of his physical body to a particularly flammable grease and then ignited it. At least that is the current explanation for the phenomenon. Current as of 1903, that is."

"Do they all-"

"No. Most just quietly die, if you call convulsions or a massive stroke a quiet death. And this is the last I will expand upon the subject of the end of Mister Snow. Good night Mister Braxton."

And he drifted off. I washed my face and hands, used the necessary and washed again. Then I took the bed closest to the door and settled down to sleep, with one node awake and aware. I got up later to use the necessary again and Wolff was sleeping peacefully on his bed with his ancient weapon held across his chest like the sword on a knight's effigy in a cathedral.

CHAPTER 21

Come midday PC41 woke me by the simple expedient of sitting on my face. >hungry< Was the push.

Being well trained I did not groan or throw her across the small room. Wolff was still sleeping in the pose of the knight, and while I could hear activity in the corridor, the ladies' room was quiet-except for contrapuntal snoring. I rolled out of bed, dumping PC41 to the floor and, quietly, rummaged through my dispatch bag for a can of food. I went into the bathroom, turned on the light which turned on the ventilation fan and opened the can. Tuna. I put it in the shower tub and sat on the stool thinking while PC41 daintily consumed the can.

I was rather fond of this world, as well as the others in its sheaf. I was perhaps not native to this line of possible worlds, a story for a later time if time allows. I had lived the majority of my youth in Alba of the Little England-or Greater France-world line. Living in what we called the 'Smoke' or the Estuary Wharfs, that was echoed in London on AngTerra. Just as Alba of the Three Crowns was echoed in the United Kingdom.

I had become more English in my habits and affections while alternating residencies between the two Londons than the rest of the inhabitants of the Three Kingdoms or the UK. I rather cherished the people and the best part of their cultures.

If Snow and his owners, handlers, what have you, were

right, this line, AngTerra was in grave danger. Which I could do nothing about. Nothing directly.

And if I walked to the 'zeme, let alone anywhere beyond it, it was my death.

There were very firm regulations, *Dikaions* amounting to a *Decretum* in Canon Law, about bringing any unlicensed biologicals into a Leaf-world. Unlicensed organics that were not native to that world line, or modified native organics, were strictly regulated and mostly prohibited. The definition and list of such prohibited imports was sixty pages of small type, with addenda published every quarter. The penalty for breaking that was contained in one word, Death.

Before the Eisenring, which was what the Iron Ring of the Seven Houses became, before the Eisenring existed, there had been haphazard defenses and 'customs' stations on the various gates between the known worlds. Some of the worlds knew the Dai, most didn't.

It had depended on who owned those gates just what could be brought through them. Most of the semi-licit trafficking were innocuous varitypes of fruit or vegetables. Crossline beverages were also common. Wheat and the other grains were too bulky to hand carry through the small gates of that time so enterprising merchants produced more concentrated goods; bread, beer and later-wine. Precious items, named weapons and steeds of legend were passed through the veil of worlds-though knowing the Dai as I do, I suspect they were cheap gee-gaws, castoff ironware and walleyed horses long in the tooth.

The beer and the wine were likely better than anything local.

Then the first of the plagues swept from and through the worlds the Dai walked on, and into the 'zeme. 'Zeme was the home of the Dai. The White Plague, what 'zeme named the influenza, was the first to pass the gates. Then the Pox and the Black Pox and the Yellow Purge all laid their mark on 'zeme. All took their tithe.

In the aftermath of that cascade of sorrows, the Eisenring was formed. Ever since that constellation of plagues, a gate to bring something or someone across the veil has been closely warded, inspected and secured by an independent martial order 'The Iron Ring of the Seven Houses', which became the Eisenring.

The 'Ring was conservative and iron-fistedly empirical in its dealings with contamination of any sort; fire being the accepted solution. In the very early days, there was a lych yard at the entrance to every known gate and a burn pit. And you were searched, sniffed and prodded by every Dai with any gift at all for sifting. Minor D'draig-what I was before I partnered with PC41-were tolerated and even valued, for their ability to sift and help 'sanitize' transients and Walkers.

All the other concerns of regulating Walking through any of the worlds; taxes, politics, fugitive Walkers or illicit technology, arose after the plagues had faded into nightmares and cautionary tales. And as corrupt as the Eisenring are, Provo and Unity both, the one transgression they will not wink at is to smuggle proscribed biological content across the veil.

PC41 and I were very much proscribed content.

PC41 came out of the bathtub and jumped to the tank behind me. He settled into a standard feline meditation pose and began a light purr. >concern<

I leaned back and let the net of my aura completely envelop his.

>very< I pushed back. >duty opposes survival<

It was easier when I was very close to PC4, to converse. Much easier now than when we first interacted. Each time we nested our auras, things became easier and stronger.

For example; 'sifting'. When you 'sift' a person of interest, you ask questions of them and by observation of their auras you determine how much they are lying to you.

Once I had to place my hand over one of the major nodes of a subject, flesh against flesh, to 'sift' an answer to the question that was put to them. My limited gift let me know 'true', 'false' or 'I truly don't know.' But I had to have my hand on them. It was helpful, it was exhausting and sometimes painful to me and to my subjects. Raging headaches or profound nausea on both sides of the sifting. And sometimes the answers were not convincing, or complete. There were ways to shade an answer to the question, even with my hands on them.

Now I could 'sift' with a minimum of effort and much more effectively. Not as easy as cracking open a book and reading plain text, but as easy as say, puzzling out a text in a language you had a limited facility in. And I did not need to have my hands on the subject, just be close by. Sitting at Table, at a cocktail party, or standing over them in a dark maintenance bay. That made me a valuable resource and an appalling danger to the Dai as a whole and both of the Eisenrings. A resource because I could read whoever I was set to interrogate, a danger because I could read my betters at Table or at Desk.

The other thing I learned, in that maintenance bay, was that I could exert myself a bit more and take the memories of the subject that I was sifting. All of them. At once. A peel.

Peel. There was a folk tale that passed around the Ddirag, over drinks, in a very quiet corner where none of the common-the mundane-could overhear. That a D'draig, if he was strong enough in his gift, could 'peel' someone like you would peel a boiled egg or an onion. Or even smash them like an earthenware crock, letting their contents spill through the D'draig's hands. A peel also left the subject as empty as a broken crock, not quite dead, but empty. It was a tale to entertain, to frighten. Gilles de Rais, Vlad Dracul, or Breaker of Houses; those mythic monsters that populated telenovels in the 'zeme and smuggled yellowback books in the other sheaves. All of these monsters were native only, it was said, to the dark and bloody lands of AngTerra. These dark gifts were ascribed to the Dai who had Manifested the traits of the Sangsue. The Sangsue. Wolff the Hunter had made a special project of the Sangsue. Churched or unchurched, it is said he had an abiding interest in hunting them to extinction.

I was not just an appalling danger, something to be used but sparingly, but a monster out of legend. A legend I had written off as *bumf*, something to entertain the credulous marks. Now I am the monster. That took a bit of getting used to.

I came to an epiphany, sitting in that small bathroom. I had been avoiding the reality of my, our, situation.

PC41 and I, were now Unchurched.

We had known the Dai, the hidden worlds, had sat at table among the Eisenring and walked the Notes of this sheaf. Now we were a threat to all that.

Sooner rather than later, someone like Wolff would be detailed to resolve our status.

"Are you all right?" Wolff asked. I opened my eyes.

He had awakened and was at the bathroom door. The antique was in his hand but pointed well away from me.

"I am reviewing my status, with the Eisenring."

"Um." He paused. "May I use the facilities, waking early

and old age, don't you know?"

"Sorry." PC41 dropped to the floor. I stood, sidled past Wolff and went to sit in the only chair in the next room. PC41 head butted my knee and then faded through the connecting door to consult with the ladies. I leaned back in the chair, designed to be as uncomfortable as possible without being upholstered with razor wire, and dozed. I needed to talk, and I did not want to talk. I could not sleep. And so, I slept. It never fails.

"Your status?" I woke with a jerk, the sort of jerk you have when you are mistaken about the number of steps of the staircase you are descending in the dark.

Wolff was sitting on the bed; cross-legged and with his back against the wall at the head of the bed. His gun was in his weak hand and he had a glass of tap water in his right hand.

I changed the subject. "You are looking markedly better. How do you feel?"

He acknowledged the shift in topic with a slight smile. "If I had but known the advantages of working alongside a D'draig, I would have requisitioned one much earlier in my career."

I noted his change in terminology for me. "I am not certain that encountering me has improved your condition. But I'll take that compliment." I stretched my back, letting my gift, my talent, ease the knots in the flows of my charkas. Ease the pain in my back. "What is your intention?" I snagged another pair of glazed doughnuts. I was always hungry now. The hunger, another glittering scale of the legend. The never satiated hunger. And the wounds I left in the living, if they followed the legend, they would not heal.

"I have contacts in this section of Kansas," He gave almost a gallic shrug, one you might have practiced before the mirror when you were at school, but his was genuine. "Purely from long habit I recruited and developed a network. Why, I couldn't tell you. All the tricks of the trade; I never thought or intended to use this ad-hoc network, but I was uncomfortable not having one." He drank from his glass. "This part of the Great Plains is noted for having several crossings, small-bore and primitive and mostly unwatched."

I pricked up my ears, out of habit. An unwatched crossing is anathema, to either of the 'Rings. No customs, no transit control and no reports up and across the web. In another time I would have been interested for the Firm's purposes, now I was fascinated on my behalf.

"My plan is to approach a crossing with a small footprint, transit to the Ford and then quietly lay to and consider the situation and our options."

"There is a problem, actually there are two problems." I held up a hand, pointing my forefinger at the celling. "Dama Ledhrad is a Citizen of the Hanse and an Agent of the *XternBuro*. She should have a *Skirbref*, a let pass, to enter the 'zeme; notifying the locals that a Hansatic is in their area and notifying the Hanse that one of theirs is abroad."

Wolff nodded. "And that notification will set off alarms across a shuffle of bureaucrats."

I laughed. I had not heard that particular formulation before. It was the first honest laugh I had known since PC41 came into my life.

>sorrow< Came the push. >what it is< I pushed back

I wiped my eyes with the back of my hand. "A 'shuffle', that is marvelous. Did you coin that gem?"

"Alas, no, I cannot take the credit for it." Wolff was broadly smiling again. "And the second problem?"

I sighed. "I, we, are proscribed; we will be proscribed. The *Dikaion*." He nodded. I did not have to outline that to him. "After the event where PC41 found me and the subsequent firefight, they brought us to a secure facility. Near New York City and Croton-on-Hudson of the here and now, but not on the grounds of that House. We were closely held, closely observed and isolated. Any attempt to separate us was unsuccessful, spectacularly unsuccessful on two occasions. No fatalities but... There were factions in the corridors of the Joint Eisenring Taskforce that advocated a quiet and tidy end, other factions in Croton and the Provo Eisenring were avidly fascinated at the implications of the...partnership. It was unprecedented. Platoons of scientists busied themselves drawing blood, ordering x-rays, cat-scans and other invasive and non-invasive procedures. Mostly of me, PC41 did not lend herself to such prodding. They did not clear us of any present danger to the Dai, but the expanded 'gift' I suddenly manifested recommended an exception to the *Dikaion*. 'For further study'."

"And study involved putting you in the field?"

"I think that 'putting me in the field' by having me surveilling you was supposed to be harmless make-work. It did get me away from the boffins and it did lose me in the thicket of Eisenring and Registry bureaucracy. Allowing the various factions of the Unity and the Provo as well as the factions in Croton House room to conspire and maneuver."

"It appears to me that a faction or a coterie of factions were trying to solve problems by hanging the problems out to dry. In particular me, Ledhrad and you."

"I was not singled out by The Gotha and the other conspirators." I pointed out to him. "You and Ledhrad were marked when the pair of you bubbled up in the Blinders, appearing often in the several matrixes according to Snow. I think the decision to wish me on you was unthinking. Not uncommon in the middle ranks of either of the Eisenrings. 'Don't just sit there, do something.' Competent my arse." I rubbed at my face. "In any event, if and when I pass through a properly manned wicket with PC41 and without an official escort even more alarms will propagate through the various bureaus." If we manage to live through the hue and cry.

He shrugged. "Then we shall have to pass you through an improper wicket. There is a 'soft spot', not known to many, to the North of Dodge City. With the right guidance, and a bit of help at both ends, we could find our way to the Ford without disturbing the beauty rest of our bureaucratic keepers. Getting from the soft spot on the 'zeme side to the Ford, might be more of an issue, but I know a man..."

I looked at him for a while, then I nodded. "I think it is time to step over a bright line."

He looked up from his study of his antique needler.

PC41 nudged my hand, back again. She was a black and white shorthaired tabby now. I rubbed at the right spot behind her ears, she rewarded me with rumbling.

"Field agents don't last long in any of either Eisenring's operational bureaus," I remarked watching PC41 enjoying her scratching. "particularly any of the 'gifted' agents. Not in the Provo nor in the Unity 'Rings. We learn this fact in the unofficial sessions of our training, what the field instructors relate over their beer and sausages at the Gasthof or the beer and skittles at the Pub. An agent either moves up and into a Desk, they are used up and given a quick burning and a proper inhumation, or they attempt to take a Scots Leave. I would have had sixteen active years in the field with Unity this fall, a long time comparatively. And I am very much not on the Desk track. My gift was moderate and of a sort ill-suited for advancement and I did not come from a qualified house." I licked the sugary glaze from the fingers of my free hand. "I would have come under suspicion rather sooner than later as 'unreliable'. Then I partnered up with this rogue." PC41's purr ramped up.

Wolff's face darkened. I found it odd that he was unaware how the Eisenring, of either strand, ordered its ranks.

"I manifested much later than most," I said, "in my early

twenties. And under a peculiar situation. Although I think, looking back, that I had been under observation since primary school. Shortly after that, I was 'impressed' by the Unity Eisenring." I moved about in the chair, trying to find a way to sit that wasn't uncomfortable. "When I was first assigned to field work, once I had passed a probationary period, I began to establish a 'suitcase' for when I was no longer trusted or needed either by the Joint Eisenring on AngTerra or the Unity establishment in Alba of the Three Crowns."

"A retirement account."

I blinked at that. "Well yes, the Eisenring version of an old-age pension plan." I smiled at the thought, I had sat through several agonizing lectures on the myriad basic varieties of pension plans on offer when I had once been tasked to penetrating a business in London.

I wondered if I was attempting to teach a Lobsterman how to tend traps, telling Wolff about suitcases. "We all learned the basics, officially, in classes at the academy. And in more detail on our own time. You establish simple identities in a world line that is not particularly 'regulated'; The Royal Remnant Colonies in the Greater France-Little England sheaf is considered a good place to consider for exile. It has a low population with a large percentage of odd-cod refugees from the Continent and the Hispanic Establishment in South America. You acquire a minimal proficiency in a common language of that sheaf, a proficiency that your handlers should not know you have. Low German or Portuguese are suitable in the example of the Colonial Remnants. You just learn to speak English with a reasonable accent and if challenged by a native speaker of the language you are legended under, apologize for your rusty proficiency-blame it on too long an absence from the homeland."

I got up and walked around the room. I expanded my net to sweep the local area, something that I could not do before

PC41. Ten yards now, where once I could barely manage a meter. Johanna Marie was lightly sleeping; Lyn was only dozing-a proper Medji will insist they never sleep. There was a couple in the hotel room on the left side, arguing bitterly. And there was Wolff. A bonfire of auras rose up from him.

"You sock away money and small valuables-" I continued, chattering. Uneasy. "in caches throughout the intended refuge, specifically caches that are not known to the Firm or to your peers. And you always try to carry some funds and identity papers with you, in case you make a run for it on a moment's notice."

"And your handlers do not-"

"Suspect? They suspect everyone, since they have their own suitcases in the event they need to 'retire' suddenly. They are well aware of the effect on morale and efficiency if they would attempt to indiscriminately sift the operational cadres for 'disaffected' agents. If they have proof, say from betrayal of a confidence made to a fellow agent, they will swiftly modify your relationship with the 'Firm'. And not in your favor. They will empty your 'suitcase' of what funds and items they can claw back, try to expose your network so that they can flip or burn your co-conspirators and make a bloody public example of you."

His face was set, a muscle in his left jaw twitching. I focused my awareness and read Wolff's auras. Anger, shame, anger, disgust, shame. Emotions blinking off and on.

"This was how the *Allemagne Noir* ordered their ranks, not-" He looked away from me. "How long have you been in the 'Ring?"

I thought for a bit, the years varied from line to line. "More than eighteen, maybe twenty-two years total what with school and such."

"It was not this sort of-what in bloody hell are they thinking; this is how we turned The Gotha, the *Allemagne Noir*, to work for us! By showing them that they could have a future that did not end with a bullet at the back of the neck."

"You still have that future, just not as a D'draig or some of the other, problematic, 'gifts'. Vertis are no more tolerated than D'draig, for some of the same reasons. Binders on the other hand are always on the fast track to a Seat at the Table." I thought about Vittorio, who had not been gifted in any sense of the term. "The fast track can still end with the bullet to the back of the neck, or to a long and tedious existence carrying the can for the accomplished highflyers." I looked at my watch. Just after two in the afternoon. "And there are a lot of Fain-the Dai who have not manifested but who are in a stud book somewhere-who hold a chair at a Desk without a lick of sense or talent and who advance slowly but surely up the ladder to a seat. Deftly avoiding all the slippery rungs as they climb. You say it wasn't like this when you were at Table?"

"No. Not like this. Or if it was, it was subdued. Or we were cozened. I had a suitcase, we all had suitcases when we were in the field; but they were established and supported by High Tables of the Houses." He wiped at his face again, wearily. "We used 'suitcases' between the wars, on AngTerra; to facilitate operations on several other Lines where the Dai were entirely covert. Greater France, Imperial Sindu, Cartago Royal. I had established identities on all of those lines, as well as on AngTerra."

"I have my primary 'suitcase' in the Remnant Royal Colonies of Little England, the 'sheaf of Alba of the Three Crowns'. Which are neither Colonies, nor Royal and are not particularly a remnant." I sat again. "AngTerra would locate the Colonies in North America. The funds and identity papers cached there would be enough to let me establish myself in one of the harbors around the great lakes of the interior. I could live a year or so without a job but not in any style. I conceal my primary suitcase in a thriving port city on the river most of the different English-speaking Sheaves call the Hudson, in the Free City of York-on-the-Hudson." I grinned at him. "Co-located with New York on AngTerra and the Port of York in the 'zeme."

He blinked, rubbed his eyes some more and shook his head to clear it. "Isn't that hella close to Hudson House, the Provo Eisenring, the Registry Marshals and the lot?"

I shook my head. "I have often been tasked with hunting down Churched absconders, as well as unchurched crossing enterprises. Here on AngTerra and in Little England of the Three Kingdoms; the one thing I have consistently noted in these operations was that there was a failure by the Joint Eisenring S2 to look for them in plain sight.

Our briefing presenters always instructed and encouraged us to search for elaborate operations and well-hidden bases; with secret tunnels to the docks, autogiro pads on tower blocks, false walls, hidden rooms and suspicious characters hanging about aimlessly." I snorted. "Field operatives said that the Rear-Echelon: Mark I-Bench-Sitters, our S2 briefers, all had the super-villain virus vectored from Hollywood in AngTerra." Wolff did not laugh.

I continued. "Joint establishment higher-ups did not think an ordinary warehouse with mundane goods flowing in and out daily would be a smugglers den." I continued. "A smuggling ken with a time clock, a break room, a credit cooperative automatic teller and a HR office with yearly performance reviews was quite beyond their conception. Even after we proved several times that you could easily hide more than a half-million pounds a year in the accounts of a moderate wholesale plumbing supplier, they kept looking for Largo in the docks and seeing James Bond in the mirror when they shaved." I leaned back in the uncomfortable chair. "So, I put the 'suitcase' in a neighborhood credit cooperative strong room; some cash in a passbook account at another cooperative, and a moderately large deposit box with paperwork and 'other' items in a Royally Chartered Bank. On holidays I occasionally visited the Free City of York, on an excursion steam liner from the Estuary along with a hundred other pasty-white denizens of the Smoke and stayed at a small hostel there. Went skiing up river in the Catskills in the winter holidays, in the summer I went to Cony Island and swam in the ocean or rode on the entertainment rides, took in a few Music Hall extravaganzas-they were cheaper by far in 'The Free City' than in the Smoke. And when I was certain I was not being surveilled, I visited my 'suitcase' to update and improve it."

We sat in silence for a while.

Wolff got off the bed and collected his watch and wallet from the desk. "Nietzsche was right," he said. "I am sorry."

CHAPTER 22

We idled in Dodge City for two days. No one bothered us, no one noticed us. I escorted a wide-eyed Johanna Marie through the tourist traps, trailed by Lyn who was just as wide-eyed. Wolff did networking, which amounted to breakfast meetings at a chain coffee house and making notes at night on a steno-pad. One morning he had us shift the contents of our luggage into a half dozen duffle bags. I was not particularly maudlin over leaving my leather dispatch bag, it was a rarity even in my Albia and if we were crossing veils, it would not do to attract attention lugging it about. But I did leave it in a safe deposit box with a five-year prepaid box rent. I kept all of my current ID-both local, Albia and Remnant Colonies on me, and most of my AngTerra currency. I did not expect to be back, but leaving the cash felt wrong. I brought a trucker's wallet, with six different card pockets, and I bought a money belt. I filled it with the paper money I had been issued when I got the dossier on Wolff. I had more cash stowed in the duffel bag, UK pounds and Yankee dollars, along with clothes and cat food. Never enough of the good stuff.

Wolff lifted an eyebrow at my renting the deposit box, but he didn't make a comment. After I dropped the dispatch bag off, I left the rental with full fuel tanks and scrupulously clean, inside and out, at a freestanding rental office. Took a cab back to a motel a block north of the motel we were staying in. Old habits can keep you alive.

That night, we piled into a large SUV, duffle bags and all, and we were driven west for a while. We'd left the keys to the rooms on the TV; and a twenty-dollar bill on the pillow as a tip. We were paid up through the next morning. So, no check out through the front desk.

The SUV doubled back and north east for three hours towards the 'thin' spot that Wolff spoke of. Turned on a dirt road, drove over a slight rise that masked the lights of the paved road behind us. Then stopped at a wide place. The driver dropped us there and then, drove off into the night with no lights. Not three minutes later seven horses came out of the dark, led by a couple of teenagers. Which I did not perceive, even with my expanded ability, the teenagers, not the horses.

We were not dressed for horseback work, jeans and trainers were not what I would have chosen as riding habits. But we all found steeds and climbed on. Ledhrad had a very placid mare, Wolff and I had business like geldings and Lyn was on a cutting horse that was very glad to see her. It was mutual, that delight.

The auras of our reception crew were clear and simple once they formed up around us, horse and rider were calm and focused. The duffle bags were loaded on one of the horses and off we walked, into the night. One teenager at the van, one at the rear and the packhorse in the middle with Lyn leading it.

PC41 had crawled inside my windbreaker, right next to the 9mm pistol. She was a very small, black, kitten this night. And nervous. >what< She queried.

>crossing< I pushed at her. Curiosity and some worry came back down the push. I worried too. The smugglers ken had been on AngTerra, in the Carolinas. So, no gates since PC41 and I had partnered up. And how the shipping boxes got there I had no idea.

>could tell<

That startled me. >from box< I questioned.

>was some *where*, was some *when*<

A memory of dropping and spinning came to me, riding on a tilt-a-whirl in a warm night. Lights swirling in the distance. This came across the push, into me, and through me into the horse. The horse stumbled and shook its head till the bridle rattled. >later< I pushed back and got a faint reply.

"Trouble?" Lyn asked in a clear but very quiet voice.

"I don't think so," I said, and thought soothing thoughts about horses, threading my 'fingers' through its auras. Motors. I was comfortable with motors. Horses were not my particular choice of transport. I was a boy of the 'Smoke' after all. Motors were my preference.

Half an hour later, maybe; by the setting moon it was late, we paused at a dry creek bed, barely visible by the quarter-moon. There was a rustle from the left. A heavy-set man and a small woman walked out of a clump of dried up reeds six feet high. She had a shuttered bullseye lantern in one hand and an air carbine in the other. A pump action carbine that could fire a cluster of flechettes. He had another bullseye lantern, an unlit carbide lantern on a soft billed cap, and an antique double crossbow tucked under his arm. It was loaded and spanned, and I knew it and the air carbine from my time in the Eisenring gate watch.

He nodded to Wolff and walked to the back of the line, followed by the lead teenager on horseback. The crossbowman gently patted Lyn's knee with his free hand, and silently walked past me. Both of them, Bowman and Walker, had very faint almost invisible auras. Like Lyn. And the teenagers.

"Wolff." The woman with the pneumatic said in a low voice. "What have you brought to my hearth?"

"Passing through, wakeless if we are fortunate."

"Heard you were declining."

"Don't feel like declining. You going to carry us through?"

"Ten for the lot of you. Ten more for the trouble."

"Done and done." Wolff said and dropped a pouch into her outstretched hand.

She stepped forward, pitched her voice loud enough to carry to the end of the file, not loud enough to echo over the field. "Listen up. Bag your watches in the sacks on the saddle horns; bag any pagers, bag anything else that has a battery. Do not draw or brandish a gun. If you have transited before, you know why, if you have not walked before this-it is an excellent way to get a bolt in the back or a 'chette in the face. We will cross in single file, a meter separation between the horses, I will lead on foot. Gregory will follow. Any questions? None? Good."

Then she took Wolff's horse by the bridle and led us down the dry creek bed. The other riders dropped back and disappeared into the night, they faded away both in vision and in my other senses. I knew Gregory was at my back, only because I could hear the carbide lantern hissing. The woman at the head of the file was a shadow against Wolff's horse. Impressive.

We walked along in silence, broken only by soft crunching of the pebbles underfoot and under hoof. And Wolff faded away; and Ledhrad faded and Lyn and her pack horse faded and then PC41 and I and my nameless gelding walked through the veil.

And we walked up a trickling creek with the smell of spring about us.

The Walker paused for a short time, her head rolled back on her shoulder and looking at the full moon above us. I felt Gregory close up and I knew he had slipped the safety off his bow; I swung my net wide and had him if need be. She threw her lantern on to the bank of the creek and swung her gun on Wolff. "Wolff," She said, anger in her voice; fear, anger and confusion in her blooming colours. "What have you done in heaven's name?"

Wolff was looking at the moon as well. "I don't know. There was an incident-"

Her colours faded slightly, the anger bled mostly away. "Damn. That crossing fuckup."

"We heard that things were calm."

"They were calming." She waved her gun at all of us. "Git off, now." She was quickly up in a saddle and had the reins of all of the horses but the pack horse. "If I see you again, Inquisitor." And the threat was plain in her voice. "Keep the pack horse and pray I and Gregory go when and where we should, else the boys will come calling when they are of an age." They trotted down the way we had come, in to the dark, into the gate and gone. She'd left her doused lantern; he'd walked backwards, covering us, into the darkness.

Lyn had charge of the pack horse and Ledhrad. I splashed over to Wolff, whose gaze was still fixed on the moon. PC 41 was nowhere to be found, having jumped from my windbreaker when we had come to a stop.

"Fifteen days," Wolff said. "Or more…"

"You think?"

"I don't know." He nodded. "With luck, with the gate still open behind us and all, she might be home and dry."

"And if she is not?"

He rolled his neck around on his shoulders, cartilage cracking in the moonlit night. "She has three boys, if I remember rightly, and they know of me. They would come looking when they are of an age. I'd hate that."

We walked on up the trickling stream.

Elf hills.

CHAPTER 23

We got to Cantry Ford two days later, after spending an uncomfortable day and night at a Wain stop on the Horse Creek Trace three miles north by a trace from the 'soft spot'. The stop was clean, the food was acceptable, and its staff paid no attention to us walking into their laager after enough 'white metal' changed hands. Dama Ledhrad was quiet, her eyes taking everything in around her, her minimal conversational talents even more contracted. Lyn was quiet too, resenting the loss of her cutting horse and the bundle she had behind the cantle when the walker had ordered us off the saddles and left us standing in the creek. I was on her list again, so was Wolff. So was every male in the Wain-wagon station; human, dog or horse.

Wolff and I were just as quiet. He bought a broadsheet digest of news, run off on a wire printer that had a direct connection to the Ford. Bought fifteen pages; that digest covered the last six months; in the 'zeme, on AngTerra-a milieu that had a particular dark fascination for the locals, Little England, the Seven Islands, and Imperial Hindi. The digest covered particularly the eternal scandals Hind-Sindhu 'high society' generated, but it also abstracted the high points of low doings among the rest of the lines. He went through that digest with a red pencil and a cup of coffee, as if he was solving the Time's crossword puzzle. Very intense.

PC41 and I just spent that day sitting outside of the Wain station, watching. I was not sure what PC41 was watching, but I was watching the auras trail past us. Eating my fill of lean, rare, buffalo steak and lots of dark bread, feeling the creaking hollow under my ribs start to fill in. Crossing the veil had a new-found effect on me, a drain I did not know about. Anything to do with auras was a drain.

Nothing leapt out at us, nobody came strolling down the trace with ribbons of blood red auras trailing after them. Nobody came by missing auras, either. Except Lyn. Some people are born or come to maturity with colorless or absent auras, some people learn to suppress them by endless practice. Or so I had been told once upon a time.

Lyn and Gregory and the Walker that had brought us across. They were Ghosts.

An acquaintance tried to describe that phenomena to me, once. He asked, "Have you ever seen fish raised in a cave. Fish that have been in the cave for so long that they're transparent."

"No," I said. I was fifteen and the only fish I had seen were wrapped in yesterday's newspaper.

"Well that is what a 'suppressed' looks like, if you were a Sensitive like me, you'd know. They're not as rare as you think, those alba auras."

"Right," I said. "Pull the other one, Jax, it's got bells." In my defense, the gormless Jax, in the very same conversation, had tried to convince me that he knew an absolutely brilliant way to coax a girl out of her nickers on the first date. Reading Auras and getting laid on the first date, not on the programme as they used to say. Jax was a Mod then; chinos, dark wire rimmed sunglasses and desert boots. He was also hanging about with the local Scions of Avalon-an entry into the Elders of Avalon. Hollow earth, hidden truths, aura reading, crystal healing, elder civilizations and secret societies out to rule the world; all part of the pitch of the Elders. I thought he was about a half bubble off dead level. Reading auras and nattering on about hidden powers and dominions. The Elders of Avalon. Bah.

It was a Unity Eisenring front.

Funny, isn't it?

Very full of himself, Jax was. Still is. I once heard, while at Table, he was a desk sitter for a Joint 'Ring Taskforce in a covert station in one of the Muscovy Lines. Not a good station, it wasn't particularly comfortable, but it was a living. Better than being a 'stand-over thug' back in the Smoke, or better yet a bookie. Which is what he was aspiring to be.

"And how is your day?" Wolff was leaning against the post holding up the veranda.

I blinked away the image of Jax behind a reception desk in an Import/Export house that had never had better days. "The coffee was acceptable, and the crullers better than I deserved, other than that." I shrugged.

"We left AngTerra in the last days of August, we are here for the last month of spring of the year following that August."

"Really." I was sitting already, or I would have plopped down in shock. "Seven months?" Not fourteen days, or forty.

"Near as dammit."

"Nothing happened?" Visions of mushroom clouds rising from horizon to horizon sprang up.

"General Secretary Brezhnev died in November. The Central Committee anointed one Yuri Vladimirovich Andropov as the General Secretary. He lasted until March the following spring. Renal failure was the official cause of death."

"March 1983? Assassination? Two assassinations?"

"There is nothing in any of the broadsheets that even hint at that." He rolled up his sheets and sat on the stoop next to me. "Near as I can figure out it is late April 1983, or maybe early May at my home. At my home in AngTerra. A couple of the sheets are fond of using the French Revolutionary dating schemes, the Mayan Haab, Lunar-Solar calendars or other oddball systems just because they can. Some of the broadsheets use the Julian Calendar instead of the Gregorian, which further confuses the issue. But I think May is the current month. Now there is a Chairman Konstantin Chernenko, appointed to the exalted post of General Secretary in late March or early April."

"You got that fishing on the Wire?"

"Yes, I had to set the net very broad at first, but I did get some of the more relevant news when I refined my search queries."

"Our news is old."

"Perhaps. No one has tried for Reagan again."

I stood up and brushed off the seat of my pants. "Are we going to tell the ladies?"

"Our ride is due, and I'd rather have that conversation in a slightly more secure place."

He did not want the brawl to happen in the rest area. "Agreed."

It was another day of travel on the Wain, to come to the outskirts of the Ford. The Ford was a Free City, the largest in the continent. A Free City. It was not controlled or owned by a House or a constellation of Houses-or under the Confed House political regime. How it functioned was, to quote Churchill, " -a riddle, wrapped in a mystery, inside an enigma." And someone else once compared the Cantry Ford to the Serene Republic of Venice, hinting that the Venetians lifted the idea of an oligarchic republic from the Ford. This was also the merchant that thought that culture faded out west of the Kaatterskills, so take that how you will. In any event, the Ford had a very uneasy relationship with the Eastern houses.

There was a Confed House office, with registry Marshals and the attendant Eisenring lice, but their writ ran only to their office space and their own people. And they had a continual loss of people, going walkabout and fading into the Ford. So, they had a large number of Marshals and a larger number of Provo lice than you would think. To keep the desertions down. Or at least to a manageable level.

We unloaded our scant baggage and settled into a four-bedroom cottage; one of six cottages attached to a modest restaurant hotel. We all had our own bedroom, one large bath with shower and tub as well as the commode, a mini kitchen and a sitting room opening onto a pocket garden. Much nicer than the Motel 6 in Dodge City. Worlds better than the one we left Captain Snow at.

After a room service meal and an after-dinner round of drinks, Wolff opened the lecture.

"I have found several things out about the walk we made from AngTerra to 'zeme. First: we transitioned seven months into our future." Lyn and Ledhrad, were stunned. No one spoke for a while. I poured another round of drinks.

"Several significant things have transpired on AngTerra since we left it. Nothing as yet devastating, but all disturbing to say the least. Primarily, the Soviet Union has had three heads of state in the time it took us to cross the veil."

Lyn recovered first. "You knew?" She growled. Wolff moved to the head of her list. "And," She swung her glare on me. "when did you find out?" I regained the pole position on the list.

"I suspected," Wolff said, "but I needed to come for my information in a roundabout way."

Dama Ledhrad was calm. Which concerned me, I threaded my net through her auras. She was calm. I thought that the rapid-fire shocks she had been subjected to in the last seventy hours of real time had numbed her. If not broken her. I was wrong.

"Is this a normal hazard, while crossing veils?" Ledhrad

asked.

"No, not to this degree." Wolff did not look to me or to where PC41 sat observing. But I had an idea that he had the same opinion I did. What triggered the leap was PC41. And there were several other things that PC41 might have influenced. Snow's demise among them.

"Tomorrow I will begin to contact some old acquaintances, if they are still here in Cantry Ford. I respectfully request that you, Dama Ledhrad, refrain from contacting the Hanse Consulate Steelyard here until we know what they have made of your disappearance on AngTerra."

Lyn cussed under her breath. "And what do you want Illya-" She hooked a thumb at me. "and me to do? While you stroll through the casbah?"

Wolff blanched a bit. Then stared Lyn down before she worked herself up into a right insubordinate temper. "Devise and document an explanation for you and me turning up here. Braxton is not here, Lyn. Braxton never was here. Braxton is never going to be here. And you haven't a clue as to where he might be, or what happened. Have. I. Made. Myself. Clear?"

Lyn, to give her due, gave me the briefest of sidelong looks and settled back in her chair. She looked at PC41. Then folded her hands in her lap and focused on Wolff.

Wolff went on to outline what was happening in AngTerra and specifically in Soviet Russia, more for Ledhrad's sake than for Lyn and me.

A half hour later, after a short explanation about the role of a 'General Secretary' in ruling Soviet Russia, we all went to bed.

Come late morning, PC41 woke me in her usual fashion. I opened the last can of the 'good stuff' I'd brought over, fed her and started a kettle for tea. Cantry Ford, being a crossroads for many worlds, loose tea was well supplied. No tea cakes, but croissants and loose tea. Three-and-a-half stars out of four.

I needed a day to make and mend; I needed to get some more of the 'good stuff' for PC41 and some new clothing and kit for me. My shoes had not been intended for cross-country strolls in a damp springtime. A watch in particular was also required, mine had remained in the bag on the saddle horn of the gelding. Lyn appeared as I was jotting down a list.

She set a coffee maker to brewing and taking a croissant sat across from me. "Benjamin read me in, on your situation."

She was polite. This was a sea change.

"Oh," I said. Watching her hands, as my close quarters combat instructor advised. "He, did?"

"What are you going to do?"

I shrugged, slightly. "Run as long as I can for as far as I can, with my partner." I looked her in the face. "We don't know what is happening to us, between us. Or why. But I know we will be hunted; we are certainly hunted. Seven bleeding months since they last had us on their maps or in their hands. They must be shitting bricks." PC41 appeared at my elbow on the tabletop, inclined his head for a regulation scratch. "With Snow's spectacular demise and what dregs, we left of The Gotha-the Allemagne Noir-operation we scuttled, my ex-employers, and the more vigilant un-Churched but knowledgeable Secular agencies are searching for us. We are very much in demand."

"West of here, in the foothills of what we call the Rockies back home, they are very unfriendly to the Eisenring, the Confederated Houses or the 'Unity." She got up and poured herself a cup. Offered me and I waved her off. "They have a habit of shooting Eisenring and Blackleg Marshals on sight. And if you are on the run from either of the 'Rings-"

"A refuge?"

"Maybe." She looked at PC41 and grimaced. "You might not be forthcoming to them for any of the reasons you have gone off the porch, or for that matter your late history as an

Eisenring."

"Is he out walking the Casbah?"

She gave me a flash of a smile. "Just after dawn. Had a cuppa and a roll here and took a trolley into the center of the Ford."

"Never been to the Ford. Just to the eastern coast of this continent on occasion." I did not mention the year I spent in the north of Albion on 'zeme being shaped up as a Unity Eisenring; I did not go near the Provos or any Confederated establishment that year. I poured myself another cup from the tea cozy. Coffee is alright, but I prefer a good cuppa tea when I can get it. "Much in the way of surveillance?"

"What are you planning?"

"Shopping. Canned kippers, shoes, trainers and the like."

"Hmm." She drummed her fingers on the tabletop, copying Wolff. I resolved not to mention that 'tell' to her. "How are you fixed for cash?"

"What passes for cash about here?"

"Anything that isn't blatantly counterfeit and is from a line that is not wildly inflationary or sealed off. But cash, no plastic."

"I have silver bars, English pound notes and American dollars."

"Dollars and Pounds. Suitable. Does he come with us?"

Us? I looked to PC41 who was now he and smoke grey. "Since we met, we have never been successfully, forcibly, separated. When we were being assessed, they attempted to put us in separate holding cells and under observation 24-7. In less than an hour their observers would 'see' PC41 ensconced on my pallet." How she did it, I did not know but I suspected the time-honoured trope of 'crawling through the ventilation system'.

I didn't bother to expand on how 'he' would sometimes patrol the perimeter of the holding cells or go foraging.

Sometimes he came along with me to the men's room, butting my leg with his head and having a serious conversation while I was on the loo; sometimes I wouldn't see her for half-a-day. It varied.

"I am surprised that they didn't get rough."

"They did, once." PC41 rumbled, loud enough that the cups rattled on the tabletop. "That was enough to discourage any further attempts."

She nodded in approval; of PC41, not me. She considered him a proper Medji.

Cantry Ford was much like London in AngTerra or Smoke on the Thames, or any of the York-on-the-Hudsons. Small self-contained villages embedded in the greater city. The Ford had no motorized transit, only horse drawn trolleys between the villages and to the Wain and River terminals. They did have electric driven street cleaners, having a desire for clean pavement over crusty tradition. There were several terraces to the Ford as well, with broad stairs leading down and up from one terrace to the next. "When they started planning this place," Lyn said, indicating the stairs. "the Local Powers in Being decided they wanted to limit expansion up and down the sides of the ravines. So, no cog rails between the levels of the terraces. They wanted to slow the expansion of the city."

"Pleasant in spring, Wintertime?"

"Have you noticed how many buildings have expanded up the sides of the canyons and ravines." Many two-story expansions, some three. Nothing above three stories.

"Elevators?"

"Escalators; you can use them as stairs if the power goes out, where elevators are not useable in that event. I suspect there are generators in the buildings, but they are not obvious and rarely used. The Escalators are turnstile controlled, dirt cheap and they run right through the main levels of department stores, apartment houses, offices and various schools. But they are not a transit point, officially." She pulled the stop signal and our horse stopped at the corner. "There are free elevators in the buildings, for those who can't safely use an escalator-the handicapped or someone seriously encumbered with small children. But the operators decide if you actually need to use an elevator."

Bouncers that operated elevators, an appealing idea on the whole. "And if you buy something, they comp you the escalator fee?"

"And everybody said-" She started to say Eisenring and caught herself. "you Little Englanders were dense."

There was a doorman at the place we went to. He was sturdy, quietly armed with truncheon and gun, smoothly formal in his interactions. Think a Butler with a hog leg pistol strapped on.

Lyn gave him a token, a token that she had gotten from the desk clerk when we left the hotel. It was the size and the shape of a gambling chip, the name of our hostel on one face, a crest on the other face. The doorman passed it through a slot machine by his kiosk and gave it back to her. Then we went through two sets of doors into the department store proper.

"Armed doormen?"

"Cantry Ford is light on police. Many of the blocks have their own patrollers, funded by the establishments of that block. Private police, whose writ runs to the middle of the boulevard. They turn over the serious fuckups to a Bench Magistrate Malefactors team, but the drunks and lackwits get street justice and lump it. The doormen keep the knuckleheads down and mostly out."

I wasn't too easy with that. One block's gormless lackwit might be another's block's master criminal-or less. But it seemed to work, I didn't see people stuffed into stocks on the street corners, crumpled in the gutters or strung from the lamp posts.

She tucked the token into a slot on her outer belt, picked up a cloth sack from a rack by the inner door with the store logo on it. "Right. I think we should begin with a supply of rations for our mutual friend." And she led me to a section in the basement of the store, navigating by signage. It was mostly in creole and supplanted by pictograms of fresh produce, cans and hams.

We found the small well-equipped grocery in the basement; I bought a flat of tinned food; kippers and salmon. Lyn bought a flat of jerky packets, a flat of cookies in tins and a large tin of trail mix. We paid for it all at a counter with a cash register that looked to be a hand-cranked antique but wasn't. The clerks took my American dollars with nary a twitch. They wrapped our purchases tightly with brown paper and thick twine. Lyn gave them the token again, from her belt. They ran it through a machine at the side of the register and gave it back to her. And they slapped the register ticket on the side of the packages.

"They'll deliver it all to the cottage," she said as we walked away.

I picked up a watch, a reading lamp and a battery-operated electric shaver. My shaver, which I had little use for, had died in the transit. The batteries had looked ten years old, crusty with discharge when I unpacked the duffel bag. I had not thought to secure it before we crossed over the veil, poor practice on my part. I put on the watch, wound and set it to local time, sent the rest to the hostel. Lyn grimaced at me, bought herself a watch as well, muttering about what she lost on the saddle.

PC41 rubbed up against my ankle, while we were waiting in line for the escalator. For the first time since we left the cottage, he had made an appearance. I opened the five thresholds and swept the area.

We were being watched, but in the usual way for the usual reasons. Lyn was a more than presentable lady, if you pass by the slightly bent nose. The blooms of the men watching us were no more than the usual. There were some women watching us as well, or should I say, watching Lyn.

We bought small-clothing, shoes for me, some toiletries for all of us and a selection of current news broadsheets from AngTerra. The broadsheets I folded under my arm. "How did you know what to buy for Dama?"

Lyn did not bother to look at me. "I asked her if she needed anything washed or replaced before we left. She had a concise list." She stopped to finger a distressed Bison leather jacket at a display. "We have a follower."

I opened the five thresholds again. "I see." The shadow was predatory, and he was not alone. From what I could also gather he was not official. "I think they are planning the usual box in, for a bump and grab. What do you know about the Ford and their attitude towards casual punch-ups?"

"They run closed-circuit cameras in this store, use broadcast quality magnetic videotape to record the event. They won't pay much attention unless there is a lot of blood or a big heist. Small-time boosters get a beating and a warning when they catch them." Heist. I had not heard that in a while. They won't whistle up the local constables then, if I punch up a couple of knuckle draggers.

"Right. I'll take the one at the rear, when he makes his move."

"Letting me do all the heavy lifting. Typical." Poor oppressed Medji, I could hear the smile in her voice.

I lagged behind a half step, screened the sight of her pulling a collapsible baton out of her coat sleeve. Not three steps later one shadow tried to rush us from behind.

I stepped aside just enough, then raked him with the net I'd brought up as he bumped me. The rake hit him like a flashbang stuffed up his sinuses. He lost his footing, dropped the sap, put his head through a rack of jackets, knocked over a display of boots and then opened his scalp on the display support. Lyn laid one of the blockers out cold, hit the other one with the back swing and folded her baton in the same motion. Medji. I sniffed. She flashed a grin at me. I was off the shit list for now. I smiled at her, tucking the wallet I'd lifted from the mugger into my trouser pocket.

Medji get cranky if you don't let them occasionally slap heads in the line of duty. Which is why you shouldn't take them to a saloon without firm rules of engagement. Or you can take them to a saloon and cry 'Havoc!" as a change of pace and a reward for good conduct.

We didn't scamper, guilty people run; the floor walkers came up at a quickstep looking for an explanation while staff straightened out the mess. She told them what happened in well-spoken Creole; when they turned to me, I used a broad Low German accent and lots of hand waving when the Creole failed me, which it did abysmally. They had a quick look at the camera feed-from that video tape, a novelty and a worry to me, shook the two semi-conscious ones down, photographed them and placed them on a 'No Admittance' list, thanked us and sent us on our way. The lout I'd raked was still snorting through his nose and bleeding from the scalp wound. He was concussed, I saw their medic check his eyes and whistle up a stretcher.

I shook hands all around, twice, and let Lyn pull me away. I was avidly entertained at this excitement. "An attempted robbery and the Medji had to fight them off. Marvelous, simply smashing." I chortled in *Hanoverdusch*, a distant branch of the High German Wolff was fluent in.

Two long blocks away, with PC41 trotting at our heels and intimidating the pigeons, Lyn started to snicker. "You are a shameless piece of work, Braxton."

"I had a Medji with me, I was but a poor sod of a cross-veil principal and not able to find my bum with both hands. They did not look any closer than that at me."

"You think they were really just on the prod? Trying to strong arm us?"

"No, but let's save the after-action report for later."

I handed her a wallet with a lot of folding money-

Canadian AngTerran I think-some dogged business cards, a

Cantry Ford ID.

She goggled at what I gave her for about two steps. "What the hell? You flat boosted it, under their noses?"

And under their cameras. "I had several possible careers before the 'Firm' impressed me. And I have gotten better over time."

She had bouts of suppressed laughter the rest of the way back to the cottage. Medji, they are so easily entertained.

CHAPTER 24

Wolff was not waiting for us, but Dama Ledhrad was up and drying her hair while wrapped in a heavy terrycloth robe. Her old German gun was close to hand and she looked better than she had for the last three days, a long bath, good sleep and good food will improve almost anyone's outlook. Lyn nodded at her and went to the box-lock by the entrance. Using her token, she opened the interior door. The locker was stuffed with brown-paper parcels.

Lyn sorted through the lot, handed Dama her packages. With a soft thank you, Ledhrad withdrew to change, clutching her robe about her.

"I'm for a shower and a change as well," I said picking up my parcels by their strings. "You are comfortable with holding the post?"

"Ten minutes and then my turn."

I took fifteen, feeding PC41 his due before I got in and out of the shower, I dressed in trainers and fresh shoes and then sortied into the sitting room. Wolff was there. Not looking happy at all, his parcels neglected at his elbow.

Lyn had just finished her after-action report. "The local security forces took our account at face value and I think we did not merit more than two lines in the daybook."

"You think it was just an opportunistic thing?"

She shrugged. "One had priors of smash and grab,

according to the house security he'll be up before a low stool tribunal for certain. The one that Fearless here-" And she hooked a thumb in my direction. "tripped was copped for no identification, possible drug abuse-his eyes when the medical techs pried them open were pointing in different directions-and carrying a cosh."

"And what of his and your ID?"

"I'm registered Medji, he's my goofball charge and I showed them we were dossing here." She made the token roll across the back of her knuckles. "So, can I go hog the shower?"

He waved her away. Poked listlessly at the ID I'd copped.

I sat down and declined a cup of tea. "What news?"

"Disturbingly little. The Hanse diplomatic directorate, both the *XternBuro* and civil affairs, don't know that Dama Ledhrad is not where she was placed. If I can trust my sources, they don't have her on any of their muster rolls at all."

"That is not good." Hanse will banish their citizens for things the 'zeme ignore, they can just erase someone who is out in the barrens without a writ.

"Lyn and I are in the wind back home, hiding from both Croton-on-Hudson and the Joint Eisenring. There are traplines out for us through most of the worlds; detain and interview."

"And me?"

"You are the man who never was."

I winced at that. I had a very good idea of what came next, if they got hands on me. But. Since I did not exist, they would not stir the pot looking for me away from a gate on any of the worlds. "And our Walker and her crossbowman?"

"Two weeks displacement. She is pointedly and obscenely insistent, through backchannels, that I not darken her door in this lifetime or the next."

"Does Lyn know that she got home alright?"

He blinked at me. "You made them?"

"There are damn few who can Ghost, I suspect fewer still that have a close friend who is a cutting pony."

He smiled at that memory. "I reported to Lyn, first thing, before she told me about your dust up."

"Good to have your priorities straight. But we do have a problem."

I pulled the wallet I'd lifted to my side of the table. I emptied it on the surface and spread the business cards, money and photos across the tabletop. I picked through the litter and found what I was looking for; a small photo, wrinkled and slightly stained.

It was Lyn, at the door to the bookshop.

"Damn." Wolff exhaled.

"I thought we would find something like this." I sorted the pile, found nothing else that stood out. "When I dropped the thug, he had that image of Lyn fixed in his mind. Back in AngTerra, not here."

"We are rumbled."

"Not necessarily," I slipped the other trash back in the wallet. "He caught a glimpse of her on the trolley, tapped two of his boys and intended to get closer. What he thought he could achieve in the aisle of the store is beyond me. He did drop the cosh; perhaps he had something else, a location tagger? Particularly if the Hanse are remotely involved." I placed the photo in the center of the table. Lyn was wearing a light jacket, the sun was setting, her hair was slightly shorter than now. "From what I could glean-" I looked at Wolff, put my finger along my nose. "when I 'tripped' him, he had not had time to send a note up the line."

Wolff nodded. "And when he comes around?"

"His mind will be like a runny, soft scrambled, egg. He should come around, killing someone in a department store is too memorable, but he will be hard put to give an account of his week-let alone the scuffle in the aisle."

"You have an idea of who is handing out these-" He tapped the photo. "in the Ford?"

"He did have another image uppermost in his flabby brain, Director Vittorio. Handing out money. Anyone offering a bit of silver will be well remembered. And I have a notion of where that meat sack might be festering."

"At the Confederated Houses?"

"I think not." I pushed the photo about. "After the ambush, when Lyn caught a spray, Vittorio suddenly was not my handler anymore, in fact none of his people came on the line the last times I contacted the Desk. The man who assumed his position wasn't Eisenring. He was Unity Cadre."

"Political Cadre?" Wolff wrinkled his nose, the scent of a rat.

"Slightly more capable than most, but yes, political cadre. He would have been suspicious of any of the manifested Dai as being unreliable. Ah-" I tapped the tabletop with my knuckle, "he did not know that I was a D'draig! If he had known, there would have been an action team coming down the pike at me. None of the Five Black Gifts were supposed to be without a 'proper' close supervision."

"How would that have gone over, I wonder?"

"Not well for any of us-I doubt that the Commonality as a whole knew anything about PC41 and I, and certainly not the Cadre Desk. The Unity Eisenring tells them just enough to allow them to wipe their bums and tie their shoes."

"Your comments earlier about your happy retirement were not misplaced."

"Remember that I did not enlist but was impressed." I got up to get something to drink, tea, water, anything. "In any event I think that Vittorio scooped up his lot of fuck-ups, the dossier that the Desk issued and what funds he could lay his hand on and left. Caerton was behind the ball from the tick." I found a pitcher of water in the refrigerator and poured me a glass, set back down at the table.

"Vittorio is unlikely to be perched at the Table of the Confederated Houses." Mused Wolff.

"No." I agreed. "He was Unity Eisenring and the Confeds and the Provos will not be particularly welcoming. He might accidently shoot himself three times in the back of the head. He is here, has been here since before we left Dodge City. Been here long enough to pass around some of these." I tapped the photo again. I turned it over. It had a watermark on the back, it was not from AngTerra. "Long enough to make copies of photos he'd brought from AngTerra."

"Cantry Ford is a large place to hole up in," He waved his hands at our surroundings. "for example."

I drank some water. "Well, he's cheap. Legendarily cheap. You know the Ford, where's the low rent neighborhood?"

"Up on the rim, to the east."

I smiled much in the way PC41 smiled while successfully coaxing a pigeon closer. I checked the time, not quite one in the afternoon. "I think I will make a sortie in that direction after sundown."

"I think I should join you. The Ford is safe, safer than Kansas City or any of the large cities at home, but…"

"Less of a chance to be noticed if I have a partner and a guide."

He nodded, scooped up his packages and left.

Come sundown we gradually made our way to the eastern rim. We didn't take Lyn, which sparked a riot-one Medji, one riot. But Wolff put that down, showed her the photo and had her stand-to as a security force.

She put her killing hand in my face and promised. "You get him hurt, you'd best be dead before I find out-Mr. Turner!"

I blinked. I understood the threat, but not the reference.

"Dork. 'Day of the Condor'." She punched me on my shoulder. "Do keep up!"

"Right."

Wolff had legged it after telling her no, leaving me to the rearguard. I took a backpack with a change of clothes for the both of us and hustled out the door as an empty bottle whistled past my head.

We walked up an external flight of stairs to the terrace above us, got on a horse drawn streetcar and made our way to a casino that extended up four terraces. There, we engaged a suite for the evening and changed clothes. Wolff did a bit of makeup, darkened his hair and face. I just pulled a watch cap down over my forehead and found a bit of grime under the headboard of the bed to dirty up my five o'clock shadow.

We were not disguised enough to defeat a line-up, but it would make a casual glance miss us.

We took one of the casino escalators to the upper-most terrace, hired a two-place cabriolet that took us to the south. In the Smoke, where I was raised, we would have called it a hansom cab. Here it was a Cabriolet. The driver was at the back, the reins draped over the hood that sheltered the passengers, steps that folded up and a dashboard to keep the road off us. Very 1820s; except for the electric running lights, and a radio whip antenna.

We got in. Wolff opened the judas hatch and told the driver where he wanted to go, paying him in advance, then settled back, took out a pipe and began to pack it with tobacco.

PC41 was with us all along, through the casino and into the cabriolet. A very thin, black, alley-cat. Curled up on the floorboards between our legs.

"What do you plan on doing?" He asked me as he fiddled

with his pipe.

I sat back, watching the horse and watching the terrace go by. To our right, we had a view down the five terraces to the riverine. The rooftops were lit up, many had gardens or lounges that had customers dancing and dining under the lights. There were rooftops that were dark and silent, you could see tables stowed away and chairs tucked up against them. On the river were boats, some fast air cushion craft throwing roostertails that shone in the lights of the riverfront, some slow barges crowded and merry in the nighttime; all moving up and down river or ferrying across the flow. No bridges, and the bottom most terrace had no buildings, just a wide promenade. Full of horse drawn vehicles, pedestrians and food carts.

"Awaiting developments." I discreetly pointed at the wide promenade. "Why are there just landings and wharfs, no bridges; and no permanent commercial establishments along the riverfront?" I could see broad and deep arcades on the far side of the river, brightly lit and busy with cargos going in and coming out on hand carts to the riverfront. At the center of each of the arcades there was an illuminated spot, that when loaded with pallets and containers, rose up into the celling and disappeared from view. A cargo lift.

"There are no bridges for the same reason there are only horse drawn conveyances. And flood control is the reason for the lack of development."

"They let the river flood where it will?"

"On the most part." He lit his pipe. "Where we are going is where the vulgus live. The hewers of wood and the carters of water." He drew on it, tucked the lighter away in a pocket of his coat, blew a broad smoke ring that instantly dissipated in the wind of our passage.

"Show off."

He smiled at me. "Long practice. They have

accommodations that the tourists don't use and usually don't see. Cheap housing, maintained by the Ford on the whole, cheap food close by their houses and a Transit Pass along with a working document that gives them free rides on the streetcars and the water taxis. The Powers that Were cottoned on quite early that the secondary livelihood of the Ford-fleecing transits through the gates-relied on people that worked behind the arras. And unlike the Houses that controlled the east coast of this part of 'Zeme, they decided to buy their loyalty and not compel it."

Luring marks and fleecing them, then having them return for another go. The Powers-that-Were were minting white metal on a wholesale level. Likely made the Confederated houses livid.

The houses to our left, row houses with a postage stamp garden in the front, were uniformly tidy. Warm lights behind curtained windows. There were occasional taverns with a biergarten in the front, well-lit and merrily populated. There were a few houses that showed hard times had come and stayed, but only a few. "Better than the streets I came from, you say this is not the norm? In the 'Zeme?"

"No," he said. "The Houses on the tidewater and in the riverine settlements inland wanted to emulate the establishments they came from, just with them on the top shelf and someone else on the bottom."

"Hm," I said. I opened the five gates and let the net free, it was better than twenty yards in its reach now. At least for scouting purposes.

Twenty minutes, maybe a mile and a half down the road and I had Vittorio. He and a couple of hangers-on were in a two-story saloon cum boarding house, alongside a dark section of row houses that'd had a fire sometime in the very recent past. You could still smell the creosote.

It was luck, but in the wad of trash I lifted from his minion we'd found a card extolling a Bierstube on this side of the river. So, we trolled this side first.

"Pick a spot."

Wolff tapped the judas hatch. We came to a stop; the driver dropped the steps that had folded over our legs and we left the cab about fifty yards from the tavern. Wolff tipped the driver.

"Thanks," the driver said. "You change your mind about the neighborhood or want to chance your luck elsewhere, call on channel 16. Ask for Ray-Ray the Skua." He clucked to the horse and they ambled off down the road.

"CB radios and horse drawn carriages," I said.

"The 'zeme's a duke's mixture."

"More pleasant than the chuff you smoke."

He clicked his tongue at me.

The Tavern was n'Akos Grill, the name was in the Creole and it was a bit of a clicking mouthful. The outer garden was hopping, the barmaids zigzagging through the tables with beer and platters of food. There was a dining room to the rear behind a sturdy wall with windows and a double door, with a greeter and a pair of bouncers.

"What's with the dining room at the rear?" We were heading for the door to the restaurant proper, I was drawing in the net and watching all the auras trailing through the place. The greeter and his bouncers had seen us; they didn't know us, but they had an idea that we might be trouble. Wrong clothes, wrong walk, just off. Not their kind of chum.

Out of the side of his mouth. "Keeps the rabble out, and lets the place charge the quality more." He put a bit of swagger on, gave a big smile to the greeter. "And would you be having a table for two, a round of ale and the best platter of bison from the Empty Grass." And he made a coin dance through his fingers, an eagle. Not an AngTerra gold coin, but close enough.

The closed face of the greeter blossomed into an oily grin. He lightly back handed one of his bouncers and led the way deeper into the taproom, through men and women who were professionally working their way through bison platters and large tankards of beer.

Wolff bought a round for the leaners at the bar with the coin and got us a table at the back, by the jakes and the stairs and a hallway to the kitchen doors.

We ordered a large medium rare between the two of us, red potatoes, greens and a loaf of bread. And a pitcher of beer. "Now," He said in German, after the waitress left. "can you penetrate the upstairs from here?"

"You want me to drift up the stairs in front of the gods and everybody." I shook out my napkin and aligned the silverware. PC41 drifted off into the room, under legs and heading for the back of the bar. "No, but I think I can cause the fire alarm to go off-as it were." I smiled at him. "Let's wait a bit, eh?"

And they brought us out a three-pound slab of bison to share.

Have I mentioned that after encountering PC41 my appetite increased? Wolff got a respectable share of the steak, but I had the greater portion and another pitcher as well.

"I'm glad I am not paying your mess bills." He asked for a cup of coffee for the both of us. Lit up his pipe. Nobody noticed, the room being thick with smoke. No one had picked up on us being here, after we got through the door and settled in, only the waitress kept an eye on us.

Once I paid a visit to the jakes, there was a closet door, a mirror that was rusting under the glass and a vent in the celling. There was a man sitting in the back of the hallway, in an alcove, just out of sight and holding a short pump shotgun across his lap. I didn't acknowledge him; he just gave me a flat stare.

"M'yes. Do you want to pay for this, or do we decamp in the coming riot?"

He blinked. "I'll pay, it's easier." He waved the waitress over and passed her a nicely folded bill and a silver cartwheel as a tip. She beamed at him and then...

Something fell above us, hard enough that dust and the odd splinter came down from the ceiling, the hanging lights bounced on their cords and we could hear shrieks of pain and anger. A thunder of boots and then down the stairway and through the dining room came a stampede. Some were clothed, some were wrapped in sheets and towels and some were as nature found them. Among them and behind them were a ribbon of rats, running for the door to the biergarten. Some of the fleeing humans were shooting at the rats; hitting the floor, the walls, each other and randomly, a rat. The shotgunner had nailed three of them before the kitchen emptied and he was knocked arse over teakettle.

Three humans came by, from the upstairs, that I had marked. Vittorio was at the rear and somehow tripped to faceplant on our tabletop, shrieking and waving a small pistol about. Something ran up his pant leg and, in the excitement of the moment, he lost his pistol, his late dinner and a schooner of beer. Then passed out. I grabbed an arm, wiped his face with my napkin and horsed him on my shoulders in a fireman's carry, Wolff collected his hat and cane and we hustled our injured friend out.

Outside in the street there was a crowd milling about, tables turned over, random shots and smashing crockery. I turned to the south and started dog-trotting away from the grill.

"I am healthier than when you met me, but-" Wolff

gasped. "I am really not up to this."

I looked over my shoulders, spun the net out and drew it in and kept hustling us away. "Another fifty yards and we'll find a bench with a crank set." PC41 appeared out of the dark, darted between my legs and trotted ahead. "We'll drop him there for the morning garbage run to find."

"Dead?"

"All but," There was a hollow thump and the road lit up around us. "now that's a turn." I turned to look behind us.

The Grill was on fire, a bubble of fire came rolling out of one of the upstairs windows. Then a thump and another window blew, scattering glass and burning flinders over the crowd.

"I don't like the looks of that." We could hear sirens off in the near distance. The Ford had streetcleaners with electric motors, they also had water tenders with ladders, foam pumps and large diesel engines. Wolff pointed at a shelter with a cranker about five yards off. "There and take a rest."

I dropped Vittorio on to the seat, grabbing him by his collar to keep him from cracking his head open on the lean-to's wall. We watched as a set of yellow fire tenders thundered by, dispersing the mob and blowing in the windows with suppressant foam, dropping off men in turn-outs to charge the burning structure.

"Impressive," I said. "Not five minutes to arrive on scene."

"I take it," Wolff said, "you didn't notice the fire brigade station when we came up in the cabriolet?"

"No."

I pushed Vittorio upright and went lightly through his pockets. Money, spring knife, a wallet with papers in it and a packet of safes, sheepskin. Then the three of us sat admiring the firemen knocking down the blaze. "What have you gleaned?" Wolff asked me.

"Vittorio was bent." Wolff snorted at my comment. "But he wasn't *Allemagne Noir*. Remember when Snow was having a literal melt? When he was listing the players in the game."

Wolff was watching Vittorio breathing. "And?" He poked Vittorio, no reaction. "Are we leaving a trail of corpses, now?"

I was watching the chaos at the fire scene, muffled secondary explosions. "No. You worried about my rules of engagement?"

"Somewhat." His emotional overtones bled over into my net; recalling a treasured cat who once left songbirds as gifts in his slippers.

"Vittorio. He was a mug with no flipping idea of what was about, he had not been adequately read into the situation. Just to keep an eye on you until you died, then toss your various hides and keep Croton in the dark as much as possible. He knew you were fading away and was patiently waiting for you to expire. Then Croton House sent me and an Eisenring watching brief, along with a lot of *bumf*."

"Well then. And?"

"What Croton or the Unity 'Ring didn't know was that Vittorio had ties to a Sable house as well as the Streltsy. What is the Streltsy, by the by?"

"Romanov version of 'The Gotha'. Not as accomplished, but with similar operatic notions." He pushed Vittorio back towards me.

"He was waiting for guidance from both of his controllers-Streltsy and Croton House-when the shit got into the fan; Hanse *XternBuro*, the Eisenrings, Uncle Tom Cobbleigh and all. He thought I was a wet work team from the Unity 'Ring fixing to lance the Provos in the Wichita station; after the fuck up with his needle-boys he pulled the plug, did a runner to the east and out into the 'Zeme through a gate the Sable house had a hand on."

"Mnh. Then who was at the storage units?"

"Our Mr. Snow and the *Allemagne Noir*, which explains why they didn't know about the back gate. "

"What more do you know, now?"

"The house in sable, Bettenmann? They might have had a sleeper in the inquisitors according to Vittorio here."

Wolff nodded. "It would fit, they had a hand in the first war and paid dearly for it."

"They still have an edifice, but they are reluctant to make any more investments. Good capital after bad. So, they sent a 'burned' agent to watch a mouse hole in the Ford. If the agent turns up missing…a solution they might not have to pay for."

"Speaking of which, rats?" His turn in conversation made my headache. More than it was already.

The fire was mostly out, the firefighters were bringing out lumps that might have been people once. We could smell the acrid smoke a house fire puts out and the under tang of accelerant. "There were quite a few rats in the walls, I and PC41 encouraged them to swarm." I pushed the body upright one more time and gave a pulse to the fading auras that locked the muscles in rigor. "There was only one easy exit from the upper floor, a dozen rats and panic ensued."

"And the fire?"

I looked at the dark spot on the terrace that was PC41. "I have no idea."

>blameless<

We left Vittorio there, walked two rods away and called on a CB radio from another biergarten, Ray came by. We had a bit of a conversation about the fire and the panic at the last place, then went back to the casino. Showered and took a tram back home.

Lyn met us at the door, inventoried Wolff and then gave me the stink-eye. "Fire?"

"I'll have a night-cap and off to bed." Said Wolff, handing

her his cane and his hat. Casually. The effect was spoiled by her finger through the hole in the brim of the hat, the size of a pistol round. "Now how did that happen, eh?" He wondered. And drifted off towards the kitchen.

She gave me another dead level look. "There will be an after-action report, right. Commander Bond?" Turned on her heel and marched into the kitchen.

I hope she will give that jest a respite; she is beginning to run out of credible secret agents.

CHAPTER 25

In the morning I was awakened as usual by PC41, I showered after I fed him a can of the 'good stuff'. We had a bit of a conversation about last night and the rats. She insisted that neither the fire nor the explosions we heard were our fault. Maybe a dumped over lantern, although the place had electric lights.

What I pulled from Vittorio was what I'd laid out to Wolff. He was in exile; he'd screwed the goose and was going to be hard done by his owners for the rest of his life. Well, he was hard done by; I wonder if it kept him 'keen' that last seven months or so.

I went for my breakfast, found Wolff and Lyn already at sup. She had a half dozen crullers and a coffee on a tray by the divan in the common area. He had a cup of tea, a teapot under a cozy, a lonely triangle of toast and a notepad. She was reading, out loud, a scandal sheet detailing what had happened at n'Akos Grill up on the eastern rim last night. "Mass panic, a fire of suspicious origin. Several people killed in the fire and the panic. Twenty rats recovered-RATS!" Lyn gave me her number eleven glare, warranted to peel paint at fifty yards. "You dragged him through a rat's nest?"

"Good morning Wolff," I said, not rising to the lure. I poured myself a cup from his teapot and sat at the table with him. I could have read his notes but refrained. I could hear our other member stirring. Lyn returned to reading the sheet.

"No origin of the fire known," She rattled the newsprint as she followed the story. "hmm. No arrests of the usual suspects. What the hell were you up to, Braxton?"

"Tidying up." I dropped a sugar cube in the tea and waited for our Hanse to appear.

Dama Ledhrad came into the sitting room and politely asked for a cup of tea.

I poured her a cup, then set about brewing another pot. She was bright and cheerful, and I manifested my net. I was still worried about her. The memories of Snow melting away disturbed me.

>not similar< Came the push.

>agreed< I pushed back. >still<

"We did not have the opportunity to have a serious conversation yesterday." Johanna Marie said, sitting at the table with both feet flat on the floor, looking only at her cup and saucer. A bag hung from her weak shoulder. "You have made inquiries about my current status?"

Wolff sighed. "Yes, to the best of the knowledge of the people I talked to, you are not assigned to any station. Nor are you marked as missing." She was down among the never-was, like me.

She didn't flinch. Her auras flowed from her like gently rolling water in a clear stream. Focused, calm and intent.

She nodded. "I should confess. I violated certain protocols, when I came through the last series of gates. I retained my *XternBuro* credentials." She produced from her bag another wallet, the dimensions of a folded American dollar and not much thicker than a coin.

"Well now." Wolff said, perking up.

"I have been briefed that my *XternBuro* credentials are not readily forgeable, they are not useable by anyone but me, that they will confirm my identity down to the cellular level and that they will allow me free access to a consular message center. To be precise, to the Concierge. Even a freshly struck *XternBuro* agent outweighs a Consular-" She gave me one of her infrequent smiles, "dogsbody on the steelyard." She sipped at her cup. "So, when I make an appearance at the steelyard, things may be quite different than you expected, eh?"

Wolff smiled broadly. "You are beginning to come along. To come along right smartly."

We sat in a comfortable silence for a bit. She was positively glowing at his approval. Then I asked Wolff. "So, are you going to make an open approach to Confed House?"

"I am reluctant to take that step. There would be questions on how we got here that I am not prepared to answer."

"Blame me," Dama Ledhrad said. "I wanted to return to the Common Land, and I was reluctant to trust myself to a crossing point controlled by the faithless and obviously incompetent Eisenring." She sipped daintily at her tea, holding the cup and saucer to her face. "So, I used an exit-full resource cutout to gate to a secure location and I required you to escort me through the gate so that I could debrief you properly upon the issue concerning Herr Snow and the infiltration of the Common Lands. A gate you, of course, know nothing about but that I have been appraised of by my handlers."

Wolff and I looked at her, then each other. "Exfiltration?" he hazarded.

"Yes, I exfiled with help from dozers."

Exfiled. Dozers. Sleepers?

"Dama, you were provided with an escape plan when you were sent to AngTerra?" I leaned back against the chair. PC41 had stopped purring and his ears were focused on her. Surprise was not an adequate word for either of our reactions.

"Oh no. No, no. No. I was issued only the identification for being a West German minor functionary, an obsolete pistol, some clothing and of course a purse with some useless items. Nothing more. But I have read many excellently terrible spy novels of the AngTerra intelligence services." She beamed at us over the rim of her teacup. "It is not widely known that *XternBuro* has active detachments operating in many of the worlds that the Dai touch. It is not known, not even to *XternBuro* Operations or the Over-Government of the Hanse."

We goggled.

>very different< Came over the push to me.

>m'yes<

Wolff buried his face in his hands. "What have we done, Braxton?" He laughed at himself. "What have we done?"

I shook my head. "And Confed House in particular will be very eager to drop the entire question of how Lyn, you and Dama Ledhrad got to Cantry Ford, while they frantically start turning over rocks looking for Hanse operatives in their territories on AngTerra and the other lines," I said. "Can we produce suitable legends for her 'dozers'?"

"In an afternoon." Wolff stood. Picked up a light jacket from the back of his chair and patted his pockets: wallet, keys, knife and pistol. "What about you?"

"I will loaf about; PC 41 will watch our neighborhood and Lyn should accompany you to the Cobbler in case she needs more exercise. To work off the pastries from this morning. Have her do a little camouflage in case there still are people looking for her." The scandal sheet rattled like a snake about to strike. "Dama Ledhrad and I shall refine the structure of the Table that she sups at alongside of the hapless *XternBuro*."

"Cobbler?" Said Ledhrad. "Shoes?"

CHAPTER 26

Johanna Marie and I put our heads together to produce an absolutely fictional, but tenable, table of organization for the *XternBuro Dai Betrekkingen Provinciale*. Also known as the DBP.

We made a list of Seven departments, labeled one through number eight, all tagged in a sub dialect of Afrikaans. Which I found she could almost piece out without prompting, it being evidentially very distantly related to Low Hanse. How or why it was related tickled my interest, but there wasn't time to work on that question.

"Why are you listing-" She tapped at the tabletop where I was fabulating the table of organization and the responsibilities of the various DBP sections.

"Anyone who comes across this document-and we will eventually leave it where someone appropriate will come across it-they will think that there is really a hidden department somewhere in the *XternBuro*. The over government will expend time, personnel and energy trying to find it. And running into real counter-espionage operations by the *XternBuro* Internal Affairs who will be ripping up the floorboards trying to find the DBP who are embedded, evidently, within their offices." I explained, while drawing the table of organization up in my best formal hand on fine paper. Meg bless the 'calligraphy for beginners' tutorial at Scarsbourgh Uni.

"*Afdeling* Seven, the Missing Section." I produced a

redacted footnote. "Labeled 'direct action' but not detailed in any way." And used a very small nib on the pen to scribe the footnote. "So, they will assume it is the Special Operations branch of the DBP tasked with 'wet work'. A section that is even more covert than the DBP itself. Which of course does not exist."

Her eye lit up with glee. "'Wet Work', like James Bond?"

I wondered if every person drawn to intelligence work among the worlds the Dai touched, had that sort of mania. Since 'Bond' had propagated across the various lines, in direct or indirect entertainments, he had become a standard for spies. Before Bond, it was Richard Hannay or Nayland Smith, but they did not seem to make as great an impression as Bond. I didn't have much of an interest in Bond, but I was 'impressed' and not called to the Standard.

"Yes. Much like Commander Bond, or my particular favorite, Modesty Blaze. And do you want to have a number assigned to you?" Please Lady Murphy, not double zero.

She thought for a moment, nodded her head. "Thirteen-eighty."

Four numbers. "Why?"

"It was the number of the house I lived in when I was very young. Before I was declared a foundling." There was a story there, which I doubted I would or should ever know. I saw a new facet that echoed mine.

"Very well, as of now you are one Agent Dertien Tagtig of *Artikel Agt*, Dama Ledhrad."

"*Artikel Agt*? But that is Bookkeeping?"

Department 'eight' of the seven listed in the DBP Table of Organization was Financial. Not an exciting title. Not like 'Wet work'.

"And bookkeeping 'keeps accounts'," I said. "'Settles

records', 'expunges debits, 'handles double-entry transactions' and often "disposes" of surplus or 'excess to requirements' items."

She thought about the double meanings I had just laid out for her. Low Hanse being a more rationally constructed language than most common tongues, did not often use the trick of saying one thing to imply another. If the Hanse intended to kill someone, they said so simply and then did so with an appallingly efficient dispatch. No working up to it, no explanation that this was a necessary but regrettable course of action. They just did it. Much like crumpling up the newspaper that had wrapped the chips and fish, with no ceremony and no hesitation.

She nodded, accepting the idea of indirection in her newly acquired tradecraft. Then she looked at the tabletop covered in notes, organizational flow charts, titles, and operational responsibility layouts. "This is a lot of work for documents that we may never use."

"Let me tell you a story from the history of AngTerra. During the Second World War…" And I spent an idle hour outlining the Ghost Army and how they distracted the enemy with less than two thousand troops pretending to be two divisions.

"So, if you, 'inadvertently'," I made quotes in mid-air. "disclose the existence of the DBP at the consulate for example and it appears to be substantial from what you disclose, it will give them-the *XternBuro* or any other players on the board-a great deal of agita when they cannot find the DBP or a trace of its other agents."

"Agita." She puzzled on that. "You mean anxiety?"

"Less or more." I was enjoying leading her through acquiring the tradecraft of 'misdirection'.

Johanna Marie was inadequately trained by her original handlers. She was but a discard in their eyes and had very little knowledge of the world she had been unceremoniously dumped into. But Ledhrad was not a 'flat'. She only had to have a lesson outlined for her to flesh it out into a useable tool. Or a weapon.

It also kept her busy. Sometime very soon we were going to present her at the Hanse Consulate here in the Ford. She would have to overrun the doorkeepers and then over awe the 'dogsbodies' of the consulate staff to get to the Concierge terminal and present her credentials. And then she would inform the Government Structure over and above the *XternBuro* about the infiltration into and through the Pure Land, with the connivance of the *XternBuro*. A violation that had occurred through the last two Long Generations, by their count.

And that would be the last we'd see of her. Fail or carry the day, it would be the last we would see of her. I was beginning to greatly regret that. In a way we would be abandoning her as well, to her own devices.

Wolff reappeared with Lyn not long after I had taken a series of photos of the fabricated documentation of the new DBP. They were hungry, we were hungry and PC41 was bored and not at all hungry.

Which concerned me to no end.

>pidgeons< She pushed at me. >only<.

Over another delivered, and excellent, meal we exchanged notes. Wolff had several suggestions for how to place the fabricated table of organization into the hands of the Consulate staff. Most of the suggestions relied on her being new to the game and not accustomed to hiding things from her fellow agents.

"Hand them a generic business card with a microdot of that fabrication-we can provide one tomorrow-placed in the typical location on the card. After that tin-hat accepts you as a bona fide *XternBuro* operative, the business card can legend you as being from DBP and the Auditors." Wolff was enjoying a free-range roasted chicken, with dumplings. He marveled how his indigestion had eased appreciably since becoming acquainted with me. Lyn had a bison steak with a baked sweet potato. "Being from a hitherto unknown Bureau and from the Auditors deployed by that unknown Bureau will absolutely put the wind up every member of the Consular staff. And it will give the *XternBuro* agents the fantods, they will be looking at each other sideways." He tapped at the other packet of 'cobbled' documentation. "When higher authorities want to know how, why and when; give them a taste of your DBP's network in AngTerra and some of the other Dai touched worlds."

"And one lie will support another." She was none too sanguine about that; it broke some very important mores of her culture.

"Don't rely on the legend," Lyn said. "Just enough of a taste and then take it off the table as beyond their remit. They will flesh the fabrication out in their own good time, sending apologetic reports up the wire and reprimands down the line."

Dama Ledhrad scraped pudding from her cup. "A wonder that any of your organizations function at all."

"They follow the spirt of the regulations and break them at need and at will. Unlike your homeland," I said, stroking PC41 and threading all their auras with mine. "And really some don't function well at all, which can be an absolute blessing."

I don't think they realized how open they were to me.

Most, if not all, of the Sangsue in their experience-or in Johanna Marie's' case, the entertainments she avidly consumed-needed to be hands-on to work their mayhem. And I was a good double arm's length away today.

It was obvious to me that PC41 and I had an effect on them. Most of the physical damage that Wolff had shown was now gone, all of the effects of the spray that Lyn had caught were also gone. And Dama Ledhrad was not as clumsy nor gangly as she had been when I first met her.

And then there was Snow.

I pondered the changes to me.

CHAPTER 27

P resentation is all. We took Johanna Marie to a local haberdashery, flashed considerable dosh and turned them loose. They fitted her out top shelf 'Office Casual' clothing. A local knock-off of the Burberry, slacks, undergarments, shoes-the lot. And not just one outfit, three sets from the skin out. She had her hair done, her hands tended to and a faint scar etched into one cheek, down to the bone. I gifted her the 'clean' 9MM pistol I was issued from the Old Firm; Lyn donated her own well used belt of many pockets, it's pockets full of incidentals that would help secure her 'legend'.

She acquired a couple of business cards with microdots, we provided her a professional set of conventional ID for West Germany. Then a set in *Frankii* for Greater France, legending her as a member of the *Maréchaussée*-the National Police of that region. She retained her credentials for the *XternBuro* and a further set of microdot credentials for being an "Auditor" for the DBP. The DBP credential set will decay in a day or so to gibberish after being read by any Concierge. A Micro flake in the DBP credential that decayed over time.

I was impressed. With the decaying credential set. And what was a Micro-Flake? I asked Wolff.

Wolff shrugged. "I have no idea what exactly our Cobbler did, they asked me what I wanted to achieve with the legend and when I told them we would have to fox a Hanse Concierge, their eyes lit up and they scurried about the shop. They almost offered to pay me for the opportunity." He snorted. "Almost. Cooler and older heads ultimately did prevail in the negotiations. They will pay me handsomely for a report later."

"You think they might-?"

"Sell her? No. They well know me." He suddenly had a hard look about his eyes. "It would not be a prudent thing on their part."

He gifted me with a one-pound AngTerra coin, with the head of George V on it. "This is a microdot reader and storage."

"Inside the coin? Your Cobbler is something marvelous."

He laughed. "No, this is an antique. Issued to me after-" He waved a hand, dismissively. "Well, after things went pear shaped all over my Europe. I had it salted away in the storage safe and brought it along with us. It has a built-in lens that magnifies 160 times, more than enough to read a microdot or a microfiche. In case we couldn't stroll into a library." He handed me a three by five card. "All of the files we carried with us through the veil. Just in case."

I nodded. In case he was 'disappeared', and we needed to pass the information up a different route.

Johanna Marie was cautious while easing into her new Legend, but she was delighted with her fresh kit. She walked and stretched, did yoga and shadow-boxed in her new clothing. She stripped and dry-fired her newish gun under Lyn's close attention. Then they went to a range that Lyn had used earlier in our stay and Johanna fired a box of rounds through it. Then she cleaned it under Lyn's tutelage. It had a history now; the throat of the chamber had been buffed and the pull of the trigger adjusted. She had a spare magazine for it, both magazines had signs of wear as well and were full of cartridges. She had a small box of cartridges we procured locally, tucked into the bottom of her purse. Lyn showed her how to don the holster and advised her on walking with her purse slung casually over the weak arm's shoulder.

"Wearing it like that will let them take it casually from you, without a fuss, and they will then go happily through the trash in the bottom of the purse. You have a restaurant stub from Dodge City, a tenner coin from Cantry Ford's Marcus Emporium, shuttle bus ticket stubs from AngTerra, lipsticks, random hotel keys, a set of motel keys from Dodge City, tissue paper packets from an Alba tobacconist shop and from a convenience store in Wichita. And if they get stroppy about poor tradecraft and the like, tell them this is what your handlers issued you. Excepting the coin." She patted the leather bag. "These things will collect anything and everything we handle and are a pain in the tuches to keep sterile."

"It still goes against everything-"

"Yes," I said. "It goes against everything you learned when you were a cadet. But you are not a probationer, regardless of what one set of credentials presents. You are an Auditor for an *XternBuro* Internal Affairs Agency that is a closely held secret within the closely held *XternBuro*. You are walking into a shop that you wholly own. Period." I continued, sitting with my feet up on a divan. "Did you have an intake camp or base during your training for the *Buro*?"

"Yes."

"If it was like mine, there were endless inspections and we

never performed to our instructor's expectations. Never. Now you are the Auditor and the Consulate is sadly slacking off its responsibilities in this benighted land."

It took a bit longer, but she got it.

Wolff had located the Confed offices in the Ford, then found a suitable go-between to escort him and Lyn in, to come out of the cold.

He picked Helen McDermid, a friend of a friend of a distant connection. She was wealthy, had connections with DeGrace House back in the tidewater and closer connections with the local heavyweights. This meant that the Provo Eisenring section couldn't just disappear McDermid, Lyn and Wolff, to lighten their Desk loads and improve their quarterly metrics.

The plan was to have Wolff, McDermid and Lyn deliver Dama Ledhrad to the Hanse Confederation Consulate portal, with all her documentation. After that, McDermid would escort Lyn and Wolff with their dossier about BRIXMIS to the Confed offices.

I was supposed to hang back when McDermid escorted Wolff into the Confed offices. He didn't think it was prudent for me to brave the doormen. I agreed, but I set up a fall back. It involved the rats, you see.

After the half riot at the n'Akos Grill, the local sheets and the low powered radio stations that dotted the Ford became stridently hysterical about the threat and menace of a rat infestation. Black plague, rabies, hantavirus, anything that they could find in the books that would inflame the public. Then pest control companies popped up like weeds after a good rain, guaranteeing to eradicate any problem.

I looked at the first half-dozen of the services and then I looked at PC41.

>proposal<

He looked up from his meditation upon a sunbeam. He was a tiger striped bully this morning. >mmmn<

>set up rat eradication close to the confed<

He blinked at me. Twice. >within reach< He got up and stretched, mouth opened and full of teeth. >like it<

We went into business. Got a narrow room with a narrow tabletop, a directory phone, a cardboard filing box. A business card on the door and a shared receptionist. I sat it up the day we outfitted Johanna Marie, got a boiler suit made with a logo and bought a largish tool carrier. When I told Wolff, he approved, with one proviso.

"Things go to hell, you walk away. It's more important to get the information to good hands then to save us-or revenge us." We were sitting in the garden at the cottage. He had his pipe going, PC41 was intimidating the pigeons, I was sitting watching the sun go down.

"We won't risk it." I lied. We might not get Lyn and him clear, but they would have a proper escort to Fiddlers Green. My organization, my rules of engagement. Kill them all, inventory later.

>no worry< Pushed PC41. >kill them all<

CHAPTER 28

The day came. We closed the account at the cottage, wiped all the security tapes, tossed the bedrooms and shared spaces for items we might have forgot. Packed Dama Ledhrad's roll-on luggage, set up Lyn's backpack. Helen McDermid arrived, had a cuppa of what she liked-coffee-and was introduced to us all. The story was that we were having to do a double penetration. Place Dama Ledhrad in the Hanse Consulate and then place Lyn and Wolff in the Confed House offices. Why was not broached. Wolff was vetted by people Helen trusted, the organizations being penetrated were despised by her and the money was good.

I was supposed to displace to a coffee shop and await developments. I gripped Johanna's hands, shook Wolff's hand and hugged Lyn-to her great unease-and saw them off in a carriage. Then I went down the street to the shared offices. I keyed the door, nodded at the receptionist and slipped into my office.

I didn't follow them to the Hanse Consulate, I made my way instead to the strip mall that had the Confederated Houses offices embedded in them. Cantry Ford was a Free City and the Powers only grudgingly allowed the Confed and their minions space inside the city. They had forced them to set up a secure compound a half day's ride away, when they first tried to over awe the Ford. They did provide the Confeds a graveyard by their compound, with perpetual care. Only recently had they become more accommodating. They had to pay rent, pay through the nose, and they had to provide their own, meager, security.

Earlier, I had given them, the management for the mall, a prospectus for inspecting and eradicating any rats within their properties. PC41 was part of my arsenal. To his disgust. He was resembling a stoat this day and not a proper cat.

He was crouched in a small cage, with a latched door and a mesh floor. I got it from a pet store. >angry< And he pushed hard at me, spiking the migraine. We presented ourselves at the office for the site, gave them the newly counterfeited license for rat hunting, signed a limited contract in Vittorio's name and started snooping through the back gangways of the mall with an escort of Mall staff. Teenagers. Young girls, they were cooling over PC41. >much of the good stuff< She pushed at me. >much<

We were stopped from venturing into the offices of the Confed House, by their security. They insisted they did not have a problem, one of the Blackleg officers told us in very stilted Creole that they were meticulous in their habits. Or that was what he thought he said. Our escorts nodded and giggled behind his back.

And there were rats, to my real surprise. PC41 flushed a pair from a HVAC access duct into the middle of the Confed House offices in his first reccy. Much shouting and banging on, needle-gun firing and all that. We, PC41 and I, drifted to the other side of the complex and started another mischief of rats into the open. She darted into the scurrying mass and killed five of the six, losing one under the front door to the Confed offices. More needles, angry phone calls and an adult manager made an appearance, blanched at the trophies we had laid out on the tiles. We retreated to the business office and began negotiations in earnest.

>entertaining< PC41 pushed at me, curled up on a towel on the mesh floor of the carrying cage and pretended to go to sleep. >overwatch<

This was while Wolff, Lyn and McDermid were at the doors to the Hanse Consulate.

CHAPTER 29

According to Helen McDermid they escorted Dama Ledhrad through the portals. She ran her basic Hanse credentials through the entrance kiosk and the receptionist allowed her and her escorts into the waiting area, not offering any refreshments or seats to the grubby *Auslanders* or the dubious but very well-appointed Citizen. Dubious, because no well-adjusted Citizen ventured into the grubby backwaters of the Sheaf of Worlds without an escort and a pressing reason to be there. But she was presentable and well-spoken, so they gave her the benefit of the doubt instead of turning her away.

She then presented her *XternBuro* credentials to the desk and the ever-present Tin Hat. The attitude change was breathtaking according to Helen. Seats, coffee service, light refreshments and three consular officials appeared. Instantly. Magically. They had a twenty-minute interview in formal Hanse with rotating officials and a mobile secure terminal of the Concierge-the Tin Hat. Helen said she got less than one word in ten, Wolff and Lyn appeared to be catching less than that. Wolff was smiling and nodding at the very spooked and obviously well-armed staff, whose grasp of Creole was as limited as Wolff seemed to be with functional Hanse.

At the end of the interview the Concierge begrudgingly confirmed her status in the Consulate pecking order; Johanna Marie being *XternBuro* trumped all including the Consul

General here at the Ford.

Johanna then turned and graciously thanked Lyn and Wolff in English for their help, shook Wolff's hand, shook Lyn's hand in an excess of sentiment. Nodded to Helen and touched her hand, slightly.

And Dama Ledhrad then instructed a consular officer to escort Wolff, Helen and Lyn off the premises, and to adequately compensate them for their time and trouble. Johanna Marie Ledhrad, Auditor: DBP, then walked into the embrace of the State without looking back.

McDermid said later that the staff shook hands with Wolff, nodded politely to her and ignored Lyn. "I think that was a mortal insult to that one, to be ignored." I agreed. Although if they had paid attention to Lyn, she might had taken insult anyway.

Twenty minutes later Wolff limped into the office of the Confederate houses leaning heavily on Lyn and McDermid and the three of them were escorted to a quiet anteroom. Lyn was not split off to a separate holding area, though she was disarmed at the office door.

Another mortal insult to Lyn. Of a certainty, her auras were the bright crimson of imminent violence. She, Wolff and McDermid were well within my net. I was getting ready to set PC41 on another sortie through the halls and access ducts, although we were odds on certain the four-legged rats had decamped or been disposed of.

Lyn was Wolff's sworn Medji and was carrying a battered rucksack that had medicine Wolff required. Helen had remained with them, chatting with the Head of Station and ignoring any mild suggestions that she could just go on about her busy day or come to his office for a cuppa. She settled in for a long public gossip with the Head of Station, who'd she had given the 'cut direct' to before, while keeping a weather eye on Wolff.

The Confed Houses staff and the Marshals' Blacklegs were only mildly interested in Wolff when he limped in the door. The Provo section couldn't be bothered at all. All they could see was that the elderly gentleman needed traveler's aid, medical care, and a place to rest; and they were only concerned that he had white metal to pay any hostel or medical costs.

Then his ID came back with a host of flags; Hanse, Unity Eisenring, Provo Eisenring and Confed House all had a claim on him. They became much more interested, if not aggressive. The Provo Eisenring appeared from the woodwork like the louse he was and tried to split off Helen and Lyn from Wolff. Helen was not having any of this and tore Head of Station a new one. She rang in several Cantry Ford administrators, using the Confed House telephones and adding insult to injury. This frustrated the Provo's desire to take Wolff into a back room to begin an inquiry out of the sight of meddling hayseeds.

Prior to this cotillion, Wolff had deftly side-stepped the local Registry remittance men by sending a suitably edited and weakly encrypted report to a Desk in Croton, a Desk concerning itself with AngTerra, before he presented himself to the bureaucracy at Confed House. He sent it over an antiquated and mostly unmonitored communications path, the Morse wire telegraph. And thus, he bypassed any filter traps anyone might have set for messages referencing BRIXMIS over telephonic or other means.

He'd transmitted it a finely calculated ten hours, in the middle of the night on the Hudson, ten hours prior to his appearance at the Confederated House offices. That time lag allowed for initial decrypting, alarms and excursions at the relevant Desk, and that Desk dispatching a Registry Marshals

Rapid response team to Cantry Ford to 'sort things out'.

Wolff then had a sudden relapse of his 'old trouble' while he was being aggressively questioned by the Provo Eisenring in front of god, Helen McDermid, Lyn and all the rest of the station. The Provo wanted to know my whereabouts and were getting pushy with Wolff. So, he took a dive.

"Toppled right off the chair with his eyes rolled up in the back of his head and hit the carpet like a dead cat. Lord what an actor we lost when he went on the confidence pull!" Said Helen. "Scared us one and all."

Five yards away I was not scared, but the urge to manifest and rip them all was strong. PC41 began to lose his stoat like appearance, more cat like and he'd ghosted through the side of the carrier. One of the putzs was a Sangsue, a very weak Sangsue to be sure, but he should have felt something in the nets. And he might lay hands on Lyn, who was not reputed to be as resistant as Wolff. I focused on that gobbet of shite and had a net ready to drop on his black veined auras.

Wolff was then placed under doctor's care, a doctor summoned from an independent practice across the lobby from the Confed station and retained beforehand by McDermid. He was not the band-aid bandit of the station, who did not look capable of treating a sunburn according to Helen. And the proper doctor promptly gave Wolff a sedative and loudly demanded that he be released to a proper hospital. This made the Provo officer present get stroppy and try to strongarm Wolff away from the doctor, Helen, the Head of Station and Lyn.

Lyn was but the simple Medji of song and story; all knives, needles, muscled and thick-headed. She was fluent only in English, struggled with Creole and had no idea at all of what Wolff or Dama Ledhrad were doing here in the Ford. Or how they all got there without going through customs. But she knew her duty.

The stroppy Provo Eisenring Proctor at the station lost teeth and much face over trying Lyn on, disarmed as she was. Helen McDermid reminded everyone and sundry that she and the doctor were residents of the Free City of Cantry Ford. And not at Table in the Confederated Houses. And not beholding in any way to the gormless Head of Station. And certain influential people knew they were attending Herr Wolff, who was-by the by-also well known to the Cantry Ford elites. And Herr Wolff was not, as Helen understood his situation, at Table with Confed House either.

Much shouting and drama as the station Blacklegs tried to restrain and eject Lyn, McDermid and the unnamed doctor while their band-aid bandit was tending to the unconscious Proctor. Who once was a Sangsue and now was a potato, PC41 having had quite enough of him trying to harm Wolff or Lyn.

Wolff was under the table, dead to the world by all appearances. He was simply dozy, had his hand on a four shot derringer and was willing to wait it out.

Then the Fast Response Team appeared on the doorstep, from Croton House proper. A half-hour behind the finely calculated time, but still a prompt response all things considered.

McDermid said everything came to a screeching, gear stripping, halt and things started to rapidly improve for Wolff and company. The Fast Response Team turfed all of the Civil Staff and the Custom and Enforcement Blacklegs out of the building and ringfenced the local Provo detachment-all four of them-in a commercial lockup, with FRT 'escorts' to keep them company and incommunicado. Then they started in on sorting out just what sort of clusterfuck was transpiring here. Beginning with Head of Station.

I was on the backside of the Mall, collecting my 'white metal' from the anxious manager and rescuing PC41 from his admirers. I'd picked up the Fast Team when they came through the net, pulled it in to just skimming my skin and started getting us away. They had two *Sangsues*, moderate and nowhere as strong as we were now, but it was time to vacate.

But I got the story in all its operatic glory from Helen, over a rack of pork roast with a side of oysters, a tossed salad and a brace of red wine in dusty bottles. I was very hungry for some reason. Her house had a splendid apple tart on the table as well along with some smuggled coffee.

McDermid had been tasked to provide me a safe house away from the site as well as 'aiding' Wolff when he came in the station. She was supposed to give me three days grace from when he went to the Confed offices to when I should be on my way and out from underfoot. I got to the safe house while she was still observing the Confed getting buggered by their own side.

She was very accommodating, providing good food and better booze and excellent yarns over the next few days. She was mildly curious as to what that 'Jolly old Pirate' was doing to cause such a commotion. She hated most of the Blacklegs and entirely all of the Eisenring with a cheerful passion. Helen thought the Hanse were officious prigs not worth the effort to insult. McDermid enthusiastically filled me in on the actions and events she was privy to and worked hard to uncover the things she was not. And if she could not uncover anything salacious or entertaining, she invented it; passing it on through the local rumor mills to inflame and dismay the Confeds. The rats in their offices for example. She was tightly connected with the local political structure, and that structure had a lot of influence in the halls of Confed House proper. She had a solid tap into what the Fast Response Team knew about the situation before Croton House knew it back on the Hudson. She did not know about the business with BRIXMIS, everyone kept her in the dark about that topic, but she made up for it by generating convoluted conspiracies.

None of the Confed officers, at first blush, could determine how Wolff and his Medji turned up at the Ford.

While being escorted by a Hanse *XternBuro* agent.

Without going through a documented entry-port.

And there just could not be any illicit posterns in the Ford…the Ford was so well self-regulated as the Confed so well knew to its frustration. It just had to be an inside job among the Confed Civil Staff or the Customs and Security detachment, or the Provo Eisenring, or any combination of the above.

Suborned by the snooty Hanse no less. With their infuriating habit of using gates that the Eisenring were not welcomed at. That the Eisenring couldn't locate.

And the Hanse were being more stroppy and un-cooperative than usual. The Consulate Steelyard was not replying to any messages; telephonic or hand delivered. Not answering the door, or they answered the door with their version of a Fast Response Team. Armored up, with large guns indiscreetly displayed.

Twenty hours later, or so my hostess gleefully told me, the FRT had purged all of the Customs and Security Blacklegs at Cantry Ford. When they couldn't prove a particular Provo Eisenring or Blackleg officer's malfeasance, and they did find some of the Blacklegs that were on the general pull, they still sent that person to one of the Confed posts out in the foothills of the Western Ramparts.

Where the Pika used Eisenring and Marshal Blacklegs for live fire exercises and the career life expectancy was measured in weeks.

The remaining Confed House political officers and the few Registry Marshals that survived the cull began to treat Wolff like he was solid gold. No more attempts at intimidation, they kept the local physician on call, they even gave Lyn her weapons back. Nothing was said about the battered Provo, it hadn't happened, nobody saw it, and it was obviously just a misunderstanding. Besides which, he passed on from an aneurism, while under treatment from Croton House medics.

Which indicated to me that the information Wolff brought over was accepted and being acted upon.

Helen, knowing nothing of what information he had passed the bureaucracy, thought Wolff was running an elegant scam on some deserving scum and that the Hanse were also getting scammed. She was particularly delighted in bidding an oh-so-regretful good-by to the ex-Head of Station as he left for the Sunset range and a career change. Mentioning to me that she had 'cater-cousins' out of the Grass in need of exercise and the former Head of Station was a 'worthless piece of grubby shite' in need of ventilation. Never did find out what he'd done to annoy her.

I watched the newswire for another day beyond my grace, enjoying the elaborate farrago of charges and insinuations that Helen concocted and broadcasted. Then I packed my bag to head east.

The cobblers had done well by me, as far as that went. But I wouldn't get past a competent squad of Eisenring at any gate. Even if I could fool the document scanners, they were sure to have sniffers of some sort at every type of gate; postern, narrow, and broad. I was stranded in the 'zeme for the foreseeable future.

I had some ready money to buy the good stuff, for PC41 if not for me. Wolff had washed my American dollars and English Pounds into 'white metal'. I could manage a good year out on the tiles in the 'zeme before I had to surface or get busy on the side.

I intended to get busy and await developments.

CHAPTER 30

I rode the wain lines east, the cheap ones. The Wain roads didn't run straight. They ran along county or House boundaries, heading for BigRiver or towards the Northern Lakes and then you'd take waterways to the old implanted steadings or to some of the newer independent or semi-autonomous cities. If you were insisting on cutting across country, they got even more twisted and slower.

I rode two days in a diesel wain that rattled my bones, then stopped in a burg that had been a market town for three modest Houses seven or eight short generations back. It was still the middle of square miles of cropland, pastures and orchards, but the House chops on the Granaries and the warehouses were faded or effaced. Those Houses had gone under, one at a time. Their Fain, what AngTerra would have insisted were peasants, were still here and there was likely a framework of Table and Hearth still embedded in the population, but the Houses and their Holders were gone.

Nothing bloody like the Unity overturn, nothing dramatic like that. The binders and most of the other 'gifted' had been recruited, adopted or married into larger establishments; the not-so-gifted had been given a hiltless knife and a modest donative and they had left for the coasts or to cross the veil into the worlds. What was left were the hewers of wood and the drawers of water and people whose gift was growing things and shaping things with their hands. The people who loved and were loved by the land and very loath to leave.

They threw 'gifted' children every generation, but less and less often. And their 'gifted' would up and leave not long after manifesting, if they lived through the change. They, the remnants, were Fain, but they didn't have the spark of the Dai.

And if you had the foolhardiness to ask, they just might feel better about it all. About the decline.

Dai don't actually live long lives on average, at least the manifested Dai. Some don't survive the stress of manifesting; others manifest but don't survive the mastering of their gifts.

Then intrigues and dominance struggles within a House, low level conflicts outside the bounds of the House and the occasional all-out war between Constellations of Houses; these thinned the Dai out right smartly. But these struggles also had collateral damage to the Fain. A Dai walked at the head of a warband, at least in his dreams, with bonded Fain at his command and allied Gifted at his side.

That was the adolescent fantasy, but it did kill. Particularly the adolescents. Fain and Dai adolescents, brought up on a thousand years of legend and romance. From Anyr's Saga to the Breaker of Houses. And someone always tried to emulate a legend. So, the remnant population of the Fain, where the bright, shining, dangerous, Dai emerged less and less, were content. They got to watch their children grow up and they got to know their grandchildren.

I'd bought a hiltless knife and a black presentation case when I was in the Ford. To blend in. No sigil was etched into the blade, and it would be terribly rude to ask about it, if someone was to see the presentation box and the blade. This explained why I was out on the 'ways'. I found a house just a street off the square, took a room for a cheap price, and looked for a short-term job. I looked over the pegboard at the tobacconists, picked up a free paper at the corner shop; I asked around in a pub and the two chip shops, said I was turfed out and heading for the coast and maybe go a wandering across the veil.

"What can you do?" Said the Host, leaning on the bar and polishing a glass.

I sipped at my lager. "'Bout anything. Got a steady hand with cattle, not so much with horses. They are just smart enough to be dumb, am I right?"

The others at the bar snorted knowingly.

"Can do some shade-tree mechanic work, shingle roofs, run a ditcher."

"Why didn't they keep ya, if you're so handy?" One at the end of the bar. Always the one.

I gave that one a hard look. Everyone else at the bar hunched and looked embarrassed, like someone farted in the sauna. "There is that. I got the knife. You want to know more?" And I pushed the half-schooner of lager back at the Host. The jackass asking rude questions didn't look or sound Eisenring, but you never know. "Want to come along, outside? And ask again?"

He blinked and his Adam's apple worked as he swallowed. I had the height on him and the reach, and more importantly I had the nerve. I felt someone at my back, not threatening, not yet. PC41 was close underfoot and she was very calm.

"Duncan you are a drunken, mouthy, ass; pay up, go home and stay home." A deep voice behind me.

I didn't look away from Duncan; if 'deep voice' was a danger from behind, Duncan would be the one from the front. What neither knew was that I had them cold. I was slowly manifesting, bringing up the net but keeping it low. I didn't want to attract attention, but small towns and their hard boys…

A hand clapped on my shoulder, I flinched but PC41 was

quiet and I just cracked my knuckles. Duncan threw some white metal on the bar top and stiffly turned away.

One of the drinking men stepped to the side and Deep Voice sidled into the gap, leaning on the bar. He was bigger than me, wore a light brown uniform and had a star with four points on each of his collars. And he was a D'draig. But a very, very, minor one. I let the auras melt away and relaxed. PC41 was closer, but still not concerned.

"And you are?"

"Deputy for the County." He held his hand out for me to take and I shook it. Felt him lightly sweep me and knew he made me for a talent, but not how strong, or what kind. "Sorry bout Duncan, he drinks and hasn't the sense to pour the piss out of his own boots."

I nodded at him. "My name's Josiah Risley." My bunkmate's mother's maiden name, back in the Smoke. Always easier to run a legend when it has as much truth in it as you can stand. "Came from-"

He shook his head. "Nah, no real need. Passing through?" The under thread was are you planning to stay?

"Ran out of ticket and the ready. Like I said. I need a job and a bit of a pause, then I'll drift on out the line."

"Hard separation?"

I let my eyes get cold. "They were eager enough to see the back of me, but that is how it goes, isn't it?"

"Y'know there is a ditching job coming up at the old grange. Go see George Clayton tomorrow and tell him Deputy Calvert sent you."

"I will," I gave him my hand again and shook it once. "Thank you kindly." Nodded at the host, said my goodnights and with my news sheet in hand walked down the street to the rooming house.

I stayed there a ten-night doing the ditching job, eating at the grange, sleeping at the rooming house. I stood a round at the pub the night before the morning I left. Thanked the Host. Went to bed and got on the Wain with enough visible money to get me to a town ten counties away. Never saw the Deputy again and never saw Duncan, though PC41 said he'd had a good sniff of him once or twice lurking about. Back stabber.

I had thought of traveling all the way to the coast by slow Wain, but that stop put the wind up me. Not that they were actively looking for me, but that there was always going to be some fool looking for entertainment. I was passing through and I was not kin nor was I 'mobbed' up, so fair game.

And if I stuffed his fool head up his ass, I would generate gossip even if the locals liked the thought of me stuffing his scabby ass with his head. I did not need any attention.

I took a jog sideways and got on a slow excursion boat, on one of the Lakes, sailing along the shore and then down a canal to the Hudson river and down the river to Bellingham-a suburb of York-on-the-Hudson, loafing past Croton House and all the merry bands of Provo Eisenring and Registry Cadre intent on climbing a slippery rope of reputation.

A good two months after I got crossways with Duncan, I had arrived on the western side of the Hudson. I was looking for a particular place in a particular part of that riverfront.

There was a postern gate, one of many that the Eisenring had 'lost' long before I was born, but the approximate locations of the 'lost gates' had been orally handed down. Much like the 'suitcases', it was a fallback that no one in the 'Firm' wanted to acknowledge or burn, you never knew when you might need it. Even if you were made director of the Eisenring tonight, the wheel could turn tomorrow, and you might need a quiet trip through the veil the day after. It made the Eisenring uneasy, just as uneasy as knowing there were gates that the dissident houses controlled. But there it was.

I got off the barge at Bensenille, which was three miles north of where I thought the postern gate might be. Bensenille had a dozen piers thrusting into the Hudson, a ferry connecting West York County with York City proper, and a cluster of brick and mortar buildings filled with businesses that grew to handle the commerce that came from being close to York City. And the commerce that came from seamen; bars, moneylenders, chandlers and bordellos.

I changed out my clothing at one of the moneylenders, swapping my slightly used and western styled clothing for well used but sound dungarees, a canvas jacket, some shirts and steel toed boots. Went to a chandler's shop and nosed about, but I didn't get anything other than a solid footlocker. I knew enough about the merchant marine to convince a Sunset Range Pub I was salty. A real seaman would rumble me in a minute.

I found a credit cooperative with a strong room, that had boxes for lease. Put everything I brought over from AngTerra there, what I couldn't let go of, and started a 'book account'. Seaway Trust and Exchange handled small accounts cheerfully, had branches up and down the river in the County of York and across the river in the big city as well. I stayed at a cheap hostel for a week, looking the ads and flyers over and then moved on down the river to where I intended all along to settle.

Wat's Ferry. The Ferry was long gone, the piers it had docked at were gone. The only way you could tell that there had been a ferry there was the broad street down through the middle of the town from the Wainway, a street that ended at the river.

I found an inexpensive boarding house, just off a smaller cluster of piers and jetties that still served the river. It did not allow animals, that was the only drawback to it. Not that rule would hamper PC41.

I bought a set of mechanics tools at an auction in Bensenille before I came to Wat's Ferry. I started making the rounds of the local job shops. I did not want to have anything to do with a 'livery' shop, most of them would have done a cursory background check on me. I didn't trust the Cobbler's talent back at the Ford that far.

I got a place doing repairs on 'small' engines, it helped that I brought my own tools to the job and knew more than a bit about motors. The 'small' motors were big diesels for barges and the like, but the technology was seventy years old. At least. Maybe older. I'd seen them, or something very like them, when I was apprenticed at the Estuary docks long before I got impressed into the bleeding Eisenring.

PC41 cut a wide swath through the local vermin and kept me company at night. I kept myself to myself and learned the in-and-out of the workshop. The rooming house had a scant breakfast and an adequate dinner, linen service, laundry service and a common washroom and shower.

Somebody gently tossed my room twice in the first months I was there, but I had all the more interesting items already salted away in another town, in another safe-deposit box under another name.

I did leave the presentation box of the 'knife' out after the first time my room was searched. Wasn't interfered with the second time they tossed the room, but it was moved slightly in the sock drawer. I figured it was an inexperienced nosey Dot, a cache of coins-white metal- and local script was also moved about but left intact. Not theft, just curiosity.

We located the Postern gate, when it fired up occasionally. It was not known to any of the local authorities, as far as I could tell.

PC41 said that she knew it was being used, once or twice a month. It was also close by to a broad adit, a type of big commercial gate, and when that gate opened and closed it masked the postern operation completely with the backwash for several hours. Which often determined when the postern was operated. The commercial gate was to the north and inland of the postern.

Wolff had given me a couple of cutout mailbox addresses. I used a Morse telegraph dispatch, sent from York-over-the-Hudson to activate one giving it a postbox address in Bensenille. The cutout mailbox would blind forward his messages to a chain of mailboxes from Cantry Ford. The last one being the box I had opened in Bensenille.

He didn't have my exact location, just that I was near the east coast and still in the 'zeme. If he quit using it, it would go dark and not forward anything to me.

I got a postcard the week after I opened the box, supposedly from somewhere to the southeast of York. I took it 'home' and that night after dinner I steamed the stamp free over a votive candle and a teacup and found the dot.

I broke out the lucky pound coin that Wolff gave me, unscrewed it and set up the 160-magnification scope. And bob's-yer-uncle I had a letter from Wolff that made sense. It only took about an hour.

PC41 sniffed. >wasted time<

I agreed, but everyone needed a hobby. His was running a network, I was happy to play.

I kept tabs on him and Lyn, getting postcards and the occasional letter from them and a wad of trash from all and sundry. I didn't send anything back, of course. I trusted him to send messages out from under the watchers but getting one to him through his minders might have been chancy.

The postcards had a microdot under the franking coupon-what they called the stamp hereabouts, so did the letters when they came. The cover messages were innocuous, supposedly being from the House on the Sunset Range that I left under a cloud. No complete names, just a bit of news from a world I'd had lost and had not quite completely cut myself off from. I didn't pay any attention to the cover letters, I read them in case I was ever asked about them, but it was all *bumf.* I think Lyn was recycling soap operas and posting the mush to me. At least she had dropped the references to spies and secret agents.

But the microdots were replete with real news and gossip about the Ford and the churning hysteria among the Hanse, the two Eisenrings and Croton House.

Wolff, eventually, was given a clean bill of health; ascribed to Dama Ledhrad and the Hanse knowing precisely what the cause of his decline was and how to counter it. The Croton Registry, the Confeds, kept him on ice in the Ford for a while, waiting for another shoe to drop. The odds were on for another attempt on Reagan. The Russians seemed to be very closely warding Chernenko, who was ensconced in a hospital with the KGB sitting on him. Wolff thought that someone had 'leaked' more threats against Reagan to several different desks in the intelligence silos in Washington; ascribing the threats to Iran, or Nicaragua, or the DNC. And so, they got very protective of Reagan and Bush.

There were more statistically unlikely deaths tabulated in AngTerra and Little England that Wolff was consulted about. Or badgered about. Most were not related to the post-war period at all, but the powers that were in being had begun to see every unexplained death or disappearance as being involved with the end of civilization as the Dai liked it.

There were some surviving-wanted-fugitives uncovered from the dregs of the second world war, but there were many more that were found to be safely buried in quicklime.

Relations with the Hanse central government, the *XternBuro* and the DBP were tense or non-existent.

In fact, the DBP seemed to be not available for any sort of debriefing with the Unity Eisenring or the Provo Eisenring. The Joint Eisenring commission. Wolff started calling them the Ghastly Twins.

And the network the DBP had in AngTerra had also seemed to have gone to ground completely. Baffling, simply baffling.

The *XternBuro* as well as the Hanse *Oor deRegering*-their central government- was stiffly adamant that the DBP did not exist. None of the Eight Sections of the DBP existed. The notorious and very secretive *Afdeling* Seven did not exist. Or the Auditors of the Eighth Section. Or anything else in the Table of Organization that the Registry confronted them with. The *Betrekkingen Provinciale*. Did. Not. Exist.

This was making everyone at Croton House barking mad, because they knew full well that the DBP existed and it was blown, and it had been operating in AngTerra and Meg knows where else in the Sheaves. Covertly operating, up to no damn good. Like the Joint Eisenring did everywhere, but in the Hanse.

The Unity and the Confederated Houses, as well as the Joint Eisenring, had paperwork proving that the DBP existed, a detailed table of organization with all sorts of management and communications pathways. And for a short while they had a DBP operative exposed and working alongside a Joint Eisenring operator. Who they also couldn't find, the Eisenring operator that is. And the subsection he, the operator, had been in had likewise gone to ground. Or it was suddenly dispersed, the entire joint operating section, Unity and Provo. Nobody brought up the subject of Vittorio, the absent Director. He was simply missing.

But the section I had been in when PC41 bowled into my life, it was scattered to the hundred worlds? Now that caught my interest. My old section was dispersed? That made all the tradecraft that Wolff had insisted on much more of a necessity than a joke. And it made me much more cautious about moving about between Bensenille and Wat's Ferry. Dispersal implied intrigue and counter-operations between sections, and in the Ghastly Twins that was serious business. Messing about with other worlds and nations was just workaday paper pushing, but putting the knife into another Desk, now that was real.

Wolff had made copies of the table of organization for the DBP, supposedly taken from a microdot on a card that Dama Ledhrad had slipped Lyn when she shook hands with her at that parting. It was a microdot that he had made personally several days before. He gave the copies to the Croton Fast Response commander, and not the local Eisenring dupes, with a wink and a nod. And they took those table of organizations very soberly.

The *XternBuro* itself underwent an extensive public reorganization, further hampering any cooperation. The Hanse did not make Dama Ledhrad available to be debriefed by any of the Dai bureaucracies. The Hanse *Oor deRegering* did admit she existed, and they did provide a summary of her version of the events she witnessed. Suitably and extensively redacted and without any further comment.

The *Oor deRegering* and the *XternBuro* wanted full access

immediately to Wolff, to J. Braxton and Hugh Snow. They snubbed Lyn, which Wolff said made her extremely difficult to live with for a week.

They, the Hanse, were as apoplectic as they could get, without bleeding at the ears, at the refusal to produce Herr Wolff and Herr Braxton. When they got the report of Snow's death along with a coroner's verdict of legendary misadventure-a highly redacted autopsy-they went barking mad alongside of the Dai.

The traffic between the Hanse and all the other World Lines in the sheaf dropped off dramatically with knock-on effects on all the economies except the Hanse. They liked our trade and what we traded with them, but they really did not need us. They would have liked to incorporate us into their society, because our culture wanted 'rationalizing' and needed to have our peculiar biology explored for the betterment of...well for betterment at any rate. They did try to extend their cloak of a rational society over us once, but that was a long time ago and it ended quite badly for everyone involved so it wasn't mentioned in polite company.

The last Wolff had definitely heard of Johanna Marie was that the Hanse had slotted her into an *Oor deRegering* office, an office with a title on the door and a Personal Assistant in the reception cubby. This was on the home world in their version of the Hanse Foreign Office-which was not the *XtemBuro* at all.

The Foreign office had never been staffed with any of those uncivilized deviants who actually worked or associated with those foreigners, thank you very much. The F.O. did compose reports and generate blue binders about the nefarious goings of those foreigners, but talk to them-oh no. No, no, no we don't do that.

Wolff suspected they had her embedded in a web of observers waiting for the DBP to make contact with their Auditor. And I suspected Dama Ledhrad was taking them for all they had at this game of liar's chess. Bully for her.

Wolff and Lyn were finally sent home to AngTerra and the bookstore when World War three didn't immediately break out. The Existing Powers; the Confederated Houses-Croton House-the Unity and both sets of Eisenring decided that Wolff had uncovered a tremendously dangerous situation and did so only by happenstance. Thereafter the professionals would be keeping the situation well in hand with their modern methods of investigation. They likely had rings of watchers circling Wolff like the planets in the Ptolemaic charts of the heavens that circled AngTerra.

That goodbye was the last I heard of them for a while.

What I had come to think, over those months drifting through the Eastern waterways, was that PC41 was an amplifier. Wolff said that 'our bodies were an uneasy amalgam' and though he was not referring directly to PC41 and I, that concept had a resonance to our situation.

I wasn't much more than a minor D'draig that could with some effort affect a subject's charkas and auric flows, monitor the flows for evidence of subterfuge and intent and 'enhance' the interrogations. I could also give some auric medical aid, more than an icepack or elastic bandages, but much less than a qualified Battle Medic could have offered. Those abilities were enhanced with rigorous training in close quarters combat and I was a valued utility player in the Unity Eisenring. For as long as it would have lasted, that is.

Then PC41 appeared and everything changed.

Even after I understood and accepted that 'we' were bonded and that bonding affected my talents, I did not notice the effect that bonding between us had on everyone else within my expanding range. Not until Wolff and I bumped heads.

Maybe the ten weeks or so of PC41 and I slowly learning to live immersed in each other's auric field expanded our linked abilities. Or perhaps someone else being immersed in our field for a longish period of time enhanced or repaired their charkas. Wolff was not dying when I last saw him, not of the sophisticated poisoning nor of simple old age. He was not rejuvenated, but he was a vigorous gentleman of a certain age.

Lyn. Wolff had quietly, very quietly, let me have the sketch of a back story on Lyn. It involved an extremely traumatic assignment that had come apart disastrously. An assignment that injured both her body and spirit. An assignment that had her brush up against a psychopath that happened to be a Sangsue. And lost her a posting and some of her immediate family in the aftermath.

Wolff took her on, as his Medji. He really did not need her. She was a bodyguard and assistant to a superannuated intelligence agent who was passing as a bookseller and a semi-retired Philosophy Professor. In the flyover country. It was a quiet post and except for occasional petty criminals and lovestruck college boys, she was not challenged or stressed. As Wolff's health declined, he despaired of her recovering her balance in the time he had remaining. He owed a debt to this Medji. One he never elaborated to me.

And one of the open 'tells' to the issues Lyn had was an eating disorder. I am not well versed in these disorders and Wolff was reticent about the details. But Lyn was both concealing 'emergency' supplies in her kit and around the apartment and store; at the same time, she was not eating what food there was on offer. Or not eating well.

Then she quit caching food all through her environment and began to openly enjoy her meals. She also lost much of her reflexive disgust and fear of me, I was no more than an ally-of-convenience but that was all right by her. Her easy acceptance was a 'tell' to her recovery's progress.

Then there was Johanna Marie. PC41 and I smoothed the transition from an anxious probie to an assured and competent agent-in-place for the *XternBuro*. The raw material had been there, but the *XternBuro* had not wanted to spend the time and materials to shape her properly. They intended to simply discard her after the crisis was past. And again, I was not intending to change her, it just happened. As did Snow.

Snow was when I began to grasp just what sort of danger we were, to the people around us. Skrenner Adepts were unstable to begin with; perhaps of all the talented or 'gifted' Dai, including the Walkers, they were the most likely to just lose the plot and curl up and die. Being able to see and experience many of the multiple pathways from mundane decision points had a cumulative effect on their minds and eventually their bodies. Adepts ended their careers in suicide or catatonia. Others simply lost the ability to follow the possible pathways.

Somehow, I had dumped just enough energy into Snow to send him over the edge of the precipice he had been dancing on for a long generation. I'd never heard of 'spontaneous human combustion', but it almost made sense knowing what I had learned about auric fields.

What I had learned. They didn't teach us much in the intake classes and even less when they sent us out to our first assignments. Not about being a D'draig. We got a good grounding in armed and unarmed combat, a reasonable exposure to tradecraft and how to blend into a community just long enough to do our job. What indoctrination D'draig got in auras and charkas was in the field. Very rough and ready and no theory to speak of. Hard on us and immensely worse for our victims.

Now I knew much more.

CHAPTER 31

In the early winter there was a new face in the neighborhood.

I'd been quiet, spent the late summer and all of the fall getting accepted. Kept myself to myself. I stood drinks on rare occasion at the pub that the waterfront mechanics favored, the Cracked Cylinder-Head, also known as the Cracked Head. That pub had a rusting, cracked, eight inch in diameter piston hanging over the door and a scattering of engine parts on the walls like fishing trophies.

This part of 'zeme kept what they termed the Alba measurement system alongside of the metric. The reason they retained it was simple, retaining it browned off the Commonality to no end. So, in everyday parlance, 'eight inches' was used instead of '10 centimeters' because any of the 'Unity pollywogs in hearing would get a slow burn at the term. Or the pollywogs would try to educate the hapless rubes in the utility of the metric system. I guess you had to take your entertainment where you found it.

I had nothing much to say to anyone about where I came from. I was here, I'd been somewhere else before I came here, that's all.

I faded into the background, once they had an explanation for me. The nosy Dot in the rooming house, probably the linen service kid, had spread the explanation around. 'Someone sent down from the West and oooh he had a 'hiltless knife.' So that was the reason I was out here all alone, no house and no obvious connection to any house. Once they had a reason, they quit bothering to speculate. Or investigate.

It was dead easy to fade into the woodwork. I'd lived on a waterfront most of my life, just in another world. In the Smoke, what we called London back in the Three Kingdoms.

I was abandoned when I was about one year old, on the doorstep of a Salvation Army mission. No note, no signet ring on a thong about my neck, no tattoo or birthmark. Just a baby wrapped up in an old wool blanket, not even a military blanket. Nothing special.

The Sally Ann's didn't raise me; like suicides and absconders, orphans were the particular concern of the Court of the Lyon. The Sally Ann's called the local Lyon sheriffs-constables with a fancy red and gold badge-and I was passed into the procurator fiscal's hands, being a child of unknown provenance and inheritance.

After being proven an orphan and destitute, I was presented with a Certificate of Live Birth, a name, an address and a small donative from their Majesties. Then I was bundled off to live in a Royal Orphanage. They sent me to Wanstead House down close to the Thames; it was a manor seized from one of the exiled Royals and converted to a government establishment at the turn of the realm long generations before my birth.

When the Thistle came back from the continent, leaving the Hanoverians plotting and squatting in the Westlands, it became a Royal Jacobin Orphanage and Infant School. By the time I turned up in its drafty hallways Wanstead was just a Royal Orphanage and School, no longer closely associated with the Jacobin Thistle or any of the other Royal lines.

There were good points about being in Wanstead; being an official ward of the Court of the Lyon was better than being dumped out on the street like a bushel of kittens. They closely warded us at the old ruin; three meals a day, safe bunking, warm togs, school, a Nurse on the grounds, a Doctor on call, and sports-lots of sports. We also got the occasional clout about the ears or more formal corporal punishments for really screwing the goose. It wasn't a cheery place, but it was much better than any of the other places I've seen. The Ley Gardens for example.

It was also a recruiting station for Their Majesties Armed Forces, the Royal India and Caribbean Company, the Parliamentary Service. And the Eisenring, the hidden world's Iron Ring, which didn't have a recruiting office in the old ruin, but still kept an eye on the orphans.

After the first round of exams, when you were ten years old, they filtered out the high-flyers and put them on a University track. Then they cycled the rest of that cohort through commercial and apprentice introduction courses.

After you turned seventeen and six months, they gave you several choices of how you were going to earn your bread. You could go for a Trooper or sail with the Royal Merchant marine, they'd take you in an instant and you'd have bed, board and be outfitted right there and then. Or they'd send you to intern with your choice of a trade; machine shop, furniture refinisher, baker, or the like. At Eighteen, they handed you a scrap of paper and turfed you out into the world. The donative the crowns gave you when you qualified as an orphan, that coin had been banked for however many years you were at the Manor, then they handed you it on the day you went out on the cobblestones. That tided you over till you found a job, but you were on your own, sink or swim. Usually the place that interned you, if you suited them at all, would take you on. Apprentice, or clerking, or driving a truck. If you had a clean sheet from the orphanage, you'd find a place. If your sheet wasn't clean, you'd still find a place but, on the fiddle, as it was.

I suppose I was lucky they didn't tattoo the Broad Trident on my bum when they found me on the doorstep. A lot of foundlings went straight into the service of the thrones. But it wasn't Their Majesties that ended up owning me, but the Eisenring. Funny old universe isn't it?

There were always a good number of recent castoffs on the Hudson riverfront. Some with presentation boxes and hiltless knives in their bundle and some just with their old lonesome selves and a gunny sack. The wharfs were always looking for casual stoop labor; chandler's shops and the like wanted literate hands that were steady and could pass muster under the aegis of the Aunts-who were choosier than a Regimental Sargent Major. The repair and rebuild shops might take you on spec and if you worked out-you had a job and a place as long as you liked. Within reason; you could always get up crossways with the boss or the boss's nephew or get feloniously stupid in public. But it wasn't like working in a House. Politics, Houses were always politics and who was in the studbook and who was at the Hearth or who was sleeping with who or who was seated at the Table and... politics. I watched it all from afar when I was jumping through the hoops for the 'Unity Ring. As bad as the 'Ring was, it was easier than being a cadet in a proper House.

There were several House underwritten establishments, heavy machine shops maintaining Liveried vessels or tending to the independently Flagged consignment ships. But there were a lot of smaller places that tended to 'small' craft and hired anyone who could turn a wrench or run a mill. No one bragged of having once been part of a Major House. They didn't bemoan being cut loose either. It was what it was.

In the small places you formed a loyalty to the shop, bonded with the people you worked with and the people you worked for and the people you lived around. The discards made places for themselves, started families. Started minor houses, if you please. Some of the 'minors' were three or four generations old and had an establishment that covered three city blocks or an entire section of the wharf to themselves. They were good at being prosperous while keeping their heads down and not making a wake. They excelled in not making a show where the Major Houses might take an interest, and a Major House might demand a cut. The small houses also kept a close eye on the waterfront and any strangers walking the docksides.

And there were a lot of strangers on any given day, coming and going. Dai and Fain and unchurched and what-have-you. Discards, Minors, and bindlestiffs were all very aware of the wharves and the streets behind them.

Much like the small towns I'd drifted through in the spring, but with more slack in their dealings with strangers.

They had patrollers, Township Constables, strolling along the wharf and up and down the backstreets. Keeping the peace between the Back Water-Street denizens, or thumping heads to discourage the more obnoxious wharfies. Every township, a township was about a two and a half miles square parcel inland of the river or a mile of river-run that had a one hundred and ninety-five rods deep backstreet, every township had a low Sheriff; most had a Curule Bench that bound over significant breakers of the peace for the Magistrate Benches and passed low justice on bog-common knuckleheads with too much to drink or too little to do. All these predated and sometimes clashed with the more organized and systematic legal systems of the Confederated Houses. The higher lawdogs were just Croton House Marshals, the Custom and Enforcement Blacklegs; lately Provo Eisenring were becoming common sights. To everyone's disgust.

The rivers were still the principal arteries of trade and traffic in the 'zeme. Just like they were at the beginning of the "Implantation." They were teeming with all sorts of powered and unpowered craft.

Ranging up and down the water, stopping at jetties built of bamboo, docks made of cast-off PVC pipes or bobbed wharfs of rusting steel shipping containers. Shipping job lots of food and cottage industry products, passengers and freight, up and down the river. And over the ice in the winter.

Ducted-fan hovercraft were becoming familiar, just as common as skiffs or barges, at least on the eastern rivers that I saw. The Skimmers, the local term for a hovercraft, allowed their operators to move farther up barely navigable streams, 'skimming' on the water surface. They were taking the place of the pirogue, the skiff or the sampan for small boatmen. And in the winter, the skimmers were faster and safer than snow sleds for going up and down the river. If you found a polynya-a hole in the ice-the hard way in a sled, you might be recovered in the spring thaw. You might not. A hovercraft would just skim right over the open water. They were not as expensive to maintain or run as some of the more traditional motor watercraft. The smaller air-dinghies with light fans were ideal if you didn't need much in the way of speed or seaway.

A lot of the work I did was on skimmers and air-dinghies serving as tenders for larger cargo vessels. They could come alongside of the merchantman and net a load or enter a washway hatch, hand load a pallet and buzz across the river and up on the bank to deliver their cargo to a waiting truck.

Turn right about and do it again in less time that it would have taken a lighter boat to take on cargo with a net. Much quicker than docking at the wharf and it allowed for small volume cargo drop off operations.

Which attracted the Gentlemen.

A skimmer needed at least two motors running to keep the plenum inflated and a much larger one to drive the ducted fans that propelled them. Noisy, like overrevved dirt bikes. Which could be a problem when the 'Gentlemen', with their customs-free cargos, skimmed by in the night. The Gentlemen's Skimmers were much faster than any legitimate concern needed, three times the engine and half the cargo was the rule of thumb. They were hella louder than the Customs and Enforcement Cutters, but they could skim by on a drop of dew or a smooth strip of marsh where the cutter would rip its bottom out following them. So, the Blackleg Cutters drifted through the backwaters and estuaries on quiet electric trolling motors or lurked with their petrol V-12s rumbling at idle just out in the middle of the river.

The dark grey skimmers of the Gentlemen went howling through the night carrying what items the Gentlemen did not intend to pay tax on and the Cutters roared after them. A game both sides enjoyed playing, more than the rewards at the end. Smuggling was more a civil infraction than a crime, depending on what you were attempting to slip past customs. Dangerous drugs and some proscribed technologies got way more than a slap on the wrist, while alcohol and luxury goods earned just a fine and trash talking in the pub afterwards.

The smaller air-dinghies were very forgivable of sloppy handling and catch as catch can maintenance. The plenum bags on the dinghies were just cheap rubberized sail fabric, fixable with waterproof hundred knot tape; navigation aids were a light fore and aft. There was a small tiller cuddy in front of the ducted thrust fan with a short-range radio and a bit of rain cover. The engine ran both the lifting fan and the thrust fan, max speed was about twenty miles an hour. That was your typical air-dinghy. Carried about a half ton of cargo, though that was pushing the envelope.

The wharfies often turned their kids loose with a cheap air-dinghy for their first job. Most of them made a go of it, they'd been on the river since they could walk and working an air-dinghy was easier than a skiff or a punt. And was on the whole, more pleasant than clerking in a shore establishment.

I liked them, fast skimmers and putt-putt dinghies; they weren't horses. And except for the Gentlemen's Skimmers with overrevved and overpriced AngTerra engine imports-the bleeding Datsun inline six was the most popular smuggled burner-they really were small engines. Four cylinders, alcohol or petrol four cycle, carbureted. The skimmers and the dinghies were tiny compared to the hulking devils that I was tearing down and rebuilding.

I got a reputation for not turning my nose up at the truly 'small' jobs or charging the world for a repair done on the wharf-side. Brought us more of the proper jobs by word of mouth, which was funny in a good way.

I was getting comfortable, here. Too comfortable. It smelled like the Estuary, looked like the Estuary and except for the accents and some of the fashions in clothing it was the Estuary.

The paperwork that Wolff's Cobbler produced couldn't withstand a close inspection, but I could finesse a more than casual look over now. I had settled in and I was no stranger, the local constables didn't see me as a new face anymore. The acceptance that would have taken twenty years living in a small town fifty miles inland of the coast, took less than six months on the river.

I began to rethink moving on, there was the question of walking through the veil. I could drift away upriver or down the coastline, there was always a need for a machinist. And I did not have an attitude about being 'churched', I came late to that status and it was not part of my self-image.

But I also knew I couldn't discard it completely. PC41. We were both looking for something.

A discard came off of one of the dinghies; not quite dressed for cold and wet, but not wearing sandals and shorts either. His dungarees were out at the knees and had grease stains, he wore two sets of heavy cable knit sweaters and a sleeveless yellow hoodie. Close shaven, short hair and a portwine mark on his left chin. He had a small knapsack slung over his right shoulder, that made him likely left-handed.

A discard, I thought, like a dozen others I'd seen since the summer turned to fall. Cast off in the spring and hard done by over the summer. Like kittens dumped out on the wharf. Young and thin and very, very, watchful of his surroundings.

>watch<

I didn't flinch, but I was surprised. Usually PC41 would surface at the end of day, sidle into the rooming house with me and then into my room on the second floor. I'd wash up, go down and eat supper in the common room and be friendly with the other boarders. I didn't spend much time in the public room after supper; had a cup of tea and a pipe of tobacco, read the paper and comment on the weather or the way people abused perfectly good hardware and then off to my rooms. I was quiet, I was clean, I paid my bills on time. I was not particularly cheap nor was I a spendthrift. I blended into the tatty wallpaper.

PC41 and me. We'd spend the evening after supper sitting close to each other on the bed, watching the night fall outside. Letting the flow knit slowly around us. We worked hard at not knowing anything about the other boarders. Just enough to know that they weren't interested in us. He rarely ventured out at night, now. I didn't know why. And he was more regular in his conformation. He favored a Tomcat now, with a short grey coat. And he only occasionally asked after a can of the 'good stuff'. A can I fed him out on the wharf, since the boarding house banned pets. I think he had a trap line running through the fishermen on the dockyards as well as thinning out the rats and gulls.

>who< I asked.
>walker<

I was taking a break from a very old Briggs-Thompson two stroke that I was reviving. Sitting outside on an empty five-gallon paint can and wrapping myself around a thermos of tea. It was afternoon, not too cold and little wind. But the clouds to the north were darkly bruised and promised cold rain if not snow.

The man, or boy was it? The boy walked past me and up the street, his auras faint and gauzy in the afternoon light. He walked past two pubs and a chip shop then went into our Sally Ann's.

I nodded to myself. Flat broke, or near as damnit, he was. The Salvation Army would give him a wash, a bowl of stew and a chunk of bread with tea to wash it down and a safe place to sleep. All for the cost of a sermon. The Sally Anne's were just about everywhere; AngTerra, Little England, Hindi Imperial, Picardy-Normandy, all of the Muscovy Lines except the Trotskyites-they all had Sally Anne's. The Dai knew that the Sally Anne's had originated in AngTerra and drifted across the sheaf of Worlds without anyone knowing quite how or just when. And as far as we-we being the Eisenring-as far as we knew nobody coordinated the missions and their operations across the world lines. The missions had simple rules; no alcohol, no drugs, and no fraternizing. There was a Men's side and a Women's side. And no-nonsense chaperones. They took donations, the staff would do odd jobs and turn over most of their outside pay to the Mission, sometimes they ran small scale canning and salting operations for the local subsistence fishers. They had a heavy mob of bouncers, low-key preachers and Christian bibles in Creole or whatever. Good people on the main, some nutters, but good people. The locals on the wharf thought they were flakes; Christianity not being widely accepted, or understood-Buddhism seemed to be more popular-but they're our flakes and you'd best leave them alone. I remembered them from the Smoke, AngTerra and Little Englander both.

I finished my mug of tea. Screwed it onto the thermos. >interrogative< I pushed at PC41. I got up and went back to my cranky two stroke diesel, a 'small' four-cylinder engine that weighed seventy-five stone and was a favorite of barge tug owners.
>walker< Came back on the push. >won't be home<

That brought me up short as I stepped across the threshold into the shop.

CHAPTER 32

I don't remember the rest of that day. Not really. I finished work, downed tools, walked to the boarding house and followed the usual routine. Went to my room and sat at the head of the bed, leaning against the wall.

Waiting for something to come across the push.

Fell asleep in my clothes, woke up at dawn and PC41 wasn't there. She was always in the background of my awareness, since we bonded. Now she wasn't.

I went down to breakfast and then walked to work, almost walked past the shop. And slowly I knew she was within my reach. And that she was a She again. A weight lifted off me.

I felt better. When I had woken up that morning, I'd opened the push to her. I hadn't realized that we'd connected. Then I looked at my bench.

"Bloody hell?" I muttered under my breath as I stared at the half-assembled blower for the two-stroke sitting on my workbench. I opened my toolbox and began the day, installing the parts I had left out of the turbo-blower when I buttoned it up yesterday.

"Bad day, eh?"

I looked at my boss. Shrugged. "Had a bit of news I didn't expect. Took me aback and well-"

She laughed. "Eh, a cuppa tea and a smoke will make it right soon enough." And she wandered on off through the shop, heading for the break table. I just turned to and sorted out the blower and redid the gaskets.

>?< I pushed.

Satisfaction came back over the push.

CHAPTER 33

The castoff came looking for a job later that week. Cleaned up well; had a newish set of overalls on and had a well-scrubbed look to her hands and face. Hair pulled back under a kerchief.

And it was a her. I gave her a sidelong look as she made the pitch to the boss. I opened the doors of perception and had another minor shock. She had little in the way of colors flying from her. Not totally washed out, but just about as faint as a child's auric signature. I went back to my diesel and kept my mind on my job. She was gifted and hooded. Well hooded.

She made a good cigarette pitch, gave a job application while the boss smoked a cigarette. Boss took her on as a helper and cleaner. She had some experience, working in the blackgang on a fishing canner as a wiper. Boss introduced her as Cally, shook hands all around and Boss gave the usual talk about keeping your mitts to yourself "or I'll break your fingers like, one at a time. Get me?" We all nodded.

Cally looked us all in the eye, one at a time. Not as tall as most, brown eyes, rail thin and her hands were rough from hard working. That portwine mark on her face drew the casual gaze, you would be trying not to see it and then not see her for it. She didn't say much, that first day, and none of us prodded her. She had a slightly cracked tea mug and a place in the nook at lunch, someone had shoved a tin of cookies-they didn't call them biscuits here and now-out in the middle of the table and someone else gave her a castoff shop apron to keep the gunk away from her street clothing.

Nobody made a big deal about it. Most of us had been there before, one time or another.

End of the day, she went back to the Sally Anne's and I went home the other way. And out of the corner of my eye I saw PC41 slinking at her heels.

Two days later PC41 was waiting on me at the door to the shop when I came to work. I opened the door; the Boss had come in about an hour afore time to open up the skylights, shake the clinkers through the grates and stoke the stoves. Coal was cheaper than electric and safer to deal with than coal-gas. So, we used electricity for running the machines and work lights, natural light for the rest of the time.

This was not unusual for the 'zeme. The Houses always had a mix of technologies in their establishments and their cities. What worked cheaply, was easy to maintain, and was well suited for the task was preferable to shiny and expensive. Horses instead of IC engines when horses would do the job-riding fence for example. When you needed to cover a square mile of crop quickly, then you went to mechanized implements. As simple a kind of implements as you could get. Tractors that were forty years out of date on AngTerra were highly regarded in the 'zeme; simple, durable and easy to maintain.

Cally was working alongside the Boss like she had for the last two days. Tending the stoves and filling the rag barrels by the machines. I nodded to the two of them as PC41 slid past me and vanished under the benches. The rest of that day Cally pulled parts from inventory, de-gunked cylinders, attached paperwork to jobs, spread oil clay on the floor and basically worked in the background. We knew she was there, but we didn't see her, or watch her. Boss gave her an advance on her week, told her to get a second set of overalls and a lunch bucket, told her bright and early every morning. She had the stoves to tend to, pull the shutters back from the skylights and make sure the floor was well salted with oil clay before the start of work. Gave her a key and waved her off to go home.

That evening she went back to the mission and PC41 came back to the rooming house with me.

CHAPTER 34

It was quiet for the rest of the year.

I asked PC41 over the push what was brewing between her and Cally. I got nothing much back in return, >satisfaction< and a migraine. Cally was settling in well.

We had three women and four men, counting me and the Boss among the crew; Cally made eight. She wasn't togged out for winter, and winter on the Hudson was nothing to fool with. I had spent a bit of 'white metal' that summer on a heavy coat, lined gloves, a watch cap, muks and leggings when I knew I was going to be here over the winter. She had arrived just before the Hudson Hawk, the winter storms, had come rolling in. She had 'sweet-fanny-adams' for any sort of harsh weather kit. We all knew this.

So, the women produced a locker full of mended clothing, one of the lads had canvas leggings that would turn the winds that he'd outgrown and never got rid of, coarse wool shirts and wool trousers came from the hope chest at the Sally Ann. The Boss had contacts among the 'Gentlemen' and got her a pair of insulated boots from across the veil-I was amused to see they were an LL Bean knock off. And PC41 and I 'happened' to have a set of lined mittens that had been mis-sized when I bought them. So, she was well set up for the Hawk.

It wasn't because she was a girl, this casual outfitting. They'd done it before for anyone that came in off the wharf to work with them. Anyone who needed a coat or a place to kip or a couple of meals on the cuff, they'd get it. If they got a foot inside the door and a taste of a job, they got more. "You work for the Shop. The shop provides." It had something to do with the House system the Fain and the Dai were born into. Once you were working in the House, you were more than a stranger and only a little bit less than blood.

It cut the other way too. If you were on the outside, you weren't likely to get squat or more than the back of a hand. A lot of discards and bindle floaters lived off of casual theft and begging. They slept rough, at the Sally Ann, or if they got up crossways with the local tunship-in Gaol. People fed them like they fed feral cats, if they looked harmless and appealing. If they looked more like pydogs, rough and ready to take a bite out of anything or anyone, they got the Patrol sicced on them and a bum's rush off the wharf and down river. Or worse. There were a few dead bodies every fortnight, here and there on the wharf. It was common enough, no one noticed.

If you walk in cold, like I did, but set up for the job and for the wharf, nobody made much of it. Didn't cut you any slack, but they didn't push you either. They watched how you worked and when you took a break, how you lent a hand and how you accepted a bit of help or a piece of advice. After a while, they took you at face value. You might not be much of a 'mate' and kept yourself to yourself, but you didn't put on airs and you kept your word. That made you all right.

Cally, she worked hard, thanked us quietly for the stake we gave her, gently fended off offers of bed and breakfast and watched over her shoulder all the time. Sat with her back to the wall when we coaxed her into the Cracked Head, the pub we favored; she drank carefully, watched her glass, watched the people around her. Especially she watched closely the Host, the Gimp who tended the place.

Word got around that he had tried to 'help' her when she hit the wharf-side. She'd turned her back on him and his offer.

Jambo, the bouncer, had words with his supposed employer over that. And the Gimp backed off. Made me think that Jambo was much better connected than the Host.

She carried a sailor's lock blade knife, razor sharp; she didn't wave it around but casually showed us that she knew how to use it. She didn't walk carelessly through the backstreets when shopping, had a good situational awareness. Street-smart, is what they would have said in New York, or the Smoke. And she tried to stay off the dockside proper night or day, stay out of sight of the river.

Whenever a Constable strolled down the dock side or a pair of them worked their way through the backstreets, she made herself scarce, faded into a friendly shop front or arcade and out of sight. I knew the second time I saw that move; she was on a list somewhere.

After the Hawk finally came down from the north to stay, things got slow for the small shops. We finished up all the major rebuilds, took on a double handful of small jobs-skimmers and the like-and tended to our workshops. That year we needed to refit the big lathe, for instance. The Boss paid about a third less for maintenance work, but it kept us all in bread and jam and kept us close at hand for if-and-when the season picked up.

This was normal; everyone laid up white metal in season for the winter's end or if they had an 'establishment' they opened the cellar storeroom and lived off of the larder they'd salted away.

I had more than enough in the way of hard cash tucked away that I didn't have to worry; PC41 was just as well off, ambushing pigeons and gulls, abusing the naiveté of the local rats and cozening the fishers. Cally, now Cally would be hurting come winter.

Boss, her given name was real dutchy and hard to

pronounce, so we just called her Boss. Boss didn't own the shop and had to answer to the owners; a third generation up from the wharf and not particularly sympathetic.

She could keep all the long-time hands on and give them make-work jobs to keep them on the books and available when the work spooled up, but casual labor like Cally and new hands like me she had to eventually let go. There wasn't enough work to justify keeping us on the till.

"Risley, Cally." She'd called us back into the break cubby at the end of that day. It was just after the Solstice. We had the lathe trued up, the place spit shined and all of the small engine jobs were finished and buttoned up. We stayed behind and the other workers somberly nodded to us as they left the shop. They knew.

I knew what was coming, Cally did too. "I have to let you go, until the spring thaw at least."

"Figured as much," I said, cradling my tea mug. "Can I leave my tools in the strong room?" I had a small rolling tool-chest that I wasn't going to try and horse up the stairs at the boarding house.

She nodded. She looked at Cally.

Cally had known this was coming. We'd told her how seasons went on the wharf and told her to keep things sweet with the Sally Ann's and put away as much white metal as she could. She just nodded. Thanked Boss and took the end of the year pay-packet. She nodded to me, looking me in the eye for once.

"You need anything, Cally, you can touch me anytime." I looked at Boss, she nodded. I nodded. "No funny business," I said, to Cally. "Right?"

Cally blinked. We hadn't said six words directly to each other in three months, and I was offering a stake in front of a witness. "No funny business?" She had an accent that I couldn't place, but it wasn't local. She'd filled out some, three months eating regular and sleeping safe helped, but she was still starvation thin.

"Nah, you can trust Risley about twice as far as Jambo can throw him." Grinned the Boss.

Cally smiled. Jambo liked Cally. Jambo was the bouncer at the pub the shop went to, the Cracked Head. The same pub whose Host had once tried to turn Cally out on the 'walk' as a revenue source. Jambo had a reputation for trying to throw dickheads across the wharf and into the river from the pub door. Never quite made the throw, but he was still growing. And he was connected, everyone knew that now, including the Gimp who tended bar at the Cracked Head. No funny business.

"Okay, I will remember that Mr. Risley."

"Josiah," I said and offered her my hand. She took it and shook it once, and I read her from topknot to heeltap before she left the shop. Walker. Like PC41 said.

I'd know her in the dark, even with her washed-out auras. And she had a lot of burned over spots in her auras. Burned almost to rags.

CHAPTER 35

I locked up my toolbox, put it in the strong room, shook Boss's hand again. "Keep an eye out for her," I said. "She's going to be going through a rough patch."

"I will. See you in the spring?"

I shrugged, nodded.

That weekend night I swung by the pub and stood a round of drinks for the shop, told the lot that I was going to enjoy my down time loafing about the docks and pubs while they worked their fingers to the bone under the hard, hard, Boss. They razzed me about coming into my donative from one of the big Western houses-Mihaly or the like. I laughed it off, stood another round and noted that we had a strange face in the background. It wasn't unusual to have a stranger drinking in 'our' pub. But he made me uneasy.

He wasn't watching us; he was watching the door and our Jambo and the Host. The door opened and a girl came in shrugging off her heavy coat in the sudden warmth, handing it to Jambo to hang it up at the cubby by the entrance.

Jambo cut down on theft and other transgressions, working as a doorman and bouncer while he kept an eye on us-and on the Host. The change never came back light or the drinks watered when Jambo was about. And the fights were rare and brief.

The watcher marked the girl at the door, then turned his

gaze on the Host who was lurking behind a battery of taps, the Host shook his grizzled head slightly. The watcher dismissed that girl and went back to watching the door. I turned to finish my beer and lightly swept the room.

PC41 rubbed against my leg. I pushed. >careful<

>hunter<

>agree< I pushed back. The watcher was by the hallway to the toilets. I finished my beer, made a remark about leasing beer and not purchasing, then made my way to the toilets.

The hunter sat with his back to the wall, still wearing a heavy peacoat in the warmth of the snuggery and a black lambswool hat with a short visor on the table in front of him.

For anyone to leave by the backdoor they'd have to go past the observer, anyone coming in the door would have to face him. Jambo was sitting at the cubby with his back to the man, chatting up someone, watching all the people in the snuggery and at the saloon bar at the same time. He was watching the corner where the stranger perched by a mirror on a wall of the snug, but no more than usual. Jambo was not in the loop. The Host was.

I brushed by the stranger, gingerly trailed the net of my auras through the edge of his, went to the toilet and then back to the door. I collected my coat, slapped Jambo on the back and slipped out the door.

It was early evening yet, cold and the snow crisp under foot where it hadn't been trodden into freezing slosh. PC41 collected me and led the way, away from the pub and past our boarding house. The watcher was an Eisenring Proctor. I'd thought as much from the hat, it being identical to the issue head piece for the uniformed 'Ring. But it was good to be sure.

He wasn't a D'draig, or much of anything really, but he'd been set to watch a mouse hole. And I had an uneasy guess at which mouse he was after.

>agree< Came the push.

>she<

>bring< PC41 faded into the darkness.

And I slipped into a tea shop close by the mission, took a table and ordered some tea, sandwiches and cookies for two. I sat at the back of the shop, in the darkest corner of the shop and waited. I kept touching the place at my hip where my needler rode, when it wasn't locked away. Discards didn't carry a needler usually, but I'd felt the need to carry a weapon lately.

Cally came through the door, wearing her secondhand winter finery and looking both wary and bewildered. PC41 will have that effect at the best of times. She saw me, started to shy away and then lurched slightly, as if something pushed her. She sat down at my table, with her back to the windows and doors. She made to doff her heavy coat and muffler.

"Don't, you're cold. I can tell. Take the gloves off and warm your hands on the mug."

"What…"

"You've been shying at shadows since you got off the boat. Now there is a shadow on the wharf. Somebody is looking for you, and I have the notion it's the 'Ring.'" I didn't bother to differentiate between the Provos and Unity, both were equally a threat.

Her face drained and her birthmark stood clear against her pale face.

"Take a drink and have some of the bacon sandwiches." I drank some tea and had a bite too. "Down in the pub, there is a proctor eyeing them that comes through the door. Every woman."

"Mother…Meg" She stopped breathing.

"Drink and have a bite. Don't draw eyes. She brought you to me."

She blinked rapidly, frowned. "You see her, Bast and her brother Baig?"

Brother and sister?

>mirth< Came over the push.

"PC41, yes."

She relaxed for a moment. "I thought I was losing my mind, no one else saw-" Then she tensed up again. "Proctor, I have to go-"

"Take a calming breath, have a sip of tea, take a bite and keep your bleeding head down. He has a description, I think, from that pig-bugger tending the bar at the pub." I took another sip. "For some reason Jambo isn't in on the deal."

"Jambo's sister has-" She made a gesture to the mark on her face. "Jambo told him to sod off and threatened to have him kneecapped and turfed out." Bravo Jambo.

"That Eisenring will have Jambo on toast and give the Host a pouch of white metal and the freehold to the pub, if he gets you. If you rabbit and they will see you rabbit, runners always draw hunters, you will take Jambo and likely the Boss and the shop down with you. Proctors and Blacklegs like that sort of solution. It discourages scum like us and it makes the paperwork simple."

"What to do? What to do?"

I just smiled at her. "We'll let Bast sort it out." I finished my mug and ordered another one.

>well< I pushed.

>happy not< And I got an image of the Eisenring from the pub leaving, heading towards the mission. I about spilled my tea in my lap. This was new, pushing images.

>she taught<

Right. Eisenring first and then sort out who taught who. "Now, I am going to leave you right here; you are going to have another mug of tea, finish the tucker, make the last mug last. Bast and I are going for a walk." She took a deep breath. "No argument. Bast will come back and take you to the Sally Ann's, when it is safe."

I got up and patted her face, on the unmarred side. "Take

this however you want. Bast likes you. And that will make a difference."

More than you would ever know, Cally.

CHAPTER 36

PC41, Bast if you will, joined me outside of the tea shop. >watch her< I got a sullen agreement, I think, back over the push. Bast shimmered and was male and pitch black. He drifted through the doorway and in my enhanced awareness, I felt him take up a position under her chair.

I turned my collar up to the freshening wind and the spitting snow. I swept the street around the mission and picked up three bindle floaters who were nothing more than what they should be, a lock rattler pretending to patrol the block and the thrice-damned Eisenring strutting in the cold, intending to roust the Sally Ann's no doubt. By his own self.

I fell into step behind and then drew alongside of him. He shied when I came out of the shadows to his right, started to draw a weapon.

"Will you be going away or coming back, and your ownself?" I asked him quietly, looking straight ahead and walking at a quick step. He formed on me; a habit ingrained in response to a challenge phrase.

"Coming back, away from away." He was staring at my profile; wondering who the hell I was, what the hell I was, where the hell I stood in the Croft. I'd gave him a challenge for the midlevel degrees. A challenge he knew but was not passed to initiate. Dai worried at who fed you, the Eisenring calculated where you stood in the Croft.

My eyes were focused, a thousand yards away. "Ware'

reckless eyeballs." I muttered, and his head snapped around to look straight ahead.

In the great hall, they would have fair rang his chimes on him breaking lock like that.

"Follow, Hasrai." And I turned to the right and went down an alley not much wider than my shoulders, an alley I had marked before I'd come up on his blind side. He hesitated, then turned and followed me in. I think he did draw a weapon, a baton or club, but it didn't do him any good.

Ten yards into the darkness of the alley, I had him on his knees before I turned to face him. I had him peeled to his soul's center shortly thereafter. I gathered his name, his position, his brief, his support and what news he had for his handlers. We were in luck, of a sort.

Milburn, the Eisenring, had a hunting brief, with a wide and vague description of Cally leMere. And an order to seize and extradite her across the sea. The portwine stain figured largely in the description. The Unity Eisenring had traced her as far as York on the Hudson, here in 'zeme. And the Provos decided to help out the Unity Eisenring in bringing their runner home. Professional courtesy, from one nest of rats to another nest of rats. The Host had heard about them looking for a portwine bint, fresh from overseas and hooked up with Milburn the proctor.

Milburn was a Radman proctor, an entry ranker within the Provisional Eisenring, who was liaising with the Customs and Enforcement Blacklegs. Fancy term for being Mobbed up.

He was about two steps above a lock rattler and a long ladder below a Township Constable or a Registry Marshal. The Radman didn't want to share with his squaddies, it was going to be his righteous collar alone and a step up the ladder. And maybe share a bit of overseas strange with his mate, the Host, before they passed her on to the Unity Eisenring.

He was pissing himself at the end of the peel.

I stopped his heart. Robbed him and bundled the corpse down a convenient hatchway in the boardwalk, into the river beneath running cold and dark. Then I drifted through the neighborhood ditching the contents of his pockets where they'd do some good or not be found.

And I went back to the pub to have a heart to heart with Jambo, outside, where the Host couldn't see us chat. I'd make sure that Jambo knew Milburn's plan for a little bint from overseas, including sharing her with his good mate. The Host.

Bast took Cally back to the mission and slept at her feet that night, calming her. Keeping her from doing a bunk. I went back to my cot and washed my hands three times in very hot water in the washroom. Peeling is dirty work. Dirtier than working on a diesel.

The next day I met her again for a meal at the tearoom. She was escorted to me by PC41, we had a light lunch and I rested my hand a respectable two inches from hers. With PC41-Bast-sitting under her chair. She didn't see my manifested webs drift over her, but she felt them. She didn't shy away, but she was wary.

That was good. It meant her auras were strengthening. I was going to be encouraging that. I was also going to have her eating better, on my tael as it was.

And I was going to introduce an old family remedy to her, known by my people for long generations, a poultice bleaching the portwine mark on her face. A remedy I made up on the run, as it was. Corn Meal and a bit of lemon juice soaked into a plaster, to fade the mark. Not erasing it, that would draw notice now, but fading it. One of the hardest things I'd ever done with the auras, to be so delicate at it. I started it at the tea shop that day.

There was a new Host at the pub two days later, Jambo

was still the chucker out, the new Host was a kissing cousin of Jambo, I think. The old one, the Gimp, was just gone. The Customs and Enforcement jacks nosed about looking for their missing Eisenring but gave it up as not worth the lantern oil.

'Somebody will eventually brag about doing a jack and then us and the fooking 'Ring would have the sorry bugger on toast.' Was the opinion of one of the Constables, at the snug after we bought his third round that night.

And I spent more time with Cally and Bast or Baig. It varied day to day. A much as we could manage and not overstep bounds and draw attention.

Which was a foolish notion when you look back at it; not drawing attention.

CHAPTER 37

S ix weeks after the high solstice Cally and I sat down to dinner again as was our habit. Bast, PC41, was curled about her ankles and I was sitting close to her at a four-top. She was on my left; I had my dominate hand free for anything. I was facing the doors.

Late tea had become a regular thing for all of us. She sat close within my auric net, and I continued to knit the many burned-out places in her auras. She spent her time trying to pry into my dubious background while I patched her talent.

This got us a lot of knowing looks and minor kindnesses from all the nosey Dot's on the harborside. They had a definite, but wrong, opinion on what was brewing in the teapot. Cally knew their opinions too, but she felt safe with me and Meg knows I never put a foot wrong.

I had made two trips to Bensenille to close out the deposit boxes and thin my caches there. Disposing much of Josiah Braxton, of faded memory. Keeping all the weapons and what little folding money from AngTerra I had left. I brought it all, bit by bit, back to my rooms, in the boarding house. The down season was ending, but we couldn't go back to the shop. I knew we were going to have to move on, very soon. All of us.

Cally glared at me over a glass of cider. "Who feeds you?" Oi, that again.

"You know, I hear on AngTerra the opening conversational gambit is 'what's your sign?' instead of asking whose table you have your knees under."

"Clever arse."

"Hmm. That is a new one, haven't heard it before." I cut another morsel out of the chop I was worrying at and swept the local. We were not in the Cracked Head; it was still getting much too much open attention from Customs and Enforcement Jacks wearing badly tailored street wear. I didn't want them getting a better look at me, or Cally. That Rat Bastard Milburn was long gone, but there might be other lice hanging about.

"Bast talks to me, at night, in the dormitory."

"He does?"

Cally frowned at me. "She does. She says your story is not hers to tell."

"Courteous of him. You want a short explanation or a shorter explanation?"

She grunted and glared at me out of the corner of her eye.

She was brighter than I had given her credit for, when she first came off the skimmer. Too bright by half. And knowing what I, and PC41 were all about, would likely get her killed. But not knowing was just as likely to end in her getting killed.

"Nobody feeds me," I tore a yeasty roll in two, slathered honey butter on it. "I am houseless."

"And you were of a house, once?" Houses. For the 'zeme it always came to Houses and who your people are or were. For AngTerra the question was what you did for your living, the Hanse wanted to know how you fitted into the community; Alba wanted to know a bit of all that about you, told over a pint and toad in the hole and maybe a bit of backgammon. I liked Alba; it shows doesn't it?

"You ask much and risk more." I looked in her brown eyes and wondered if PC41-Bast-was having me on. Auras and hormones. I placed my left hand on her dominant hand, to my left of the table, and manifested fully, just in case. She did know how to use that long lock-bladed knife. I leaned in close to her, she leaned across to me. "Ich bin vom Eisenring," I said, just above a whisper, in her right ear. Not an endearment you would expect, would you?

"Ah lalala Meg," she whispered, she turned to face me fully, her eyes darkened, and she shivered. The auras swirled and strengthened about her. Freeze, flee or fight-all the primary colours. She closed her eyes, took a slow deep breath and her auras stilled and faded.

"Oh, my lady," she said finally, and I took my hand from hers. "And Bast led me to you?"

PC41 I thought. "And how is your flounder?"

She blinked twice, then heard the footsteps approaching. "Very good. But the fresh vegetables are most excellent. Out of season but most welcome." She still had the accent, but her Creole had expanded. Not from rubbing up against the wrench turners in the shop. Or me for that matter. Sally Ann's?

"More cider?" The server had brought a carafe.

"Please," I said. "And the tart." The server nodded and topped off our glasses with a knowing smile. Then she left.

I turned to Cally. "Now your story."

"From a House," she began, "from a lineage within a proscribed house. In the homelands." She picked up her glass and sipped at the cider. I could feel her pulse racing at the memory. "I was going to be a Veterinary Practioner, large animals. Six months in lecture halls, six months in labs and tutorials, twenty months in practicum assignments and I would have had a cert in Veterinary practice. I would have been supervised by a degreed Veterinary, but that would have been fine. Less paperwork, less responsibility. Then I manifested, late and weakly, thirteen weeks short of completion of the programme."

"Walker."

She nodded. "For the Common Good I was placed in

reserve. They found that I was not suited to service, but I might have potential to pass my talent on to a new generation."

I made a very short, obscene, description of those Eurotrash bastards. It sounded better in *Frankii* than it would have in Creole or Spanglish. She flushed.

It was an accepted practice in the Unity Commonality; the Dai were owned by the *burgrij*-what was called the Fain elsewhere-in common. The Great Houses were disestablished; after a war, a civil war and a revolution. And a terror. A fair number of the old Houses, Great and Small, were broken on the wheel and the bulk of their talented folk who survived fled to the west. Others had sworn to the Unity-what later became the Unity Communality, then later still just the Commonality. To the disgust of the Unity the Houses in the west had gleefully absorbed the refugees and refused to join with the Common Good. They had sent the Unity representatives back with a flea in their ear, or sometimes they sent just their ears.

It happened in the Western Hemisphere Houses as well, North and South, this breeding for talent. It was an occasional, shameful, abuse and not an accepted practice. One House might have that twist incorporated into their Stud Book and the folk a half mile down river would spit on the ground at the mention of that Book and that House. Duels and blood feuds occurred over that twist. But that attitude faded as time brought changes. Less and less embracing of runners and more tolerant of projects to 'enhance' the gene pool. In the last hundred years the Unity or Commonality, if you will, had forged closer links to the Confederated houses. And not for the better, in my opinion. I had a close acquaintance with the Commonality, through the Unity Eisenring. I despised them on the whole, more than I despised the Eisenring. Which was saying something.

A constellation of Great Houses, mainly standing West

of the Big River, had a stated policy of offering refuge to any manifested Dai fleeing that sort of abuse or anyone just fleeing a house that tolerated that practice. This had caused a lot of stiff notes between Croton House and the houses on the Grass and in the Sunset Range. The Registry Marshals would send out Blacklegs to extract or convince the runners to return. This never ended well for the Blacklegs, tar and feathers were the best they could hope for. If the Pika found them on the Grass, their bones bleached underfoot.

East of Big River, the Registry writ ran stronger and Croton-on-the-Hudson was courting the favor of the Unity. "They will be back," I said.

"Yes. I was just high status enough that my escape would be noticed by the authorities. And remarked on by the wrong sort of person, longing for a revanchist time. An example made for the rest to contemplate, no?"

"The wharf can conceal you only so long. So, you need to go under the hill."

She shook her head. "I'd thought about the Sunset Range."

I shook my head. "Long trip and many eyes and, forgive me, you are marked."

"Nothing to forgive. The poultice is etching it away, but it will return. It always does."

PC41 pushed at me. >linked talent<

I formed an image of me kicking a can into the river. Kicking three cans in the river. Kicking a ceramic cat into the river.

>mirth<

"Right. I have a set of rooms hired, around the corner and up a flight of stairs. You doss there for the night, don't go back to the mission." Or longer. I pushed a key to her. And a small packet of white metal.

"And you?" Her eyes narrowed at me over the key and the

packet.

"I'll be going back to the boarding house. You have anything you need or want from the mission?"

She thought about it. "Clothing. Some sundries. Nothing more."

"Maybe I can wrinkle them out of the Sally Ann's, but if needs must we can buy more."

"Why?" She waved her left hand slightly over the dishes, like shooing away a fly.

"We have enemies in common. I need to go 'under the hill' as well." They brought the tart and the tab. I think they undercharged me.

Outside it was, if anything, colder still. I walked with her around the corner, to the threshold, opened the outer door and escorted her up the stairs. She opened the door and PC41-Baig-slipped through and cleared the room. Neat as any entry team ever did, with less fuss.

"Coal heat, electric light, running water and an ensuite loo. You have an electric hob to give you hot water. Stay put unless PC41-"

"Bast."

I bit my tongue. "pulls you out. There should be tea and cookies and a tin of food for-" I paused. "Bast in the boatman's pantry."

"Take care." She was sincere.

I paused for a second. "I will." And I left her there, she double locked the door behind me, and I went back to the boarding house.

In the morning I loitered in the public rooms at the boarding house. A gentleman of leisure drinking tea and skimming through the scandal sheets and the local rag of record. Making lists in my head.

Everything I thought I needed, would fit in the duster I had in the back of my closet. White metal, weapons, my identity papers for the Remnant Royal Colonies. I didn't have anything for Cally in the way of papers, but in the RRC I had my own contacts and cobblers that I had developed relationships with when I was constructing my suitcase. And once across the veil I planned to take a motor coaster up to the Hanoverian Establishment and a steam train to the Lakes and their own set of wharves. I was taking Cally along.

Why. Couldn't say. PC41 was insistent that this was the optimum thing.

Bast. I was uncomfortable with the name, but PC41 was too much of a 'tell' if I had to discuss him with…somebody.

We, PC41 and I, were working together very well and yet I still had no idea of how or why he landed in my lap. She was unclear on that event as well. It wasn't random, from what I could gather, but it wasn't organized.

>best choice< Was all the explanation I got. And as how the partnership worked, her guess was no better than mine.

I finished the list late in the afternoon. Went to the shop and called on the Boss.

"I'm moving on."

"With Cally?" She grinned at my open consternation. "It's a small bleeding town, the riverfront, and everyone knows everyone else's' dirty business. Nobody knows nothing about you or Cally, and everybody knows everything."

I knew the folks at the tea shop were knitting webs for Cally and me, but the Boss? Romantic? "I think I followed that. But the Rat Bastards will be back." The Eisenring.

She nodded. All serious now. "They are back, just being on the low about it. The Cracked Head has a new long-term tenant in one of the rooms over the bar. The Rat Bastards think Jambo had a hand in that one tosser going in the river."

"The river?" Butter wouldn't melt in my mouth.

"Yeah, they found a bloater with a Rat Bastard tattoo floating in Ratan Bay, where the river tends to drop trash for the crabs to cycle. It was our own wee rat bastard, a disgrace to his mother's memory. So, the Constables and the black-hearted Eisenring are investigating his demise. Together in the same bunk."

"Feel sorry for the Constables."

"Well they are having the Provo squaddies 'consult' closely with them on every floater the Harbor Constables recover. It will put you right off a good crab boil, it will."

CHAPTER 38

I couldn't get past the doors to the mission that Cally had sheltered in. They were sympathetic, but wary. One of the porters came to me at the entrance, shook my hand and was openly friendly, calling me by someone else's name.

"Thomas Jackson, lord bless me, but it has been a long time."

I picked up a name from his blazer, a dark blue with thin red piping at the sleeve. Hoskinson. It wasn't the name I picked up when I, gently, sifted him at the handshake. But it would do.

"Hosk! Well, you are working for the Sally Ann's. I didn't believe that for a moment when they told me. An old rounder like you?"

"Changes, they come whether or not you wish them to."

"Come have a pot of tea and a bite with me Hosk, tell me how you came to the Sally Ann's and what's happening in your life now."

"Gladly, let me tell the new Head porter." And he flicked a glance to the side. But I still had his hand in mine, and I had an idea of what he wanted to tell me. Eisenrings.

He ducked in and came out with a heavy wool overcoat on and carrying a stick that would do for stunning cattle. We walked up the lane away from the river and the mission, talking quietly as sober men do, not hiding our conversation. Two acquaintants long gone from home.

At the patisserie, a pot of tea between us and his back to the street, he told me what was about.

He began to spin his legend. "Can't stay long. If they ask, I know you from the Sunset Range; I got the knife the short generation before you. Went about and around and hit bottom, came to the Sally Ann's up on the Seaway." I nodded. Always shade a covey of lies with the truth. "This very morning the Marshals, the Provos and a pair of lice from across the water all stuck their noses into the mission. Took the SA officers away for questioning. Dressed up the lice and all as our officers; fools. Thugs not knowing how to hold the Book let along hold services."

I flicked my eyes to the side as someone came towards the table, gave him a spiel about liking dealing with motors better than horses. A waiter came and swapped out the tea pot, put a turnover in front of each of us and left the tab. I palmed the tab, which was two sheets of paper, one handwritten. 'jacks outside.' The handwritten one said.

Hoskinson went on. "The girl is what they want. The lice want her damn badly and think the mission is hiding her. Tore up the place and went to roughing up everybody."

"Eat the pastry Hos' and I'll tell you what I've heard from the old House." And I started in with the latest gossip manufactured by Lyn in her last letter to me.

I had the two rat bastards outside clocked; even lurking in the street outside, I had them clocked. I felt a nudge at an ankle and knew PC41 was about. They were at the very limit of my extended range now, but I knew where they were.

I finished my pastry and motioned the waiter over, paid the tab and left a little extra. "I got to be on my way, thinking of pulling up stakes and off to the south and away from the Hudson Hawk." We both laughed at getting well away from winter. I shook hands again with him, and took my time bundling up at the door, looking over the lane outside.

On the way up the lane I had the jacks well spotted. Thought they'd pass for bindle floaters while wearing clean shoes. Pissy tradecraft.

I turned into a convenient doorway out of the wind and tried to light my pipe, teasing them closer. Then I let the net thread through their auras. I didn't need much, I was not intending to drop them on the walk. That would draw attention. I just made one of them violently sick.

The sick one fell to his knees, dropping his bindle and throwing everything he'd eaten for the last day on top of it. Too well fed he was.

I turned and looked at the jack being sick all over the boardwalk not ten feet from me, then cussed in Creole and quickly walked upwind, like anyone would have done, holding a fold of my muffler over my face.

His backup was torn between following me, tending to his partner, or following Hoskinson who'd popped out and then back in the patisserie cussing the 'drunken bastards' fouling the walk. That brought three people out of the shop with buckets of steaming water, brooms and foul language, washing the pair of jacks out into the middle of the lane and threatening to call the constables on them.

I was away and around the corner quickly and alone. It was time and past time to get out of here and 'under elf hill'.

We, PC 41 and I, went into the boarding house by the back door, the one that didn't get used much. There wasn't anyone there that I had to worry about, but people being people I figured one of them would drop a casual word to someone about me walking out with Cally. If the jacks knew she was bunking at the Sally Ann's, they'd be around to see me right soon.

I got my duster out of the closet, made sure I had the loadout I wanted in the pockets and webbing, left the coat I'd been wearing behind. I was down the back stairs and dropped a pouch of white metal on the counter in the kitchen.

The Lady of the house, nodded, scooped the pouch up and said, "Never saw you this day at breakfast or last night after supper." She sniffed, spat into the waste bin. "Fooking jacks." And went back to stirring the kettle.

And I went to collect Cally.

CHAPTER 39

I let PC41, Bast, lead the way into the hide I had Cally in. She wasn't armed as such, coming from the Commonality and being doubly suspect coming from a proscribed House, she wouldn't have had arms training. She wasn't a trustworthy citizen in their eyes.

But she had that knife. Someone had given her the basics in filleting and gutting, and she had the attitude. Did not want to get stuck on accident.

>come<

PC41 pushed at me. I came in and told Cally she was rumbled, we were going to just leave all her stuff behind. She wasn't too broken up, she'd run before.

"Where to?"

"There's a postern, nearby."

She stopped gathering what things she had, tucking underwear and socks and other items in her coat pockets and her bag. "I can't-"

Bast nudged her, hard.

"Don't worry, let Bast and I worry. Off we go.

And we went down the stairs and out the back into the narrow lane. It had dustbins and sheds and the occasional outdoor jakes all along it, and it was dark as a mine now.

PC41 slipped ahead and I brought Cally along, not letting her out of my reach and keeping her calm. Six blocks along the back streets, north and then three blocks west to the postern that PC41 had located.

The postern was in the back of a pawnshop. It was not a part of the shop; you couldn't access it from the pawnshop as far as I could tell. You came in a narrow door at the back of the building, inside there was a hall with a stairway leading to an apartment on the second floor. Under the stairway was a low door, apparently to storage.

That was the entrance. You ducked through the door and you were in the postern. The postern was thirty feet long and ended in a wooden wall with a sun wheel painted on weathered planks. The sun wheel, a circle with a cross encompassed within it, was there to help the Walker focus on the path. For anyone not gifted with Walking, it didn't do a damn thing. I knew, I'd been in there once.

There was a table, a wooden chest on the table with a lining of copper mesh, a set of oil lamps, a bucket of sand and a coat closet at the end by the entrance. No guards, no wards and not an Eisenring to be seen. Grand.

"Can you feel it?" Cally asked.

"No." I could feel it, through her. But I wasn't going to confuse the issue.

"I couldn't feel a gate, ever. I had the 'gift', but I was blind to the paths."

The postern was responding to her, the air between us and the sun wheel began to ripple like heat waves over cobblestones or asphalt. I could 'feel' the gate building around her and in front of us. I heard footsteps overhead on the stairs, someone in the building had felt the gate start to open. I couldn't sense them, even with PC41 tucked up under my duster.

Cally walked forward, into the waves. I was behind her, a spring needle gun in my hand, facing the doorway behind us. Halos formed around the oil lamps, polychromatic halos. Shadows fluttered in the half light and the door began to swing open.

Whoever it was, they had a long gun in their hands. And my 'gift' could neither see nor touch him. I dumped a short spray of needles from my spring gun high into the ancient planks of the postern *adit*, over the door and over the head of the keeper. Whoever it was jerked back and shut the door with a thud.

Then I bumped into Cally.

She was very slowly feeling her way towards the Sun Wheel, glowing at the end of the passage. Carefully stepping, like walking on slick stones in a knee-deep stream. Arms out for balance, white mist trailing from her fingers, her head thrown back facing the wide and dark timbers of the ceiling, her eyes closed. I bumped into her, but she didn't falter or stumble.

I pocketed my needle gun. To free my hands. There were many Cally's before me. One wore a light blue smock, two had heavy sea coats with salt crusts; two had long hair braided with some sort of wire and one had close trimmed hair under a watch cap. And then, with the next step, all changed. The blue smock vanished and one of the apparitions lost the sea coat and gained a parka with fur trim. And they took another step forward, alongside of Cally and before me.

I had a flash of insight, Walkers and Skrenners were aspects of the same 'gift'. I tucked it away, the insight, and placed my right hand on her shoulder. Only our Cally with the watch cap remained, she was deep within my aura, but only when I touched her. I walked behind her and close in step. She knew I was there, and Bast. And she pushed that knowledge aside, following the path.

The Sun Wheel was at our back and we were walking towards a high door with a half-moon transom back lit by the sun. There was a heavy table to the left of the door with a twin goosenecked lamp, a box a foot on a side, a ledger and a pen case. The heavy timbers to our sides were gone and there was a white ceramic tile wall with patterns fired into the tile. No one was waiting at the door, but I knew there would be a reaction. Soon.

We passed through a shimmering membrane; at a border marked by a broad silvered line in the tiled wall. Then Cally was one person again. She sagged into my arms. Bast climbed out of the front of my duster over the top of Cally, landing on the tiled floor in front of the door and then leaping to the ledge at the base of the transom.

>guards< I pushed at Bast.

>not< He nudged at the transom window. >yet<

I got under Cally and deadlifted her across my left shoulder. In three steps we were at the table, I sat her on the inlaid top next to the unlit oil lamps and pushed the ledger and the pen case to the floor. She slumped to lean on the wall, and I moved closer towards the door, pressed my hand on it.

The door started to slide, into a pocket on the left side. I punched through the opening gap with my right hand and pulled hard on the door with my left to sheath it home in the pocket. The guard went down with a clatter, dropping a long wide blade on the tiles. One behind him had a spring bow, a leather cuirass, and dark goggles. As I thrust through the door my 'gift' manifested and I swept the building and dropped the bowman with the same breath.

>clear< I pushed.

>done< Came back from PC41 and she pushed through the transom above us, dropped on the other side of the pocket door and began to clear the rooms above.

Neither of the guards were dead, but they were out cold. One had a concussion, by the way his auras bent and puddled; the other I'd simply pinched a flow in his third Charka. Another cognac hangover without the pleasure of knocking back a glass. I searched them quickly, listening for PC41 or reinforcements to the guards. Except for their bronze age weapon load out, they were unremarkable. Silver coins in the belts, Hanoverian Exile Pounds with George Rex IV of England stamped on them. Key rings. Working knives, much like the Swiss made on AngTerra. Wallets on chains, with local currency and papers. Spring Needle guns, small diameter and short range. I swept it all into the pockets of my duster.

Bast slithered down the stairway, tile steps and hardwood railings. >nothing<

I nodded and went back through the pocket door, having my auras thin out as I did. I didn't know that could be done, never happened before but I'd never crossed through a postern before. Never had my 'gift' up and manifested when I was transiting either. And then the ha'penny dropped. This postern was not the match to the one behind the pawn shop on 'zeme.

The walls were tiled, the floor inlaid wood and the guards well turned out, if indifferently trained. I stepped out into the hallway again, knelt and ran my net through one of the guards. Carefully.

It was not a lost postern, at least not to the Provo Eisenring. And I had kicked the proverbial paraffin tin over into the campfire. No time to waste.

I got Cally to stand and dumped as much energy as I dared into her. "Come on," I said, rubbing her neck and coaxing her auras back into line. "Up and off we go."

We got out of there with just one more dust up. I sucker punched the doorman, who was wearing more conventional body armor and carrying a big bore spring needle gun along with an evergreen 10mm automatic. I scooped up his wallet and keyset. I tucked the 3mm spring gun into the duster, left the automatic. I was making such a collection that I was beginning to clank when I walked. I'd left the bronze age weapons behind, since I wasn't planning on doing any bloodletting in an *adit* gallery anytime soon.

Outside the sun was setting to the west and it was Summer-late summer. I knew we'd walked through time again. At least we'd come out where I'd hoped.

The silver Exile Five Pound coins told me we were in the Remnant Colonies in the Western Hemisphere and the cityscape to the east told me we were across the river from the Free City of York. But I knew the here and now we were in. It was home.

I peeled Cally's coat from her in the foyer of the row house that contained the postern. emptied the coat's pockets into the big purse she'd taken to carrying across her body. I got her down the stairs and out on to the street with the coat draped over her shoulders, two houses down I dropped the coat beside a dustbin. She was still wobbly on her pins, leaning into me, Bast was nudging her along.

A few people gave us hard looks as we walked down the street, towards the river. But I gave as good as we got, and they decided it was not their problem to claim. It helped that about a block down the street from the entrance to the postern she turned to the gutter and vomited. I held her up, put on a long-suffering face and then gently wiped her mouth and chin with a handkerchief from my pocket.

"She's not at all well?"

I looked up at a Grandmother, the sort you see on the telenovels. Grey hair, proper frock, sensible shoes and an umbrella sturdy enough to break rocks. She was eyeing me with intent to do grievous bodily harm if I was after needing it.

I shook my head. "Sloe Gin at the hen party, for the cousins' wedding." I'd dropped into the broad accents I'd had in the Smoke.

She nodded, her eyes lightened up, clucked her tongue and commiserated. "Ach, that is a terrible drunk."

"It is that, they called me on the blower for a pick up and an escort. There will be sharp words when she is at home, out on her own and drinking so early to boot."

She nodded again. Told me to be sure and hydrate her and passed by between me and the building we were stopped in front of. She was what I thought she should be, her auras trailing along behind her like flags on a ship.

After she had the shout into the gutter Cally was better. "I'm thirsty Jos, my head aches and I'm thirsty."

"We got a fair bit to go, but the first place we find we'll have a sit down and a cup of tea."

"Alright." She gobbed up another bit of sick. "I am so thirsty."

We were in West York across the river, in an up and coming stretch of waterfront. I was overdressed to a degree, Cally since she lost her coat was conservatively underdressed in wool slacks and a long-sleeved top. But we didn't draw much notice; she was walking better, and she had her arm tucked into the crook of my right arm. I didn't like that, much. I was right-handed. The Firm did train us to be competent with both hands, as far as use of weapons. But my best scores with a gun were with my right hand. Knives, now knives were a different matter.

The neighborhood changed as we got closer to the river. There were fewer three decker row houses that had been cut into flats. Those row houses had a foyer tacked on at the top of the outside stairs that had an open mail cubby. A cubby that had six or so mailboxes, for the tenants. No doormen that I could see.

The row houses that had the postern among them had been better maintained than I remembered any of the flats in West York being, the trim freshly painted and the bricks newly pointed. The mailboxes at the house containing the postern had been polished brass, the names printed on the cards and not scrawled on a scrap of paper. The mail cubby had a substantial door to the street and another one leading to the foyer where I cold cocked the doorman. Again, a pointer that the postern back on the wharf was a front. We were lucky. Now to copper our bets.

There more low fronted commercial shops, some with a multi-story house behind the shop. Some used to be chandlers or other maritime suppliers, by the names carved into the lintels over the bay windows or the doors. But they were upscale clothing and notions boutiques now, or trendy tea shops. This area was on the rise.

I found a coffee shop, it used to be a rope chandler by the carving over the lintel, ushered Cally in and seated her. The proprietor was uneasy, I was wearing a long canvas duster that had very full, lumpy, pockets. I walked up to the counter, it was self-serve which was odd, no waiters or attendants with an apron on. There was a Mermaid printed on the coffee cups, a bleed over from AngTerra?

"My principle has been taken ill," I leaned in close to softly spin the lie. "I would normally take her back to the Residence across the river but-" I invited a comment.

"Perhaps a discreet hostel with a spa? To restore her spirits?" He looked at her with a considering eye. Drunk in the afternoon, on foot, but fairly well dressed and sporting an armed escort: upper middle class?

I smiled, slid a one-inch stack of five-pound coins across the counter. "I thought you might be able to steer me straight."

The coins vanished, a cup of coffee appeared, and the barman smiled for the first time since I darkened his door. Before Cally took two shaky sips of the coffee, we had a link girl to guide us to a nearby spa-hostel.

I settled Cally in the hostel, cautioned her to keep quiet as a mouse and to let them pamper her. Then I prepaid her bill, said I would be back in two hours or less to take her home. I slipped them an additional stack of coins and instructions to freshen her clothing and touch up her makeup. They were uncertain about her, they could tell the clothing wasn't right for the way we were fronting her, but the money was right. They smiled and told me they'd do their best.

I left her with Bast, PC41, lurking in the shadows.

I wasn't known here, in West York. I had an active account at a minor credit cooperative and caches at two other banking houses. Clothing, weapons, identity papers and such were in deposit safes at the banks. But I hadn't stayed on this side of the river when I came over from the Smoke on holiday. I wasn't familiar with the hostels on offer here. And they were definitely not acquainted with me.

In York proper I had a history at a couple of middling hostels, connected to tourist surface traffic across the ocean. In passenger steamers and not the newish turbines. And I currently did not look much like the James Braxton that had stayed in those Midtown hostels.

The Firm knew I came here to the Free City, from the Estuary as they called the Smoke. I occasionally liked to have a bit of a holiday away from the Firm and the City. They knew the papers I used and the banks I washed my money through, and they were happy on the most part with me being there, in the Free City of York. They thought that they could reach out and take me anytime, at need.

The Firm did not have the slightest inkling I had money on the West side of the river. If they did, things would get difficult, to say the very least. But in the last twelve years that I had been building my 'suitcase' I'd not had a nibble at my block of cheese.

I walked northward, keeping the river and the riverfront to my right hand and browsed for a place to hole up. I was maybe two to three blocks inland from the riverfront proper. The path varied as the drunken cow that laid out the lanes had wandered. It was getting on dark; the streetlights were coming on and the lights over the doorways indicated what places were open for custom. There were linkboys and linkgirls, costumed appropriately for two centuries past and well coached in archaic English. There were Sedan Chairs in front of the Royalist Exile hostels, that were taking costumed marks to themed pubs and clubs.

There were more contemporary hostels that boasted that 'the party never stops' and had head-splitting music rattling the windows fronting the street.

There were business chain hostels, with discrete entrances and gold lettering on the single window at the front. A window that let passers-by see only a couple of chairs, a table, and a potted plant. The front desk and the receptionist and the stairway or lift was out of the line of sight, as were any customers.

A local bed-and-board was what I wanted. A hostel with a restaurant and pub, solid doors, thick walls and a no-bleeding-nonsense bouncer to keep the merrymakers clear. I found one three blocks on from where I had stashed Cally and not far from a freestanding teller for one of the credit cooperatives I had an account with.

The freestanding teller was in a solidly constructed kiosk, employing a cashier behind inch-thick glass and an armored port. The kiosk was furnished with limited but ample enough ready cash, no access from the street and an escape tunnel for the cashier. It was an ATM that was not automatic.

It had a blower connected to the local telephonic system and the Constabulary station and no way of easily breaching the armor. I assumed someone brought the concept over from AngTerra. Once all the banks used to keep 10 to 4 office hours and a long lunch where they closed shop and had cake or tea or fiddled about with the help. Now, everyone was on the hop.

I took about two hundred Exile pounds in paper currency from the cashier stationed in the kiosk, using one of the IDs I had with me. The young man didn't bat an eye, counted the stack of twenty-pound notes twice, passed them through the lock and went back to his reading. I went back to the bed-and-board I'd chosen.

I reserved a two-bedroom suite, with three plated meals in the room, spa, and door-to-door jitney service. For three days and close to a hundred pounds; cheap, really. In the Smoke it would have been two hundred and fifty pounds, In New York it would have been six hundred Yankee dollars. Then I took the jitney on offer, a three-wheel taxi with a driver at the back of the vehicle-a setup intended again to attract tourists. It had a wide and enclosed cabin at the front that could seat three easily and four at need. Interior lighting, mock lamps and a hand-out in an interior door pocket listing all the venues on the avenue. Food, liquor, music and cinema screens. All likely with a back hand to the bed-and-board for steering the customers there.

It was tidy and comfortable inside, but the motor badly needed tuning.

CHAPTER 40

I got Cally out of the spa and into the taxi, then out of the taxi and into the bed-and-board I'd chosen. She was wobbly from the gate and wildly hungry. I had the establishment give us a late meal of roast venison and early summer vegetables with a lite gravy and today's bread. She ate her half and a good portion of mine.

She lingered over the wine I'd ordered. "What happened?" She asked.

"We traveled."

"I know. What happened?"

I sighed. "You manifested, fully. Took us through a gate you did not know, on your first run on that path to a destination you hadn't the Book for."

She stared at me. "Bast."

Damn the woman. I got up and turned down the oil lamps. Turned on the electric lights instead. We didn't need the romance of soft light. "PC41," I said.

She was holding PC41, stroking his head when I turned back to her.

I returned to the table. "What do you know of the worlds that lay adjacent to 'zeme?"

She looked over my head, remembering. "AngTerra, Hanse, Little England, -" Ticking them off on her free hand. "the three Muscovy's, Imperial Hindi, Island League, Five Nations-" I stopped her.

"The Five Nations? What do you know about that sheaf?"

She recited. "The Five Nations has a crooked book, the 'Ring closely holds the *adits* that lead to the 'Nations. Few go there and fewer still return." She shrugged. "When they took me under the robe, as it were, we had a short lecture about all the worlds we could and could not walk upon." She took a sip of wine. "That one was listed as restricted."

I was shocked she even knew the name. English Measles was pandemic on that sheaf. Of those sent across to the Five Nations, one out of twenty survived and there was no prophylactics for the virus.

"How many more did they brief you on?"

"Perhaps five more, twelve in total. They said there were many, many, more than that. Grains of sand on a beach. But those twelve had the simplest paths, the highest number of known *adits* and a host of exploitable resources." She pushed her glass away from her. "I was blind to the paths; I've told you that. But I came from a 'suitable' linage and they were going to see if they could 'help' me contribute to the Unity."

"Eisenring or Commonality?"

"Two sides of the same leaf, at least from where I sat."

"Hmm. PC41 had an interest in you from the day you set foot on the wharf, you know?"

"I found her. I didn't know where she came from, in the mission dormitory. She was under the blanket and-"

I held up a hand. "Doesn't matter. It was much the same with me. I am gifted, but my gift was more problematic."

"Binder? Skrenner?"

I hesitated. "No. D'draig, or a Sangsue if you prefer."

She didn't flinch. Nodded. "Accounts seem to exaggerate. You are not two meters tall, darkly handsome, and habitually well dressed." She smiled at me. "And lethal to everyone you encounter."

I sniffed. Frank Langella. "I was a very modest exemplar

of that gift. Then PC41 bonded himself to me-"

I gave her an abbreviated version of how PC41 and I came to be hunted across the sheaf of worlds. Wolff and company, I left for another time-if we had another time. I told her I 'knew' I was going to have to escape 'zeme and the Wharf, I had not planned on recruiting a Walker. Or using PC41 to amplify that Walker.

"Bast." She corrected me, then yawned. "I have had enough education and excitement for the week. Where shall I sleep?"

"Back bedroom. There is a lock on the door-"

"Pffit. It is not needed among outlaws such as we." She stood up, with 'Bast' tucked under her arm like a cherished teddy bear and walked to her bedroom.

I was dismissed. She was of the quality; I was but an honest Yeoman with manure on my boots and straw behind my ears. I finished my wine and saw PC41 slide out of her door. Ears laid back and radiating miffed embarrassment. Handling him like he was a beloved stuffed animal. How rude.

>query< I pushed at him. And tacked on an image of a very popular bear, from AngTerra's London. He pushed back, hard and I had a migraine for the first time in months. It was worth it. Bast, eh? I think I might prefer Paddington as a name to conjure by.

I pulled the bell cord, tipped the steward for clearing away the dishes and knew that PC41 accompanied him out of the suite. I felt sorry for the local fauna, besides being hungry he had a ration of annoyance to express.

I sat up for a couple of hours, waiting on him. Thinking on what we were to do next. PC41 batted at the window that opened on to an escapeway and strolled in when I lifted the sash.

>and< I pushed at him. He was a rangy black tomcat

now, with one ear ragged and an eye weeping.

>quiet< He sat down at my feet and proceeded to wash his eye and his ear back into shape. >but active< And over the push I had images of small detachments of Franklins-what they called the local street constables-quietly turning over the streets surrounding the postern. They focused on warehouses, abandoned houses, back lots, stables and garages on the back streets. Every place that the 'book' said hapless fugitives would lay up and hide out.

Which is why we were openly in a mid-range bed-and-board. I planned on three days stay here; long enough to send me to a couple of casual but conservative fitters, then let her have a run at a second rank boutique. Then take a water taxi half an hour up the river, find another bed-and-board and settle in for another hide. I'd clean out a suitcase, tap a cobbler and fit her with some plausible paperwork, and think about heading for the Lakes.

By that time, the security details that were mobbed up with the Eisenring might have second thoughts-assuming they had any thoughts at all-and start canvassing more broadly. The Eisenring might bring in Dowsers, to see if they had another postern within reach or to find an unmapped soft spot. Or if we were criminally careless, to pick up an undisciplined Walker's trace. Cally appeared to be anything but undisciplined.

The next day I fed her a substantial breakfast and half of mine as well and I told her to stay put and stay quiet. She muttered a bit, scooped up PC41 and retreated to her room with a pot of tea and a scandal sheet that had been tucked under the suite's door, it came with the suite.

I got the concierge to give me several places to go about touching up my wardrobe. I needed slightly more upscale clothing. Oh, I'd keep the duster, it was odd but men in this milieu and on this coast had more latitude with overcoats. But I needed at least a good pair of pants, a blazer, casual but dressy shoes and a half dozen shirts. And a box of those damned collars, with studs. There were a lot of things I missed about Little England, the food and the beer for instance, but not the separate collars for the shirts.

I'd left the lethal hardware with PC41 and took the wallets and all the local cash I'd lifted from the gate staff when we crossed over. On the way up the high street I came across a Green Box and dropped two of the wallets in it for the post to deal with. I discarded the other one in a sheltered corner by a pub entrance, leaving three ten-pound notes showing from under the flap. The ID papers I cut up and flushed in a handy loo, at the first men's wear shop.

I didn't care for any of the trousers on offer in that shop, but the shirts were cut the way I liked-much more freedom of motion than conventional and they were suspiciously well woven. Smuggling is universal. I got a half dozen off the shelf, of seersucker fabric, and a box of collars. I donned the exemplar I'd tried on, had the resident tailor touch up the other shirts and forwarded the package to the bed-and-board. Much the same regime as Wolff and company had enjoyed in the Ford. I wondered for a moment, looking at myself in the shop's mirror, where he and his more than a Medji was.

The tare for the shirts was about sixty pounds, here-and-now. Would have been twice that in the Smoke and easily four times that in the London of AngTerra. All on the Feckless Provo's tael, as it was.

Three blocks on I found a shop that carried what I wanted: I bought three sets of linen trousers, with generous pockets and room for a money belt as well as a set of braces. I waited on a pair of the trousers to be hemmed and sized by the onsite tailor. The rest would be delivered to the bed-and-board Hostel along with a blazer a half size bigger than what the tailor thought I needed. I'd need the room for a shoulder holster and more. All lightweight fabrics for summer. I purchased a pair of casual shoes in the same shop, not steel toed engineer boots. Had my old boots boxed up to be sent along with the tailored items. Bought a hat as well, gentlemen wore hats here-and-now, only mechanics slouched around in watch caps or flat leather caps. It was a snap-brim, wool, fedora and I wore it out of the shop. Didn't get a cane, that would have been a bit much. But I wore the hat.

I wanted to pass as a gentleman, today.

CHAPTER 41

I drifted back toward the bed-and-board I had Cally stashed at, through the High Street, browsing the shops and taking the pulse of the streets. I'd stopped and had a small coffee, small pastry and bought a paper to read-and to carry. A gentleman often carried things; papers, briefs, canes or a briar pipe. Gave him something to do with his hands, kept them out of his pockets. Then I passed a half hour over the coffee and the shipping news.

There were more uniformed constables about, walking in pairs. They were looking still in the dark corners and shaking down idlers with threadbare coats. And I began to ponder why the streets were busy.

And just how concealed the postern had been.

The Franklins of the Remnant Royals were not particularly rigorous in demanding identity papers from all and sundry; for one thing, they knew that a substantial number of the people on the wharf had sod-all in the way of papers. Well-dressed or not, most of the freemen on the waterfront didn't carry identity papers. They bristled at the very idea and this made policing...difficult. The indentured and the impressed, the sailors and entered apprenticed mechanics, all carried a wallet containing their identity papers; this was an attempt to cut down on absconders haring off for the interior. Most of the indentured wore blue dungarees and a brightly colored vest-linked to their shops and factories; sailors wore whatever they liked, but they walked like men who'd spent their lives on the oceans. Folks who were better dressed or locals known to the constables were not bothered.

When I'd finished my cup, I left a modest tip on the table and tucking my paper under my arm continued on my way.

A pair of Franklins walked by me, touching their bills with a finger and nodding politely. I nodded back, distantly polite as a gentleman would. I trawled my nets through their auras and found them to be just what they appeared to be.

Out in the roadstead, in the mid-stream of the Hudson, powered launches were calling on the moored ships. Sending squads of harbor police up the gangways and, gently, turning over the ships complement. Gently because the ships could up hook and give their trade to a wharf a mile downstream. There were ships from all over the world moored there, flying pennants from all the maritime nations-and a few from absolutely landlocked States. From what I could see, at a half-mile's distance, they were going through all of the sailors and idlers on deck. With very little fuss visible at the distance. And there was always among the Harbor Police an awkward bird, a figure in HP togs who climbed up the ladder from the launch with all the grace of a drunk pig on ice. Eisenring, likely a Verity. Verities sifted for 'honesty' when rubbing up against people suspected of being less than forthcoming. Knowing what I knew now, they were a subset of D'draig; they could sift but not coerce an admission. And they were less likely to present a problem for their superiors.

I saw one of the Eisenring lubbers slip off the ladder and take the plunge into the river. The Harbor Police were slow to rescue, letting the launch drift over the top of the thrashing figure. Nobody likes an Eisenring.

I was complementing myself on how well my scheme was going, when the ever-celestial Murphy raised her head.

Down the street, at the entrance to a corner pub, there was a trio of Eisenring agents-Unity Eisenring no less and not the hapless local lice. I knew this because I knew one of them, entirely too well. They hadn't seen me as yet; they were too focused on someone coming from the pub. They were not in uniform; rough trade but presentable with flat caps and all. Pretending to be civilians. Pretending to be human.

I was in front of another clothing store, and I paused for a minute, as if I had seen something interesting in the window. Then I went in.

It was full of casualwear, athletic themed pullovers and trainers. I wore warm-ups and the like when I was actually going to exercise, not when I was going to the pub for a pint or off to a movie. I was of the generation that wore chinos and oxford cloth to go out on the town, and not jerseys and running shoes. I know; I sound like the Governor at Wanstead House, groaning on about all his charges dressing like a 'bloody tearaways'. I got old somehow.

I pretended to browse through the offerings. They had the usual football and rugby gear, different from the AngTerra teams but the same. No cricketing merchandise; for some reason Alba, the Free Caribbean and the Royalist Remnant never really took to Cricket on this sheaf. And of course, no Yankee Football or Baseball tie in merchandise, the milieu here did not know of that particular fandom. Or shouldn't know of it.

I felt the Eisenring stroll past the storefront.

They never broke step, as far as I could tell they never stopped talking. But I was not best pleased that the Unity Eisenring had a presence here, in West York.

The one of them I knew, Ty Ballantine, was a proper Dai. Not an impressed wayfarer like me. His House was covert, but well established in the Little England milieu's Free Caribbean islands generations before. Refugees he said from the establishment of the Commonality on 'zeme. They came through the veil to here-Little England-and settled on the islands as opposed to buying into the Confederated Houses in the 'zeme. Medium fishes in a very small pond, was the implication he gave me.

Ty said his family seconded him, sold him really, to the Unity Eisenring as a way of fobbing the Commonality off. His people had an edgy relationship with the Unity, they sent them their second string 'gifted' as a way of buying them off. He wasn't in the studbook as suitable-either in the quality of his gift' or his place in the house. The Unity 'Ring was happy to have a close connection to a House, even one as rustic as Ballantine House and Ty was content the last I knew, with his place at the Little England Desk. Which made his appearance here a red banner.

I'd went through the intake classes with him and many of the advanced programmes. We...weren't friends. I came from a very rough place and until the Eisenring sanded me down, it showed. But I was acceptable as a foil to his sophistication. And I learned more from him than I ever let on. Clothing, food and drink, music-although I never turned my back on Pop and Rock for his taste in Opera. He helped the Eisenring smooth my rough edges, without knowing that he was tutoring me.

Ty was a Dowser. He was charming, educated of course, fair with a gun and barely adequate in hand to hand combat. He could sense a soft spot within fifty yards. Used or abandoned or never opened, he had it clocked, the only thing that made him a second was the short reach of the gift. He also could spot a Walker, though that gift was more haphazard.

If he touched a possible Walker, put his hands on them,

he would certainly know they were 'gifted'. Elsewise it was hit or miss.

I didn't know if Cally was disciplined enough to hide her talent under a bushel. And I was afraid we might have to find out.

CHAPTER 42

When I ventured out of the shop, the trio of Eisenring operatives were not to be seen. I made haste slowly to where I'd settled Cally and PC41, trailing my aura as wide and as thin as I could. Eisenring are like cockroaches, you see one, there is usually twenty you don't see.

But there wasn't a one to be seen on the way. I checked for messages at the front desk, extended our stay four more days and took the stairs to our floor.

>bored<

"I am about to go absolute dingo; there is nothing to read, nothing to listen to, nothing to watch. Nobody to talk to!" She threw a cup and saucer across the room, channeling some of the telenovelas she'd consumed back in the 'zeme. The cup was empty, the set did not break since they were thrown at a couch, but her intention was pure.

>hungry< And Euston chimed in. I had resolved to call him Euston, or Miss Euston as the day required. I suddenly got a headache, but it was worth it.

"I want to go out of these rooms and see if the world still exists!"

>agreed<

"Sit down and shut up." I told them both. I sat next to Cally and, to his surprise and dismay, scooped Euston up and held him firmly in my lap. His claws were beginning to unsheathe when he picked up my unease. And the reason for it. "Cally, there are Eisenring about."

She rattled off a lot of gutter *Frankii* that I had no chance of understanding, the auras translated just fine.

"Right. So, keep your voice down and try and tuck your auras under a basket."

"What shall we do?"

"Stay calm. They are thrashing about. I don't think the *bâtards de cochon* know who they are looking for, but they intend to beat the bushes until something runs out."

She sat well within my penumbra and thread by thread wrapped her auras close about her. "Hunter's see runners."

"Right. And one of them is a particular *bâtard de cochon* I know. He is a Dowser."

"Mhn?"

"A gifted that can find 'soft spots' or operating gates, and upon occasion, Walkers."

>walkabout<

I pushed back. >shortly< and let Euston drop to the floor.

I got the impression that there was going to be a reckoning for that new name, but not today. I patted Cally, got up and opened the balcony doors. Our suite was on the second floor and had a tiny balcony overlooking the back streets of West York. Two chairs and a table that could just hold a pot of tea and tea service for two. Euston, formerly PC41, slipped out and was gone. Next balcony or down to the alley I could not tell, but gone he was.

I was not quite as confident as I 'fronted'. If Ty saw me, if he recognized me, he would know I was loose upon the sheaf of worlds and definitely without leave. Or perhaps not, I was a non-person when Wolff made discreet inquiries about me. But certainly, if and when Ty made his weekly report and mentioned that he encountered J. Braxton on the shoreline of West York, things would get warm. Someone would know that I was on the List and send someone to handle the matter, expeditiously. Maybe Wolff.

Awkward.

This meant that quietly moving upstream and eventually inland was not a good idea at the moment. Cally was still memorable. I could, I think, blend in and not be found. Cally, with the mark on her face and her accent was not going to blend into West York.

Maybe if we got to the Great Lakes and settled in as refugee free holders-she with her practicum knowledge of large animals and my ability to tend to motors-we would have been welcomed in most of the small burgs. We'd hint that she was on the run from the Terror-over-the-water and they would put down any odd behavior on her part to being a *Frankii*. I'd pass for an ordinary entered 'prentice that come out of the Smoke, but common as a mudlark and not a skint.

We were not leaving Cally behind. Both PC and I were firm on that point.

There had been no 'funny business'. Somehow, and I don't know when, we became a pair. Trio, if you counted PC41. Maybe because of PC41. We slept in separate rooms, unlocked because we were outlaws, but separate. But when I woke up, I swept my penumbra over her, when I walked the four corners of the suite just before sleep, I swept her auras.

Unsettling. It was completely new to me.

Euston, PC41, returned just before ten o'clock curfew-honored in the call but not in the observance. He was still Euston, not particularly banged up and had fed well.

>rat bastards<

Cally was tucked in bed with a half-bottle of wine. I was sitting on the balcony with a glass of wine and rubbing my lucky coin. "Well?" I said to him.

>about< He pushed a series of images at me. The Franklins and their embedded Eisenrings were still combing the high street, the back alleys and nosing into courtyards and carriage houses. But they were less frantic than earlier in the day, almost lazy.

They hadn't a clue, but they had to tick off the checklist. That was good. PC41 knew who Ty was, PC41 knew everything about me. Euston, PC41, hadn't seen Ty or the other two *bâtards de cochon* about.

I could have dropped them, when they walked past the shop I was lurking in. Or with a bit of luck, tonight if they were out on the tiles. Just an odd sod mugging. But that would just bring a fresh flood of Eisenrings combing the streets, even if it was an obvious stand over robbery.

Ty didn't know it, but he was bait.

The Desk handling this had him staked out like a baby goat. Which meant that they were looking for me, more than Cally. Which also meant that they had D'draig sweeping quietly through the streets. Ty was bait, he knew me mostly by sight. They put him out on the tiles and trailed him up and down the street to see if anyone reacted.

At a guess, one of the Eisenring out walking with him was keeping his head down and sniffing the air. Looking for me. It was just habit and luck that I tucked in my auras and didn't try anything on.

I was hoping that Ty didn't just trip and break his neck.

But…

>go wake her< I pushed to Euston.

PC41 blinked at me from where he was perched on the rail. Then dropped to the balcony and slipped in through the doors.

She came out of her bedroom in a long tunic and carrying her knife, open and ready. I resolved in the back of my mind to query her on weapons familiarity, once we were past this.

"Jos?"

"Let's talk about Walking and soft spots."

CHAPTER 43

In the Eisenring they try to keep us ignorant in our boxes or silos. Much like Vittorio, in memory yet rancid, they want us to know as little as possible and still fulfill our roles. So, I knew that a 'Walker' could open and transit through a 'gate' that passed through the 'veil' between the worlds of this 'sheaf'. How a 'Walker' did this, how it was possible, I did not need to know as a minor operative in the Firm. The less the 'gifted' knew about the other talents, the better our superiors slept at night.

I knew that Cally, as stunted as her training was, knew a lot more about Walking through the worlds than I did. So, I ordered late tea, sent PC41 out on walkabout and nocturnal foraging, and I sat down with her to explore 'Walking'.

"After I manifested and was 'offered' a place in the Commonality, they ran me through a precis of what a Walker's role is within the commons." She was curled up on the divan in the parlor. "They ran all of us 'revealed' talents through orientation classes. Propaganda primarily." She had a glass of wine. Turned her nose up at tea, ate all of the small ham sandwiches. "Then they separated us out into clades of talents. Always with minders, we were not 'reliable' coming late to the Commons as it was."

"You got shut of them, I should say you weren't reliable."

"I was most certainly not, reliable that is. As a Walker, I

was dropped into a stifling tutorial and subjected to a mind-numbing explanation of the Sheaf of Worlds. We had six tutors to our four candidates, no breaks for any reason and no questions permitted."

"And was it enlightening?"

"Pfui. I got more from the penny rags they used to pass around at year eight in the lyceum. After three hours and a dozen different explanations on offer, they agreed that nobody knows why the Sheaf of Worlds exists, just that it does. And they don't know how the Sheaf is ordered, why one world is harder to 'Walk' to than another World, why three adjacent Sheaves might have wildly different histories and cultures and two other world lines are close copies." She finished her glass. "And then, after a break for plonk and pâté, they got to the nubbin. With two Master Walkers and an Eisenring proctor telling us how to open a gate, close a gate and what not to do. Ever."

"Cascade effects."

"Among several other catastrophes. Weapon usage, electrical effects and wandering off the plot. They also took us into the cellar of the school we were at, let us experience a postern gate opening and closing. That was when I was classified as too weak to be of purpose."

"Now, things have changed."

"Obviously." She waved her empty glass at the suite. "I seem to have improved my evaluation, no?"

"Could you find *un point faible*, an un-exploited passage?"

"I...don't know. Perhaps. But you wanted me to keep my-
"

"Your 'penny dreadfuls' ever mention 'wreckers' or 'smuggling'?"

She blinked. Looked at her empty glass and then sat it carefully on the end table. "Smuggling, yes. Wrecking?"

"Luring ships to run aground on a coastline, then looting

the wreckage."

"Oh yes. On the coasts of Albion and Brittany, much smuggling, wrecking and romantic risky behaviors. She giggled.

I closed my eyes. Giggled, oh Lord, she giggled. I let my net expand to mesh with her auras. She was a happy drunk, I should have known. I didn't know how far a Dowser, Ty, could sense a Walker's aura. But Cally's aura was blooming, like a bonfire on Guy Faulks night.

So, I put her to sleep.

She slowly slumped over and curled about a throw pillow on the divan. Her auras blinked and then sank back into her skin, like film of a bloom of ink in water, played in reverse. I covered her with a blanket and swept my net through the building and the streets close by.

The hostel was quiet, some activity but nothing to do with us. The streets had penny-packets of Constables and attendant Eisenrings. But they were doing just enough to not catch the attention of someone higher in the chain of their organization. Ticking off boxes in their end-of-shift reports.

I had to sort out if they were looking for me, specifically. Or it was just Murphy's luck that sent a Dowser I was acquainted with out on the streets of West York.

CHAPTER 44

The next morning Cally was embarrassed at finding herself in bed, with the clothes she worn last night. She had a mild hangover and wanted croissants and coffee, with cream and sugar. I got that down her, then a small omelet as well. She eyed my sausages and eggs over easy but refrained from raiding them.

"I am going to do a little cosmetic work on your face."

"Mnmh?"

"You need clothing and other items; I propose a shopping expedition."

Her smile lit up the room and made my purse ache.

Two hours later we were at large on the streets of West York.

I'd touched up her face, blending the portwine birthmark into her complexion so it was barely visible.

>won't last< PC41 was sitting on the sink watching me working on Cally's face.

She grinned at me. "You know, if this D'draig career does not prosper, you have a likely situation available as a cosmetician."

"Sit still, keep still, will-you-please?" It wasn't as hard as blending makeup with a fine brush. But the trick had its own issues. Body auras were malleable, but they tended to return to a resting state. Which was a fancy way of saying the glamor would wear off over time. It was an accidental sleight of hand

I'd picked up while adapting to PC41 bonding with me. I woke up one day in the brig early on, badly in need of a wash and a shave. Without thinking about it, as I washed my face, the three-day stubble melted away.

Distressed my keepers to no end, I had not been issued a razor. So, they tossed the brig, stuffed me in an orange jumpsuit, and did a very invasive search of my body in search of contraband. They left PC41 alone, even then she was able to shred Kevlar, and very willing to do so.

Shaving was easy. Changing the color of your skin was another case. I did it as an experiment after the Eisenring stuffed me away in a different holding pen, while the factions tussled over me. They did not keep a very close watch on me, just gave me a case of cold MRE's and left me to my own devices. So, I fiddled about with my newly improved auras. I ended up hairless and piebald. Which was the end of that.

It took two days and I was uniformly pasty-white again but with very short hair. I did learn to use that particular twist, sparingly, to amend my appearance. I never liked shaving anyway, I kept the razor and kit to blend in.

I was trying to blend the portwine mark. Her hair was not an issue, but the birthmark drew the eye.

I had rethought my concern over Ty recognizing me on the Riverfront. It was almost twenty years ago that we were in the intake camps, and I had not gone to the Croft he was formed at. He had not changed, but I had. What he is going to be looking for is a thin, pasty-white, wharfie. An ill-bred delinquent wearing a distressed black leather jacket, black trousers, engineer boots and a cable-knit sweater of the type Their Majesties Naval airship crews favored.

I wasn't thin, I wasn't pasty, and I didn't wear those togs. So, unless he had a recent photo of me, he was going to be clueless. Unless he laid hands on me. And that would be unfortunate. For him.

They could be just looking for Cally. She had popped up in the 'zeme and near to a postern that was concealed but not hidden. That postern was then forced, and it did gate to Little England and West York. So, they might be hot on her trail.

But.

There were other Dowsers, much better than Ty. Ty was Unity Eisenring and sits for a Desk in Montbrillant Chateau in the midst of the 'zeme Commonality when he is at home. Why is he in Little England trolling through the streets? Roughing it, as he would insist? He still might just be a goat on a short length of rope. But, why him and why now? Vittorio would have been a better choice, talentless though he was, he had seen me face to face quite recently. Of course, he was unavoidably absent.

Alas.

I got her face more or less in order and we set off, to refit Cally as a proper West York heiress.

She was nervous the first time we crossed paths with a pair of Franklins. PC41 and I gave her a bit of a nudge to keep her from bolting. They nodded politely to me, touched the rim of their bowlers to Cally and walked on down the street. The second time, an hour later and after we had spent two hundred of my pounds in a spray of shops, she nodded to them and sashayed on down the pavement. They nearly broke their necks observing her passage.

I linked arms with her and leaned in to speak softly. "Remember, we're looking for *un point faible* and not to entice poor honest policemen."

"Mhn. They have so little joy in their lives, eh?" And radiated an innocent satisfaction.

I kept a light myst net trawling, not enough to throw a hook into anyone, but enough to know what was passing.

We were better, PC41 and I, much better than any of the

D'draig I had encountered since the Carolinas and our bonding. Our net was not noticeable, no wake as it were, as we trolled down the street. I sniffed at the wakes and the smuts the rest of the traffic left behind. There were Constables. There were Eisenring, Unity Eisenring in fact as well as the Feckless Provo 'Ring. There were Sworn Dai from several notable Houses, who were watching the Eisenring closely and being watched in turn. All milling about, watching the crowd flow by. Some of the Eisenring had talent, some were just rough boys who worked for the talent. But the one thing I picked up from the myst net was that they all were bored.

Three more shops and another tap on my account, I called an intermission in the expedition.

I was, to a modest degree, flush. But not flush enough to endure this drain on my funds for very long. PC41, Euston, suggested that I join him in prowling the wharf and the back streets come nightfall to replenish my roll. I was not quite ready to take that step. But the notion had its attractions.

We returned to the bed-and-board, had a light tea, egg salad on rye toast and settled in for a doze on the divan. She was tucked deeply into my auras; Euston was curled up on her lap.

>gate< Euston pushed.

"Jos, somebody just opened a gate." Cally's eyes popped open, as if someone had poked her with a sharp stick.

"You know what direction?"

"Towards where we came from."

"Can you pull in your auras?"

"Uh?"

I took her hand, it was sweaty. PC41 and I let her 'see' how to draw in her auras, leaving just a faint slick upon her body. Like any other talentless unchurched mundane.

"Good," I said, after she mastered the trick. A trick I

knew before I'd partnered with PC41, but now I could fade into the woodwork, become one with the paint. "Now let's sit and 'listen'."

For twenty minutes we huddled in the suite. I delicately swept the halls and the alleyways, looking for a wake. Fear or anger or something on the hunt.

There was a wake, like a drift of smoke from a snuffed candle. It wasn't anything I could read, it wasn't close. It was from a talent, but even so it was too faint to discern what talent emitted it. A drifting smut from a candle in a ballroom lined with candles. I had no clue.

>any track< I pushed at PC41.

>possible< And he flowed off the divan, padded to the open door of the balcony and disappeared into the afternoon shadows.

I held Cally close. I knew this was not wise. It had never been wise. Each time I gained a little from her and she took a little from me and it was not wise. A day might come that I had to leave her behind or send her away and…

"No," she said. "My paladin of the chapbook sagas, that will not happen." She tucked her head under my chin and settled, matched her breathing to mine.

An hour later, PC41 came through the balcony doors.

CHAPTER 45

It was a short squad of Senior Proctors, Unity Proctors, dressed to blend in with the local Constables. PC41 informed us. They had baggage, which they handed off to the unlucky Constables told off to 'work' with the rat bastards. PC41 didn't know them, by sight or by 'sniff'. They went down the high street, according to PC41, then disappeared into a prosperous warehouse on the wharf.

I knew that I was going to have to cut one of them out of the pack. We needed information on what the hell was going on. I knew I could single one out and peel him like a boiled egg, but I wasn't sure I could do it and not leave a D'draig's tracks all over it.

Cally had an idea. "Don't be subtle. Get your information and then-" She produced her knife and opened it with a flick of her wrist. "carve him up."

"There are ways to trace that."

"Misdirection?"

"Maybe," I said.

>agree<

I sighed and rubbed my head. "Right. You might not be safe tucked away here."

"Safer here than on the street with you. You are just an opportunistic thug with a taste for blood as well as silver. You bring me onto the scene, and it gets…interesting."

"You had an odd 'finishing school'."

She got a distant look to her face. "I said we were proscribed, didn't I?" She folded her knife, tucked it away somewhere in her drawstring lounge pants. "The house survived. We survived the Terror and the denunciations that came after with the Permanent Terror. The house was preserved, as a caution to its peers, the linages survived. It was a very hard school."

"Hunh" I grunted. "I have been remiss; can you handle pistols?"

She smiled, shrugged. "Up close, yes. But anything over three meters is chancy. A target on the other side of the street, I would spray and hope I hit something."

I went to my duster and produced a three mm needle gun, the large bog-standard gun that hadn't changed in two long generations. It wasn't a Borchardt, but it derived from Wolff's preferred weapon. I removed the magazine box and sat next to her to demonstrate. "The gun is now set for five-needle bursts. Pull the trigger, five needles spray out. These will penetrate most leather, 15 mm soft wood planks, a layer of tempered glass or very thin metal doors. The needles have toxic loads, so you don't have to be very accurate. No recoil to speak of, not much in the way of noise."

"Why didn't you-"

"I forgot where you came from. You are a proper Dai. I am just a straggler without house or hearth." I handed the gun to her. "And the 'Ring didn't let us fraternize with the Dai, much. Might give us ideas, might give them notions, I suppose."

"And do you have ideas, now?" Her deep brown eyes held mine for a long moment.

"More than is wise." I patted her hand, the one not cradling the gun. "There is enough money in my satchel to get you clear of West York, upriver or across the Hudson to York. I'd not go inland, strangers are noted."

She gave me a level look. "Come you back, Paladin."

CHAPTER 46

I was wearing my working togs, from the wharf back on 'zeme. Flat hat, steel-toed shoes, denim mechanic's trousers and a mac. I had two long knives, a short 2 mm needle gun and a double wool sock with a good handful of ball bearings.

That was just for show.

PC41 and I went down the back streets and the gangways, working our way close to the warehouse. I was hunting.

If they had a station here in West York, in the warehouse, it would have posted guards. Local hirelings or their own people, walking a perimeter or just watching from vantage points. In a pinch, I could take one of those down and get some of what I needed. But it would be obvious, a targeted attack on an Eisenring watchman.

If I was lucky, someone in the station was going to break protocol and slip out for a night on the tiles. In local togs and carrying a bit of money. More likely a pair or a trio, numbers make you bolder. They knew they could whistle up backup and they knew that the Eisenring basically 'owned' this sheaf and they were Eisenring Drakes. No worries, a bit of fun off the clock as it were. Ask forgiveness and not permission.

It was raining when we got close to the warehouse. That was good and bad; a bit of rain to keep the noise down and witnesses indoor, but it might keep any targets inside out of the wet. PC41 moved off, trotting down a narrow gap between two small stores that looked to have been built on the ruins of a larger one. I huddled in the lee of a loading dock, listening to water running down the drains and into the gangway.

It was bigger than an alley, large enough for a horse drawn cart to carefully turn around, but not a proper street. Real cobblestones and not ginned up paving slabs, mud between the cobbles, garbage in the gutters and three centuries stink overall. The sort of place I grew up playing in, when I broke curfew.

Still cleaner than I remembered, hard coal and not the cruddy lignite that was common in the Smoke. You could see the lights of the Free City reflected off the clouds, giving a soft half-light to the gangway.

I waited an hour past curfew and got a push from PC41.

>two<

The hint was that they were coming back towards the station. We were at the rear of the warehouse, which was a solid brick façade thirty feet high with a low-pitched roof. No doors, no real windows-just narrow skylights hinting at the floor layout inside. But there had to be a way in and out. No burrow had only one entrance.

There wasn't two, there were three. Two men and a woman, though by her auras she was very young and very, very scared.

And the men were mean drunk, drunk with liquor and intent. Lust for more than a hurried coupling out of the rain.

They were dragging her between them, laughing and telling each other how lucky they were. What they were going to do with her. She was a whore. But they weren't interested in that form of entertainment. Sangsue. Young Sangsue was my guess.

>watchers< I pushed.

>no< Came over the push. I nodded and slipped the sock

full of bearings out of my pocket. They came up on me, where I crouched, and just past the dock's edge I came up out of the shadows.

The first one I took with a solid blow to the widow's hump between the shoulder blades, the second one I dropped on the backstroke swinging over the head of the woman, smashing his startled face in. Blood and teeth sprayed out and the girl gave a strangled, terrified, squeak; dropping to her knees between the two. She was very careful to not be seen watching me, her face focused on the dirty cobbles in front of her.

I was quiet; my auras slid over hers and with a soft touch I did not know I had, I suppressed them. Calming her. I dragged the closest one to me, quickly went through his pockets and took a wad of folding money. Local pounds, I could tell from the size and the embossing. I stepped closer to her, she started babbling that she'd 'seen nothm' over and over. I stuffed the pounds down her minimal cleavage, tucked her wet wrapper about her and hoisted her up on her feet.

"Run." I whispered in her ear, turned her around and pushed her away. She did, both hands holding the pounds to her chest and running for the end of the gangway and not looking to either side.

I watched her go.

>soft< came over the push.

I nodded. >optimal<

Sad agreement.

I left the one I'd smashed in the face on his back in the rain. I slit open his clothing, stripped his weapons, papers and money belt and left him face up, choking on his blood and the rain. He died while I was bundling up his partner. I wrapped the one I'd stunned in his own coat, threw him over a shoulder and went back down the gangway behind the fleeing woman.

There was a ruined storefront two blocks away. I'd marked it earlier; it was being used as an occasional crib from the bottles and trash about the broken doorway. I swept it, it was clean of the usual vermin, two or four legged. I took my prize inside, to peel it out of the wet and any interested eyes.

I worked quickly. His name was Daniel, Daniel Penzler. From the fucking 'zeme. Out of the Unity Commonality.

He was a low level Sangsue, brought here for muscle and a little bloodwork. He liked the bloodwork and he liked the status being an Eisenring Drake gave him. He and his mate-the mate was "just a bit of muscle"-had gone out on the tiles for a bit of fun; they drank a lot, bragged about being "Kingsmen" a bit in some of the sketchier holes, which got them nawt. Their money was good, and the locals were happy to charge them triple for watered plonk or raw alcohol. And only the understanding that topping these two would cause more trouble than profit, kept their heads attached to their necks.

They were on their way back to the station a bit poorer and about half-seas over when they encountered the girl. "A bit of trash that no one would notice the less of." and they could have a bit of fun that none of the Seniors would know about. That was uppermost in his mind, not getting caught and having a bit of free-range bloodsport.

I let that go past, what I wanted was why they were here.

CHAPTER 47

The Eisenring had given them, the pod he was assigned to, an operational overview. They had been brought through the veil that very day, by a Desk that was administering joint Eisenring operations on 'Little England and in the Colonies. The Desk was looking for several different *'contrabandistas'* that were thought to be crossing through 'Little England'. It was a joint operation between Alba, the Remnant Colonies and the Eisenring. Mostly putting more men on the job, padding the payroll.

Most of the names on the list he'd seen I didn't know, he had a fair memory of the list but, it was only fair. I was on the list. That was to be expected. I wasn't safely dead or in the bottle, so I must be on the run. I suspect that I would be on that list for the next long generation. And I have a history with 'Little England', so all the little drakes could keep a lookout for me here and now. But there was one name-or rather an ID-on the list that was a shock. *Standartenführer* Karsten Tauber.

They had a description of the *Standartenführer*, and he remembered seeing a slide projector of a fuzzy photo identification card. The card dated from the end of '46 and he knew there was a set of prints and blood type attached to the card. Tauber was presented to the drakes as being of The Gotha, a proscribed Dai constellation. He was supposed to have avoided capture and summary execution by becoming an apparatchik for one of the Three Crowns Services. Then

Tauber was denounced as a traitor to the Crowns as well as being wanted by the Eisenring directorate.

No mention was made of him dying in the Hanse, or even having been in the Hanse. Just that he was dangerous, and no attempt was to be made to take him alive.

Me? I was a three-line footnote, a middling operative who was noted as 'run', to be taken and sent to Unity House upon recovery. No interrogation needed. Nothing about PC41 or Cally. Or the Hanse.

I had what I wanted from him. I snapped his neck and let his aura drain away into the night. Cut his throat and let the blood drain into the punk-rotten floorboards and stuffed the corpse up the fireplace at the back of the shop. Took his shoes, his cash, the weapons-they let both of the worthless pig-fuckers out with 'zeme manufactured needlers and .40 Glocks from AngTerra; an absolutely shocking lapse of tradecraft. I took his ID folder. It had pristine Eisenring, Alba Three Crowns and Royal Remnant paper in it. That, that would be useful.

Tauber. I wonder if I could gin up something from the Thistle to lay a drag trail with his scent on it. He had been in the Service of the Crowns, and I had paperwork that could be repurposed-badly-to document him.

The Eisenring paperwork, that was bonus. If I could find a cobbler that I trusted enough to let him fiddle with it. Or trusted enough to sell it to him.

I sloped off home.

At the bed-and-board I found Cally waiting up, with a small bag by her side on the divan, and her new gun in her lap.

"How went it?" She asked.

"Found two of the pigs about to have a party with a local whore." I shrugged. "I dropped them and sent her on her way."

She gave me the stink-eye. "You left her alive?" She sighed. "Ah well, that is one of your admirable traits." Faint praise. What I should have done was let them have her, then have one kill the other in the bloodhaze. It wasn't in me, not before, not now. I cut her loose and hoped. One reason I was considered a moderate Sangsue, I really did not have the taste for it.

"If she is wise, she will not advertise her good fortune." I sat down and started sorting through the haul. "But I doubt she will be wise." I'd ditched the Glocks in a sewer before I had gone three blocks from the spot where I'd taken the Eisenring down. The needle guns I'd thrown up on a handy rooftop, his shoes I threw into an alcove. Everyone on the back street needed sturdy shoes more than weapons or white metal. Even if the Eisenring didn't have serial numbers for the weapons, and I knew that would damn well not be the case, I didn't want the items anywhere near us. One of the somewhat uncommon talents was a 'sniffer' who could possibly read the history of an object. It varied wildly, but he or she could have fondled one of the needlers and said, 'this was associated with one of the persons who broached that postern.' We didn't need that. Didn't need more weapons anyway.

Money. The heavy muscle I'd left to choke on his own teeth had a roll of ten pound notes the size of my fist and a belt of silver Alba crowns. Enough to cover the last week's expenses three time over. He was nothing much on paper. He had an ID as a field agent for the Remnant Colonial Office. The ID was bogus as the day is long and he had too much dosh for a field agent. I made him as a supervisory Proctor, tasked to watching Penzler. I mildly regretted having not taken the time to 'peel' him, upon reflection he might have known a lot more than the one I'd peeled. But, spilt blood.

Penzler, from his paperwork was a highly talented

Eisenring, who had been covertly brought out from under the cloak of the Commonality into the service of the Eisenring. That was a laugh. He was bottom feeding trash with more appetite than talent. It was his origin that piqued my interest.

He supposedly was procured directly from a freestanding house embedded in the Unity. A house not held by the Unity *burgrij* in common, but by a Desk in the Eisenring itself. I was going to have to ask Cally about that.

What I knew about the Commonality I got from my time in the Unity Eisenring and I'd heard nothing about freestanding houses remaining in the Commonality. Not even Freestanding Houses owned by the Eisenring. From what I knew about the Dai as a whole, the idea that the thrice-damned Eisenring having a House would have united every single one of them in a pogrom with the Eisenring as an honoured guest. They tolerated them, barely, as long as they kept a firm hand on the Eisenring's collective throat. Or as long as they thought they had their hands on the Eisenring's collective throat.

That was his story at any rate, that he came from the House of the Eisenring. He never went even near the Commonality bureaucrats, not that I could glean from his memory. Born and bred on a largish canton in the north of the continent. Near the Baltic. House schooled, culled at manifesting and indulged in his talent; and then off to the Eisenring intake and then to the Croft.

Why was he not culled at the first month, when they noticed that he was a Sangsue? He wasn't particularly strong or effective, the Proctors had inflated his value to a ridiculous degree. 'could be another breaker'.

My. Scabby. White. Ass.

He was a worthless git, even by the Eisenring's low standards. He could serve the purpose, but only under the close supervision of a stronger talent, or the tight control of a binder. The Croft I suffered through would not have kept him longer than it would've taken to scrape a shallow grave in the potato patch.

And Penzler had a lot of coin in the belt around his middle, too much coin for a small drake like him. Alba Crowns and Remnant pounds and a scattering of anomalous currency. Silver and gold from other sheaves and nations. More than any Eisenring, let alone such a pissant, should've had. And the anomalous coinages, pfui. Like wearing a sign on your back saying investigate me!

At that thought I smiled. Wolff. He would have been amused at my contempt for such a paltry, piss poor, Sangsue. And at my use of the epithet.

>yes< Came back over the push. A remembered image of Wolff at the way station, also came over that push. Thumbing through his tear sheets, trying to sort out what was happening on AngTerra by the shadows it threw on the Sheaf of Worlds.

I looked over at Cally, PC41 was ensconced on the arm of the divan. Her free hand absently scratching at his, her, head. Her head tilted back and her eyes tracing the antique tin ceilings. His were slitted in sybaritic pleasure.

I frowned slightly and looked back to the haul of specie and documentation.

>trust< I pushed. >her< Interrogative appended to the push.

We were getting quite good at communication over the push. The blinding migraines were mostly a thing of the past and images were becoming common and informative.

Mirth came back. >bonded< The image came down the push. Small, furry, needle-clawed kitten. Battered, ragged ears, slitted eyes, slow stalking very large prey. >ours<

Big ham-fisted country boy with a large club and a straw in his mouth. >hers<

I turned over the Eisenring identity papers, thinking over

what PC41 implied. I grinned to myself.

I pushed. >not Wolff< Interrogative.

I got up and went to shuck my stalking clothes. Looked them over for trace, not much blood, not much in the way of any other dirt. I manifested and let my net pass through them, like flowing water. The blood lifted off the fabric, crumbled away, evaporated. Another perk of the talent, dry-cleaning. Like the other tricks I'd learned since Euston and I partnered up. Things no one had mentioned when I was a duckling in the intake center.

I washed my hands, washed my face and then washed my hands again. Peeling back auras, when you mean grievous harm, always makes me feel dirty. Letting my nets cleanse me was not enough, I needed the hot water, the harsh soap, to feel clean. Just like when PC41 had brought me trophies, long dried rats or pigeons, mummies that I cringed to handle. And a minor 'lift' in my energies.

>talent< Came from PC41. >absent< Wolff in his chair, pipe in hand.

I looked at myself in the mirror. Lyn. Lyn could suppress her auras; was that a talent? PC41 did not think so. Johanna Marie was Hanse, they prided themselves on being absolutely 'untalented'. Wolff was robust, resistant to 'binders' and supposedly proof against the kiss of the Sangsue. Not just a Fain, but he was not 'gifted' either; not a Walker, a Skrinner, a D'draig, or a Binder was he. Wolff was something else, something not in the three-ring binders the Desks were fond of.

Fain live longer than the average mundane, if they keep their wits about them. Live better lives than either the Dai or the mundanes, if the truth be told. Dai, well it varies, day to day. A Dai, whose gift was a quiet one, might live well past a long generation. Providing she stayed away from the Great Game between Houses, or the lesser games within a House. A

Binder played at intrigue and power without much choice in the matter-if they were not using Fain and Dai, they were being used. But a Sniffer, for example, could live to a very pleasant old age if he chose his patrons cautiously. Antiques was a good line of work for a Sniffer, book dealers as well.

I thought about Wolff and his books store and wondered.

A powerful Sangsue, well, she'd live like a flaming arrow shot across the night sky. Manifest at menarche and be on the pyre before her twenty-fifth year, that was a typical career of a more than middling Sangsue. A middling D'draig might live longer, but if my experience is any guide, he would be on a very short leash. Not trustworthy, you know. Not our kind.

PC41, she trusted Cally and Cally trusted her. Euston had enveloped Cally in his myst, for longer than anyone but me. Cally was a Walker, which was not a quiet talent but with care, an enduring one for a Dai. Well-kept property and not something to be expended in a pass of the Great Game-unlike a D'draig.

I kept circling back to Penzler, running my fingers over his papers, his trash and his cash. Something was off, ever so slightly about him. He was just not worth the care and the privileges lavished on him. Not from where I and Euston stood.

I'd fiddled with his document case, then sorted through all the odd trash he had in his pockets before I stuffed him up the chimney. Breath mints, 'safes', wipes. I sorted his currency, then picked up a heavier coin, an anomalous coin, out of the stacks I had made of his money belt's contents. This anomalous coin was silver with the profile of the AngTerra Emperor Wilhelm I of Germany, dated 1878. And it was very heavy, much bigger than a similar coin struck in 1875 that he also had in his belt. Bigger diameter, thicker. A commemorative strike, not intended to be circulated.

Much like the English pound coin I had in an inner

pocket of my duster. I carefully set the German coin aside, swept the rest of the money into a sack.

I went to the closet where I'd hung the duster, took Wolff's coin from the inner pocket and came back to the table.

Interrogative came over the push from Bast.

I put the two coins side by side, then opened Wolff's gift. A counterclockwise twist and it gently opened; I flipped the lens up out of the finely machined pocket it was nestled in. It was the size of a .22 caliber bullet, just the bullet standing on end. You would put the microdot under one end of the lens, put your eye at the other end of it. It took a bit of fiddling with it, like getting comfortable with a telescopic sight on a rifle, but when you found the proper placement you could clearly read the microdot.

Then I tried the Imperial German coin. Counter-clockwise did not work, but clockwise did. And there were three microdots in a pocket in the middle of the sectioned coin.

"What are you looking at, Jos." Cally asked from the divan where she was cuddling with Bast.

"Perhaps nothing, perhaps a great something."

There was no lens assembly tucked away in the German coin. Just a pocket for the dots. I gingerly took one of the microdots out of the pocket, put it on a clean sheet of paper-the daily bill for the suite-and picked up the coin Wolff had given me. And I began to read what Penzler was carrying, all unknown, across the veil from the 'zeme Commonality to the Remnant Royal Colonies.

CHAPTER 48

I got through the first microdot. I secured the microscope, secured the microdot and closed both of the coins. Then I rested my head on my hands. I had a raging headache, among other things.

I could read 'The Gotha' High German, to a degree. It was close enough to my strain of German that I could puzzle out the meaning of most of the sentences. The font was what was causing my headache, it was a heavy Gothic script-that figured-compressed and archaic.

The information contained in those microdots was monstrous.

Cally touched me. She put her hands on my shoulders and lightly rubbed at my rigid muscles. Euston, or Bast, or PC41-whoever- jumped on the table and rubbed against my head with a low rumble.

"Cally," I asked. "do you remember the cautions they gave you? At the seminar on 'Walking'?"

"Yes."

I tapped the table, by the sheet of paper where I had placed the microdots. "There is a plan in motion, to detonate at least four, perhaps five, very large explosions, in each of several Broad *adits*; open *adits* between five of the sheaves."

Her hands stopped. "That would-"

"That would break the paths between those worlds, for several long generations, if not permanently."

"Who-why?"

"Who, The Gotha. And it is for revenge, and a final triumph."

"Gotha?"

"They were a Grand House, on AngTerra and their machinations failed grandly. Their puppets lost the World Wars and the survivors of The Gotha were hunted through the myriad worlds."

"The Breaker of Nations?"

"No. That is a myth; The Gotha failed in the First World War, then again in the Second World War of that sheaf-AngTerra. There are no romances spun about them, unlike 'Breaker of Nations'. They did not break nations, they butchered them. The only explanation I have ever heard of them, is that they were a House ruled by Sangsue, blood drinkers."

"You cannot bind with-"

"It is an explanation, not a fact. The generation before mine broke The Gotha once and then a second time. None of their High Table nor their Inner Hearth were taken alive at the end of that long war; some were never taken at all. Fled into the sheaf of worlds." I looked over my shoulder at her, our auric fields swirling about us. "Now they throw one last cast of the dice, they intend to crash all the gates within their reach."

"It will destroy 'zeme."

"Perhaps. It will destroy all of the Houses, major or minor. Leaving The Gotha as the only House standing. And I suspect The Gotha, table and hearth, is concealed within one of the Houses in the 'zeme." And the more I thought about it, the more I favored the Commonality as the pond The Gotha lurked in. Not just because I heartily disliked the Unity, but because the Gotha had a lot of entangled connections with what the Unity sprang from.

It was a long night. I told her everything: Wolff, Lyn, Dama Ledhrad and Snow. The series of deaths associated with BRIXMIS. The disruption of the gate from the Commonality to the Hanse. I told her more of how PC41 and I came to bond with each other, and my suspicions on what was happening between us and her.

In the morning, we had coffee and pastries. And conspired on the divan, her head on my shoulder and Euston draped over the back.

"As foul as they are, the Eisenring need to know of this atrocity," she said softly.

I nodded. "But I think they are compromised. They are compromised here in the Remnant colonies at any rate. Why else would there be someone passing information by a courier in the service of the 'Ring?"

"Some of the 'Ring is compromised, but not a large fraction." She corrected me. Cally rested more of her weight on my shoulder, held her cup on her knee and rested her free hand lightly on my hand. "If the 'Ring here was completely controlled by The Gotha, they wouldn't need to use couriers with artfully hidden documents. And I suspect you have netted only one of the couriers, they would have sent multiple coins."

I nodded. I was tactically competent, not politically accomplished. "They will be looking for their Courier, and the microdots."

"Frantically, and in great secrecy at the same time. They will be suspecting that opposing forces have the information and are moving against them-so they might advance the timing of their strike."

"How reassuring."

>Johanna<

Euston pushed at both Cally and I. Cally winced and hid her face in my neck, spilling her cup. It hurt me too, but no more than eating too much Italian ice on a hot day.

I pushed back. >Hanse< Interrogative.

>ghost army<

I sat. Silent. For a long time.

"Jos, are you all right." She stirred from her cuddle with me, trailing her auras through mine. Her migraine was eased, by my closeness. I was eased by her closeness.

I nuzzled her hair, huffing her scent. We no longer needed two bedrooms, last night she had put paid to that affectation.

"Yes. Our comrade in Outlawry might have a wonderful idea, if we can get to Cantry..." I stopped. "Or maybe we should go to AngTerra instead."

"You are not at all well." She sat completely up from where she had been nestled at my side. Reached out to touch my head, trailing her fingers through my auras. Auras that she could read, slightly.

"Wolff," I said. "He has several hobbies, one of which is operational networks, another is killing Gotha vermin."

"He is retired, so you said?"

"Apex predators never retire; they just change their hunting grounds. How did you find this end of the postern?"

The jump in topics phased her for a moment. "I did not find it; the gate, the veil, found me. It was the closest one and I was drawn to it. From what I know that is the way to walk to a world you do not have the book for-" She paused. The woman who had thrived in the backwash of Unity intrigues was not slow on the uptake.

"Did you have other worlds, other veils, other gates within your ken?"

"Perhaps. There were lights on the horizons in every direction, like the flashes you see at the corner of your vision after a sharp blow to the head. Only these flashes were outside of my vision, just beyond my fingertips. Arcs in the darkness."

>memory<I pushed at Euston.>crossing<

He replayed to me, in a push that made me sick, that hurt more than anything we'd come through before. And at the end, I had in my mind a shimmer of lights.

That might be AngTerra. Outside Dodge City.

CHAPTER 49

We made haste, slowly while I burned through almost all of my cached funds.

I outfitted Cally and me for winter; which was a wild-assed-guess for when we might come out of a gate on AngTerra, if we came out at all.

I converted as much of the local money as I could to anomalous coins, coins the local collectors had as curiosities. Yankee silver dollars for a common example, some Krugerrands were almost as common. In the back of my mind I was avid to find out how in the sheaf of worlds these particular coins crossed over. But I tucked them away in a belt and soldiered on, suppressing my insatiable curiosity.

Not long after I had made these exchanges there were flyers and ads in the West York tabloids, soliciting 'exotic' coinage. They were offering fifty pounds for some of the rarer examples, which they had printed images of. A number of the coin and gold shops I'd used closed up suddenly. Then new ones opened, perhaps with much more 'reliable' proprietors. I think I had been a half-step ahead of the investigators. Who were looking for mundane stand-over robbers, with coins that were not easily resold to coin dealers.

I avoided the constantly patrolling Constables and their Eisenring attachments. There were posters up, with a fair likeness of Penzler, a 'missing citizen of Alba'; reward of two thousand pounds for his return. Which I thought was very peculiar, the phrasing was just 'return' and not 'safe return'. There were slow but constant searches up and down the riverfront and in the back streets. They had all the sewers tore up along the gangway where I had ambushed the pair, excavating the antique outdoor jakes at the back of the shops as well.

I went back to the postern gate, the town house that we'd come through just ahead of the Eisenring detachment. It was much more heavily guarded than it had been. Three doormen, one at a kiosk at the street level and two apparently in the foyer. PC41 said there were more on the rooftops, next to the town house and across the street as well. Guarding well the barn after the horses had left.

I would have been entertained, except that we would have liked to use it again. That was not going to happen. Well then.

A week later I closed our account with the hostel, took our luggage and hired a water taxi to take us across the river and into York proper. Cally was well dressed, I was turned out as a gentleman should be, no one paid much attention to us. We were not running, we were strolling away with baggage and tipping properly as we left the establishment. I checked us into a middling hostel in the south end of the island. The accommodations were nowhere near as comfortable as where we had been, only one room with an ensuite bath, a wardrobe and a convertible couch with a very thin mattress.

PC41 went out on a reconnaissance sweep through the neighborhood.

I knew there was a postern in York; there were several, in point of fact, along with four large *adits* with broad galleries. But only one postern opened into AngTerra. It was, as I recalled, within three blocks of the middling hostel we were in. I hoped that postern was lax in their security, lax enough that we could get past their doorkeepers and through the gate. Then we would have a quarter hour to disappear into AngTerra before the gate would cycle, leaving a string of dead Eisenring behind us and no descriptions.

It was going to be a close-run thing, particularly if we attracted attention rushing the gate. They could use a blower and contact someone at another *adit*, have them send a blocking force into New York. Sent from West York to the Smoke and on to New York City in AngTerra. If we dropped them without much fuss, it might be an hour or two before someone noticed the gate was not secured and raised the hue and cry.

The time slippage though was going to be critical. If we cut our way into the gate and transited to arrive six months later, we might walk out and into a reception platoon of bronze age heavies. They might not know who we were, but they would have known we went through the postern.

I spoke to Cally.

"You have any idea what is causing the slippage in time?"

She shrugged her shoulder at me. "Bast. From what you told me she is the only common factor. You went through, by all accounts, several gates, several times with only minimal errors in time."

"Yes, we had to reset the watches by ten or fifteen minutes at the most."

"I never was sent through a gate, but what I did hear-or read about in the romances-it was never more than a half an hour of slippage." She smiled at me over a clean towel where she was field stripping the heavy spring needle gun. "Of course, there was a lot of other things in those romances that I know are absolute tosh, now, so take that account of slippage as you will."

I know I blushed.

"After the attack in the *adit* between Hanse and the

Commonality, everything went to hell and the gate 'scrammed' as the Hanse said. Afterwards there were reports of problems with calendar synchronization across the veil."

"Synchronization," she said. "I would think there were issues with timekeeping that were lost in the calendar being mucked up." She deftly reassembled the spring gun, wiped it lightly with a bit of oil on a tissue and went to her knife. "Bast is at the window ledge."

I looked up and saw a cat shape against the glass. I slid the window open; it was one reason I'd chosen this hostel, it had windows that would open and a lot of external fire escapes. More necessary for Cally and me, then for Euston.

>gate present no activity< He pushed to me. >salmon< And a hopeful nudge.

I got a can from one of our knapsacks.

While he carefully consumed the contents, I turned back to my own weapons.

From what I was informed when they cycled us through the gate operations workup, anything other than clockwork or Bronze Age weapons was absolutely verboten. They didn't tell us why, although I did witness some outstanding calamities from a safe distance. No use of firearms, no walkie-talkie, no electric torches. They took everything electrical from us and put them in coppery boxes with lead seals before ushering us through the *Adit*, into the gallery and along the path. I'd known, from being a fortunate witness, what having an electrical device unsecured in an *adit* could mean.

I had two Ceramic knives, a smokeless powder ten mm pistol, two electric driven two mm needle guns, a single shot spring dart with a poison dart and a sock full of ball bearings.

Outside the *adit* proper, anything was useable; inside the gallery, that was a different thing. Most weapons were highly restricted, confining combatants to edged weapons or clockwork needlers. No gunpowder, no battery-operated items at all; so, my pistols were useless. And we had found that some of the electric watches failed spectacularly, so we used none of them either. We used fine Swiss clockwork chronographs. Or purchased or were issued cheap watches every time we transited, purchased from the local cultures and discarded them before we left.

Now it appeared that I also might have limitations in using the 'gift', limitations I encountered at the doorway to the postern in West York. Something else they never mentioned.

I was not certain of why this, this restricting my auric fields, was so. It may have been that I couldn't reach across a threshold for some reason-though it had never happened before...

Cally spoke dryly. "Vampires, or Sangsue have to be invited over a threshold, so the story goes. So maybe that rule applies to crossing the veil?" I blinked, looked over my shoulder at her lounging on the lumpy couch in the hotel room. "You are talking to yourself, Jos. That's a sign of encroaching age, you realize. How old are you, again?" She flicked her knife open, lightly oiled the hinge with a bottle and then flicked it open and closed several times in quick succession. The razor-sharp edge gleamed in the room.

"Which myth came first, madam D'Conde?"

"I would not possibly speculate, my paladin. Are we to make another reconnaissance, or may we lay up in bed tonight?"

>smirk< Came over the push.

I blushed. Cally had that effect on me, it was unsettling. It was pleasant, but unsettling. I was not thirteen again, but she put me on the back-foot time and time again. It was what it was.

She slept now, when we slept, with her head on my shoulder and her knife under my pillow. Bast, or Euston or PC41 slept at the foot of the bed or patrolled the room. And we all were in the middle of my auric net at night, when we slept.

>?< I pushed at Euston.

>quiet< He had been watching the postern. We had felt it open two days ago, then nothing since.

"Sleep. Then we go, across the next night."

She sobered, the way she could suddenly change her mood was often breathtaking. She looked about the room. It was nothing much to speak of; ensuite bathroom, an am radio, dim electric lights on retrofitted gas goosenecks, coal oil lanterns on a dusty sideboard for when the electricity failed. A freestanding wardrobe, a folding couch, a wingback chair and a small occasional table. "I will miss this."

I understood. "The nosy dotties back on the wharf knew all what they were about, didn't they?"

She laughed, softly. Put her knife in a soft leather pouch that rode at the small of her back, tucked the gun into a soft leather holster I'd brought with me from the Smoke. It would nestle into her purse, in a cross draw. "No matter how it ends, it has been better than I deserved, Jos."

I cupped her face with my hands and kissed her.

Bast approved.

So did I.

CHAPTER 50

I chose the hour. Just before midnight, at the turn of a tide and in a waning moon.

We strolled down the street, small knapsacks draped over our right shoulders and riding on our left hips. I had settled up at the hostel, then we ate a late supper and tarried over tea and dessert. York, as a major city should, had no curfew. It did have constables, mounted and on foot, to keep the peace and to rattle the doorknobs. But, again, if you dressed the part and were calm and composed, you were not stopped by any of the police nor noted.

We left the luggage at the hostel. I had my duster on; Cally was wearing a winter coat, greatly overdressed for the weather. She also had a largish purse across her body, full of munitions and cans of the 'good stuff'.

We exited the hostel and walked arm in arm down the pavement and past the darkened storefronts. Until we got to the postern.

Murphy smiled on us, as we arrived there was a boisterous party ascending the stairway to the foyer door. Three couples in clubbing outfits intended for another world, then two more couples ran up and pushed ahead of us to join the party at the door. We simply followed in their wake, then down the interior stairs and to an open *adit* sited directly under the front stoop.

The door was open, the *adit* was clear and we were the

end of the queue. Cully looked at me, her eyes wide in the semidarkness and I nodded. I dropped all of the clubbers, the two wardens, a transit Walker and an Eisenring Proctor in the gap between one breath and the next. Cognac hangovers for all. I wasn't being squeamish; it was simpler to stun them and let them hamper the investigators. It also took significantly less effort. We were in the anteroom of the gate, the *adit* door was open.

Cally walked into the gallery of the *adit*, stepping over an Eisenring sprawled on his back. I picked him up, dragged him six feet and draped him over one of the clubbers, I did not want the possibility of a stowaway on the crossing. I quickly went through the billfolds and purses of all of the eight in the transit party, acquiring cash that matched the venue they were transiting to. American dollars, subway cards and a handful of change. No weapons, no plastic, no watches.

"Hurry." Hissed Cally, St. Elmo's fire dribbling from her outstretched hands. I slipped through the entrance to the gallery, dogged the door behind me and jammed it with one of the broad knives the wardens had worn at their backs. It would buy us five minutes at most, but it was five minutes prepaid.

The sun wheel at the end of the passage was flecked in gold and lit by bullseyes coal-oil lanterns. The walls were worked marble. I tucked Euston, PC41, into my shoulder bag and held the spring dart in one hand and rested the other hand on Cally's shoulder.

"Away and under we go," she said. That was the thing her tradition said, when they stepped off into the veil. Mine just said 'get on with it.'

The three of us took a step forward, then three steps, then more steps than we could count. Holding tight to Cally, keeping Euston in my bag and within my net and watching for a familiar arc of light at the edge of my vision. She was intent on the Sunwheel, I was intent on turning us away from that path.

We had discussed this possibility, that while she was focused on the Sunwheel I might be able to nudge her away from the path and through the veil to another destination.

I proposed it. After the first gobsmacked reaction, she was adamant that it was a novel way to commit suicide without the satisfaction of knowing your witnesses would be impressed at your ingenuity. She was also of the opinion that I was crack pated, terminally inbred, oxygen deprived, moon addled and-well it took her a quarter hour of non-stop fulmination to exhaust her ready-rack store of invective. In English, Creole and *Frankii.*

I handed her PC41, in her Bast form, and pushed at both. >show<.

PC41 and I had reminisced about how and when we had come across the veil, from AngTerra to the 'zeme and from the 'zeme to Little England. PC41 remembered exactly both crossings. Remembered clearly enough that I could feel the veil tremble. And I brought that to a full stop, immediately. We moved away from the quayside of the river, where we had been having a quiet pipe of tobacco and a skull session and headed inland at brisk stroll.

Someone should have noticed that flutter in the veil between the worlds. I certainly noticed it and I was not a Walker, nor a Dowser. Though I was closely acquainted with Cally, and Bast. Someone should have noticed that flutter, and someone did. Ten minutes later, from a convenient sidewalk pastrie blocks away and up the hill, I saw six constables-two of them likely of the Talent-converge on the Riverwalk. They were casually quartering the Riverwalk and chatting up the idlers along that stretch. Looking for a Walker and a soft spot.

I finished my cup and turnover and left at a ramble, PC41 weaving in and out of my legs.

After Bast calmed Cally down and showed her what we had conjured up at the riverside, she grew very quiet.

"Jos. This goes against everything I have ever heard about Walking-from formal instruction to Yellow Novel fantasizing."

"But we are here. You had never perceived a gate, let alone walked the path to that particular destination."

"Three impossible things before brunch." She cuddled Bast against her neck. "And you propose?"

"To jump the tracks and go forth to a different destination."

"Pfui. I should have remained a brood mare, in the commons." She turned and stalked off with Bast glaring at me from her shoulder. "If we are to be scattered from breakfast to hell, I require a good soak, clean clothes and a proper meal." And she took Bast to the ensuite bath we enjoyed at that hostel.

Now we were in the gallery of the gate. Cally was in the lead and I had a hand on her shoulder. Off to either side I saw flashes of light PC41 lightly pushed at one.

>there<

And I leaned towards it, like riding a racing motorbike.

That's all I can say; like steering a sled down a snowy hill, he pushed, and I leaned and Cally slowly came that way. The Sunwheel was still there, ahead of us, but it changed shape and colour. Receded into the distance. Then it was gone. Like a discarded cupboard sinking into dark water, to our left. You could see it beneath the water, fading as the light lost it in the darkness.

All that was ahead of Cally was a smear of light, a faint phosphorescent smear on a tree, in a dark thicket. Three steps more. She stumbled. And we were there.

The thicket was dark, we were in a shallow trickle of water, there were lights on the horizon to the south. PC41 was out of the bag and questing about, Cally was retching, one hand wrapped about a sapling to hold her up. I knew where we were, but not when. North of Dodge City.

But it wasn't winter.

CHAPTER 51

We moved away from the marked tree, to get clear of the gate in the event someone noticed the veil opening and came to check on it. It was the same primitive gate Wolff and I had crossed through on our way to the 'zeme. I followed PC41 away from the site, headed towards the drop off point. I planned to den up to one side of the creek, wait for daylight and while I was waiting sort out what I'd culled from the people I'd dropped at the gallery. Buried the plastic and ID's in a cat hole at the side of the creek, folded the money into my wallet. Keys and other items I'd left at the scene.

I found a dry place, ten feet off to the side of the creek bed and behind a thicket. I spread a drop cloth, I'd tucked it into her bag on the loadout, and I sat down with Cally by my side, a gun in my hand. Cally was better; I kicked myself for not thinking to bring some water. She was very quiet, cuddling Bast when she allowed it, leaning against me when Bast was not available. I had a headache, there were flashes of light off to the side of my vision and my ears were ringing softly. Other than that, I was functional. PC41 didn't report any side effects, he did inquire about the possibility of some of the 'good stuff'?

Beast that he was, I did have a can to give to him.

Just before dawn, we had company.

There were two people riding slowly down the creek bed.

I'd picked them up about fifty yards away, more from their horses than from them. They had their auras dimmed and the hooves of the horses were muffled. Scouts.

>guns< PC41 pushed to me. And an image of the last time we came this way. I nestled Cally into my arms and coaxed her into a semi-doze. She didn't want to, but I wanted all of our auras under a bushel, and the best way for her to hide was to let her be half asleep.

They walked past us, the horses began to be uneasy when they caught our scent and then I was among them.

"Let's not have any drama."

They froze. The horses shivered and began to bolt, and I pushed at their charkas, staggering them but not quite knocking them down. The riders were just as startled as the horses, but they knew they were toast if I wanted them.

"We have -"

"People waiting for you. That's fine. There are people waiting for us-" And they heard a bit of a rattle off in the thicket to the south, PC41 being clumsy on purpose. "so? No drama. A 'rand for a lift into Dodge, four 'rands for a lapse of memory?"

"Who are you?"

I clicked my tongue. "No names, no pack-drill. If you feel awkward, I do know you have a fine cutting horse in your string."

We waited a minute as the sky got lighter above us. "Right." The boy said, not looking to either me or the other rider. "I send her back, with two Krugerrands. I stay here. She comes back, two mounts and an escort and four Krugerrands. We take you into the city. We don't know you; you don't know us."

"That's a bargain." I handed him two coins from my belt.

He turned to the other rider, the girl. Handed her the coins. "Go get 'em."

She turned her mount around and walked, then trotted away. I didn't look at her or look in her direction until I couldn't hear the horse.

I whistled at Cally and she came out of the thicket, shaking off her fuzziness and letting her auras bloom about her as she maligned me in artful gutter French. The boy on the horse was carefully not noticing anything. But he did pick up on Cally, his horse gave him away.

"Yes," I said. "We came across the veil."

"Wasn't supposed to be a crossing this turn of the moon."

"It was, unplanned. You'll understand that I would not like to elaborate."

"Any one coming after you?"

"Possible, but not likely." One of the things we had discussed, when I was cuddling Cally after the crossing, was that she felt the gate was no longer useable. Felt, but she was not certain. She thought that bending it disrupted it.

The escorts did not include the Walker and her bowman, that had brought Wolff and company over, but they were the same crew. I forked over my 'rands and clambered on a horse. Cally was not a particularly accomplished horsewoman, but she wasn't a complete duff either. Veterinary school encouraged some familiarity with horses. Two hours later we were in the north edge of Dodge City. PC41 had paced us all the way to the truck, then snuggled himself into Cally's bag. Out of sight and never in their minds. They were carefully marking me, for future reference. Cally they considered as my customer as well as a Walker, but I was the danger to them and to their enterprise.

We got out, shouldered our bags and walked away. They got in their truck and left in the other direction. They could have dogged us, but I think they were not comfortable with doing this. A couple of them had sniffed at the edge of my net, and I gave them a bit of a pushback. Slight hangovers, auric pepper gas, if you will. They were not D'draig proper, but they carried some of the gift, enough to know one when they rubbed up against one. And to not want to do that again.

It was just before noon, local. We found a cheap motel, checked in and paid in advance. Washed up a bit, changed what clothes we had. Then called a cab and went to another, pricier motel. The first one was interested only in our money, reading the situation all wrong, with Cally's help. The second one took my cash, backed by a credit card and glanced at a Delaware DL that backed the credit card. The card was good, had about fifteen hundred dollars I'd abandoned in that account when we crossed over. The DL was fake, it just lent a bit of gloss to the card.

I took a cab to the bank I'd stashed my Alba courier bag at when we crossed to the 'zeme. I'd left PC41 and Cally at the motel, told her to sleep lightly and told him to sit on her.

I'd prepaid the safe deposit rental for five years; it was not quite three years gone by. I had a key and a different ID matching the account at the bank, tucked away in my duster. I guess I went to the 'zeme with about three complete sets of ID tucked away in a portfolio, photos and supporting paperwork. Wolff wasn't the only creature of habit, he spun off networks, I assembled identities. On the way back to the motel I picked up a Sunday KC Times and a weekday Wichita paper.

The newspapers were nothing special, no war in Europe, no assassinations in the States. Much bloviating about missiles. Chernenko, the General Secretary Wolff had gone on about at the Ford, has been dead for about a year, I thought. Gorbachev-who I don't remember at all-is the current General Secretary. Reagan is still President of the US. That made me happy, things hadn't come all pear-shaped. It was late April in the Gregorian year 1986. Well enough.

I got back to the motel, ran Cally through a shower and

then showered myself. "We going to kip here?" She asked.

"No, soon as you catch your breath and I can get a bus ticket, we are on the way to Wichita."

"Which is-?"

"About a hundred and fifty miles east of here. Two and a half hours by car, maybe six to seven hours by bus."

"Bus? Why not hire a car?"

"Anonymity. If anyone is keeping a more than casual eye on that crossing, they will be looking for people appearing out of nowhere-particularly if the crossing is closed. They'll find the first motel and eventually this one from the taxi service. But we will be gone. Using a bus. They won't think to look at the bus lines. Airport, or limo service from city to city, any flash transport would draw their eyes; but the bus lines are for Very Unimportant People. Very Unimportant People do not cross over the veil between the worlds. It is just not done."

I went on, drying my hair, which was much shorter than it was when we arrived and darker as well. "They will look for someone picking us up from the motel, when they find us gone. Looking for someone in a black sedan with tinted windows. They won't expect us to walk to the bus station and buy round trip tickets to Kansas City via Wichita."

"I think I want to see a map."

"Trust me." I smiled at her. "Ask Bast."

>another can< Interrogative.

CHAPTER 52

It took all of seven hours to make our way to Wichita. The highlight of the trip was introducing Cally to the toilet at the back of the bus.

My schoolboy French allowed me to understand about one malediction in five, but it was to the point without being repetitious. PC41 was highly entertained so were several of the passengers.

We got into downtown Wichita about nine pm to change buses for the rest of the trip to Kansas City. We filtered off the bus carrying our scant carry-on bags and just kept going. No fuss, no bother. No questions. There were a number of cheap, anonymous, hotels close by the bus station. I got us settled in one, with even less attention than was afforded us in Dodge City, then I put us to bed. PC41 was stretched across the doorway, I was sleeping in the only chair the room had and Cally was sleeping the sleep of the truly pissed-off. I was not welcome to cuddle her, the toilet on the bus had trampled on her last nerve.

I got a cramp in my back.

In the early morning we left the key on the bed with a twenty-dollar bill under it and walked to a diner on the highway that cut through the edge of the downtown. From there I took a cab to the airport, hired a car, came back and picked up Cally and Bast. Neither one was speaking to me. Which was just as well, I didn't want to be sociable. I hadn't had time for a coffee or a bit of yoga to ease the cramp in my back.

I drove over to Wolff's bookstore, in the strip mall with the dry cleaners and the Chinese restaurant. The bookstore was still there, the liquor store was closed, which was a puzzlement. I cruised slowly through the neighborhood, trailing my net as wide and as thin as I could. There were watchers, none churched. Predators, minor ones, more interested I thought in the rims of the rental's tires than us. I parked a block to the north and Cally, PC41 and I walked to the alley at the back of the shops.

"Jos, you take me through the most attractive alleys."

"If I we can, I'll take you on a walking tour of the Smoke. It has a much more historic sleaze than this."

She glowered at me. I went to the back door to the shop, popped the rudimentary lock with my knife blade and ushered us into the back hall and up the stairs to the door that opened into the kitchen. Tripping the alarms of course.

PC41 quickly cleared the rooms, I left our meager kit at the top of the rear stairs and had Cally sit at the kitchen table.

"Nobody home?"

"Wait a bit."

The door to the front landing swung in and I felt rather then saw Lyn at the edge of the doorway.

"Hullo, Lyn. Got any coffee?"

PC41 was out and in the hall and I heard a muffled squawk. Lyn stumbled into the doorway with a heavy needler in her hand. "You," she said. "I thought we were done with you and your..." She saw Cally. Looked to me. Her gun went away. "Wolff is down in the coffee room, an informal gathering with some people from the university. It is immediate?"

"It's important, but it can wait."

"You are Lyn, of course." Cally said in her best butter-would-not-melt, I-am-just-delighted-to-make-your-acquaintance tone. "Bast and Jos have told me about your hospitality." She gave Lyn a fixed smile that they taught her in fourth form, 'to be used when meeting servants or other inferiors', for the first time.

Lyn smiled back; the long knives were out. "I'll just bet." She glared at me. "You know where the coffee is, fix it yourself and cleanup after, I'll tell Wolff the bad seed is back." And she left.

"She is such a pleasant conservationist." Cally smirked at me.

"She has her moments, she also will play a large role in getting you a proper bed, a warm meal, proper clothing and a clean bathroom. Or not."

Cally lost her smile. "Mmm. I will remember that."

>kippers< And an overtone of delight came through the push.

I made coffee and warmed up some leftover sweet rolls in the microwave oven. Bast was perched on the windowsill, as still as an ebony statue. I heard Wolff and Lyn come up the stairs.

"Braxton," he said, pausing for a second at the doorway. "It does me good to see you, that it does."

I rolled my eyes at Cally. "Cally, this is Benjamin Wolff. Wolff, this is a new partner of ours, Cally D'Conde, she is on the run from the Unity Commonality."

"I am pleased to meet you." He walked over to her, took her hand and shook it once in the continental fashion. Then he sat between us, Lyn got a saucer and cup from the cupboard and poured him a cup. "I take it Josiah has told you about our association?"

"Yes. In the middle of things, as it were."

"Always a good place to begin a story." He turned to me. "Now, would you like to be brought up to speed on events, since we last saw you?"

"No. No, in truth I need to bring you up to speed on what hell The Gotha is planning to unleash." I took the heirloom pound coin out of my watchpocket, placed it on the tabletop and gently pushed it his way. Then I extracted the German Mark and laid it next to the pound coin.

"My," he said. "I hadn't expected to see that again."

CHAPTER 53

I t didn't take long. I laid out what The Gotha intended to do. Their plan was to destroy most if not all of the known gates to the 'zeme. To do it in such a way as to break all the Houses.

He did not blanch at this, nor did he scoff. He took the pound coin and the silver mark, accessed the micro dots and drank his coffee. Wolff took a good hour, and three cups of coffee, to read all three of the dots I had. He carefully stowed them away, closed the coins and sat back in his chair rubbing his eyes.

"How much of this did you read?"

"The first microdot only. My German was not up to scratch and the Gothic typeset was-challenging."

"Mmm, yes." He pushed his cup away. "The first microdot had the overview of their plan, the second dot concerned logistics and tasking of the various operational teams and the third microdot was an abstract of progress reports to date. It would appear, from those abstracts, that we eliminated all of the competent operational planners in the last war."

"They aren't as far along as they'd like to be?"

"No. And there seems to be factional struggles within The Gotha that are throwing sand in the gears."

"More power to them."

He tapped his fingernails on the tabletop, the tell he had

for when he was working through a problem.

"And how stands your credit with Croton-on-Hudson?"

"Small beer. They were very appreciative of our aid in opening the investigation of *Allemagne Noir*, gave us a hearty handshake and a pat on the back. Sent us packing back to AngTerra, then sent along an itemized bill for keeping us at the Confed station in the Ford."

"And the Hanse involvement?"

"Hmm? The Confeds and the Eisenring send someone by to chat, about once a quarter. Still turning over rocks for you and the *Dai Betrekkingen Provinciale* networks that are supposed to be here in AngTerra. Not as industrious as they were, but, it's a living?" He grew very still. "You haven't spoken to Johanna Marie, have you?"

"Just her spirit. My partner-"

"Bast." Murmured Cally.

"Bast" I echoed. "had a suggestion. Have this-" I pointed at the courier coin. "come through a network from the DBP to you because you are considered reliable. And then from you to the authorities, such as they are."

He smiled. "You know, Braxton, every month I spend in your company seems to take a year off of my age."

"He is a corrupting influence." Lyn said from the couch.

"Yes, he is." Agreed Cally and winked at Lyn. Lyn glowered, I blushed, and Wolff tried very hard not to smile.

Lyn put us up in a small house on the street behind the strip mall. Closer than I liked, but they had an open and furnished rental and it was quickly done. A change of sheets, a delivery of food from a local grocery and we had effectively gone to earth.

If, and I stress if, any investigators were to attempt to track our movements from Dodge City. They would not find much information. The rental car, but it was procured at the airport by a credit card that none of the players knew. It was not even the one I had used back in 1982 when we went to Dodge City.

Lyn and Cally eventually came to an armistice. The issue was not me, I thought, but PC41.

Bast's first reaction to that notion was amusement, her second reaction was to find a reason to leave the arena. I wished I could do the same. But, like I said, they came to an eventual peace—by blaming me for the ruckus.

I fed myself and Cally; admitted PC41 when she slapped the window screen, fed her.

>anything< I pushed at PC41.

>no< She daintily finished the bowl of salmon, followed me to the counter as I set the bowl in the sink, then escorted me to the loo.

>don't need help< I complained.

Mirth came back over the push. I stripped to my boxers, put a gun to hand by the bed and settled in behind Cally.

"Jos," she said a bit later.

I came completely awake and my nimbus flooded the room, the house and a fair part of the yards about the house. Nothing. "Cally?"

"You and Lyn?"

Oh. Enhanced Interrogation. I was in for a long night.

>aid< I pushed to PC41.

A stick figure of a man with an anchor about its neck and bubbles coming from its head came back over the link.

I think I convinced her that Lyn, while a boon companion, was not an issue between us. I think.

CHAPTER 54

We put the microdots, after copying them, back into the German Mark coin. Then gamed how this would transpire. Wolff got boxes in the mail and from several shipping companies each week. UPS and the like were more traceable, you needed a valid return address, or it would not be shipped. But the US Postal Service needed only a plausible return address when you sent packages through the mail. So, if a package came through the post office ostensibly from a used book dealer on the west coast, no one would likely bat an eye. He had been getting packages on a weekly basis from several different dealers and they all looked to not be tampered with.

So, he gets a package in the mail, waits a week or less and opens it. Instead of a rarish book, it is a silver German Mark commemorative and a typewritten letter addressing Herr Wolff. And since Wolff has experience in this sort of tradecraft, he reads the letter and then immediately contacts someone from Croton on the Hudson.

Now the question is, who is the boy in the barrel, and since we have multiple examples of the microdots to spread around-who gets the extras.

"I think," I said, "you should contact your man in Croton house and just give him the coin. I could send a letter to that blind drop box I told you about. That would go to the Unity Eisenring, informing them that Croton house has documents from both the DBP and the *Allemagne Noir*, my message authenticated with extremely out of date pass-phrases."

"And-?"

"Then you, if you can, give McDermid a copy of the microdots-or print them out. Original documents and translation, perhaps into Hanse? Would she-"

"Three hours after she got the packet, it'd be translated and all over the Western Range." Lyn spoke up. Cally was giving her a practicum on makeup, working with her and a mirror. Once Lyn found out that Cally was 'horsey', needed practice with guns, was comfortable with knives and did not lord it over a 'simple' Medji-they united against me. Woe.

"She's right. Anything to embarrass the Eisenring and give hindrance and discomfort to the Confederated Houses." Said Wolff. "What she cannot wrinkle out of the *Allemagne Noir* documents she will fabricate."

"She won't be in any risk?" I had a fondness for McDermid, even though she would have cheerfully cut my throat when I was a Churched Eisenring. If it comes to that, I might have cheerfully done the same thing, if meeting my doppelganger in the Eisenring.

"Some. But she is hearth-kin to several circles of the Pika. Not someone you would casually come after."

"We might want to have her be in possession of the documents prior to your receiving the Mark?" I was making random notes on a pad of paper; ammunition needed, cans of the 'good stuff', plots to contrive, underwear to purchase, that sort of things.

Wolff stared off into space. "I'll tell her to sit on them and then, say the day after I will reveal it to the House, start spreading it around. Have a possible source that has vague connections to the Hanse consulate in the Ford?" He nodded to himself and stopped messing about with his pipe. "That would do it, The Gotha would really not want to get up crossways with the Hanse, before they shut off the gates."

"Yes," I said. "I would not want to have the Hanse seriously unhappy with me." I rearranged my cup and saucer. "How is Johanna Marie?"

"She is well, astoundingly enough I receive the occasional letter from her through the postal service." He shrugged. "Evidently, she stumbled into another issue, for the *deRegering*. Corruption charges that led to a 'simply shocking' suspicious death. Resolving that case led to a better office and, I should think, even closer surveillance."

I grinned. "They think she is definitely mobbed up with the DBP as an Auditor-they just can't prove it."

"And, whatever their faults, they follow the absolute letter of the law and the regulations."

Swiss.

CHAPTER 55

Cally and I decamped two days later, not wanting to be anywhere near Wolff when he contacted Croton House. We had made a concerted raid on several department stores in the area. Replaced the luggage and items we'd abandoned and bought a flat of kippers. I took her to a cobbler Wolff had vouched for, got a set of papers for both of us. I paid gold for the set, in advance. I wasn't worried about being sold or bilked. Wolff knew them.

Passports, properly stamped and countersigned, she was from the South of France and the Fifth Republic and I was from the Smoke of AngTerra-London. They were forgeries, and they were top notch-for AngTerra. The Eisenring were better at this sort of legending, but only because their papers were not forged by a cobbler but produced by the proper agencies. It helps to have a partial controlling interest in certain countries.

I thumbed through my new identity and thought, again not for the first time, that Wolff was not as retired as he avowed.

We drifted south east, into the Ozarks. Did some touristy things, went to Branson and spent a fair amount of dosh there in attending shows and buying trash. Every day I touched up her birthmark, every night Bast guarded us while we slept.

I got a ping on my new pager one morning. To call a number. It was in the area code for Wichita, but I didn't recognize it.

We got in the rental and ran up the highway from Branson towards Springfield. I found a convenient truck stop and called from a payphone, with a phone card I bought at the stop.

Lyn answered.

"Yes?"

She was beside herself, for a Medji. "They took Wolff at the university. Left two dead, unchurched. We have unchurched and churched working it, but the House thinks he's been snatched across, the unchurched is thrashing about."

"Five hours." And I hung up, I wiped down the handset and laid the card on the ledge in the phone booth. I'd wiped the card as well. Might not have needed to wipe it down, but...

I got back in the car. PC41 was between Cally and me. "Bad?" She asked.

"Yes, someone has Wolff and has killed two to seal the deal."

"Right," she said and settled in her seat for the trip.

I thought about a lot of things on the way there. Not Wolff. Either he was dead, in which case there were debts that I would be calling in, ankle deep, or he was alive, and someone had him for a reason. A reason that I could only speculate on and speculation was not going to help.

If he was still on AngTerra, and close by the shop, then I could find him. If he had gone across-maybe Cally could find him. I know there was a postern gate at the airport, I didn't know where it traveled to. If Croton House thought he'd gone across the veil, they should have a notion of where he'd gone to. And that gate was possibly blocked now. I didn't know just how much energy could disturb a gate or for how long.

If I had been indifferent to the collateral damage, I might have left a squib charge on a clockwork timer in the gallery after we cleared the gate from 'zeme to Alba. I hadn't left that charge, but I could have. I didn't for the same reason you don't dump bodies in wells as you raid an enemy's territory. For one thing, you might have to retreat across that territory.

What they didn't know, was how Cally, Bast, and I worked together. I hadn't told Wolff just how we turned up at his back door, just that we'd come across at Dodge City. I let him assume that we'd somehow came through the gates in the usual way, likely leaving a scatter of dead Eisenring. And I didn't tell him that we'd scrammed the postern gate when we arrived.

We got to Wichita. I used another phone booth, another pre-paid card. Didn't get Lyn, got somebody with an official tone and I hung up. I cruised the place, swept the block with my net. Cally curled up on the floor in the back seat. They had people on the bookstore, but they were unchurched. Not a talent among them that I could see or sense. I thought Lyn was there, but I wasn't sure.

I had a phone number for the Chinese place in my black book, I called them from a booth a couple of blocks away. Ordered a sweet and sour shrimp combo, sent it to Lyn.

She hated shrimp.

She came out of the Bookstore with a keeper, stalked down the front of the strip mall and into the Chinese place with a plastic bag, held as far away from herself as she could. Yelling at the counter girl about mucking up the order. PC41 was in the take-out shop, I was outback by the dumpster.

>here< And I felt him push at Lyn.

I came in through the back of the restaurant, my face blurred a bit with the auric web and under a bandanna, showed the cooks a gun, showed the proprietor a gun and dragged Lyn out the back. She had sucker punched her keeper, I added a double cognac hangover to what she'd done. He'd be out of it for the rest of the day, if not to the end of the week.

"Jos?" She had a hideout knife ready to carve on me if I wasn't.

"Yup, the bad seed." I grabbed the dumpster and pushed it across to block the back door to the shop, threw her in the trunk of the rental. Cally put it in gear and we drove sedately off, on the right side of the road for a change. Five miles to the mall, we parked in a fairly busy part of the lot. I got out, then climbed in the back seat, pulled down the split-seat back and motioned Lyn out. The mall wasn't really busy, but it wasn't dead either; just enough traffic milling about that their security patrols wouldn't notice us for a while.

"We won't have much time. Brief me."

"Wolff went to talk to some people in the University. In the History department, talking to them about Paris in the thirties." Lyn was sitting up right, one arm across the back of the seat and just as calm as you please. She'd combed her hair with her fingers, she had a faint bruise on her cheek. Her eyes were everywhere but on my face. "Someone tried to snatch him as he went to lunch, they did snatch him. But one of the History staff and a campus PD officer got mixed up in it. They were killed."

"Weapons?"

"Local." Which meant no needles.

"Croton have a clue?"

"They think he was taken to a hide, then across. They had a Dowser overwatching Wichita from shortly after Wolff made his report about DBP activity, he felt a small gate come open for a short time, then close."

I thought about it. "If he's across the veil, there is not much we can do." I had an idea about that, but I was not about to lay it out in front of Lyn. What she does not know, she cannot reveal. "I think you need to go to ground." She stopped her scanning and focused on me. I held up a hand to stop any recriminations. "If they have him and are putting pressure on him, a Verity or even a D'draig as an interrogator, he will hold as long as he can-then he will give up as little as he can before he dies. Correct?"

She nodded; her jaw clenched until I heard her teeth grind.

"But if they dangle you before him-"

She was silent. Then she slumped, her head dropped back against the seat, her eyes closed. "Fuck." She wiped at her face. "I told him, and told him, and told him he needed a change in-"

"Yeah. He had his reasons." I patted her knee, carefully. I did not want her to lash out. "So, they will want you close to hand. And they might not have taken him across but brought a specialist to him."

We both sat there for a long while. We knew what sort of specialist they might have brought.

"That makes sense," she said, finally. "Now you have me. And who ever has Benjamin needs to find me…"

"One disadvantage is that I don't know this town, but neither will they. You know all the cranny's, hmm?"

"And they don't know you are in play."

"They know someone is out there, just not what, or who. I think we should plan on Wolff being still in Wichita or just outside the metro area. Then take them down when they come looking for you."

We needed to den up, so Lyn took us to a very modest motel on the south west side of Wichita. An improvement from her usual haunts. We waited on getting Lyn into the room until dusk, not that anyone would have paid any attention short of a marching band with flaming batons. I asked her, Lyn, if any of the people sitting on the Bookstore were Dai or Eisenring.

"Maybe. There were two that were supposed to be FBI from Washington. But the other Federal agents, the ones from the field offices, didn't know them and I got the impression they did not trust them."

"They didn't trust them?"

"They thought they were one of the other alphabet agencies." Lyn said. "Your aborted call had them spinning in circles, two of the district agents and one I made as an Eisenring took off in a sedan. The rest were chattering on radios. One of them opened the door to the delivery boy, poor tradecraft. So, when I hit the celling, the rube they sent with me was the dumb one of the pair from DC."

"He didn't know? He didn't know you were a Medji?"

"Oh, he knew I was a bodyguard. He had a low opinion of me, as a guard and as a woman. He just didn't believe I was more than a secretary and bed warmer to a has-been."

"Ow." Said Cally. She was sitting by the window to the parking lot, her heavy needler in her lap. She had the curtain pulled just enough that she had a sight on the car and the entrance, but not enough that you could see her. "He going to walk again?"

Lyn grinned. "Maybe."

"Where can we ambush them?"

"Not the bookstore, not the storage center either. One of the reasons they were sort of rough on me-" And she flicked her fingers at the bruise on her face. "was that they couldn't get into the safe at the storage center. That Rube decided to slap me about a little to get me to 'cooperate' on getting into the safe. He got dressed down by his handler and the Senior of the district agents, that piece of work was one reason they didn't trust the two from DC."

"You have any suggestions?"

"Let me think about it." And she went off to the bathroom.

PC41 was out and about. It was dark and I left most of the lights off in the room.

Wolff. I sat on the bed and let the auras sweep about me. I know where Cally was, how she was feeling. I knew where Lyn was, but she was closed. No auras, none that I could tease out. I could have forced the issue, swept the net through her but that was not something to do casually.

Wolff. He was a friend. Hadn't had one since…since the Smoke back in Alba. And maybe not even then. You live in an orphanage; you don't have friends. Allies maybe. People you can trust to a point. But no further, and you never know just where that point is.

If Wolff didn't trust you implicitly, you knew it. What you saw on the table was the deal. When you crossed over the line from questionable to trusted, he never looked back, never second-guessed his acceptance. Somewhere, from the night he showed up in my apartment, to the night I left him in Cantry Ford, I crossed over that line.

He was that sort, if he accepted your loyalty, he gave you his. Unconditionally.

I just sat there in the dark motel room, waiting. For something.

Lyn came out of the bathroom, sat on the bed next to me. "There is a gate in Hutchinson, close to a salt mine there. We knew about that one. There was another gate in MidContinent Airport, at the Aircargo end of the field. Mid-size, fully staffed. Has a Book for the 'zeme as well as for Little England. We did not know about that one until after we got back on Earth."

"Hmm." Eisenring and Croton action teams, long knives and needlers, paperwork.

"But they did not think either one was where Dama Ledhrad came through."

"I knew she didn't come from Hutchinson. She was dropped off at the store by a limo, your Eric saw her get dropped off at the door, so I assumed she came through ICT."

"He wasn't my Eric; he is not my Eric. Both of those gates are fully staffed, and both were gone over by Croton with a fine-toothed comb. There were no irregularities. The gate in Hutchinson is from the Islands. The one at the airport is from the 'zeme and has a book for Alba as well. They questioned us at the Ford very closely about where Dama Ledhrad came over at; they were unhappy at how little we knew."

"And the limo."

"Poof. Nobody had one working the airport on that day and at that time. And no one had any in Hutchinson at all."

"Anyone think to check the local funeral homes?"

"No." She chewed on her lip. Said something slightly obscene in Creole. "I didn't think to suggest that."

"Wolff might have had a notion, but he didn't want to make things easier for the 'Ring."

She looked at me, in the half dark and her auras bloomed ever so slightly. "You think the airport?"

"Perhaps." I rubbed at an ache in my lower back. I needed to eat. "It isn't easy to work a large covert gate within a major airport perimeter. Even if you own the airport, the FAA keeps an eye on the operations with officers that are not so easily suborned. So, you have to have the local officials on board, convinced they are working for an arm of the government."

"The Men In Black."

"Mhn, yes. Someone would have to be significantly cozened to turn a blind eye to the activities around a gate and bringing the CIA into it would serve." I got up and retrieved a box of biscuits-cookies-from a bag. I sat down and started methodically going through the box. PC41 wasn't the only one perpetually hungry. "I was told, when they brought me into the States, I was told that there was 'significant' cooperation between lower echelons of the US government and the Eisenring, but that the upper echelons had 'deniability'."

"We don't know anything when the trolley runs off the tracks."

"Something like that."

PC41 was batting at the window in front of Cally. She looked over her shoulder and grinned at me. "The Boss wants you," she said. I got up from the bed again, drew my needler and leaned against the door. It was PC41 out there, and no one else was around. I opened it just enough for a cat, then closed, locked it and put the chain on again.

>salmon< Hopeful push.

I walked to the corner where I had dropped my bags, got a can of kippers out and took it to the bathroom.

>kippers< He pushed at me when I peeled the can open with the key. >soon<

"You could be foraging for your dinner. Lots of vermin about, no? Hunting builds character."

>acceptance< PC41 looked at me, then shut his eyes. >not< And an image of a cat with its eyes crossed and a tongue stuck out in defiance.

>slacker< I pushed back.

I put the opened can of kippers on the floor of the shower, washed my hands and went back to the bed. "My money is on a postern gate, somewhere in the interference screen of the *adit* at the airport."

"Why."

"No wards, no operators, just a secret door to a short gallery for the gate. And after someone transits, they close the hallway up and pocket the fare."

"So. You think you can find him." PC41 jumped to the bed and butted his head against Lyn. She scratched him under his chin.

"Two days. If we haven't got a taste of him in two days, he's gone. Close to the postern and not out of the metro area, the less distance they have to travel, the less likely to have eyes on them. And someplace that they can control the number of witnesses. In the general aviation area or inside the aviation authority division, I'd say."

"Sounds like you've done this before."

"I have no comment at this time."

CHAPTER 56

They weren't on the airport proper. They were in a RTTF, Residential Through The Fence. A small private hangar and a Fixed Base operator who was 'outside' the airport, but who had ready access to the airport. By just stepping across a line on the tarmac, you were inside the airport.

I'd never heard of a RTTF before I came across it in a magazine some years before all this hit the fan, I was escorting a principal to a dentist appointment and was desperate for something to read that wasn't about golf. I picked up a magazine about what they called General Aviation.

An Airpark subdivision is an RTTF; you have a private airstrip in the middle of your subdivision, you build your split-level with a semi-attached hangar opening onto the taxiway around your airstrip. When you want to go flying, you walk out of the house, to the hangar and into your plane. None of the 'drive to the airport, park the car, check through the gate and then get your plane out of a shared hangar.' You do have to file a flight plan and it is not as easy as taking the family sedan for a spin, but it is easy.

Industrial airparks work like that as well. They might have a light cargo or passenger aircraft in the hangar, belonging to the company and accessible through the company. You come to work, clock in, wear your badge and come and go all day from the office to the hangar, onto the tarmac and fly off on business. Cargo or chartered passenger service, you flew when you or your passengers were ready to go and not on a schedule. Employees of the RTTF went through a thorough vetting process when they were hired, and the FAA tried to keep an eye on the company as a whole.

We went out to the airport, Cally, Bast and I. Cally was supposedly looking for job applications while I trawled the net through the swarm of auras looking for a taste of Wolff. At the Airport Authority offices, she picked up a pamphlet listing all of the companies based at MidContinent, the HR office for the airport authority had a stack of them available. With a map locating the companies, their phone numbers and a thumbnail description of each of them.

We went back to the parking lot and the car and went through the pamphlet. Crossing off the custodial services and restaurants we got a list of possible businesses that were inside the interference coverage of the *adit*.

On the General Aviation landside, there were three Fixed Base Operators and two big service areas that were dedicated to Cessna and Learjet. We decided to concentrate on the General Aviation side before we tried the commercial facilities again. So, we left the short-term parking and went to the GA lot.

We intended to cruise all three FBO frontages, plus the Cessna and Learjet service area. I was out in the car, in the GA parking lot. Bast was loitering with intent just outside the offices. Between us we had a footprint of about fifty yards radius. When Cally went in each of the frontages, our footprint intruded into the building.

We started with the bigger ones-Learjet to begin with. Cally was looking for a job; she was picking up applications at the front desk and flirting a bit. She got a handful of forms and a couple business card from pilots who were hanging about the front desk. Wolff wasn't there.

It was much the same at each of the places we hit that afternoon. Application forms and come-ons from dashing pilots-PC41 was sniggering over the push at both of us. Some of the dashing pilots had, I swore, flown bi-planes in the first world war. Cally was not amused.

Then there was Laboe Air Service.

The smallest one of the FBO was Laboe LLC. They were listed as only supporting aircraft for Michigan Island Inc., which was a courier service that covered most of the middle of the country, from the Dakotas to the Gulf of Mexico.

Laboe was very bare-boned next to the other FBOs; one desk that handled reception and dispatch, a counter and a scale for the dispatch boxes, a restroom marked 'employees only', a battered set of vinyl seats and an even more battered coffee table. There was a double door at the back of the office marked Hangar, with a CCTV camera watching it and a Keycard lock station on the wall under the camera. More security than either of the Cessna or the Learjet FBO.

Cally took almost all of this in one glance when she walked through the door. We also had Wolff in the net as soon as she walked through the door.

She didn't break stride, made her pitch to the man at the desk. He told her that they had nothing for her, nobody would like to talk to her, and he didn't have any application forms she could take away with her. And he went back to reading his current Sports Illustrated, and he did not hand her a business card.

She thanked him, came out to the car, she and Bast got in and we went on to the main terminal; where she collected three more application forms and a solid offer of a position at a Pam Am check-in counter. That offer of a job calmed her down. Which was a good thing.

We hadn't let Lyn come with us. I was relatively sure they were not watching for us, if Wolff hadn't broken, but they really wanted Lyn. So, she sat in the motel room stropping her knife on a bit of leather I'd brought across the veil.

"Well?" She asked me.

I didn't wind her up. "He's there, stressed I think, but what I could suss out he is in better shape than the first time I met him."

She nodded, put away her knife. "We are going to get him, are we?"

"Yes. I don't want either the mundanes or the churched getting their hands on him. I'd lay odds someone in Croton house or the bloody Eisenring tipped him into the muck."

"We are light on hardware, Braxton."

"If we have to fight our way in, we are just bloody well up the creek. I've got three pistols, two needlers. Cally has that needler of hers, plus her knife. You can have one of my pistols, the nine-mil, it's got three magazines and it is locally sourced-Browning HP." I handed a canvas holster to her. She gave me a cocked eyebrow. "A left-over from the last time I came through town."

"It does work?"

"I shot it in, when were down in the Ozarks. Ran across a gun range and wanted to give Cally a bit of time on the local weapons."

"Thank you." She pulled the gun from the holster, dropped the magazine, jacked the slide back and cleared the chamber. Nodded. Looked me in the eyes and nodded again. Much more than a Medji.

"Quite all right. That office is open until seven PM, I intend to walk in at five till; then you and Cally come in at seven on the dot."

"You going to kill that arsehole?" Cally asked, she was sorting through the HR material and paperwork for Pan Am. Muttering about needing more supporting paper.

"Maybe, are you actually going to try to get on at Pan

Am?"

"I like horses, but I'd rather not spend my time with them with my arm up their bums." The notion I had of wafting her off to a small bucolic town on the big lake, she serving as a veterinarian and I as an engine tender, was right out. Bother.

Lyn gave me a cheerful look, then went off to the bathroom. "Braxton," She shouted at me through the door. "that cat left fish parts all over the damn floor."

PC was curled up asleep. Slacker.

CHAPTER 57

I walked into the office of Laboe LLC. with a box under my arm and a clipboard with papers in the other hand. It was five of, by the clock above the desk.

"We're closed, bub."

"Sign says seven to seven, your clock says it is five till."

"I say we're closed. Come back tomorrow."

"Pity." I dropped the box, scaled the clipboard at his head, shot him with the small needler; a spray from his chin to his receding hairline. He dropped his gun to the floor, fell out of his chair and hit the tiles. I hustled around the desk, he hadn't hit the panic button and there weren't any other cameras in the room.

I scooped up his gun, took a key ring off his belt, took a card on a lanyard off his neck. The women and PC41 walked in, making haste slowly. The women had balaclavas on when they came in, I pulled one out of the back of my jacket and put it on. I gave Cally the box for safekeeping. I needled the cable to the camera, cut the phone line, then swept the keycard through the lock and popped the doors.

There was a broad hallway to an open hangar, there were two bays with sliding doors opening out on a taxi way. There was a single engine propeller aircraft in one bay, with the cowlings open and the engine exposed. Right next to the plane was a rollaway tool chest, a stepladder and a rolling bench. To our left was a door, no deadbolt and no key-slot in the doorknob. A closet, I thought. To the right was another office, cheap desk, chair, typewriter; TV monitor at the side of the desk with a split display-one of the four scenes in the display was a haze of snow, the other three showed the hangar, the taxiway and a blank doorway at the outside right rear of the hangar. A doorway with a deadbolt keyset. There was a jacket hanging on a coat tree in the office, water running behind a door to the left of the desk. I could barely sense the man behind the door.

He came out saw the monitor and then saw me. I dropped him, catching him in my free hand before he could hit the floor.

He was not quite out and when I pushed Wolff's image at him, my hand holding his head like an actor in Hamlet cradling a skull, he brought up where they had him. Then I shut his breathing off and lowered him quietly to the carpeted floor. He had Lyn's trick of suppressing his auras. I looked at her, mouthed 'you know him?'. She gave him the once over and shook her head.

I knew that there were two in the hangar, where we couldn't see them-over by more toolboxes to the right of the hallway. There were three more deeper in the building, and there was Wolff.

I sidled up to the entryway into the hangar. Let my net bloom out and covered the two working at a bench on my right. I dropped them and went around the corner.

They weren't dead, nor were they armed. Two men, early forties, working men by their hands and coveralls. One had a metric wrench set, the other a bag of plastic ties in his hand. Car keys, wallets. I turned them on their sides while Lyn cleared the rest of the hangar to our left and Cally covered her. The men might be *Allemagne Noir*, but I gave them the benefit of the doubt, too much grease under their nails to be *herrenrasse*. I also gave them the worst hangovers they ever had in their lives, and an eighteen-hour nap.

At the far-right hand end of the hangar there was another hallway, masked by a parts rack and a tall rolling toolbox. There was an exit light above the hallway. That was where Wolff and the other three were.

We worked our way down the wall to that hallway. It seemed to take forever, but it was not more than a minute. PC41 led the way. I had the three bodies clocked by the time we got to the parts rack.

PC41 pushed me an image, man leaning against the wall by a door, reading a folded newspaper.

I put away my gun, took the balaclava off and held my hand out to the women, three fingers extended. Then two, then one and then I walked around the corner.

The man didn't twitch, just kept reading until I was halfway to him. Then it was too late. I caught him as he began to fold. Laid him gently on the hallway floor, took his gun and a badge case. FBI. Interesting. Looked real.

I hate it when we start blue-on-blue exchanges.

This hallway ran to the front of the building, had a metal door with an alarmed crash bar at the exit. The FeeBee had not been leaning on the exit door but by an interior door. What little I got from him when I snuffed his candle was that he was an Agent but had a second employer he answered to. I pulled the body over, out of the way.

I touched the doorknob, it wasn't locked, and it appeared to be just a stockroom door, like the one in the other hallway. I turned it and eased it open just enough for a small PC41 to shimmy through. I counted to three.

Then I swung the door open the rest of the way and stepped through into an improvised interrogation session. It came to a sudden halt, of course.

Wolff was pretty badly knocked around. Sitting on a

heavy wooden chair and cable ties holding him steady. They had been using several old school tactics to encourage him to talk, some new age methods as well. One new twist was that they had a reel to reel tape recorder documenting the session. I flicked it off.

Wolff opened his one good eye, looked at me and spat out a gobbet of blood. "You made good time."

Lyn hustled in, opened the box we'd brought with us and started tending to his injuries. Cally was watching at the corner by the parts rack.

"Any more than these?" I lightly kicked one of the interrogators, the dead one. I'd left one alive on purpose.

"Three, maybe four. There is a postern gate somewhere close, they are careful with it."

"Okay," Lyn was cutting him free of the chair. "you want to muck the postern up or just vanish?"

"You are not suggesting 'scramming' the gate? That would compromise the entire region." He was hurting, but he had all his fingers and he was able to stand.

"No, Cally's got a way of knocking the gate out of alignment-doesn't seem to affect other gates in the sheaf." I lied. I intended to compromise the whole bloody region if I had to.

He smiled.

CHAPTER 58

The outer door of the hangar, the one the CCTV monitor was showing was the postern, of course. After we got Wolff out of the building and into the rental, I laced the living *Allemagne Noir* into the office chair. I coaxed him awake after I got the cable ties set. He was not badged, no ID at all. Small needler, switchblade and a knuckle-backer; and a high-end Swiss chronometer, the type you had to wind.

I didn't ask him any questions, just sat at the corner of the desk in the office with the monitor. The dead man at our feet. It took him a good five minutes to get his soggy brain around the scene.

He focused on me and pushed. This was a novelty. Then he spun a cloud of pheromones through the air. I'd sent the women to sit with Wolff for this possibility. Sonny, here, was a Binder.

I hadn't run into them much when I was in the 'Ring. An honest to god Binder is hard to find outside a House. They are the 'grain of sand around which the Pearl of the House accretes' and they weren't supposed to be rubbing up against scum like me. They were also regarded with unease by the Eisenring Desks, because a Binder without a house sometimes tries to rise up and establish one. And they sometimes succeeded.

They were rare in my personal experience. What I knew

of them was anecdotal, absurd and incomplete, much like Cally's account of a D'draig, sourced from Yellow Novels. We knew 'all' about the pheromones, nobody said anything about a 'push'.

Selai, D'draig, or Sangsue were all moderately resistant to a Binder as a rule. The stronger the D'draig, the more resistant, as a rule. Our hapless Binder did not know how resistant I might be, he likely did not know I was a D'draig. We don't wear snappy little black fedoras or drape a blood red sash across our chests.

There were Dai or Mundanes who were absolutely 'blind' to Binders and were valued and feared for that fact. Valued by Desks who were tasked to handle Binders, feared by Binders for good reason. I suspect Wolff was one of those specimens.

Interrogative. >push back< PC41 was sitting on the desktop next to me, sphinxlike, with a rumbling coming from him that made my teeth ache. He liked Wolff. PC41 had hopes of shredding this Binder and leaving it for the rats to eat. And he was wordlessly passing that hope on to our Binder, PC41 had subtonics in his rumble.

>wait< I pushed to PC41.

I leaned in and took a deep breath, smiling at the Binders hopeful face. I shook my head. "Not a good extrait, I fear, not suitable for purpose." I reached out and with a tentative little finger dragged a strip off his rolling boil of aura. I saw it break red and open whitely and then crumble away into black smuts. He thrashed, his jaw gritted, and he took deep breathes through his nose at the pain.

"I can have your name, your rank and your preferences in sexual deviations in several heartbeats." I spoke to him, in a quiet matter-of-fact tone. "But what's the joy in that? It becomes so tedious, stripping off a piece at a time, asking another question, stripping off another piece of your soul; simply tedious. But if you crack-" I wrapped a cast of my web about the center of his mind and twisted it. "the eggshell and take all at once, so very often you lose important information." I twisted the web tighter. "And you forfeit all the little grace notes of the interrogation process; the begging, the screaming, the bargaining, all just lost in the surge before death ends the entertainment. Most unsatisfactory."

PC41 turned his head and gave me a silent hiss, a hiss that the Binder saw and misinterpreted. >where came that< Interrogative: interrogative: interrogative.

I smiled. The Binder squealed through his nose at that smile. But I pushed to PC41: >bond< Flat statement. >james<

An image of a cat covering up excrement on a hard floor came back over the push.

He told us his name, Petrone.

That he was of The Gotha.

A holder of a Hearth, a master of a Table.

That his task had been to break and induct Wolff to the needs of the *Allemagne Noir*.

And he had been finding Wolff obstinately resistant.

They had just begun to explore more drastic methods of breaking this obstinately resistant fain.

He was babbling variations on this, thirty seconds after I peeled the third strip from his aura nimbus and left the strip open, casting off smuts and yellow pearls of decay.

They wanted to stop Wolff, stop the DBP, penetrate the DBP here and in the Hanse and they had recently lost three of the four action teams that they were going to use. For their masterstroke. One team was left. They were going to use this postern, because all of the other gates were compromised.

They had a fifty-pound charge and it was planned to happen in fifteen hours. They were going to transit to 'zeme through the gate here.

None of the team members knew they were discards, the charge was planned to be detonated by a clockwork, but there were two clockworks.

One set fifteen minutes fast. It should suffice to scram all of the gates to and from the 'zeme and The Gotha embedded in the Commonalty and the Unity Eisenring would execute a coup d'état there and in the Confederated Houses.

I peeled him as he babbled on, fact-checking and exploring threads though his memories. He didn't notice that I was stripping off ribbons of his auras, his soul. A D'draig can 'peel' a subject and the subject would not know anything was amiss, until the subject stopped breathing. But you can miss information doing that, by not asking the right questions, and it is exhausting to the operative; it is easier if you are only fact-checking the statement rather than coercing the statement.

And often you peel the subject to 'encourage the others', in front of an audience to get them to volunteer information. Watching someone be 'peeled' is likely the source for all the Yellow Novel accounts of the Sangsue lust for blood and agony.

Not that there are Sangsue that did not lust for agony, but it wasn't effective as an interrogation. You got more with a suggestion of absolute agony infinitely prolonged, then actually grinding them up.

When we were done, he was breathing and his heart was still beating, but he was gone.

Unfortunately, he was not a Walker, so we didn't have a handle on the gate. Not directly. But I had recovered a memory of transiting a gate. And Bast, Cally and I have been known to use a memory.

It was dark outside; the airport was lit up but there were deep shadows about the FBO. Lots of noise, jets taking off, jets landing. I dragged the husk of Petrone out of the hangar, around the corner to the door of the postern. I had a key to the lock. We; Bast, Cally and I had eaten our fill of the three lunch boxes and broken into the vending machine. Bast had also gone hunting. So, we had enough energy for the planned operation. Enough energy without having to follow some of the more outrageous legends of the Sangsue. Which were true, as far as that went.

Lyn stood chuckie and Wolff insisted on backing her play as I opened the postern door and Cally and I rolled the heavy office chair through it. They had coal oil lanterns every ten feet, leading the way into the basement. At the bottom of the stairs, and it was bloody hard lugging that chair down the stairs, there was a metal door that opened into a sixty-foot gallery built from a corrugated steel culvert. Rusty and streaked with muddy ooze. There were rammed earth blocks, wooden planks over laid on them for the floor. A brass Sunwheel fastened at the end in a plywood bulkhead. The gallery was lined with coal oil lanterns, I lit every other one down the length of the passage. There was a large wooden box on a table by the door to the gallery. I opened the box, it was lined with copper, it had four high-end watches in it and a walky-talky. I strapped three of the watches on Petrone's arms.

On the floor there was a broad line painted in bright yellow, from wall to wall and up over head. This was telling us where the Gallery actually started, much like the prop warning line on an aircraft. If the gate was active and you went past that line, you might transit without intending to.

We intended to use that trick.

CHAPTER 59

"So just what is it I am supposed to do?" Cally asked me as I got Petrone lined up off center of the Sunwheel-at about its three o'clock. I had brought welding gloves and a helmet down from the hangar along with a set of tools; hand drill, rigging wire, a rigging block and a set of vise grips. I was fastening the block to the wall right next to the Sunwheel, threading some sheet metal screws into the plywood. The bulkhead was in bad condition, splintering with age-it had stencils dating from the second world war-but it would hold just long enough. I ran the rigging wire through the block and then walked it back to where Petrone slumped in his chair. He was still breathing, but it was getting raspy as his body forgot things. I wrapped one end of the wire about him and the chair, bent the wire into a loop with the vise grips and then carefully coiled the wire up at the door by the gloves and the helmet.

"Two things. Open a gate and then step back from the open gate, I'll pull it through the gate but off center."

"Brilliant, we send it off into the gap between the worlds. What does that do?"

"He's got two battery powered quartz watches on his left arm, one on his right. Running. As long as he is in the absolute center of the gallery, it should be safe as houses, but drift a bit off and…"

"That could blow us the fuck off the face of the earth!"

"Nah. I've seen it done."

"Baise moi! It's on the list of 'Never fucking do this…' they gave me at the Ecole."

"Trust me. I witnessed a pod transit and one of the gormless bastards in the pod had one of the first quartz watches, a Bulova, and nobody knew the fucking thing had a battery in it. Nobody'd seen one before." I tugged slightly at the wire, it grew taut and Petrone wobbled towards the Sunwheel. "They got almost to the end, he was on the outside of the transit pod and his watch threw an arc, then a ball of light and then a lot of sparks going up and down the gallery walls and across the ceiling."

"What happened next?"

"The *adit* went offline, the Dowsers said they could not tell with certainty if or where it might transit to. It was offline for a fortnight, everyone got investigated and-"

Cally slapped me in the back of my head. "What happened to the pig with the watch?"

"Don't know. He, the pod and his Walker went into a standing wave and never came out."

"You are a terrible liar. Simply terrible." She crossed her arms and stamped her foot. "I will not be a-?"

That was when the gate began to open. From the other side. I pushed Cally through the open gallery door, slammed the box shut and squatted down by the table. I donned the helmet, put on the welding gloves. I grabbed the rigging wire I'd looped around the table leg. I could hear Cally yelling for Wolff and pulling at the back of my jacket. I dropped the vision block of the helmet and the gallery was absolutely dark, I flipped the lens back up, so I had a chance to see what I was doing.

The standing wave came up, like a heat wave over tarmac. There were little sundogs, skittering on the top of the standing wave like water striders. Then shadows began to form in the standing wave, transit shadows.

And that is when I pulled on the rigging wire, with my eyes slitted and holding my breath. Pulled like I was landing a fish from the surf.

I felt the door open at the top of the stairs. Cally was behind me and trying to drag me through the *adit* door, shrieking all the while a mélange of *Frankii*, Creole and English. PC41 was in there somewhere. Through Bast's eyes I clearly saw:

The office chair fly apart at the joints.

Petrone's husk rear up.

The watches on his arms, all three of them, arced loops of white fire across the gallery and through the transit shadows. Ball lightening, arc flashes, shreds of cloth and other things fluttered in the strobing of the arcs.

A pressure wave surged through the gallery, a white cloud precipitating at the back of it, snuffing the lanterns stripping paint and rust from the corrugated steel, and ripping up the wooden flooring, ripping it into punk and dust. It hit me and I fell back through the door to the gallery, landing on Cally, my welding helmet ripped from my head. Curls of light swirling past my face.

The gallery collapsed into a blur of blue sheets of light and rolling clouds of dust and crud, right up to the warning line, sucking the rigging wire and the welding gloves tangled in the wire out of my hands. The table leg was on fire as the wire wound around it at speed. The door swung into the gallery and then swung back to smash against the door frame. I heard the rest of the gallery collapse, saw the door sag and warp with small blue sparks crawling over it.

Then nothing.

I was out. I was on top of Cally, our clothes were smoldering, dust was dancing in the air of the landing at the foot of the stairs, Wolff was stumping down the steps from the door above with an electric torch, the beam slashed through the dust hanging in the air. My eyes were closed, blood streaked my face, I was limp.

I was out cold and watching all this from above, crumpled on Cally. My point of view slowly panning around the landing. Wolff knelt next to me and Cally, rolled me off of her and felt my throat. Cally was sobbing, wiping at her face, wiping at me. He gave the torch to Cally, had her hold it on my face and he opened both of my eyes, one at a time. Lyn appeared, knelt with Wolff, then Bast. Bast. PC41, bumped noses with me and…nothing.

What they told me later was that Cally and Lyn and Wolff horsed me up the stairs to the outer door. They went into the hangar, found a big two-wheel hand truck in the hangar, draped me over it, wheeled me out front and with Lyn's help Cally stuffed me in the trunk of the rental with a jacket wrapped about my face. Then we went back to the motel.

Wolff said that Lyn did a grocery and food run-she didn't trust either Cally or Wolff to drive; Lyn brought back summer sausage, rat cheese, sport drinks, chocolate bars, crackers, cans of cat food and cookie dough. She went out later and got two gallons of milk, two dozen doughnuts, a box of cookies and a twelve-pack of beer. Lyn later said the Quick Trip cashiers were beginning to give her the stink eye, on the third time she cleaned them out of gedunk, cat food and milk.

PC41 stalked off into the night around the Motel, came home at dawn tubby and grungy from all of the foraging she'd done. I know this. I saw her stalk past me where I sat in the parking lot. She didn't see me.

I was out.

Cally stuffed herself with sausages, poured sport drinks and milk down me. Fed me chocolate bars and held me in her arms and cried and cussed and cried some more.

I wasn't there, but I remember all of that. I remember

hunting birds and rats about the motel. I remember Cally weeping over my hair falling out in clumps. I remember sleeping in her arms, occasional bubbles of drool that she wiped away, her rubbing her face against mine. Whispering to me in *Frankii*, tracing my lips with her fingertip.

When the fifteen-hour deadline passed, I was still curled up in Cally's arms and both of us were in the bathtub. Our clothes were rags and burnt rags at that. We later found that her lock blade was spot welded shut, my belt buckle was distorted and all the change in my pocket was fused together, my multi-tool was gone. I think I left it on the table in the gallery. She was sunburnt, the underwire in her bra had scorched the fabric, the rivets in her jeans likewise.

We'd left all the rest of the weapons up above with Lyn and Wolff, left our watches and anything else we thought that might have caused trouble, but the knife?

Wolff said later, in the same conversation that he brought up Lyn shopping at the Quick Trip, that he'd called in a few markers, got an information tap up into the Provo Eisenring and Croton House. He came into the bathroom to try and talk to me about what he'd heard.

Cally nudged me awake, more awake than I had been for a while. I came down from the ceiling, came down from the net that was drifting under the white tile. Cally washed more peeling skin off my hands and stuffed sausage and cheese and chocolate down my throat. We'd sorted out that being top drawer Walkers or D'draig required a lot of caloric input, the jump to the Remnant colonies -showed us that. Now after nearly killing my fool self, we needed a helluva lot of calories. A helluva lot of calories between the three of us. Wolff sat there and watched me nibble at the sausage, while I watched things float across the ceiling. With my eyes closed.

"Braxton." Said Wolff. "Are you with us yet?"

I opened my eye, the one that I could open, and blinked

away the fog. "I think so." I batted at the smuts floating through my vision, like the things you saw in pondwater in Biology, darting and swimming and drifting through the room. "Longue vie, aren't you?"

He snorted. "You damn near killed yourself, and Cally; and you did sorely inconvenience that bloody odd cat."

"Sorry."

"Right. Well it's a day past the deadline and nothing happened. Nothing big. They tell me a warehouse on the Estuary, across the veil in Alba, blew itself to flinders. And the Dowsers have been snooping about the airport Provo Eisenring and Blacklegs and FAA."

"Flinders." I closed my good eye and watched them both. He was solid, Cally not so much.

"Right." He turned to Cally. "He going to be worth a damn anytime soon?"

I went back to sleep. Covered us both with my light blue blanket, the net I cast with the auras I manifested.

More than a day later I did come back. I was laying in Cally's arms and watching my net drift across the ceiling and through the light. I swallowed, tried to sit up. The bathtub was cold and hard, and I had a cramp in my back. That woke Cally and she poured some warm sports drink down me, tucked a handy beach towel about my shoulders. I gagged a bit, blew my nose in the handy towel. Peeled some skin off my nose. Focused on Cally.

She was pale and bruised and scared. I could tell she was scared, she looked like the Discard I watched walk down the wharf. "Jos?" She was gently running her hand over my head, where the hair was starting to grow back in. Stroking the places where the welding helmet cut welts in my skin.

"Righ..ttt. I'm hungry, I think."

And she kissed me, nuzzled me, her tears slicking my face, kissed me and then she clouted me about the head and then she kissed me again.

Bast pushed. >welcome home<

CHAPTER 60

A week later and I could walk, stagger really. Lyn and Wolff had smuggled us directly into a safe house—more of Wolff's hobby or maybe he was just not as retired as he avowed. I keep thinking that. The safe house was down in Oklahoma, in one of the Indian nations north of Tulsa. Or so they told me. It all looked the same to me. Mud and grass and stunted trees. And horses.

Cally was fine. Sunburnt and rattled, but fine. She messed with the horses, talked to them in *Frankii*. Didn't ride them, just whispered into their ears and checked their hooves. The horses seemed to crave her attention; they came to the fence every time she showed herself.

Bast or Euston was the same, foraging among the local vermin and begging the 'good stuff' from anyone she could charm. The other cats in the neighborhood were very distant, the dogs wanted nothing to do with her. They knew Bast was a different sort of apex predator and they did not want to bump heads with her. I think a coyote did try for her, once. It did not end well for the coyote; not from the ragged scraps I saw on the ground in the back corner of the paddock.

I was not up to scratch, not at all. I slept a lot, ate four meals a day, tried to knit up the net of my auras. Walked around the paddock with a cane, with sunglasses on and a floppy hat. Rested a lot on my rounds in the paddock, there were a couple of lawn chairs placed there for my convenience.

When I slept, it was in Cally's arms.

Wolff came by once a week or so, sometimes with Lyn and sometimes by his own self. The visits started a month after he had convinced the powers that he was not hob-nobbing with the DBP and was able to be out on his own again. He did not want to have to embarrass the surveilling team by losing them when he wanted a bit of privacy, it made them cranky he said.

He gave me a more detailed after-action briefing one day. Sat us down with a pot of tea and a coffee cake in the kitchen of the safe house. Lyn had come with him that day and was getting cozy with Cally out in the paddock.

Wolff said that the postern gallery had run under the FBO, parallel to the taxiway; when it collapsed the building began to sink into the ground, not immediately but it noticeably sagged. There was a severe electrical event at the airport, most of the groundside buildings close to that FBO lost power and much of the taxiway and other lights blew out. This shut Mid-Continent down for about two days, when the electrical grid went belly up, no flights incoming or outgoing. All of the alphabet agencies showed up to poke knowingly at the rubble. They dug up the FBO and the gallery with heavy equipment.

We had gotten away before the airport knew there was a problem or where to start looking for the problem. And then there was the fire shortly after we left the parking lot. Gutted the building it did, burned up the hangar and muddied the evidence.

Wolff said he and Lyn had dragged the sleeping beauties clear away from the FBO, into the parking lot and put them in an unlocked car. What accounts he got from sources never mentioned them, they just didn't show up on any of the tallies.

Two dead officially, the jackass at the reception desk and the ghost in the office. Nobody else was missing and one aircraft was damaged badly in the resulting fire. There was an investigation into the company that owned the FBO, it went nowhere in public. The FBI Agent and the other interrogator were never there, officially.

Public notice consisted of half a page in the Eagle-Beacon, a half-column in the KC Star and a three-line squib in the Washington Post. All correct and proper by the Three-ring binder for containing an incident.

I asked Cally about the fire. Lyn winked at her. Cally shrugged and said "Lyn." As if that answered all questions about that part of the incident. Well, it would, I suppose. Medji like blowing up things almost as much as they like knocking heads. So easily entertained.

Wolff had turned up officially at hospital in Independence, Lyn dragging him in through the ER doors a month before I finally came around, three weeks after the gallery collapsed and shut down the airport. He was not as badly off as he had been when we pulled him out of the 'enhanced interrogation', but according to Cally he looked like death congealed on a greasy plate. Again, she credited Lyn; said that Lyn should go in with me on a beauty salon. I resolved to not tell Lyn about that particular bon mot. The way things were going, the two of them would unite against me for being rude.

Wolff was not available to the various interviewers, Croton House or Eisenring, that came calling while he was in the hospital at Independence. The local police were very interested in him as well, he had been roughly used and had evidence of being tended to afterwards. Lyn told them to talk to a name in Washington and then clammed up, a name Wolff had given her. A representative from the FBI soon appeared to sit impatiently in the waiting room beside the Dai representative and the Provo Eisenring. And the FBI agent discouraged the local police from getting stroppy with Wolff or Lyn.

When he finally recovered well enough to stand the stress of the interview, Wolff laid it all at the feet of DBP. It worked once, why not again? The man from the FBI took one steno page of notes about the DBP, gates, Wolff and the *Allemagne Noir*, then excused himself to use the restroom and never returned. We didn't know if he was read in on the Dai's existence and decided this was not his problem, or if he just decided this was someone's elaborate joke, but he never returned from the bog.

The local police then pretended that they never were ever interested in Wolff. Took the guard off his hospital door and lost the entries referencing him in the daybook.

Registry Marshals and the thrice Damned Eisenring were told by Wolff that he had been abducted by the *Allemagne Noir*. He gave them names and places in Croton House and in the Commonality apparat of those who-to his knowledge-were working with the *Allemagne Noir*. They took this seriously, unlike the FBI. They were not Unity cadre, but they were tasked to sort this out. I think the possibility of sticking it to the Cadre made them 'keen'.

The *Allemagne Noir* who had Wolff were intent on stripping every bit of information from him about the DBP and how much the Hanse knew of the *Allemagne Noir* schema for the coup-de-main of the Houses in 'zeme. And how much the Hanse might know of *Allemagne Noir* operations in the Hanse. Wolf was holding out, mainly because they had tried to tie him with a Binder rather than simply peel him with a Sangsue. He told the Marshals that he thought the *Allemagne Noir* might not have a Sangsue on the muster here in AngTerra, they were starting to work him over physically. He told them that he knew he would break eventually, eventually everyone breaks, but he did not know the information his interrogators wanted.

Then the DBP kicked open the door, terminated the interrogation, terminated the interrogators and took a battered Wolff along when they exfiltrated. To a location in the Hanse, of all places. They also had acquired Lyn beforehand, to be his keeper-according to Wolff's statement to the Marshals. Lyn had interpreted that role as a Medji would. She was devoted to the 'old man' all through their time across the veil in the Hanse safe house and now she was fiercely protective at Hospital. The Registry was cautious in their dealings with Lyn at Hospital in Independence. They had reports of Cantry Ford and the culling of the Confederated House Officers and the flat disappearance of the Eisenring. And the opinion of the Blackleg Marshals was that Lyn was not a 'simple' Medji, just as Wolff wasn't a simple operative from the last war, or the last three wars for that matter.

Nobody wanted more of that drama. They said they were satisfied, closed the book and offered their apologies to Lyn for her problems with some of the Eisenring agents that had been on the investigation. She had sat through her debrief, she said, answering only the questions put to her and being a ghost all the while.

Lyn was with Wolff when he spun this tale to me, chiming in with her versions of what and how she sold the investigators-churched and unchurched-the account of their stay among the Hanse. That there was a proper establishment in the Hanse; Table, Hearth and all. This made the investigators barking mad.

Lyn has mastered a flat, deadpan delivery of the most outrageous lies. My corrupting influence.

"Nothing happened?" I referred to the last throw of the dice for the Allemagne Noir.

"A number of seats at Table at Croton house opened up," Wolff was disassembling his pipe to tend to it. He still favored a brand of tobacco that knocked flies and other bugs out of the air and left a thick tar in the dottle. "I heard a section of Unity Eisenring were disappeared and a rumor of a significant turn in the administration of the Commonality. Other than that, nil." He reassembled the pipe, packed it loosely and lit it with a wooden match. "Reagan and Gorbachev are making progress with, if not peace negotiations, calming the waters. I have heard, that the Skrenners are feeling better about the end of the world as the Dai knows it."

"So, what did we do?"

"Sand in the lubricating oil, soap in the fuel tank, it's hard to say. Remember your lecture about looking in the mirror, expecting to see Commander Bond? Sometimes you just see a chap doing a job and that job trips someone to go ass over teakettle down the stairs."

"Cascade effect."

"Possibly. You know about 'Market Garden' don't you?"

"Allied version of *Wacht am Rhein*?"

"Much of the same. Excellent plans, but they both had a single point of failure baked into the scheme. If you did not take the road networks and fuel dumps in the Ardennes or the last bridge before Arnhem, your plan failed. The *Allemagne Noir* needed all the sappers to take out the galleries, while their covert forces were ready in the 'zeme to overrun the Unity and many of the Confederated Houses."

"Ambitious."

"They may have had the forces to take the Unity after such a strike at the gates, to hamper and damage Croton house on the east coast, but I doubt they could carry the rest of the Confederated houses and certainly not Nihon. They would have buggered the Houses for generations, but not overturned them."

I smiled at him. "We were caltrops before the charge of the *beau sabreur*."

"Yes. And do not even have a foot note in the Annals.

Alas."

CHAPTER 61

But there was one last throw of the dice. Wolff and Lyn had come down to spend the weekend at the safe house. Cally and Lyn were going to play with the horses and I and Bast were going coyote hunting with Wolff. We were out in the hills when Bast lit up.

>danger cally<

I held a hand out to stop Wolff. We were maybe less than a half-mile off from the house. "Something's wrong."

"Where?"

"At the house." Pain came over the push, pain and anger. We were afoot.

"Double time."

"Go." And we took off at a trot. Five minutes and we were at the back of the safe house, behind the barn and the paddock. Wolff was breathing hard but still game.

There were two extra cars in front of the house, Suburbans with tinted windows. There was also a dead horse in the paddock by an open gate. I had a person unknown in the barn, moving about, searching maybe.

PC41 went in, located the bastard searching the barn. He also knew where Lyn was hiding.

I held up a hand to Wolff, then I slipped through the paddock gate and into the barn. I had the bastard down on the floor before I went in, PC41 was close by. I whistled softly and Wolff came in.

"Lyn?" He said softly. She dropped out of the hayloft, knife out.

"They have Cally. They want me and then you," she said to Wolff. "Two of them are Eisenring-one is AN. Three more like this one." She kicked the dying man on the barn floor.

"The Eisenring you had issues with?"

"Different, but I think from the same section."

"Cally okay?"

"So far as I know." She knelt and checked the man on the floor, stripped his weapons and cut his throat. Wolff didn't flinch, neither did I. The gomer was dead, mostly, when she cut him.

I pushed at PC41. >scout< I could feel him slide out into the paddock.

"What's with the horse?" Asked Wolff.

"A demonstration, they said."

>coming< Came over the push.

Wolff faded into the stable's shadows; Lyn went back up into the hayloft. I pulled a five-gallon drum over and sat next to the corpse. They were dragging Cally by her hair and an arm across the yard to the barn's sliding door.

"Hey bitch, we got your girl here. Wanna come watch us party with her?" There were three. One with a visible gun, one holding Cally and slapping her and one strutting through the yard like a banty rooster.

I let them get just in the doorway, then I stood up. I was in a hurry, so I didn't take any time to strip any information from them. I just dropped them where they stood. What I did pull was that two of them were local talent, one was an Eisenring stringer-not much more than a hired hand.

Cally dropped to her knees, favoring an arm. I picked her up and carried her to a stack of feed sacks, stretched her out on it. They had battered her, broke her wrist, broke her nose and blackened both her eyes.

She had internal injuries too. I looked to the three louts on the barn floor. One wasn't breathing, two still were. I needed them alive for what I was about to do. I looked to Wolff.

"You should leave."

He stiffened, stepped back and reached out for Lyn. She took his hand and gave me a strange look. "Because?" He asked.

"I'd like to keep you as a friend."

He nodded. Looked at Cally. "Lyn, let's go secure the vehicles. Kill them if you see 'em."

Lyn nodded, checked her weapon. "Sir." And led the way out of the barn.

"Josh," He said to me as he followed Lyn. "I've seen worse, ordered worse."

I nodded. I waited until he was clear of the barn. >clear away< I pushed to PC41.

>not need<

And the air thickened about me, Cally and the living rat bastards on the floor. I focused my gaze on her, tracing the broken flow of her auras, highlighting the draining injuries to her Overt body. I began to work one of the other talents of a D'draig-of the greater Dragon of legend and horror. One of the things the greater Dragon was feared for. A thing the Selai was ever condemned for. I drained all of the energy from the men on the floor, leaving them husks crumbling within their clothing, pink bones under tears in their parchment skin. I spun the net of my talent around them, through me and over Cally. I knit up her wounds and restored her auras, I left her asleep.

When I looked up from her sleeping on the pallet of feed sacks, she was unmarked except for the portwine stain on her face. Around us a light blue net revolved, visible only to me and to PC41.

>finish<

"Oh yes," I said aloud. "Let us finish this."

CHAPTER 62

I could tell that Wolff and Lyn were hunting well, the net of my auras covered all of the house and the barn now. I even had Lyn clocked, with her alba aura. Three candle wicks of auras snuffed out, suddenly, silently as far as I could tell. Leaving two in the house.

I walked up to the back door, opened it and walked through like I owned the place. It opened into the kitchen. I stepped through the mess the invaders had left, walked towards the front parlor.

"Walter, you get that Medji bitch, or do I have to come help you-you dickless..."

I stepped through the kitchen archway, a gun in my hand for show. One of them, the younger one, tried for his weapon. It was resting on the tabletop next to him. But he couldn't move, he convulsed and exhaled and died. All of his muscles locked in rictus. It made cleaning up after a bit easier. I didn't threaten him, didn't dangle his fate in front of him like a noose. I just killed him, like turning off a light. He had nothing I wanted.

But the other one I didn't kill; he deserved more attention. He was paralyzed now, from the neck down. Still breathing and his heart still beating, but only his eyes could move.

I stepped past him and gently opened the front door. I did not want to startle Lyn, Medji in a close combat engagement are prone to shoot first and inquire later. "Wolff!"

I shouted. "You need to come and see this."

First Lyn came around the back of the closest SUV, her gun at the ready. Then Wolff. "What?"

I just waved him in.

He eased around his end of the SUV and shouldered past Lyn, to her displeasure. Stepped inside and came to a complete stop inside the parlor.

The Living *Allemagne Noir* on the couch gobbled something through his paralyzed throat. His face blotchy red and old, but I knew him. I think Wolff knew him immediately. He smiled broadly at the aging monster on the couch.

"*Standartenführer* Karsten Tauber." Wolff 's German was much better than mine, he had the Prussian accent well mastered before I was born.

"I thought I would give you the honour of killing him."

Wolff walked over to the couch. "Let's not be hasty, Josh, I have close to forty years of questions I would like answered. And I have, on good authority, an excellent D'draig Adept at my disposal for the questioning."

Tauber attempted to clench his jaw, to cheat the Hunter. But he didn't break the tooth of prussic acid.

We secured the scene. Lyn and I drove the SUV's to a back corner of the farm, then she dug a grave outside of the paddock with an end-loader scoop on a tractor. I stripped the dead, tumbled them into the bottom of the grave and pushed a layer of dirt and muck on them. Then we recovered the horse and with considerably more reverence laid her to rest in the grave on a layer of hay.

I carried Cally into the house. She was still out cold, Bast was cuddled on her chest under the comforter when I left them.

Lyn was skittish about me for a bit. She saw me pitch the freshly picked skeletons into the pit. But after we laid the mare into her grave then chased down and caught the ones who'd bolted, she was easier with me.

Wolff had made a pot of tea, typical; set out a cup for me and him. Sat there and stared at Tauber, with that very thin boot knife resting on the end table close to hand. Wolff never said a word. Just stared at Tauber.

I sent Lyn on a supply run. She was not eager to go but was not eager to stay. Medji are familiar with all the forms of interrogation, some grow to specialize in that particular art. She didn't like it.

It took an hour. I removed the tooth with my new multi-tool, then used my net to ease some of the paralysis. I gave him back his voice. Let him blink, let him breathe.

He threatened, he demanded, he threatened again. He grew hoarse and weary.

We ignored him and had light conversation over the tea. About my time on the wharf, both on 'zeme and in the Smoke. About his time in Paris after the war, before the war resumed.

When our 'guest' stopped raging, we began. I peeled a strip from him, not much more than Wolff would have taken with his boot knife but no blood, and the pain did not lessen. He thrashed his head and screamed, and I kept a close eye on his heart, he was old for a monster. When he calmed, I peeled another strip. Again, we did not ask a single question.

When I made a move to extend my hand, to peel a strip-although I did not need to exert myself. Wolff stopped me.

"Karsten," he said. "We know how this will end. If we want to, we can make it last a very long time, and you will break and tell us everything. Josh will know each and every time you try to evade, to lie, to shade a truth or hide a name. And he will peel another strip off of what we might call your soul."

"*Der ungeist!*" He gasped; his eyes fixed on Wolff. "*Ungeist!*"

"Perhaps, perhaps I am a demon. I have hunted you and yours for so long that I wear your skins draped over mine." Wolff smiled at him and picked up his knife. "And Josh is just a sharp blade in my hand. I know you well *Standartenführer*. I know your habits and your leavings. I will have you flayed on my tabletop will you-nil you, and you will give me everything you have. And at the end you will be nothing, all your appetites and scheming brought to nothing but a shallow scrape under some yellow scraggly pines. And I will be the only one who remembers you." He reached out and lightly slashed his knife across Tauber's face from his left brow to his right cheek across the bridge of his nose. The blood ran down Tauber's face and then stopped, the cut sealed up and faded into a red line as I knitted the wound. "And I will do this again, and again, and again."

He told us everything. He lied, he begged, he gave us the truth and pleaded. He told us everything.

Much we knew or supposed, much was old news fit only to line birdcages or worn out boots. The *Allemagne Noir* had resurrected itself a third time, with the very dregs of their organizations. They wanted 'zeme and the houses there under their hand. They thought they could make an accommodation with Nihon. They failed on all counts and a conspiracy too far.

Wolff didn't get some of the things he wanted. The names of the collaborationists who had helped the *Allemagne Noir* escape from the fall of the Third Reich, they were unknown to Tauber. He was at best a third string in the *Allemagne Noir* after the fall. Other factions in the *Allemagne Noir* had taken to carving each other up, attracting attention from the Eisenrings and other agencies. Tauber survived by being a small fish. He survived the incident in the Hanse by having a subordinate stamp him in that day, he was too drunk to come to work. And then taking immediately to his heels, into the 'zeme and the Unity. His hide was on the Estuary, in Alba. And that was where he was when everything fell apart.

Everything he touched was corrupted, every plot and expedition he had a hand in came to naught. They blamed Wolff. The *Allemagne Noir* Skrenners saw Wolff at the center of the problem eventually, they also saw the blinders as being something that they needed to secure to bring their plans to pass.

They never had a clear notion of what happened, just that Wolff and Lyn were at the center of it. And this ragged old man, this monster, thought to track Wolff down and take a revenge.

They did not know about PC41. We were the diamond dust in the gears, I suppose. When I mentioned that to Cally later, she told me to get over myself.

I pinched off the charka that governed his heartbeat, we let him die. I dragged the corpse off the couch, wrapped it in a drop cloth from the garage and took it outside.

"What are you going to do?"

"Dig a hole and bury it."

"Clever boy, I mean you, Cally and that bloody odd cat."

"I'd like to go back to Alba, but I think that might be pushing it a bit. Can't go back to the wharf on 'zeme, the Unity Cadre will still be after Cally. And hanging about with you and Lyn would be bad for my health, Medji are so easily offended." I shrugged. "We'll see."

Wolff laughed, sheathed his boot knife, took the sheath out of the boot and laid it on the coffee table. Stood up with his knees cracking and walked to the front door to see if Lyn was back.

I went and buried the past under a dying pine tree.

THE END

About the Author:

The Rest of the Story

Like his characters, JD Bell is a big persona living in a world that is too small for his personality. An early reader of SF and fantasy, Bell's stories have captivated many listeners for years – but he rarely wrote them down. The few exceptions are still out there: early sales to The Space Gamer magazine with stories that perfectly linked the Ogre and GEV game universe. These short stories were too good to disappear, and in an era of disposable electrons, his work has resurfaced in reprints from Steve Jackson Games anthologies.

JD's presence at decades of SF conventions in the Kansas and Oklahoma region is also the stuff of legend. (But as the statute of limitations has not expired on some of those exploits, it is best we do not speak of these finer moments.)

His work is a remembrance of SF and Fantasy as it was, with ringing swords and phasers that are rarely set to stun. His characters are the perfect combination of larger than life skill set coupled with a world-weary point of view, caught up in the action of the moment. With no time to consider the finer points of etiquette, they rarely choose discretion, opting for a full-tilt fight though the outcome may be in doubt.

Add to that their ability to miscalculate the passions involved, and you have a character that is larger than life and extremely competent – sometimes tripped up by matters of heart and emotion.

In other words, a person much like his readers – and the author.

JD lives in Kansas with an adorable wife and with four

daughters that take strongly after the cats he raised over the years: Fiercely independent, strong willed, extremely resourceful – and of course, beautiful.

JD currently has a second book in the Hidden Worlds fantasy universe in the publication chain. There is also a Space Opera under production – and it appears a direct sequel to Selai, in the Hidden Worlds milieu. Who knew retirement could be so productive?

PREVIEW: SELAI

TALLEN 1

It was end of summer and I was back at the Memorial Union. I'd made a delivery run from Windsor to Chicago and took the long way home through Iowa. Spent the night at a motel on the outskirts of Ames then I drifted through Dogtown and the parts of the campus I could still drive through, before parking the Chevy close to the student union.

I was just looking for ghosts.

I found them, in the Union's North entrance, Gold Star Hall. The hall where the names are chiseled deep into the granite. Abbott. Barnes. Evans. Franks, Ronald T.

I pulled a cheaply bound booklet from my leather dispatch case and opened the now ancient twenty-fifth anniversary pamphlet to the "F's".

Under Franks, Ronald T. there was a small black and white photo of a young man in a dark blazer; white shirt, high collar and a thin black tie with a straw boater in his hands. His eyes were dark shadows in the low-quality photo, his smile only hinted at. But he was there in that photo. Came from Yates Center down in Kansas to attend Iowa State as a Pre-Veterinary major. He joined the American Army in 1917and died late in 1918 from the 'Spanish Lady'. He was in the 1st Division AEF.

There was Pasaschof, Calvin M. There was no photo of him in the booklet. Calvin was an Engineering major, he died at Belleau Wood with the 23rd battalion, Sixth Marines.

Ripley, Donald Lee. College of Veterinary Science; 33 Division, Army. AEF.

Ratzlaff, Jacob. USN, Faculty member College of Engineering. No explanation given as to how an Iowa teacher ended up with a Gold Star from the Navy, but there he was.

I found the name I was looking for. Tallen, Royal A., College of Agronomy; BEF, DSO.

In the old and battered book there was a very blurry studio photo of RA Tallen, in a Canadian uniform and wearing the name of Ray Tallen. The United States disapproved of its citizens serving in anyone else's army. Thus, all of the Yanks that went to Canada for that war carried new names. When Lance Corporal Tallen went missing in 1919 it took a while for the Canadian army to sort out the subterfuge and send a letter of condolences to his American family, along with a medal. Part of the confusion was that he went missing and was declared dead after the official end of the war to end all wars. But he was on active duty and under arms, so, the Commonwealth considered him a casualty of the war. While the ISU Memorial Union committee were more rigid in their awarding a Gold Star, he had a medal from the Crown and a scroll of honor from the French. So, they let Roy Tallen into the hall.

When the Alumni Association got the Memorial Union rolling in 1922, Royal A. Tallen was listed as being among the lost students and suitably remembered on Armistice Day.

Which was odd, considering I was Tallen, Royal A.

I placed my hand against the cold stone. Rubbed my palm along the inscription. I wondered, not for the first time, if I shouldn't be struck dead. Here in the hall, under the stained-glass windows. I remembered the first time I had come here, at the Bicentennial, to look over the landscape and found my name cut into the granite. It's a queer thing to come upon your own grave marker. Particularly, while you are still among the quick.

That thought brought a chill and the stench of things long dead in black mud. But the odor was part of the here and now.

I casually turned towards the stench. At the south end, in the central hall by the desk for the Alumni Hotel on the upper floors, stood two men with stick-on badges and a map of the campus. They were tall and well-trimmed, their suits hung by bespoke tailors and their hair was strictly GQ. They'd been consulting that map for a quarter hour, folding and refolding it. Stepping back out of the general path and then wandering back into the gangway. All the while they kept watch across the central hall and down the Memorial Hall towards me. I hadn't paid too much attention to them before but, talking to the Lance Corporal tends to focus the Subtle mind.

They had no auras.

This is like having no shadow on a sunny day.

Their eyes kept shifting off me, towards the revolving doors and the bench in the other corner. I looked up and another pair was having a friendly conversation in the open arches of the second-floor landing, which overlooked the Memorial Hall. They'd got their suits from the same tailor and their tradecraft from the same cereal box.

They had no auras.

They were ghost walking.

You can suppress your aura. Sometimes this comes as the unhappy side effect of attempting to master a Subtle art quickly, without a proper grounding. The student learns all the katas and masters the throws, but it is just mechanical. Rote learning. There are several paths that seek to hide the aura, place it deep in the Overt body. The benefits from a suppressed aura lie mostly in the discipline it takes to maintain it and the lack of a wake as you move through the world.

Everyone can see auras. They just don't see them consciously. It is a quarter of the way we communicate; verbally, non-verbal cues, pheromones and auras. Auras function beneath our normal awareness, along with but stronger than, pheromones. Auras can tell us when the person facing us is friendly, intent on taking our cash, or cutting our throat.

The Adept that suppresses his auras distorts that communication. A subtler poker face as it were. You blend into the woodwork. Refuse to stand out. Wear clothing that blends in. Don't talk much. And suppress your auras. You aren't remarked upon. The suppressed aura makes you even less memorable to the casual, overt, observer. The "he was too ordinary" description. Again, useful in certain habits.

I checked out the hot corner. On the polished granite bench there was a woman with a backpack on her lap and a pair of crutches. She was reading a book or leafing through it. One hand never far from a slit pocket in the pack, her eyes drifting up to focus on the revolving doors to her left but, keeping the four suits in the corner of her vision. Her left ankle was in an air cast. Her jeans were dirtier than fashion demanded, and I could see a long scrape under a tear in her buttoned-down left sleeve. Her auras were bright and rolling in the semi-darkness of the hall. Her fear and her resolve plain if you had the eyes to see and the experience to understand.

I turned my back on her for a second to look at Lance Cpl. Tallen in the mirror of the granite wall. Then I tucked my handbook away, picked up my overnighter and turned towards the girl on the bench.

"Hello." I said, moving my body to block her from the suits.

She looked up from the book, her hand drifting towards the slit in her bag, her face pale under her coal black hair.

"Been waiting long?" I extended my hand to her and winked. "Ready to get some lunch at Hanratty's?"

She hesitated for a breath, her nostrils flaring as she gathered her good leg under her, and then she read me. Whoever the hell I was, I was not with the gents in the suits, and that was enough for her.

"Long enough," she said. Her voice a pleasant alto, crisp and clean with nothing of the public-school slop in it. She contrived to drop her book and while we both bent to retrieve, she whispered. "Two above, three outside. Where is Del?"

I just nodded and handed her back the book. She muscled herself up on one leg and positioned the crutches under her arms. I walked her past the concierge, nodding at the two suits by the desk. Then I sidestepped her through a door marked Staff Only and into a dim service corridor running to the parking garage. It had bricked up windows from when it was an entry hall in the '30s, tile floors with rough concrete patches and naked light bulbs at the midpoint and each end of the hall.

"Don't stop, I'll catch up."

And I knocked the light out, just over her head, with my overnight bag. She didn't flinch, just kept swinging on down the passage.